BEYOND
GARTSHERRIE

A novel by AJ Morris

Published by

McAlpine Media

First published in Great Britain by McAlpine Media, 2019

ISBN: 9781793491763

Designed & Typeset by McAlpine Media, Glasgow.
www.mcalpinemedia.co.uk

CONTENTS

DEDICATION

For my darling husband Paul, without whose love,
encouragement and 'nagging', this book would
never have been written.

ACKNOWLEDGEMENTS

As always my thanks to Joanne and Gary, of McAlpine Media.
They provided the wonderful cover design as well as
'All the clever computer work'
For which I am entirely in their hands.

***

My eternal gratitude to my friends Jane, Beryl and Davina
for reading my drafts and Terry for suggesting the book title.
And the blessing of true friendship.

CHAPTER 1
July 1928

The telephone rang in the hall of the elegant Blairhill home of Jennie Mathieson, former schoolteacher and life long supporter of the Women's Suffrage Movement.

The telephone operator enquired, "Is that Coatbridge 427?" Jennie answered, "Yes it is."

"I am now connecting you to a trunk call from London Madam." advised the telephonist.

Across the wires Jennie heard a familiar voice amidst the sound of background crackle.

"Jennie, Jennie, is that you? It's Mary here, I'm calling from the Savoy Hotel in London. I have just had lunch with Liz and a number of other stalwarts, we are going on to the Houses of Parliament to watch the vote. This is it Jennie, under Stanley Baldwin and the Tories we are going to get our due this time. Parliament will pass the Representation of the People's Act 1928, women will have equal voting rights at twenty one. And, can you believe, Millicent Fawcett is going to attend. Millicent has been in it since the beginning in 1867 when John Stuart Mill introduced his Reform Bill and now she will see the culmination of over 60 years work. We are all so thrilled, at long last we will have gained The Equal Franchise, can you imagine the excitement?

Jennie, can you please go down to the Long Row and tell my Ma what is happening here in London? My Mamie will be so overjoyed, after all the years of struggle our day has eventually come."

Shouting over the crackling line Jennie assured Mary she would immediately pass the wonderful news on to her mother.

Replacing the receiver Jennie lifted her jacket from the hatstand and handbag from the hall table. Just as she was about to leave she had a sudden thought.

'Liz and Mary would probably produce a bottle of champagne, I'd better take something to celebrate with'. Jennie went into her dining room and lifted an unopened bottle of Spanish sherry from the silver tray on the sideboard, before putting on her jacket and walking smartly down to the Long Row.

Although now almost fifty Jennie Mathieson was still an extremely handsome woman, tall and slim with thick auburn hair, containing only a sprinkling of grey, her eyes were sapphire blue still bright but she had recently taken to wearing gold rimmed spectacles when reading.

Coatbridge was a town of two distinct parts, the many Rows of Gartsherrie, housing the workers who laboured at the Iron Works, Baird's of Gartsherrie. And, the other parishes of the town such as Whifflet, Langloan, Carnbroe, and Kirkshaws who also had their share of poor tenement or cottage housing provided for the workers who toiled at the many engineering, steel, wire rope works and mines all over the town.

In stark contrast the professional, middle classes and factory owners lived in the leafy suburbs of Blairhill and Drumpellier, comfortable in their Victorian sandstone villas or modern bungalows, living near but yet so far from the homes of their workers.

Jennie knocked on the door of 130 Long Row, the home of her friend and fellow Suffrage campaigner Jessie Johnstone. The door was ajar so Jennie went straight through the scullery into the kitchen, she put the bottle of sherry on the table and simply hugged Jessie, the victory they had been campaigning for over so many years had at last arrived. Today would be written in history - The Vote for Women.

Both women were in tears, they had worked together in the Suffrage movement for over twenty five years, some women had given their lives, countless women had sacrificed their health and freedom. Now the day had arrived, the grey men in London had bowed to the inevitable, Great Britain was catching up with her

Empire, all the women of Britain, aged over twenty one, would be able to vote in the next election, the day of universal franchise throughout the land had at long last arrived.

Jennie opened the sherry bottle, while Jessie got out two glasses from the cupboard. Before Jennie had a chance to pour the wine, Jessie suddenly exclaimed.

"Come on Jennie, let's take the bottle down to the Laws and celebrate with Agnes Law, after all she was the inspiration for me joining the movement in the first place."

As they walked down the cobbled Row Jennie told Jessie all about her daughter Mary's telephone call from London.

"It's hard to believe Mary was the youngest of your children and just a little girl when you first joined the Women's Movement, and she is actually in London to see our triumph. How quickly the years have slipped past my friend, too quickly by far."

Arriving at number twelve Long Row Jennie and Jessie found Agnes Law in the main living room, always known as 'the kitchen' making pancakes on a girdle over the range, while her oldest daughter, Mary, was in the scullery preparing vegetables for the evening meal. Jessie told them the good news while Jennie waved the bottle of sherry.

Mary promptly brought out the glasses, this time the four women did drink to success, the success of the Suffragette movement and with it the awakening of rights for women. Not just the vote, a cross on a piece of paper, that was merely the beginning.

Agnes Law and her now deceased husband Robert, or Rab as he was know, had been Jessie and her husband Alex's lodgers when they first arrived in the industrial town of Coatbridge at the turn of the century.

Both women had lived hard lives, beset by grinding poverty but had dealt with their lot in life in very different ways.

Agnes was never a Suffragette, ever fearful of her strict husband Rab she obeyed him on every turn and bore him six children, one of whom died in infancy. However, with the freedom of widowhood she was becoming more assertive and wilful, much to the chagrin of her family.

Jessie, had joined the Suffragettes, with encouragement from

Jennie, who was then a primary school teacher at the Gartsherrie Institute and with the full support of her husband Alex, with whom she had three children within a very loving marriage. All of the Johnstone offspring had done well for themselves. Agnes, their eldest girl, married a local man, Tom Coates, who was a manager in the Gartsherrie Works. Tom and Agnes had given Jessie and Alex a beautiful and bright granddaughter called Emily, named after Emily Wilding Davidson, who was killed by the King's horse at the Epsom Derby in 1913, while promoting the suffragette cause.

Their only son, Samuel, married a girl called Maria who he met while working at Glenboig Brickworks. They were now happily settled in Melbourne, Australia, providing another three grandchildren for Jessie and Alex.

Initially there was much disapproval of this match, the couple having come from different villages and belonging to different sides of the religious divide. Parental disapproval was a major factor in them choosing to emigrate, however, Sam's War experiences and his subsequent poor health had been another reason for the move.

Drinks were poured and celebration toasts were drunk to the brave women who had contributed to the successful outcome of the campaign, not forgetting the women who had lost their lives or health from forced feeding in prison during the fight. Toast after toast; Margaret Maxwell who threw a petition against force feeding at King George and Queen Mary in Airdrie. The Pankhurst women; Christabel, Sylvia, Adela and their mother Emmeline; Emily Wilding Davidson; Annie Kenney; The Coatbridge Suffrage Group; Millicent Fawcett, the toasts went on and on. Eventually, the four ladies giggled and laughed at the unthinkable idea of them all drinking toasts in sherry so early on a week day, even if it was a very special day.

Mary decided that the time had come to put on the kettle and they all settled down with cups of tea and Agnes's famous pancakes.

The conversation looked back down the years, the small victories, the numerous setbacks, but they all acknowledged that the day of universal suffrage would never have arrived, at least not this side of the millennium, if it had not been for a bloody war, a World War that had touched its cold hand on two members of the group. Jennie lost the love of her life at Ypres and Jessie's only son Sam was permanently disabled as a result of an encounter with mustard gas in France.

The gathering broke up, with Mary and her mother resuming their work for the day and Jessie and Jennie returning to their homes.

As they walked back up the Long Row Jessie questioned her friend. "Jennie, what on earth are we going to do now? We have been fighting for the vote through the Suffragette movement since the turn of the century and now, now there is no movement."

Jennie agreed wholeheartedly. "I too have been thinking about that question, truth be told, for months now. Do I join a political party? Do I get involved in some kind of charity work? Do I return to teaching? Or, do I just live quietly and give afternoon tea soirees?"

Jessie laughed. "I can just see that happening. Oh Jennie, we need a new path to travel. I have no idea what but I hope the good Lord points us in the right direction, sooner rather than later.

CHAPTER 2
September 1928

Jessie Johnstone was sitting at her kitchen table surrounded by felt, blocks, and other paraphernalia required for her work creating hats. Her millinery skills brought extra money into the household and was the difference between just managing and a measure of comfort.

There was a swift chap on the door and Mary Law came rushing into the kitchen. Speaking quickly she said.

"Oh Auntie Jessie I'm so glad you are in, I'm afraid it's right bad news, Mrs Millar has passed away. All those years of her looking after everyone in the Rows, we all thought she was indestructible. Well, I called around to her house this morning, she had asked me to help her make up some potions and salves. The police, you know, Sergeant Chalmers and young Constable Watt, were right there in her living room. Apparently the poor auld body had a massive stroke and just passed away."

Jessie's eyes filled with salt tears remembering all the support Ella Millar had given to her personally and to all the folks of the Gartsherrie Rows over her long life.

Mary too could feel the tears rising, but she knew this was not the time for crying, she said. "Auntie Jessie, can you come with me up to the Herriot Row so that we can lay Ella out decently, it's the last kindness we can perform for her."

Jessie immediately abandoned her work and reached for her coat. "Of course Mary pet, let's get away up the road and see to poor auld Ella."

Over the years both Mary and Jessie had laid out many bodies but on this occasion it felt very poignant. Ella Millar was the respected healer, the wise woman, the local midwife. As they carried out their final ministrations they both felt the pain of losing such a very special woman from their lives.

Mary opened the drawer of Ella's mahogany dresser looking for linen. Laying on the top of the freshly laundered bed clothes was an envelope, on it was written in black spidery writing.

'In the event of my death please pass this letter to Mr A Cornwall of Messrs. Cornwall & Prentice Solicitors, Bank Street, Coatbridge.'

Mary showed the envelope to Jessie, who responded. "Well Mary I think you had better get a bus into Coatbridge and pass it on, the quicker it's out of our hands the better. I'll finish here and lock up. I can return the keys to the police."

Mary called in home to tell her mother the latest turn in events before catching a Baxter's bus at the stop across from the Institute to Bank Street and the offices of Messrs. Cornwall & Prentice.

Mary entered the intimidating offices, with their Victorian black and white tiled floor and dark wooden paneling. The inhabitants of the Rows were not in the habit of visiting professional offices and Mary sounded more confident than she felt as she explained to the secretary the reason for her visit.

Mary waited, sitting on a hard wooden chair in the reception area for a full half hour, before she was shown into the actual office of Mr Andrew Cornwall.

Mr Cornwall was essentially a kind man and recognised that Mary was nervous so he tried to put her at ease, saying.

"Miss Law, please take a seat." Mary was grateful that this seat was a great deal more comfortable than the one in the outer office.

Mr Cornwall spoke clearly in a fatherly tone. "Well, my dear, I was Ella Millar's Solicitor and I will act as the Executor for her estate. Firstly, she had no relatives and has asked me to pass to you, Miss Law, a sum of money and a letter in which she details her request for you to arrange her funeral. After the funeral, and before the house is returned to the owners, Wm Baird Gartsherrie Works, I would like you to come and see me again, accompanied by a Mistress Jessie Alice Johnstone. Now Miss Law can I leave the funeral arrangements in your safe hands?"

Astonished at this unexpected turn in events, Mary took the envelope, assured him that she would undertake the task and thanked Mr Cornwall as she left his office.

Walking out into the cool afternoon air Mary could scarcely believe the events of the day. A day that had started like so many others and was now becoming stranger by the minute.

Mary resisted the temptation to open the envelope until she reached the Johnstone home. After alighting from the bus Mary walked past her own home and hurried as fast as she could to number 130 Long Row.

Jessie had been home for some time before Mary arrived she had cleared the table of all her work stuff and started to prepare the evening meal for her and her husband, Alex.

The two women sat at the kitchen table and carefully opened the envelope. Out fell four five pound notes together with a letter addressed to Mary. Mary read the missive aloud.

My dear Mary

You have been like a daughter to me.

I know you had ambitions to nurse, actually I always thought you had the brains to be a doctor but your health was ruined between your daft auld faither and a drunken doctor. So you ended up helping an auld woman at confinements, laying out bodies, and other medical matters that the poor depend on people like us to administer, for coppers and shillings, rather than pounds.

To business - Please arrange a simple funeral, Protestant minister and burial at Monklands Cemetery. Enclosed money should suffice, anything over please give to wee Mrs Goodman, my next door neighbour. Nellie Goodman has been right good, getting my messages from the Store and doing little kindnesses.

After the funeral you and Jessie Johnstone must go and see Mr Cornwall, he will explain everything.

Well Mary, I don't know if I'll be with the Lord but I do know that I have always tried to do the right thing.

God bless you my dear girl.

Ella Millar

Mary and Jessie looked at each other in amazement. Jessie broke the silence. "Well Mary, it's just past three o'clock. If we leave now we should be able to get to the Co-operative Undertakers at Sunnyside well before they close and we can make all the arrangements this afternoon.

The day of the funeral dawned, cold and crisp with a clear blue sky. Mary and Jessie had carried out all Ella's requests as instructed, however they had not legislated for the love and respect Ella Millar had earned over the years. As the black hearse drove down the Herriot Row, followed by a car carrying the Rev. Maxwell, Jessie Johnstone, Mary Law, her mother Agnes and Jennie Mathieson. The cobbled Row was lined with women and children, many shedding tears as they said their final farewells to a much loved and respected pilar of their community.

When the mourners reached the graveside in Old Monkland Cemetery there was another two people present; Dr Murphy, paying his last respects to a woman whose skills he had greatly admired and someone who over the years he had often asked for assistance. And, Mr Cornwall, Ella Millar's Solicitor.

After the minister had completed the internment service Mr Cornwall approached Mary, as the final prayer ended and they walked away from the graveside. "Miss Law I wonder if I could ask you and Mrs Johnstone to accompany me back to my office in Bank Street."

A surprised Mary and Jessie got into the back seat of Andrew Cornwall's impressive black motor car and were driven to the offices of Messrs. Cornwall & Prentice in considerable style.

Agnes Law was most put out at this turn of events and complained bitterly to Jennie all the way home that she was entitled to know anything that was being said to her daughter Mary.

When they reached the Solicitor's office Andrew Cornwall seated them down on the comfortable brown leather chairs in his inner sanctum and poured them each a sherry, saying.

"Ladies, what I have to tell you will come as a great surprise, however, I think it best that you should hear it in the words of Mrs Millar."

He put on his gold rimed spectacles and proceeded to read aloud a testament from their friend.

To: Miss Mary Ann Law residing at 12 Long Row, Gartsherrie
and

Mrs Jessie Alice Johnstone residing at 130 Long Row,
Gartsherrie.

Well my dears,
It's all over now and I am safely in my long home.
Firstly, I want there to be no secrets between us. I was not Mrs Millar, I
was Miss Millar but the title Mrs helped in my work. What would a Miss
know about delivering wee babies?
You can trust Mr Cornwall he is a decent man and will deal with all the
legal paraphernalia.
Mary, I have left you the contents of my wee house, including my potion and
salve recipes. Now this is very, very important. I want you to take my red velvet
curtains and examine them carefully in private. I want you to have a little inde-
pendence. Your mother Agnes has become right controlling since your Pa died
and I don't want her to know you have a wee something behind you.
Now Jessie, I know how hard you and your friends have strived to get the
vote, I also know of your work to help abused women, and what's more I know
you are an exceptionally good soul.
Jessie, I have left you the contents of my Airdrie Savings Account. I would
like you to use the money as you see fit to help women in need. You must take a
decent salary out of the money for your work. No doubt you will need time to
have a long think about the best way to use the money. Whatever you decide I
am sure you will honour my life savings.
God bless my dear friends.
Ella

As Mr Cornwall finished reading the letter to the two women he
handed Jessie a blue passbook from the Airdrie Savings Bank, the
amount in the credit column read £8,756.17.6. Jessie fainted.

Once they had both got over the initial shock Mr Cornwall ran
the two woman back to Ella Millar's home and handed Mary the keys.

"When you have finished emptying the house please return the
keys to Mr McCosh at the Works. And ladies, I fully realise this is a
very unusual legacy you have inherited. Please contact my office if I

can be of any further assistance to you both."

As Andrew Cornwall drove away he thought. 'This has got to be one of the strangest cases I have ever encountered, I'm going to keep a weather eye on how it all works out - professional interest'.

Mary and Jessie entered the silent house. The house of their friend and teacher. They walked around gently touching the furniture, the ornaments, the cushions. Mary started to quietly cry. Jessie put her arms around her saying.

"I know lass, I'm completely heart broken and astounded too. Mary, we have to carry out Ella's wishes and pay respect to her memory. We must sort through the house and you can decide what you want to keep and sell the rest. I think she really wanted to make sure you have a bit of independence. We must keep our memories and grief for another time, the Gartsherrie Works will want the house back sooner rather than later so we had better get a gildy on."

Mary looked through the cupboards containing various potions and creams, together with Ella's books of remedies. Meantime, Jessie stood on a chair and took down the red velvet curtains from the window. As they dropped she saw a carefully folded ten shilling note peep through the hem. Jessie called Mary.

"Mary, will you come here and see this." Jessie put the heavy curtains down on the floor, she carefully pushed her fingers into the hem and teased out note after note, as the pile grew Mary unfurled each one, mesmerised at the amount of money that was hidden within the depth of the red velvet curtains.

"Mary, away and find a pair of scissors," instructed Jessie. "I'm going to cut along the hem stitching. All was then revealed.

The pile of money just grew and grew. By the time they had ensured both curtains were completely devoid of notes Mary was shaking uncontrollably, realising that Ella had left her a considerable legacy.

Sitting at the table they divided the notes into denominations and carefully counted Ella's cash savings. The grand total was £1,780 pounds. They also found her old leather purse, various coins in jars and a few notes in a biscuit tin.

"What on earth am I going to do with all this cash?" said Mary in a trembling voice.

Jessie, ever the practical one, replied. "Mary, we will take the curtain money to my house. As soon as we can, without your mother suspecting anything we'll go over to Coatbridge and open an account in your name at The Airdrie Savings Bank, then I think you should keep the passbook safely hidden at my place.

Much as I hate to say it, your Ma would have that money off you in the twinkling of an eye. You will certainly have to tell her that Ella left you the contents of the house, but I suggest you show her the money found in the other hidey holes and Ella's purse. That will satisfy her you are not concealing anything and she will have a field day sorting through the household bits and pieces. All you have to worry about is making sure you take charge of all the medical bits and pieces.

We will head down to number twelve now with the news. When I leave you walk me back up to my place, I want an escort while I am carrying all that money in my handbag."

When they arrived at the Law family home they found an irate Agnes with Jennie trying her best to calm her down.

As soon as Mary and Jessie came through the door Agnes hit them with a barrage of questions. "Where have you two been?; why wasn't I included?; who was that man who was dressed to kill, taking the pair of you away in his gentry motor car? And..."

She was still asking questions when Jessie snapped at her.

"Agnes, will you stop havering this very minute. Mary here is still in shock. Ella left her the entire contents of her house, including all her medical remedies. Tomorrow we will have to go up to the Herriot Row and sort everything out. Now go and make a cup of tea for everyone and, if you have any, put a wee taste of whisky in Mary's. Suitably chastened Agnes did as she was bid.

As Jessie and Jennie were getting ready to take their leave, Jessie looked over at Mary silently indicating, 'all is well, I have Jennie now as an escort'.

By the time Jessie and Jennie reached 130 Long Row Jessie's man, Alex, had returned from work.

Poor Alex, he was speechless when Jessie told him of the day's events. Jennie too was visibly shocked, saying.

"Jessie, I can't take this all in, did Ella Millar really leave you over eight thousand pounds to use as you think fit to help women who are in need, while taking a salary for yourself. And, Mary Law has been left a great bundle of money, and we are all going to conspire to ensure Agnes thinks that Ella only left Mary a few pounds together with her furniture and medical lotions and potions?"

"That's about it," confirmed Jessie. "Mr Cornwall let me see Ella's Airdrie Savings passbook. Apparently I will get a letter from him when everything is in order and he will give me a cheque for the full amount due. He has recommended that I put the money straight into a new account and keep a record of everything I spend. Jennie, will you help me with the book-keeping? I wouldn't have a clue how to go about managing accounts. Oh Jennie, where on earth do we start on all this?"

Jennie took her friends hand across the table, saying. My dear, do you remember a few months ago we were saying to each other, 'Where do we go from here?' We old Suffragettes were wondering about what life path we should now take. Jessie, Ella has decided it for us, over the next weeks and months we must work out a plan, a plan where we can feel Ella looking down on us from above and fully approving of all our actions.

Jessie, after Mr Cornwall gives you the money and we know the exact situation can I suggest we have a meeting with your Mary and Liz, and I think we should include Mary Law. Hopefully the five of us can come up with some sensible ideas."

Jennie put on her coat and lifted her handbag. "Jessie, Alex, I'll away home now, you two must have a great deal to talk about. This has been a day we will never forget and a day when I think we have all moved onto a new path and purpose in life."

Left to themselves, Alex put his arms gently around his beloved wife. Jessie was quietly sobbing while Alex comforted her as he would a child.

The following morning Jessie rose early and walked up to Ella's house in the Herriot Row in order to retrieve the red velvet curtains before Agnes saw them and put two and two together.

Jessie was sitting at her table sewing one of her millinery cre-

ations when Mary and her mother Agnes knocked the door and then
came straight through the scullery into her homely kitchen.

Mary said. "Morning Auntie Jessie, can you come up with us to
Ella's and help us empty the house. Our youngest, Alexander, has
managed to get a loan of a hand cart. We can fill it with anything we
want and he will return and push it home after he finishes work."

The three women pushed the empty cart up to Ella's home in
the Herriot Row, ready to begin what was for Mary and Jessie a sad
days work. However, as far as Agnes was concerned, her blue eyes
were alight with the promise of the treasure trove that might be
uncovered.

On entering the well loved house Mary was surprised to see that
the red velvet curtains were now missing but she was wise enough to
keep her mouth firmly closed.

They spent a full day sorting through Ella's possessions, Agnes
had many 'ooh aah' moments as she found another and yet another
of Ella's secret cash hideaways. With each find the pile of money on
the kitchen table grew, much to the delight of Agnes.

Any items which were not going to the Law or Johnstone households Mary insisted were to be given away and not sold, Jessie
backed her up on this idea. Agnes realised she was outnumbered,
and let that particular issue go, after all the money piled on the
kitchen table was more than she had seen in her entire life, that was
quite enough for her.

After his shift young Alexander came to collect the handcart,
piled with goods for the Law and Johnstone households, and helped
distribute various pieces of furniture and bric-a-brac to neighbours.
Mary then locked the door for the last time on the now empty home
of her dear friend and teacher.

As the three women wended their way home, each had her own
private, and very different, thoughts.

When at last Agnes and Mary arrived at twelve Long Row, tired
and covered in stoor, after having offloaded Jessie's share of Ella's
household at the Johnstone home, they were delighted to see that
the youngest Law girl, called Jessie after Jessie Johnstone, was busy
preparing the evening meal. Robert helped his brother Alexander to

unload the final items off the handcart and all was complete.

Well almost all. After the family meal the two boys decided to go down to the Institute and have a game of table tennis, leaving Agnes and her two daughters drinking cups of tea. As soon as her sons were safely out of the house Agnes produced her well worn tapestry bag. "Well Mary let's see how much money auld Mrs Millar has left you, it must be a right wheen of sillar."

Young Jessie looked blank. "What are you talking about Maw, 'wheen of sillar'. I thought Ella Millar had left Mary her furniture, carpets and bits and pieces together with all her ointments and potions, what's all this about money?"

Agnes opened her handbag and slowly took the money out and placed it on the table, some ten shilling notes, florins, a great handful of half crowns, a huge pile of small change, a box full of silver threepennies, pound and ten shilling notes from various banks, Clydesdale, British Linen, Royal Bank of Scotland, Bank of England. And, joy of joys several five pound notes. Seeing the money gradually cover the table Agnes's blue eyes were positively shining.

They sorted and counted the cash with Agnes notating the amount of each denomination in her little book then she added up the figures. The grand total came to £38.19.6.

"Now" said Agnes. "First go off, I don't want you two to tell the lads anything whatsoever about all this money. They, and especially our Robert, are no to be trusted with secrets.

I'll hide it away and then whenever we need something for the house I'll have the wee nest egg to fall back on."

Jessie rounded on her mother. "Wait a wee minute Maw it's not your money, it's Mary's money and she alone should decide what happens to her inheritance. I know only too well what it feels like to be deprived of an inheritance, that is exactly what the McInnes family did to me. It wasn't enough that I lost the man I loved more than life itself, I lost the inheritance he planned for me. Mother, you have no right to spirit Mary's inheritance into your old tapestry bag, she will never see it again."

Agnes snapped at her daughter. "Just you be quiet my girl. Mary can't go out earning like you because of her health so anything she brings into the house goes into my bag. Don't you dare question me Miss Jessie Law, besides Mary will get something, a new skirt and jumper or perhaps a dress, I'm always fair."

Jessie was about to continue the argument when Mary stopped her saying. "Look I've had enough of all this bickering. I've lost a good friend in Ella Millar, I just want to mourn her, not discuss money."

Mary called her wee black dog, Rags, put on her lead and took her out for a walk. Still annoyed, Jessie cleared away the tea things, venting her anger on the innocent crockery.

That night in bed Mary whispered to her sister. "Jessie, Maw thinks she has got one over on me. Well she hasn't, there was a lot more money hidden at Ella's and Auntie Jessie has it safely at her house. Tomorrow we are going to Coatbridge to open an account in my name at The Airdrie Savings Bank and Auntie Jessie will keep the passbook hidden at her place. Now keep my secret and nighty night."

CHAPTER 3
October 1928

Some weeks had passed since the breaking up of Ella's home and the opening of Mary Law's bank account.

It was a strange time for Mary and her Auntie Jessie. So much had happened and yet very little had changed. Mary still worked for Mrs Watson a few afternoons a week as a maid, and she was now starting to get requests for some of Ella's potions and salves.

Jessie was still making her hats while awaiting word from Mr Cornwall. Until she received a communication from him her secret was safely held by Mary, Jennie and her husband Alex.

Her daughter Mary and Liz were due to return shortly from their trip to London, and visits to friends in Devon and the Cotswolds. Jessie wondered if they too were at a loss to find a new purpose in life.

Although everyone in Gartsherrie knew Mary Johnstone worked as a Secretary and Companion to a blind woman who lived in Airdrie, they were unaware that Mary and her employer Liz were also lovers.

Jessie frequently had to listen to sympathetic comments from her friends and neighbours on how sad it was that her youngest daughter was a spinster. Knowing the real truth Jessie became skilful at diverting the well meaning comments with phrases such as; 'Och our Mary is a real career woman', or 'our Mary would rather type than cook'. Followed by, something along the lines of 'Did I no tell you I have just received a long letter from our Sam and Maria in Australia'? The well meaning neighbour would be so enthralled by the tales from Australia that poor spinster Mary would soon be completely forgotten.

Liz, whose full name was The Right Hon. Lady Elizabeth Agatha Banks-Wallis was ferociously intelligent, she was also very wealthy. However, she was a woman who needed purpose in her life and she too had spent many hours over the past months pondering what the future path would be for her and Mary.

On arriving back at their home in Airdrie the taxi driver helped the ladies with their cases and was rewarded with a good tip from Mary. Their housekeeper, Mrs Armstrong, had left a chicken casserole in the oven together with potatoes pealed and ready to be boiled.

After taking the cases upstairs and unpacking Mary finished cooking their evening meal, which they ate from trays while listening to the gramophone.

As the last notes of autumn from Vivaldi's Four Seasons died away Liz said.

"Well my dear, I still can't quite believe it, at last we have equal voting rights with men. In a peculiar way I suppose Millicent Fawcett was our first MP as she carried out most of the duties for her blind husband Henry. Officially, I know it's that ghastly Markievicz woman then Nancy Astor, but I like to think it was our own Millicent. If I still had my sight I think I would try to get elected but alas I just don't have the energy I once did. Mary what on earth is our next project going to be? We have been rolling this around for months now while not actually acknowledging that we are standing at one of life's crossroads."

Mary took the dinner trays back into the kitchen and returned with a tea tray. "Fancy a spot of whisky in your tea Liz?" enquired Mary. "Might give us both some inspiration. As success came within our grasp I think we were all too excited to articulate the nagging little voice within us all saying 'what now, what now'? I bet my Ma, Jennie Mathieson and all our other Suffragette chums are having exactly the same thoughts."

As they drank their tea, laced with whisky. Mary said. "Liz, let's just leave all the angst alone. Sometimes it's better to do nothing and wait to be shown the right road. Heavens, I sound just like my Mamie, that's the kind of thing she would say."

"Talking of your Ma," said Liz. "Why don't we go over to see her tomorrow with that big box of Fortnum's chocs we brought home for her and the jar of Gentleman's Relish and bottle of Glenlivet malt for your Pa?"

"Yes, good idea. Pa loves his Relish, but can you imagine if the men at Gartsherrie Works knew he enjoys Gentleman's Relish on toast with his mug of tea before going to bed? Liz, when Agnes, Sam and I were bairns the very idea of luxury foods was totally beyond our imagination. Actually that's not quite true, our luxury food was served on highs days and holidays, when my Aunt Agnes used to make little fried cakes with grated potato and onion, they were absolutely delicious.

Now come my love, we have had a long day, let's go to bed and just lets see what tomorrow brings forth."

Jessie saw Alex off to work his shift then decided to spend the morning doing housework and cooking, millinery could wait until the afternoon. Singing to herself she was in the middle of polishing the linoleum with lavender wax when there was a knock on the door. Jessie answered the interruption to her work and found the postman holding a missive, and saying. "Registered letter for Mrs Johnstone, sign here please." Jessie signed the book offered to her and accepted the letter.

Sitting at the kitchen table she toyed with the envelope for several minutes, the sender was Messrs. Cornwall & Prentice, Solicitors and Notary Public. Although she knew what the letter was going to be about she still could not quite believe that Ella Millar had placed this enormous responsibility on her shoulders.

When she could delay no longer Jessie Johnstone, whose life savings with her husband Alex amounted to some twenty three pounds, opened the envelope and out dropped a cheque for £8,745.12.2, together with a statement detailing the interest on the account and various outgoings.

Jessie returned the cheque and paperwork carefully into the envelope, placed it on the mantelpiece and recommenced her polishing.

Later that afternoon Jessie was sitting sewing when a maroon Vauxhall motor car pulled up outside her house. Although Mary had been driving for some years Jessie had still not got used to the idea of a motor vehicle parked outside her wee Gartsherrie house.

Mary helped Liz out of the car and into her family home. As always Jessie was delighted to see them and immediately abandoned her sewing to put the kettle on for some tea.

When Liz was comfortably seated Mary returned to the car and brought in a large carrier bag bearing the legend Fortnum & Mason; as well as the chocolates, the Patum Peperium Relish and Glenlivet whisky, Mary had brought her mother, breakfast tea in an oriental style caddy and a jar of honey. As she put the bag on the table she said. "Ma, I wanted to get you a box of fancy biscuits but Liz said, 'don't you dare, your mother makes the best biscuits and scones bar none', so I bought the honey instead."

Jessie finished making the tea, opening her cake box she put some treacle scones out on a plate. Even although her heart was pounding she tried her best to appear normal, thanking Mary and Liz for the gifts from London and pouring tea from her homely brown earthenware teapot.

Liz was first to bring up the 'what now' subject. Instead of replying Jessie rose and took the letter from the mantlepiece. Handing it to her daughter she said. "Mary pet, read this letter and the enclosure aloud please." Mary read:

Dear Mrs Johnstone
As discussed during our previous meeting, please find enclosed cheque in the sum of £8,745.12.2. per the attached statement.
Should you require any further assistance in your endeavour, as outlined in Miss Millar's Last Will and Testament, please do not hesitate to contact me.
Yours sincerely
Andrew J Cornwall
Encl : copy of the Last Will and Testament of Miss Ella Millar cheque in the sum of £8,745.12.2

There was complete silence in the room for what seemed like hours but was probably less than a minute. Nobody quite knew what to say or where this news was going to take them. Mary then picked up Ella's Last Will and Testament and read it aloud.

Liz was first to speak. "What a truly fine thing to do, Jessie, your friend Ella must have been a very special woman."

"Indeed she was" agreed Jessie. "However, I have no idea where to start on such a task.

Jennie and Alex know all about the money, and of course Mary Law, but we have said nothing to anybody else. I wanted to wait until I had the cheque and that would make it seem real. Can you imagine how Mary Law and I felt? We were whisked away after Ella's funeral to a posh office in Coatbridge and then the Solicitor, a Mr Cornwall, read us the Will my Mary has just read.

Oh, another thing, Mary Law received a substantial amount of money which we have secreted away into an Airdrie Savings Bank account, I have the passbook. Her mother, Agnes, thinks she received about forty pounds and the house contents. You know what Agnes has become like since Rab died, controlling, is the best I can say. It's as though after all the years of having no say in the family's finances she is now determined to hold the family purse strings very tightly indeed.

The first thing I have done for women is to make sure Mary Ann Law has full control of her own inheritance.

Liz, Mary, I'd like to set up a Committee with you both, and of course Jennie and Mary Law, this is definitely a case where five heads are better than one. Well, is this our 'what now'?"

Mary replied, in a voice that was almost a whisper. "Ma, I can't believe Mrs Millar has, has, oh Mammie I'm so proud that you were Ella's choice, not some charity run by ladies in fancy hats and men wearing gold Alberts, no you Mamie, somebody she knew and could trust implicitly, oh Mamie." And Mary, for all her beautiful clothes and Fortnum's chocolates was crying like a little girl.

Jessie put her arms around her daughter, "there there pet, I've had a wheen longer to think about all this. I know it's a shock, can you imagine what Mary Law and I were like when it all happened? But happen it did lass and now we need to make a plan."

Liz had been listening intently to every word, her quick brain could immediately see all sorts of possibilities but she knew this was a time for slow and steady, they could not afford to make a mistake.

"If the Malt wasn't for dear Alex, I would say, 'open it, let's celebrate this auspicious event'." said Liz.

"We can at least have a wee sherry" said Jessie. "Courtesy of our dear Jennie, I'll get it out of the press, then we'll have our tea and scones."

Toasts were drunk, to Ella Millar and The Way Forward.

As she poured the tea Jessie said. "Now, give me all your news, describe exactly what Parliament was like and how you all felt as they voted on the Bill, leave nothing out. I have been so looking forward to this moment, and I just can't believe that my wee bairn Mary was actually there.

Liz, do you remember when we first met at Jennie's house, that must have been around 1900, you were studying and getting degrees and I was trying to bring up a family on fresh air. Who could have thought where our paths would lead and now we are to have another adventure."

Mary and Liz then regaled Jessie with all the details of their trip to London, culminating in The Representation of the People's Act 1928 becoming law.

Liz rounded off their tale. "The remainder of our trip was partly business, I had another visit to Moorfields Eye Hospital and we enjoyed meeting up with many of our comrades in the fight. Our visits down to Devon and on our way home a few weeks in the Cotswolds were a great success. And, of course, dear Mary managed to get in some shopping."

Liz was very sensitive about her eye condition, she preferred to pretend that there was nothing too badly amiss, however Jessie asked her a direct question. "Liz, what was the outcome of your visit to Moorfields?"

"Well Jessie, they basically confirmed what I already knew from Marion Gilchrist in Glasgow. I can see outlines, distinguish light from dark and not a great deal more. There is no possibility of recovery but my consultant thinks my condition will not worsen, it is as it is. Now, any chance of another cup of tea in this house Mrs Johnston?"

Jessie took this as a signal to change the conversation. "When do you think we should have our first meeting, and where?"

They thought for a moment then Mary said. "If she is agreeable

Jennie's house would be best. Obviously we can't have it at the Laws, and can you imagine my poor daddy surrounded by women working out how to spend a fortune. Rather than you three travelling to Airdrie, we can easily drive down to Blairhill.

Can you make the arrangement Ma and get Jennie to 'phone me with the details? Thinking about it Ma, you will need to get a telephone installed."

Jessie went into hoots of laughter. "Can you imagine Alex and Jessie Johnstone with a 'phone, we'd be the talk of the steamie. Indeed we'd be the talk of Gartsherrie, if not the talk of the whole of Coatbridge.

Talking of your Pa, he will be home soon and quite honestly I am dreading showing him the cheque, it will then all seem real, a cheque for a fortune made payable to me, Mrs Jessie Alice Johnstone."

Liz stood up. "Mary I rather think we should go home now. I am sure your mother would prefer to speak to your Pa without us in attendance."

Coats and hats were put on and goodbyes said. Liz whispered to Jessie as she gave her a farewell kiss. "Be brave Jessie my friend, be brave."

After waving them off Jessie busied herself preparing Alex's dinner, she then wrote a letter to Australia, telling Sam and Maria the details of her inheritance. She had just sealed the airmail envelope when she heard Alex arrive home.

After her husband had washed and settled himself Jessie gave him the gifts from Mary and Liz. He smiled saying. "They never forget my Gentleman's Relish do they? You know I was very worried that our Mary would move away from us with all the education she's had, but no my darl'n she is still my bonny wee bairn, so she is."

Jessie lifted the envelope from the mantleshelf and handed it to Alex, saying. "I told Mary and Liz all about the inheritance from Ella today, read the papers I received by registered mail my Alex." Alex carefully put on his metal rimmed spectacles and read the letter and Will.

In a faltering voice he said. "My love I am so very proud of you my heart is fair burst'n, so it is. Auld Ella was right to choose you, there is none more honest in the whole of Scotland. And Jessie, you have a good heart and a big heart. Do the auld yin proud."

Jessie cuddled her husband of over thirty years, tears streaming down both their faces. Eventually Alex said. "Away and get a couple of glasses Jessie, I think this occasion calls for me opening the Glenlivet, what do you say?"

"I say yes Alex, I think we both need a dram."

Later that evening Jessie went down to the Law house, happily everyone was out except Mary and her mother.

Jessie breezed in saying. "Oh Mary I was hoping to catch you in, I have a block for a hat which I think would be just lovely for you, would you like to come up and take a look at it, I also have a choice of a few materials you might like to pick from, can you put your coat on?"

Before Agnes had time to work out a reason why Mary should not go out and leave her, Mary had her coat on and the two women were calling their goodbyes as they headed up the Row, accompanied by Mary's wee dog Rags on her lead.

"New hat indeed, honestly Auntie Jessie have you thought about going into the films, Greta Garbo, Mary Pickford, Clara Bow, you can out act them all."

"Actually Mary, I feel I can, after the acting I have been doing these past few weeks. However, the cheque has arrived and Liz and Mary came over today so I was able to give them the news. We are heading up to Blairhill to ask Jennie if we can have our first planning meeting at her house. It's the perfect place for the five of us to meet, just like the old days, strategy meetings in Jennie's blue morning room. Besides, she always organises good teas. And, it was partly true I do have a hat in mind for you. We can nip into my place before going to Jennie's and you can quickly choose whatever material you fancy.

As they neared 130 they could hear raised voices coming from one of the nearby houses. "Oh Lord" said Mary "that's another stooshie going on at our James's. Honestly Auntie Jessie no good has ever come of that wedding between him and Margaret. What with the debt and her flirting with other men it seems they live in a constant battlefield.

I don't say much about their goings on at home, our Jessie gets very upset. Her and McInnes were so much in love and had a wonderful future planned, tragically he dies of cancer and she loses everything, including every penny of the inheritance he intended for her. Then her eldest brother marries a floosie and its nothing but fighting, I am disgusted with our James as well as that Margaret of his. He was well warned."

They quickly passed James Law's home trying hard not to make sense of the words coming from the raised voices.

Rushing into Jessie's home they found Alex sitting by the fire with his head in his hands. Jessie ran to him and circled him in her arms, saying. "Alex what on earth is the matter you look so down?"

Alex smiled, "Come on you two, dinnae mind me, it's jist this inheritance, it's a lot to take in for an auld Ulsterman. Why are you back anyway, I thought you were going up to see Jennie?"

Jessie laughed, "We are just making up a reason to get Mary away from her mother. Quick Mary, what do like best, dark green velvet or the soft grey, I think the dark green but which do you prefer?"

Mary looked at the two pieces of material, "definitely the green."

"Right, that's it decided, let's get on our way." Jessie quickly kissed Alex on the cheek then propelled Mary back out into the night. As they walked up the Row they could still hear the arguing voices of James and Margaret.

When they reached Jennie's elegant home in Blairhill she welcomed them into the little sitting room, known as the morning room, where a cheery fire burned in the hearth.

While pouring three glasses of sherry she asked, "Well, has it arrived?"

"Indeed it most certainly has," confirmed Jessie. "I nearly died this morning, Postie brought a registered letter containing a cheque for £8,745.12.2.

Mary and Liz are home from London and their visits to friends, they came over this afternoon with gifts; don't worry I'll donate some of the Fortnum chocolates for our first meeting. That's why we are here, Jennie, can we use your house for our planning meetings? Mary can drive Liz down from Airdrie and Mary and I only have a short walk, what do you think Jennie?"

"Need you ask, of course we can all meet here, next question, when?"

Jessie thought for a moment, "Can you telephone and sort out a time with Mary and Liz, perhaps Saturday or Sunday afternoon would be a good time for Mary to get away without her mother suspecting that something is going on. Obviously we will tell Agnes when our plans are in place but I really don't want her interfering and sticking her neb in at the moment."

Jennie went into the hall, picked up her telephone and asked the operator to connect her to a number in Airdrie. After a few minutes she returned to join her friends. "It's all arranged, Saturday at two o'clock. That gives us a couple of days to think up ideas and Jessie perhaps we should go into Coatbridge tomorrow to open a bank account. I'll call for you at say ten o'clock we can get the bus over to Coatbridge from the Institute."

"Agreed" said Jessie, "The sooner that cheque is off my mantle-piece and safely into the bank the happier I'll be."

Mary and Jessie took their leave of Jennie and headed back home to the Long Row. Mary was immensely grateful that all was now quiet as she passed her brother James's house.

Saturday afternoon and Agnes Law was none too pleased. Her two sons, Robert and Alexander had gone to Cliftonhill to watch Albion Rovers play; Jessie was working and then Mary announced that she was off out, without as much as a by you or leave you, leaving her alone on a Saturday afternoon. Agnes was becoming suspicious that something was going on that she was not party to and she was not at all happy.

The 'committee' met at Jennie's home at the appointed time. Coats and hats removed they sat around the round mahogany table which was covered with a dark blue chenille cloth edged with tassels.

Jennie opened the proceedings. "Well ladies, by a completely unforeseen set of circumstances we find ourselves united in a new venture, to assist women who have been abused or fallen on hard times and in so doing honour the memory of Ella Millar.

On Thursday Jessie and I opened two bank accounts. The bulk of the money is in a high interest savings account, we have deposited two hundred pounds in a current account, a cheque book will allow us to keep track of any expenditure.

However, before we even think of expenditure and accounting we must decide what our project will be. Can I suggest that we each take a turn to put forward an idea or expand a thought and then see how we all feel about where we are heading."

Liz said "Jessie, you first, after all you will be at the forefront of whatever we decide so you have to believe in the project one hundred percent."

Jessie offered her thoughts. "As you all know I am just a housewife who left school at fourteen so I am hardly qualified to come up with clever ideas, however, I cannot see the point of simply handing money to people, what is the old saying; 'give a man, or in this case a woman, a fish, and you feed him today, give him a fishing line and you feed him for life'. Well, I think that whatever project we do it should involve training women to be independent by being able to earn their own living.

The first time Liz and I came to your house Jennie, way back around the turn of the century, the women gathered in this very room were all asked to give a reason why they supported the Suffragettes. Isa Fullerton, bless her she passed away shortly after the War, well Isa told us how she had been terribly abused by her cruel husband but could see no possibility of getting away from him, without losing her children. I would like to use Ella's money to provide a safe haven for abused women, a place where they could acquire the skills and confidence to become independent and live in safety with their children.

Also, I think we should use some of the money to buy premises rather than renting so that we can make long term plans without worrying about rent increases and we can make any changes necessary to the building without consulting a landlord."

Liz joined the discussion. "Yes Jessie, I completely agree, providing sanctuary for abused women, what better cause? Purchasing premises will allow us the freedom to run the operation as we want to, can you imagine if we rented premises and then opened a refuge for abused women, the owner could well disagree with our aims and we would all be out on the street."

"I see our ideas are on the same lines," agreed Mary, "I was thinking it would be a good idea to have a safe haven not only for abused women, but with accommodation for their young children."

Mary Law joined in the debate. "When I was a wee one, my mother always had this horror of The Poor's Hoose, it was the constant threat if we did not behave we were told 'you'll go to the Poor's Hoose'. The Old Monkland Poor House together with the Fever Hospital in Coathill was the stuff of nightmares. In fact it was just one step behind 'You'll go to the bad fire'." Everyone laughed, but behind the laughter they all knew the Poor House stories and the veiled threat of hell.

"We seem to be making progress" said Mary Johnstone. "Step one, source and purchase a suitable property, step two decide on a criteria for the women that we will help. I know that sounds terrible but better to 'cure' a smaller number of woman than to simply bandage a lot and send them on their way. As my Ma says, we should be aiming for long term independence, not just giving a woman a fish to stave off hunger, in other words, helping the immediate problem but without having an ongoing plan we will be of no real long term use."

As minute taker of the meeting Jennie opened her notebook, saying. "Friends, can I summarise our discussions so far:

Firstly we will look for a suitable property to purchase that will sleep, how many shall we say?"

Jessie made a suggestion. "We don't want to be too ambitious to start with, say 8 rooms of varying sizes, as some would also have to house children, plus two bathrooms, kitchen and several work or meeting rooms. That comes to an awfully big house so it is going to have to be in a posh area of the town, trust me there is nothing remotely like that in Gartsherrie."

The house specification was agreed unanimously.

"Next question" said Jennie. "How much do we anticipate the house will cost to buy furnish and decorate?"

Quick as a flash Liz said. "Always best to overestimate, obviously the fitting out costs will reflect on the suitability of the property. Say, we allow one thousand pounds for purchasing the property and fitting it out, we may well do it for quite a bit less but best to look on the very worst case scenario."

Jennie consulted her notes again. "For our first minute I propose we head it 'The Ella Millar Memorial'

Obviously Jessie must be Chairwoman, I am quite happy to be Secretary, now what about the other positions?"

Jessie interrupted. "No, no Jennie. I know we have to minute meetings and keep accounts but I knew Ella for the best part of thirty years. I am sure she would not want us to sink in formality. Why can't we simply say:

Friends : Jessie Johnstone, Mary Johnstone, Mary Law, Jennie Mathieson, Liz Barns-Wallis

I am sure that would please Ella."

"You are so right, Auntie Jessie," agreed Mary. "I worked closely with Ella for years, she had no time for highfalutin ways, she was a practical woman. I am sure she left her gift to you because she knew you would just get on with things, simply and efficiently."

"Back to my minute," said Jenny.

The Ella Millar Memorial
Ella's Friends
Jessie Johnstone, Mary Law, Jennie Mathieson,
Liz Barns-Wallis, Mary Johnstone
Dated October 1928

It was unanimously agreed that we will use up to a maximum of £1000 from the capital to purchase and renovate a property with say, 8 bedrooms and common areas to be used to shelter abused women and their children.

Further, the women should receive education or training, as appropriate, to assist them in finding employment and permanent safe accommodation.

From Monday first, Mrs Jessie Johnstone will receive a weekly wage of, say two pounds to allow her to work full time on The Ella Millar Memorial project.

In the longer term we should examine ways to acquire further income in order to preserve the capital.

Well ladies, can I use this to form the basis of our first minute?"

Jessie started to say that the salary was too generous and should not start immediately. However, Jennie quickly interrupted her. "Jessie enough, Ella's Will states you are to receive a salary and you can't do this work and make hats, remember 'a good workman, or woman, is worthy of their hire'. Does everyone else agree with me the wage is non-negotiable."

There was a chorus of agreement, to which Jennie responded. "Right, all done and dusted, time for our afternoon tea."

CHAPTER 4
December 1928

Mary Law heard the mail fall on the scullery floor. When she picked it up she was delighted to see an envelope in a familiar hand postmarked from Glasgow, she slipped it into her overall pocket and handed the rest of the mail to her mother who was sitting by the fire finishing a cup of breakfast tea.

While Agnes looked through the family mail Mary went into the girls' bedroom to make the bed and read her letter in private.

My dearest sister Mary

The twins want to see their Auntie Mary. Any chance you could come up to Glasgow one day next week for a bite of lunch. I will bring the little horrors with me and we can hold one each while we attempt to eat something. Miriam, by the way did you know as well as translating to Mary, means 'wished for child' quite appropriate really. She is so beautiful I could eat her. David is so like his uncle Samuel, mind you he is called David Samuel, his name means 'beloved one'. I can't believe the twins were a year old in September. I have done nothing clever or creative since they were born, I have turned into a Jewish mother, making chicken soup and admiring my darling children.

Drop me a note with which day you can come. I thought we could have lunch at Fraser & Sons in Buchanan Street - quite an easy rendezvous for both of us.

I am simply dying to hear all your news, your letters have dropped all manner of glorious hints of adventures new - without telling your Sarah all the details, tut, tut. I will worm every last little detail from you next week.

Our brother Samuel is well, although I have some BIG news to give you about him! And, my darling husband Alan who sends his love and who still chuckles every time he thinks of our mad family history. I was so awfully glad you liked him. He really likes you and hopes you will play a big part in the lives of Miriam and David.

Happy Hanukkah darling Mary
Sarah
x

Mary got out her writing materials and quickly penned a letter to Sarah, arranging to meet her and the twins the following Tuesday at one o'clock.

Mary did not mention the letter to her mother, the subject of Samuel and Sarah was a tricky one. A few years previously Agnes had confessed to her daughter about a series of youthful indiscretion resulting in her two Jewish children. Mary Law's siblings were totally unaware of their half brother and sister, a secret that Mary carried alone.

Mary had just finished the housework and was getting into her hat and coat ready to go down to the Work's Store for her messages when the door knocked and in breezed Jessie Johnstone, saying.

"Oh Mary are you just going out, I was just passing on my way to the Store, I'll walk you down."

Before Agnes could say a word Jessie and Mary had left the house.

"That was well timed." said Jessie. "I was wondering how I was going to get you on your own. Look instead of going to the Store can we catch the bus over to 'The Brig' I have something I want to show you and I would really value your opinion before we have our next Ella's Friends Meeting."

They quickly boarded a Baxter's bus, keeping the conversation very general during the short journey. As they approached the Whitelaw Fountain, Jessie nudged Mary, "Right that's us now, we've arrived."

They then walked in silence towards Academy Street and the Carnegie Library.

Jessie marched them past the library and up the hill. Several minutes later they stopped outside a large red sandstone edifice. At one time it had been a Victorian family home, however the parents were now dead and the children scattered to the winds. The oldest son had intended to put his family home up for sale, however a discussion with his friend Andrew Cornwall resulted in Jessie being given the keys to inspect the property with a view to purchasing it as a base for the Women's Refuge.

Hand trembling Jessie put the key in the lock and opened the front door and the two women entered the house, the size of which made Jennie's home in Blairhill seem quite modest. They walked around the entire house which had been empty for some years, many items of furniture had been left in situ and everything was covered in a thick layer of dust. The house had a dank, musty unlived in smell and the faded and wrinkled paper blinds were pulled down, all adding to the atmosphere of sad neglect.

Back in the downstairs hall Jessie consulted her notebook. "I make it six family bedrooms, three small servants bedrooms in the attic, one family bathroom, and one staff bathroom upstairs. Downstairs, dining room, sitting room, morning room, kitchen, scullery and a little room off the kitchen. Bonus, large garden at the back, overgrown but stocked with lots of fruit trees and bushes. Well Mary what do you think?"

"I think it is absolutely ideal" replied Mary. "I know it needs quite a lot of work but as far as I can see it's mostly elbow grease, decorating and perhaps changing the layout slightly. If we can keep the furniture so much the better, and all those fruit trees, I can almost smell the apple pies and plum crumbles."

"I think I should call an immediate meeting of the Friends." suggested Jessie. "If we are interested Mr Cornwall has promised to give me a proposal detailing the asking price and listing everything that is being left. Do you think I should say we are interested and bring the proposal to the meeting?"

"Definitely" agreed Mary. "I'd better away and get a bus home, my Maw will be having a fit by now. You take yourself down to Bank Street and get all the information we need, then go to see Jennie on the way home and get her to phone your Mary in Airdrie. I can come to Jennie's anytime. You arrange the details to suit the others. We had better lock up now and get on our way, before my

Maw sends out the search parties."

As expected when Mary returned home her mother was in a foul mood. "Why did you rush off with Jessie Johnstone? Where have you two been all this time? Why are you back home without the messages? And, what are you two plotting? I'm no stupid Mary Law, you and Jessie Johnstone are up to something and I am fully entitled to know what."

Normally Mary always cared for her mother and ignored her petulant moods but not today, the letter from Sarah and all the secrets that involved on top of Ella's inheritance was one step too many. Mary turned on her mother.

"Look Maw I have had quite enough of you and your new Lady Muck ways. Since my Pa passed away you have been impossible. Do you realise you are about the same age as Auntie Jessie and as fit as a flea. Jessie is never off the brow of the hill, does all her housework and shopping as well as making hats. What do you do? I'll tell you what you do. You sit in that chair and issue orders and we all jump, especially me. Jessie and the boys are out at work but you have me as a captive slave. Well I have had enough, next Tuesday I am off for the day to Glasgow, I will meet Sarah, the sister I can't mention or your sordid past would be round the Rows in no time. How would you like that, Mrs Respectable? Now I don't want to hear another moan from you. There is a tin of corned beef in the cupboard and plenty of potatoes and onion, I'll make a pie for supper.

Mary flounced off into the scullery and got to work, leaving a severely chastened Agnes sitting in her chair contemplating what could possibly be going on between Mary and her Auntie Jessie, for as sure as eggs is eggs something was afoot.

Meantime, Jessie had called into Mr Cornwall's office and collected the proposal to purchase Drumkiln House.

The paperwork safely in her handbag she headed for Blairhill to update Jennie. Before she left Jennie made a quick telephone call and arranged for the next meeting at her house to be held the following evening at eight o'clock.

Jessie arrived home shortly before Alex returned from his shift. He came home to find her pealing potatoes. "Oh Alex, I'm so sorry your food isn't ready, I won't be long, I had to nip into the bakery and buy pies for our meal tonight, I've never stopped all day."

The good natured Alex simply laughed. "That's what comes of hav'n one of they modern wives, just promise me you won't get your hair cut into one of them bobs. Pies I can live with but I like my wife's beautiful long hair."

Jessie giggled, "Even if it's streaked with grey? You auld romantic you, well I suppose I better tell you, I've bought you a slice of cherry cake for after your dinner so that will have to make up for bought pies. And, there is other BIG news, we might have found premises for the Refuge. I have collected all the details from Mr Cornwall and we are having a meeting tomorrow night at Jennie's place to discuss the whys and the wherefores."

Alex smiled, "You are a wee whirlwind lass, and I'm so proud of you. Now get your hard working man his dinner. I'm hungry, so I am."

The laughing banter continued as Jessie finished preparing the meal, they ended the evening holding hands in front of the fire, content in each other's company.

The following morning Jessie had arranged to show Jennie Drumkiln House. Her opinion was similar to Mary's, the size and location were ideal and it looked as though a good clean and some paint and wallpaper would work wonders.

This visit Jessie spent more time thinking about how they could use the space and examining the existing furniture. Her and Jennie also spent time measuring the windows and calculating the likely refurbishment costs.

"I've got an idea" Jennie said. "Ella wanted to help women. If we are lucky enough to acquire Drumkiln House why don't we get Jessie Law to help organise the new layouts and redecorating for us. We could pay her and being busy might help her move forward after losing McInnes. What do you think?"

"I think it is a brilliant idea to include my wee namesake. Jessie is really talented when it comes to design and decorating but she would also be a good sounding board on how we could make the best use of the house. Do you think we should invite her to join 'Ella's Friends?"

"I most certainly do" agreed Jennie. "Why don't we ask Mary to bring her along tonight, I am sure your Mary and Liz will be in agreement. In any event I'll telephone them when I get home.

On another subject Jessie, you really do need to get a telephone installed, it would be so useful and after we get the Refuge up and running the women will need to be able to get in touch with you."

Jessie burst out laughing. "Jennie Mathieson, can you hear your-self, me with a telephone. Jennie, we have an outside toilet, my man is a labourer at Baird's of Gartsherrie, get a grip on reality. Oh Jennie, Jennie, can you just imagine Agnes Law's face if we had a telephone, she would be pure beelin."

"You can joke about it but sooner rather than later you will need to be on the other end of a 'phone." laughed Jennie.

That evening Mary met her sister Jessie as she came off the train at Blairhill Station, returning from her work as Manageress of a Drysalters shop in Shettleston. She quickly updated her on Ella's inheritance to their Aunt Jessie and her part in the project. By the time they arrived home at number twelve Long Row Jessie's head was spinning but she knew she wanted to be involved. For the first time since losing her fiancé McInnes she felt there might just be a purpose to her life.

This time six women gathered around Jennie's table, each bring-ing different experience and talent.

Jessie felt confident about making the presentation, she had done her homework. Now turned fifty she was a very different person from the young woman who had first attended Suffrage Meetings in this selfsame room.

Jennie opened the meeting, welcomed Jessie Law, and promptly handed the floor to Jessie.

Jessie clearly explained that she had received a letter from Mr Cornwall. "Apparently his friend, a Mr McIntyre, was looking to sell his old family home and he thought it might be suitable for our Refuge. As you all know I have looked at a number of places but none of them have come anywhere near being as suitable. After see-ing around the McIntyre family home with both Mary Law and Jennie we all see possibilities, behind the dust that is. I will now read you the purchase proposal Mr Cornwall has given to me.

'Mr Kenneth McIntyre will sell the property, detailed above, as per the attached plans for the sum of £680, this amount to include furniture as seen. Family pieces have already been removed'."

Jessie elaborated, "As you can see from the plans, there is also a large back garden with a shed and outside toilet. It needs a lot of work but there are plenty of fruit trees and bushes, and the basis of a former kitchen garden, giving us the space to grow lots of vegetables. The front garden is very small and really just needs a bit of a tidy.

Effectively we would have nine bedrooms and plenty of communal space. I think the structure seems fine, and the musty smell is probably just because it hasn't been aired. However, I think we should get a professional man in to give the property a thorough check before we agree to a purchase. What does everyone else think?"

Liz was first to speak. "Jessie, it sounds perfect, however you are right, we must have it checked, don't want to find out the roof needs renewing after we have handed over the money, now do we?"

I propose young Jessie organises a survey and if all is well we go ahead with the purchase as soon as possible."

Everyone agreed.

"On another matter," Liz continued, "we initially agreed that the Refuge should be more than simply providing a shelter for abused women it should be a route to independence. Independence is through education. Mary and I are in the fortunate position that we can offer our services to 'Ella's Friends' without needing to take a salary. In fact we have already been working on various training courses. Now, can I suggest that our other Mary uses the talents she has learned from Ella to teach home nursing, and perhaps run a clinic to treat minor ailments at the Refuge. Sadly, no doubt some of the ladies and children who come to us may be in a poor physical state. Mary, you could also teach cookery and nutrition.

To do this you would have to give up your present part time employment with Mrs Watson so you too would require to be paid a wage, what do you think of that idea?"

Mary Law could scarcely speak, two years ago she had received a similar opportunity to teach but because of changes in circumstances and an operation that went horribly wrong, she had been robbed of her chance to escape the confines of Gartsherrie, now she was bring offered a second opportunity to escape the drudgery of housework and being an unpaid servant to her mother.

"Of course I would love to pass on the skills Ella taught me but Liz it would be wonderful if you and Mary would teach me how to teach, if you know what I mean."

Liz immediately responded, "Mary consider it done. Starting next week you must come up to Airdrie and Mary and I will prepare you and help you put together a series of lessons. I would consider it a privilege to be able to offer some practical assistance in our endeavour."

The group talked for another hour or so, throwing around ideas, before the meeting closed and Jennie served tea.

As they were leaving Mary offered to drive her mother and the Law girls back to the Long Row. Jessie refused. "Not at all, it's a nice dry night it won't take us long to walk."

As soon as they had started to walk back to the Long Row Jessie said. "I refused the lift for a purpose girls, I wanted to talk to you about your mother. Agnes is not daft she knows something is going on and she is right put out that she has been excluded. Now that you Jessie are part of Ella's Friends and Mary will be on the payroll and spending more and more time on the project we have to be straight with her. For a start she must stop this madam matriarch nonsense and start working again. Since Rab passed away she has hardly left the house and she expects to be waited on hand and foot. You know Agnes was always inclined to take the easy way out, even when your father was alive.

What say we get it over with tonight, I'll walk you home and enlighten her, however, remember girls not one word about Mary's real inheritance. Agnes is happy lording over the money she found in Ella's house, let's keep it that way."

Mary was still annoyed with her mother and was immensely relieved that her Aunt Jessie was taking the lead in informing Agnes of the Ella's Friends project. While young Jessie was dreading the hysterics that she knew would inevitably come.

Deep breath and the three women entered number twelve. Thankfully the boys were not yet home from band practice at the Salvation Army. Before Agnes could utter a word Jessie started to speak.

"Agnes, we know that you have guessed something is afoot, well you are right. Ella left Mary the contents of her house but she left me a considerable sum of money with instructions to use her savings to help women who have been abused or are in distress. I have set up a committee of Jennie, my Mary and Liz and your two girls. It looks as though we may have found premises suitable to convert into a Refuge. This means we are all going to be extremely busy. Now Agnes that means that you are going to have to take on more of the work at home and not expect Mary and Jessie to do everything. I am sorry to be so blunt but now that we know where we are going with this I think you should understand the full picture."

Agnes, who had been sitting in front of the fire with a shawl, knitted by Mary, around her shoulders stood up and pointed her finger at Jessie. "Jessie Johnstone you have been my friend for nearly thirty years and now you turn my lasses against me, you're nothing but a, a, a Judas. Now get out of this hoose with your money and fancy folderol ideas. My girls will have no part in this nonsense."

Mary was having none of it. "Look mother, we respect you, we are grateful for all you have done for us but you can't, no matter how much you would like to try, run our lives, is that clear? I am eventually going to give up my job with Mrs Watson, don't worry I will receive a wage for the work I intend to do at the Refuge. Anyway, considering what my father was like I would have thought that you above anybody would want to help women who have fallen on hard times. This conversation has now ended, Auntie Jessie is going home and Jessie and I are going to bed."

Jessie quickly said goodnight and headed out into the night, looking forward to a cuppa with Alex before bedtime. As she left Robert and Alexander were just returning from band practice so they insisted on walking her safely home.

Agnes spent the following days giving everyone in the house a hard time, she alternated between sulking, temper tantrums and worst of all tears. The ingratitude of the young and the betrayal of her best friend, the drama queen act drove her family to near distraction.

On Tuesday morning Mary dressed in her best blue coat and hat, and left the house to travel into Glasgow to meet Sarah, relieved to get away from her mother for an entire day.

Passing her Aunt Jessie's house on the way to Blairhill Railway Station Mary decided she had time to call in for a few minutes.

As always Jessie was her welcoming self. "Come away in my dear, now tell me is your Ma still creating a right stushie?"

"Stushie Auntie Jessie, you have no idea. I don't know what's worse the temper tantrums or the tears. It's been like a play with Maw the star performer but there was one never to be forgotten moment. James's Margaret called round and tried to borrow some money, did she get short shrift? It was priceless, her finest performance. I almost felt sorry for Margaret, I did really. Auntie Jessie, What on earth do you think we should do about my Maw?"

"You're dressed up to kill so I expect your Ma will be in the house alone today. I'll go in to see her on my way to the Store, she needs a right good talking to. Now away and have a nice day out Mary, you deserve a wee bit of time to yourself."

"Thanks a million Auntie Jessie, you are the only one who can talk to her, good luck and mind and wave a white flag before you attempt to enter number twelve!"

Sitting on the train Mary enjoyed thinking about the Ella's Friends project. It was now all coming together, she hoped beyond hope that the incoming year of 1929 would be the start of a new and exciting time in her life.

Back in Gartsherrie, Jessie took a deep breath, put on her hat and coat, lifted her message bag and headed down to the Law house and Agnes's wrath.

What Jessie did not know was that Mary was heading into Glasgow to see her half sister Sarah, a very sensitive subject with Agnes.

As well as her handbag Mary carried a carrier bag containing two teddies with blue and white bows, as little Hanukkah gifts for the twins. Mary had made a little blue kippah for David's and a little blue scarf for Miriam's.

As she got nearer to Glasgow Queen Street Mary could feel the excitement building at the thought of meeting Sarah and the wee ones.

Seeing Sarah standing outside Frasers Department Store Mary ran the last few yards down Buchanan Street. The sisters embraced and Mary admired the babies, she could not believe how the twins had grown since she had last seen them.

Sarah propelled them all into the store, "Right, straight upstairs to the tearoom, no shopping today with these two little monsters I'm afraid."

When they were comfortably seated by the smart waitress in her black dress and white frilly apron, and had placed their order for lunch Sarah handed Miriam to Mary. Come on darling say, May May, honestly Mary I have been trying to teach them for days to say your name. David piped up, May May, May May, May May. Miriam joined in May May, May May. Mary quickly removed the teddies from the carrier and gave them one each - peace was restored.

Three portions of scrambled eggs and toast arrived, Sarah and Mary tried to eat while also feeding the little ones, their conversation was temporarily halted.

At last the twins had their fill and were sitting happily in high chairs playing with fingers of toast.

"Mary, come clean, what is going on? You keep writing me hints but not the full story, your Sarah wants to know everything, so kindly get talking Miss Law."

Mary related the happenings of the past few months, when she got to the bit about the money hidden in the hem of the red velvet curtains, and how they had fooled Agnes into believing the inheritance was slightly less than forty pounds, Sarah burst into gales of laughter which led to the twins giggling and a lot of anxious looks from the other customers.

Mary continued the story telling her about the last meeting of Ella's Friends. "Sarah, when we couldn't work together at the hospital I honestly felt my life would be nothing else but drudgery and looking after my Ma, and now I've been given this second chance to get involved in nursing and teaching I am so happy you can't possibly imagine.

And, as we sit enjoying our scrambled eggs and contemplating which cake to have, my poor Auntie Jessie is dealing with my, sorry our, Ma. But tell me Sarah, do you miss your career at the Royal Infirmary?"

"Yes and no really, I wouldn't swop my two wee pests for anything, not even my career. But I would like to do something worthwhile when the twins are older. In a more enlightened world I would be able to work perhaps two days a week, but that's not going to happen is it - pigs will fly first - so I'll just have to hope a project like Ella's Friends comes into my life."

The waitress cleared away the remains of the savoury from the table, brushed away the crumbs and reset the plates and cutlery, she then brought to the table a cake stand with tiered China plates containing a selection of tea-bread and delicious looking cakes together with pots of tea and hot water.

As Sarah poured she said. "Mary, I am so happy to know that not only do you have financial security but with Ella's Friends a whole new career path is opening up for you. Samuel will be so delighted, he has a real soft spot for you.

Talking of our brother Samuel, you will never guess in a million years what's been happening in his life. He has found a young lady, honestly he has. As you know I was in total despair about him ever marrying and carrying on the Fischer name, then he meets a girl while on holiday in Austria.

Alan and I haven't met her yet but apparently her family are all academics and she, Leah by name, works as a translator at the Universitat Wien. Too brainy for us my dear, she speaks fluent French, English and German AND can converse in Russian, AND Polish AND Yiddish. Can you imagine? I can barely manage English, although I can trot out a word or two of Yiddish if I really have to.

Samuel is going back to Austria in the spring but meantime I believe the volume of post between Glasgow and Vienna has more than doubled."

"Oh Sarah, how lovely for Samuel," enthused Mary. "I'm so glad he has found someone special. If she speaks Yiddish, does that mean Leah is very religious?"

"Heavens no" laughed Sarah. "The family seem to be mainly secular from what I gather and the lovely Leah appears to be quite interested in politics 'don't you know'. I am not sure exactly but I think she is interested in the Zionist movement, they support the creation of a Jewish national home in Palestine. I don't know a great deal about it but I gather the movement was started in the 1890's by a young university student called Nathan Birnbaum I think it was called Kidimah but the real founder of Zionism is some chappie called Herzl who lived in Vienna, I think he died years ago. I expect that's why Leah has become enthusiastic because it all started in Vienna.

Samuel would explain it all so much better, you know he is the brain box in the family, sadly my dear, we are just the ordinary mortals."

They gossiped through tea and cake, their chosen cake of the day being a French Fancy, while the babies munched on rusks. Mary really enjoyed being in the company of Sarah, for want of a better word she was uplifting. In Gartsherrie Mary was expected to be the carer who looked after everyone with no thought for herself, but when she was with Sarah, Mary always felt that she was being cared for.

At last Sarah said. "Mary its quarter to four, I had better get the tram home before the tea time rush starts."

As they left Fraser's elegant store Sarah again embraced her sister. "My dear I wish you well with Ella's Friends, I am sure it will be a wonderful success and you will guide many women to a better life. I'm so proud of you Mary, even with all your health issues you are still thinking of others.

Now remember, if I can be of any help I will, I don't intend to spend the rest of my life making chicken soup with knadles!"

When Mary arrived home she was shocked to find the dinner already prepared, link sausages stewed in onion gravy, potatoes pealed ready to be boiled and a cabbage finely shredded.

Agnes then announced. "I've made a malt fruit loaf to have with our tea after we eat Mary. It's a while since I made one but I just took a wee notion this afternoon."

Mary removed her hat and coat thinking 'goodness me, what kind of a magic spell has my Auntie Jessie worked'.

The following Sunday morning after breakfast the four siblings left the Law house together. They walked as far as the Salvation Army Citadel at Sunnyside where the boys, Alexander and Robert, met with other members of the Band and Songsters ready to play at the Open Air Service before the morning Holiness Meeting.

Then Mary headed up Dunbeth Road, to Muiryhall Street and her final destination being the Maxwell Church of Scotland, in Weir Street, where she would attend the morning service, as she did every Sunday.

Jessie walked on up Main Street where she boarded a bus heading for the village of Carnbroe. Alighting at a little row of cottages she knocked on the door of one named Bankhead. The door was answered by a man in his sixties, seeing Jessie he immediately put his arms around her, and they both shed tears.

"Come away on in lass" said Hugh Mason as he welcomed her into his home.

"I was so pleased to get your postcard saying you were coming to see me this morning."

Hugh went into the kitchen to make a pot of tea for them both, bringing the tray into the living room. He then went into a cupboard and brought out a bottle of Whyte & Mackay Special Scotch Whisky. "You'll take a wee dram in your tea lass and we'll drink a toast to the finest man I have ever known, McInnes."

They sipped the tea for a few minutes, not talking, both reliving memories of times past. Hugh had been Right Hand Man to McInnes for many years and had taught Jessie all she knew about the drysaltery, papering and painting business.

"You know lass, McInnes was much more to me than an employer. My youngest son Fergus used to write about him with great respect during the War years. My boy Fergus was promoted to Corporal and then to a corpse in no man's land, defending God knows what foot of French soil, for politicians who played God with people's lives for their own ends. The only comfort his mother and I received was a condolence letter from Major McInnes, but not just a letter. On his next leave he came to see us and talked about our boy and sat listening to my dear Ethel as she relived Fergus's childhood. It broke my heart and it gave me comfort all at the same time.

McInnes stayed in touch and after the War two things happened almost simultaneously; I lost my wife Ethel and our daughter Grace to the Spanish flu and McInnes bought his first shop in Airdrie. He asked, no more like bullied, me into managing it for him. That act of kindness saved me from drowning in drink and despair.

McInnes became like a son to me and when he brought you into his life I was delighted, you were just so right for each other, and then cruel fate struck again and we both lost him.

Honestly Jessie I hope that evil brother of his, Fraser McInnes, never knows a days contentment for what he did to you. Mind you, I believe in the old saying,

'The mills of God grind slow but they grind exceeding small. Though with patience He stands waiting, With exactness He grinds all'.

After the day of his funeral I came home, opened a bottle of fine malt and drank it without getting drunk. It had no effect on me whatsoever, it didn't even numb the pain. I actually didn't care that Fraser had diddled me out of the shop in Main Street I was so full of grief. For weeks I lived on tea, toast and a lot of whisky. One day there was a knock on the door and standing there on the step was John Sharp and Willie Cunningham, two of the lads who also lost their jobs as painters.

They asked me to set up a business and employ them as they couldn't find other jobs. Initially I sent them packing but a few days later Willie came to the cottage again. He pleaded with me to help him find something as he had no work and a wife and four bairns to feed.

Well my dear Jessie, I am now running a small painting and decorating business from the cottage. I have a shed in the back garden where I can store paints and other materials. As for wallpaper, well I just keep sample books and order on a job only basis. The work keeps me busy and I feel I am at least helping two of our lads, oh and remember Stanley who worked for you, well I bring him in to do stripping and other unskilled work when I can. He really appreciates the money for he hasn't managed to find another permanent job either. Now lass, much as I am delighted to see you, why the visit?"

Jessie laughed. "Right to the point, that's our Hugh. It's so good to hear you talk about McInnes. I hardly mention his name at home, it's too private, too personal. But I always wear his ring, just looking at it gives me comfort. Actually Hugh I am here for some advise, back to my auld teacher."

Jessie then relayed the story of her Aunt Jessie's inheritance and the Ella's Friends project.

"Hugh, I was wondering if you would come over to the house and give us a bit of advice on well firstly, getting a proper survey then if all is well, layouts and decorating. My problem is I envisage the house as a family home and not a place where women and children will be living short term, I think practical and comfortable are the words, rather than beautiful and elegant. Hugh, will you come and have a look at Drumkiln House for me?"

"Of course I will Jessie, anything for you." replied Hugh. "Just you let me know when would be a good time and I'll meet you at the house, you know I'm always happy to help you. Your friend, Ella, has made a wonderful gift, kind of restores your faith in human nature. Perhaps it is the good Lord's balance for the perfidy of Fraser McInnes."

They spent time together talking of days past then Hugh went into the kitchen and made ham sandwiches and a fresh pot of tea for their lunch.

Jessie left to catch the Baxter's bus home before the dark set in on the cold December afternoon, feeling comforted after her visit with Hugh. No matter how kind or understanding her siblings, particularly Mary, were, they did not know McInnes like Hugh.

A few days later Christmas came and passed quietly in the Law household, although Mary and her mother made a steak pie dinner, followed by sherry trifle for the family on their return home from work.

New Year saw the traditional ritual of cleaning, dressing in Sunday best and preparing food for friends coming to first foot after the bells.

As usual Alex and Jessie Johnstone joined the Law family for the

Hogmany celebrations.

Jennie was spending the holidays with her sister Margaret and her family in Oxford. While Mary and Liz had travelled to Perthshire, where they were staying at the new Gleneagles Golf Hotel.

Glasses primed, the year of 1929 was welcomed in with Auld Lang Syne, ginger wine and sherry. As Alex downed a dram of good Scotch whisky, his thoughts were with his auld Ulster pal, Rab. Rab Law had passed away a good few years previously but Alex still mourned his cantankerous auld friend from County Fermanagh.

Mary and young Jessie passed around plates of home made shortbread, black bun, cherry cake, and clootie dumpling together with Agnes's wee tattie cakes, still warm from the oven.

Alexander put a record on the turntable of the new gramophone and everyone started to sing along to the new Ruth Etting song, Love Me or Leave Me.

A knock on the door quickly silenced the company. As head of the house Agnes rose from her chair and proudly walked to the front door. Standing on the doorstep was James, the family's First Foot, James, her dark haired, handsome son, together with his wife Margaret. Following tradition James was carrying a piece of coal, a packet of salt and a sultana cake, not home made, Margaret had bought it at Lees Grocery Shop.

Margaret put herself forward to shake her mother-in-laws hand but was ignored as Agnes put her arm around James and ensured her son was first over the front step. Saying. "Come away in lad, oor dark, handsome man, first across the Law threshold. You are bound to bring us good luck."

Everyone cheered as James came into the kitchen with Margaret walking sulkily behind her husband. The festivities got into full swing with Alexander sitting beside the new gramophone changing the records. Robert pulled his current girlfriend Helen up to dance, Alex put his arm around his beloved wife Jessie and they too danced in the New Year. James and Margaret joined the other couples but even a casual observer could have seen the coldness between the two of them.

The welcoming in of the New Year was going well, when

Alexander cried out. "Listen everybody, I've got a new record. Robert and I went halfies to buy it. Now presenting for the first time in Gartsherrie, Scotland, Sophie Tucker, singing My Yiddishe Momme.

Mary, could not believe the words of the song, there was her youngest brother, Alexander, playing a song about a Jewish mother, not knowing that his mother had converted to Judaism in her youth. Her children, her friends, her neighbours, they all considered Agnes Law to be a good Protestant, all except Mary, who knew all about her mother's past and her two Jewish children, a half brother and sister whom Mary loved.

Mary made eye contact with her mother, the moment lasted seconds but to Mary it seemed like an eternity. Quietly she made her way into the scullery, took her heavy coat from the hook behind the door and headed out into the cold night. She crossed the cobbled road to the toilet block and was pleased to find the toilet empty, Mary closed the door behind her and simply cried and cried.

Faithfully keeping her mother's secret over the years had become more and more difficult, she longed to share it with her sister Jessie, especially now the twins had arrived. Music can often set off a chain of emotions and that song had reached right into Mary's deepest soul.

Eventually the tears ceased and Mary knew she had better rejoin the festivities or risk awkward questions. As she crossed back over the cobbled road to number twelve, Margaret and James were just leaving and she could hear yet another argument was taking place as they walked up the Row towards their home, an ominous start to the New Year.

January 1st was a holiday, a celebration day, in Coatbridge and all over Scotland. The Gartsherrie Silver Band marched through the Rows playing in the year 1929. Neighbours popped into each other's houses during the day with good wishes for the New Year, and never left without refreshments. In the Law household dinner was another steak pie treat, this time followed by the remains of the Hogmany dumpling warmed and served with custard. In the evening Robert and Alexander attended the New Year Social at the Salvation Army, Alex attended a Lodge meeting and the Law

women, joined by Jessie Johnstone, blethered around the fire,
enjoying one last sherry.

January 2nd everyone was back to work and the festivities ended
for another year, back to 'auld clathes and purridge' - and the remnants of the black bun.

CHAPTER 5
January 1929

All those involved with Ella's Friends felt 1929 was going to be a very special year. And, all the members of the Law, Johnstone and Fischer families were in the main contented, with much to look forward to in the New Year.

Apart from James Law, Agnes's eldest son, his marriage to Margaret had been a disaster almost from day one. They were heavily in debt and since finding out his wife had aborted his child any lingering affection he had felt for her had completely vanished.

One afternoon, shortly after the New Year holiday, Mary was walking back from the Gartsherrie Store carrying two bags of messages and feeling fair trauchled. Suddenly she was aware of someone coming up behind her, James took the bags, saying.

"Come on our Mary, you shouldn't be carrying heavy bags, let your brother help."

"Help?" snapped Mary. "James Law you want to help yourself not me, do you think we are all deaf and blind to what's going on between you and that wife of yours. Auntie Jessie and Uncle Alex can hear the pair of you having rows nearly every night, honestly the two of you are a pure embarrassment to the whole Law family."

"Mary, I know you will say, 'we all told you so' well you were all right, damn it, marrying Margaret was the biggest mistake of my life. Do you know how much debt we owe? Well I'll tell you, over forty pounds, the tick men are never away from the door and no matter how many extra shifts I manage to work, it's never enough."

Mary thought of her Airdrie Savings Bank book hiding under

her Auntie Jessie's mattress. Her first instinct was to say, look James, I'll pay off what you owe give you a clean start but Mary was the family Miss Sensible, she knew giving the money was not the answer, James and Margaret had to face their responsibilities. Instead she heard herself actually saying. "I have an idea, why don't you give me your wages every week. I'll pay off the Tick Men a bit at a time and see to the rent and any other bills. You must go round all the shops and tell them no more credit for Margaret, if they give her any it's not your responsibility to pay her debts off. Margaret is working, she can use her money to buy your food.

I know I sound harsh, but think of our Maw, she brought us all up decently, no trips to the pawn shop or tick men for her, we never went to bed hungry and she had hardly two pennies to rub together."

They were now nearing number twelve, James handed the bags back to Mary, his head lowered down in shame.

"James, go up home and think on, come and see me if you want me to take over your money. Yes, I know it seems shaming but at least you would be doing something to improve your situation, you can't keep living on the never never."

Mary's words hung in the air as she went into the house with her messages and James carried on up the Row to a house that gave him no comfort, ruled by a harridan of a wife.

Mary heard nothing from James for several days, she had given up hope that he would take her advice. However, on Saturday afternoon there was a loud knock on the door and James called out as he came into the scullery.

"Maw, Mary any chance of a cup of tea, I've just finished an overtime shift?"

Mary stopped her ironing, "Aye, of course there is, Maw and I were just going to have a wee cuppa when I finish the ironing. Do you want a sandwich?"

Agnes looked up from her knitting muttering. "Sandwich indeed, can that wife of yours no look after you? I might no get out much our James but I am hearing plenty bad reports about what is going on up the road, you are a pure disgrace to the good name of Law."

James burst into tears. Both Mary and her mother looked on

horrified at the sight of the big handsome man crying like a bairn. Now the dam was burst he seemed unable to stop the river of tears.

Mary signalled to her mother to let him cry, she sensed that he needed a release from all the pent up worry and anger. Eventually the sobbing ceased and he started to speak.

"Mary, I've been thinking about what you said the other day, I can't think of anything else. You are right, I know you are, I've paid this weeks rent, although there is still arrears of three weeks. There you are, my wages."

He handed Mary his brown pay poke containing the remainder of his earnings for the week.

Mary took the money saying. "James the next thing I need is a list of all your creditors with the amount of money you and Margaret owe. I'll try and get all the folk to agree to receiving a fixed weekly payment. I know this is painful but it is the first step to getting your life back into some kind of decent order."

Even Agnes, who wasn't known for showing sympathy, put her arm around her son and agreed that he was doing the right thing. Then, reluctant to be thought soft she snapped. "Mary, finish up the ironing, I'll away and put the kettle on, is a cheese sandwich all right son?"

Greatly relieved, Mary put the money into the ornamental tea caddy on the mantle shelf.

Later that evening the peace in the Law household was shattered. After Jessie arrived home from work Agnes and her two daughters had just settled down to enjoy their evening meal. Without warning the front door flew open and Margaret rushed into the house like a whirlwind, yelling insults. Jessie, who had not been party to the afternoons events, was absolutely speechless.

Margaret was venomous. "What do you think you old witches are up to, taking my man's money. It's Saturday night and my Jimmy doesn't have a penny to bless himself with. How are we going to manage, just tell me that? And, as for you, the ugly baldy bitch sister..."

Even for Margaret this was a step too far. Mary, was hurt to the quick. Before anyone else could speak she rounded on her sister in law.

"If you were any way decent you would not be in this pickle of bother. My brother's money will be used to pay off your debts. You

can feed the pair of you out of your wages. Now, get out of this
house, and don't darken the Law family's door again, we don't want
to see your face until you and James have got your lives back in
order, now go, just go!"

Margaret stormed out leaving Mary shaking, horrified that
Margaret had mentioned the forbidden subject of her hair loss.
Mary, with her heart condition, could well have done without such a
cruel reminder of her constant sadness.

Mary and her mother then explained to Jessie the events leading
up to Margaret's outburst, the entire incident just further reinforced
Jessie's feeling about the unfairness of life.

Over the following weeks James was as good as his word and
handed Mary his wages, less the rent, every Saturday. However, during the week Mary often gave him a decent meal, aware that
Margaret was not using her wages to run the house properly but still
spending money on unnecessary fripperies.

Jessie and Jennie spent the first weeks of the New Year securing
the purchase of Drumkiln House. After receiving a good survey
report they had a number of meetings with Hugh Mason and young
Jessie working out how to renovate the house to the best advantage.

The united efforts of Jennie, Mary, and Liz eventually convinced
Jessie that she should apply to have a telephone installed. This did
not sit at all well with Jessie, or for that matter with Alex. However,
the waiting list was quite long and Jessie hoped that she had bought
herself some time and that she might be able to wriggle out of the
whole daft idea at a later date.

Mary and Liz returned from their holiday at the Gleneagles
Hotel in Perthshire early January and soon afterwards Mary Law recommenced her lessons with them on preparing her talks and public
speaking.

The days never seemed to be long enough for the six women
who were Ella's Friends. Led by the ever enthusiastic and hard working Jessie Johnstone, they were starting to see their enterprise, and
Ella's dream, take shape.

By the end of January 1929 the sale was complete, Jessie and
Jennie collected the keys of Drumkiln House from Mr Cornwall in

the knowledge that this time they would not have to be returned and they could start the renovations.

Jennie and Jessie immediately called a meeting of Ella's Friends. The following evening the six women met at Jennie's home. They sat around the mahogany table, and Jessie opened the meeting.

"Well Friends that's phase one over, Jennie and I collected the keys to Drumkiln House yesterday, Ella's Friends are now the owners of a muckle great Victorian hoose in Coatbridge."

The women let out a cheer and started to sing, 'For she's a jolly good fellow, For she's a jolly good follow, and so say all of us...'

Amidst the singing and laughter Jessie called out. "Please, please, it wasn't just me. We all played our part, my young namesake Jessie Law, contacted her friend Mr Mason who arranged a survey and has kindly prepared a set of plans with costings for the work required to turn Drumkiln House into a place of safety, not just that, a comfortable home from where women can gain the strength to move on to a new life with confidence and without fear." Cheering broke out, this really was a wonderful evening of celebration.

Eventually the meeting settled down to discuss the practicalities and the timescales, after much discussion the opening date of Drumkiln House as a Women's Refuge was set for April 1929.

The following weeks were busy beyond belief. Mary was now on the payroll, together with her Aunt Jessie. Jennie, Mary and Liz gave of their time and talents voluntarily. Jessie Law was the only member of the group in full time employment elsewhere, and she wished she was not. Jessie had never got over losing her business with McInnes and although she enjoyed her work at Dickson's Drysaltary in Glasgow she desperately missed the feeling of having a challenge, she wanted to develop a business, not just manage an existing one.

Tuesday was Jessie's half day off from her work in Shettleston. One Tuesday in early March, instead of getting off the train at Blairhill as usual she decided to stay on until Sunnyside and visit Drumkiln House.

By the time she reached the house Jessie was cold right through to her bones and she sincerely hoped someone would be boiling the kettle. Just as she was about to ring the doorbell Hugh opened the front door. "Hello Jessie what on earth are you doing here on this bitterly cold afternoon, you should be at home with a nice hot cuppa. Come away in before you freeze to death my girl."

Jessie laughed. "That's what I hoped to find here, a hot cuppa and a friendly face." Hugh apologised. "Sorry Jessie, I have to leave now, I have an appointment arranged. However, there is plenty of tea supplies in the kitchen and a tin with a Victoria sandwich cake, courtesy of your Auntie Jessie. John Sharp is upstairs working in the attic bedrooms, I just popped in for a few minutes to check that we were up to schedule, pity you just missed Stanley, I sent him off on a wee errand. Give John a shout, he'll give you a tour, and I'm sure he would enjoy a wee cuppa if you make one. Now, I really must rush, bye bye lass."

Jessie took herself down to the semi-basement kitchen, thankfully the new six burner gas stove was connected. The kitchen had not yet been completely decorated but it had been thoroughly cleaned and pride of place was a long well scrubbed pine table with benches on either side. There was also a second table with a marble top for pastry making and a black cast iron fireplace. Jessie went into the pantry which had been distempered white and the shelves lined with pale green oil cloth for easy cleaning, everything she required was on the shelves.

After making a pot of tea Jessie climbed the stairs and called out to John. "Mr Sharp, if you would like to come downstairs there is a cup of tea waiting for you and a slice of my Auntie Jessie's seriously delicious sponge cake."

John Sharp got the fright of his life, thinking he was the only person in the house.

He shouted down from the attic room. "Mercy me, is that your voice I hear Miss Law?"

"Indeed it is," replied Jessie. "I've made a pot of tea, would you like a cup before you show me around the house?"

John ran down the stairs and into the kitchen where Jessie was cutting slices of cake.

As he entered the room there was an awkwardness, John felt he had to say something about McInnes, to offer sympathy, but he was not quite sure of what to say. "Miss Law, I, well I just wanted to tell you that it was a privilege to work for you and McInnes and I, we, everyone was so sorry. Not just because we lost our jobs but because...er...well because it was so damned unfair what his family did to you and Hugh."

Jessie quietly replied. "John it wasn't just me and Hugh it was all of you who were affected, Stanley, Willie, Fred Watson, Jimmy Prentice and all the other guys, even Chrissie who used to come in and do a bit of cleaning. I've been lucky, I've got quite a good job managing a drysaltery shop in Shettleston but it's not the same, I really miss my shop in Coatbridge and running the painting and decorating side of the business. My new boss Mr Dickson does a decorating service but it's all done through his shop in Parkhead, I just send referrals. But enough of me, sit down and have your tea and a slice of cake and tell me what you are up to these days."

"Not a lot really, I couldn't get any work for ages after, well after. One day I ran into Willie Cunningham, he was in the same boat, although it was tougher for him, he was married with weans. I'm still staying with my Maw and Paw and I really only have myself to worry about. Anyway, we got talking and after a glass of Dutch courage at The Railway Bar, we headed over to Mr Mason's place and asked him if he could get us any work. You know Hugh Mason, he is very well thought of in the town and he has contacts everywhere.

Well, he wasn't at all keen to go back to work but eventually we persuaded him and the rest is history. Mr Mason has been great, as well as us he also finds work for Stanley who used to work in your shop.

As for anything else, not much really, my girlfriend Moira chucked me after I lost my job, not entirely her fault, I was a right pain in the neck for months. So now, other than work, I enjoy going to the dancing, usually the Albert or Locarno in Glasgow, believe it or not I also go to dance lessons here in Coatbridge. And, on a Friday night I usually catch up with some of the lads from the McInnes days and we go for a pint. Not exactly an exciting life but I'm not at all unhappy. Mind you it was a great relief when Mr Mason took to finding work for me and Big Willie, without him I'd probably still be on the dole, and as miserable as sin."

Jessie had been listening intently, John had not been one of her team, he had worked for Hugh from the Main Street shop so she didn't know him very well but just listening to him brought memories flooding back of the McInnes days. Fearful that she would start to get upset Jessie said briskly.

"Can you show me around now John? Mr Mason will be giving me my jotters if I keep you off your work for much longer."

They started at the top of the house with the three attic rooms. All three rooms had each been painted in a pastel colour and given a geometric stencil, John had just been finishing varnishing the skirting boards when Jessie arrived.

John explained. "Your sister Mary told me, the three rooms up here are to be used for single women. Downstairs there are six bedrooms, one already had an adjoining door and the joiner has made a door to join two others, they are for women with children, the two smaller rooms on the first floor will also be singles, although they could probably each also hold a cot. They have all been painted and varnished, just waiting on the furniture now. Come and have a look."

They explored the other rooms and Jessie was pleased to see that on the first floor they had adopted her idea to simply paint the bedrooms in a soft colour and omit a stencil, as the intricate Victorian cornice and ceiling rose was sufficient decoration.

"Quite a bit still to be done on the ground floor. We are going to be starting the papering tomorrow, I understand you picked out the wallpapers. Mr Mason brought them over today, want to see them?"

Back on the ground floor they went into the main sitting room and found box upon box of wallpaper. As Jessie started to look at the various rolls of paper John said. "Miss Law I'd better be away and finish the attic rooms, we have to start on the papering in the morning. Both Stanley and Big Willie will be in working with me, busy day ahead, in fact a busy week."

Jessie thanked John for showing her around, it was good to see her ideas coming to fruition, "And, by the way John, please call me Jessie, the Miss Law days have well and truly ended, the sooner I get used to that the better."

Before John could say anything Jessie had dashed into the

kitchen, lifted her coat and handbag and left Drumkiln House.

As Jessie walked home the tears blinded her, she thought she had got over crying for McInnes but at that moment she felt sure she never would.

CHAPTER 6
April 1929

Mary had kept Sarah up to date with all the goings on of Ella's Friends, Sarah in her turn relayed the change in Mary's fortunes to her brother Samuel, who was very fond of Mary. Although extremely pleased that her inheritance had made Mary financially secure he was even more delighted about her involvement with Ella's Friends. He understood Mary's nature, which was very like his own, that of being a quiet giver, and a hater of any form of injustice.

Samuel was very close to his twin sister Sarah and her husband Alan and his delight had known no bounds at being presented with a niece and nephew. However, Samuel never envisaged a domestic life for himself. The idea that he would meet someone, fall in love and marry, preposterous. No, his life was Salmond's clothing factory and intellectual pursuits, besides he was perfectly happy in his own company.

In the summer of 1928 Samuel arrived in Vienna on holiday, with the express purpose of visiting the Vienna State Opera, the Belvedere, the Hofburg and generally revelling in the architecture and art and music of one of the most beautiful cities in the entire world, the city of Mozart.

Samuel also thought this would be an ideal opportunity of meeting up with an old friend, Daniel Goldbaum. Many years previously when he was studying in Glasgow, Daniel and another Viennese student, Leon, had rented a flat in the same close as Samuel, the three had much in common, and enjoyed many happy times together in Glasgow.

Daniel was delighted to receive a letter from his old friend saying he was holidaying in Vienna. He immediately invited Samuel to spend a few days with him at his family home in the suburb of Dobling.

It was a beautiful Saturday in the early part of September 1928 when Samuel arrived for the weekend at his friends' home, carrying a small suitcase and with no thought in his mind other than how nice it would be to catch up with Daniel and also find out what was happening in Leon's life.

The door was opened by a pretty maid who showed him into the elegant home of the Goldbaum family, saying. "Everyone is in the garden having an aperitif before lunch, can I show you through to join them?" She led Samuel along the hall with its magnificent family portraits, through the library, then opened the French doors onto a picture perfect garden, where elegantly dressed men and women were sipping wine, laughing and chatting. The scene looked like an exquisite Renoir painting.

Daniel ran towards his Scottish friend to welcome him into his family, enthusiastically introducing him to the company in a mixture of German and English.

Then Daniel said the words which were to change the path of Samuel's life forever. "Samuel, my Scottish friend, this is my little sister Leah." Samuel could hardly speak, he felt he was looking at the most beautiful creature who ever walked on the planet earth.

Leah Goldbaum was in her late twenties, although beautiful the family considered her unlikely to ever marry. Clever and career minded she was also interested in politics, men admired her but they did not fall in love with her.

Samuel accepted a glass of sparkling gruner veltliner wine, laced with elderberry cordial. As he sat down beside Leah they clinked glasses, said 'Prost', and in that instant a romance started to blossom.

Leah and Samuel were as two souls that had been waiting for each other. They sat together at luncheon and talked as though they were the only two people in the room.

At the lunch table Daniel whispered to his mother. "Mama I wonder if we are actually going to marry Leah off to my poor unsuspecting friend."

During the remainder of Samuel's holiday he spent every possible minute with Leah, visits to the opera, galleries, coffee shops, uncovering to each other the layers of their interests and personalities.

They were also attracted physically and while they did not consummate their relationship there was definitely an electric spark between them.

Inevitably business called and Samuel had no option but to return to Glasgow, however, he left a part of his heart in Vienna. And, he sincerely hoped he would be able to collect it in the near future, together with the beautiful Leah.

The winter passed and the piles of letters in Glasgow and Vienna grew and grew. One day Samuel received a letter from Frau Goldbaum inviting him to spend a holiday with the family in the spring.

...Samuel, we so enjoyed meeting you last year, the family would be delighted if you would accept an invitation to spend a holiday with us at our home in Dobling. Spring in Wien is too too beautiful...

Samuel accepted with enthusiasm and made his plans accordingly.

In April a ship named Vienna was launched from John Brown's shipyard in Glasgow. Samuel for some reason saw it as an omen and he launched himself off to Vienna at the same time as the ship set sail, 10th April 1929.

Politically the 1920's were interesting times all over Europe. While to the east Russia, under Stalin, was now firmly in the grip of Communism, Italy was controlled by the Fascist Benito Mussolini. In Germany, after the hyper-inflation following the War the Nazi Party was gaining in strength. However, under the Weimar Republic there had been a great resurgence in the arts, from architecture to music, this artistic flowering spilled into parts of Austria, particularly Vienna. Vienna, in the 1920's was a city of culture, romance and excitement. Although in much of Europe, including Germany and France countries were polarised by Communism and Fascism.

The three weeks Leah and Samuel spent together in the Austrian capital in the spring of 1929 convinced them that they wanted to spend their lives together. They frequented the predominantly Jewish coffee houses in the 2nd District, where they talked and talked, about everything from their schooldays to artists, the Austrian Gustaf Klimpt, the Russian Marc Chagall, the Glaswegian Charles Rennie Mackintosh. Music, how could you not in the city of Mozart, Strauss, Brahms, Haydn and Beethoven. And, politics, from the far right in Italy under Mussolini, to the forthcoming election in Great Britain, which was being billed as the Flapper Election on account of all the women now being able to vote at the age of 21.

One bright afternoon over coffee and strudel Leah introduced the subject of German politics. "Samuel, that ghastly little man Adolf Hitler and his right wing cranks are a real force in Germany now. Apparently his party is growing by the year, well over 100,000 members now, not enough to worry the moderates of the Weimar Republic, but they are a truly dreadful lot."

"Yes, my dear," responded Samuel, "they are quite evil these so called National Socialists, abbreviated to Nazi's. I even read a bit of Hitler's book Mein Kampf years ago, an insomniacs' bible if ever there was one. However, I wouldn't like to see his party grow too much more, they are a bunch of dangerous criminals, antisemitic criminals at that, he certainly says as much in his book.

Finish your coffee my Leah, let's hop onto a tram then go for a walk in the Stadtpark, no more talk about mad politicians today."

The days were an idyll but in his room in the dark of night Samuel wondered how he could possibly ask a cultured girl like Leah, brought up in the clean, stylish and beautiful city of Vienna to come to Glasgow. Cold, gloomy, Glasgow, with its annual smogs and buildings covered in industrial pollution. Miss Cranston's Tearooms, even decorated by Mackintosh, were hardly a substitute for Viennese Coffee Culture.

Besides, he would need to think seriously about his home. During the War he had purchased a two bedroom flat in Garnethill, near the historic Romanesque revival style synagogue, the first purpose built synagogue in Glasgow. The flat was kept spotlessly clean, mainly due to the ministrations of Mrs Green three days a week, but it was hardly beautiful. The white distempered walls, were lined with bookshelves and a couple of comfortable leather chairs sat either side of the fireplace, all the other furniture was very basic, some even having been bought second hand.

For many years now Samuel had been in a financial position to buy a nice house or bungalow in one of the suburbs on the south side of the city but he simply could not see the point, he had everything he needed in Garnethill and the flat was within easy walking distance of his family clothing business in the Gorbals.

When he thought about the Goldbaum's elegant family home and compared it to his own he knew he was asking a lot of Leah to up sticks from Vienna and move to Glasgow. He certainly had to think about some new housing arrangements, a home fit for a bride.

The days were flying past, with only three days left until Samuel was due to return to Glasgow he knew that he had to take all his courage in his hands and act. In business Samuel was no slouch, if something required to be actioned, actioned it was. At Salmond's factory he was decisive and highly organised, but proposing marriage, that was altogether a different proposition.

One morning at breakfast Samuel looked across the table at the woman who had turned his life around. Leah, beautiful and exotic, almost as tall as him, she had not slavishly followed the fashion of the 1920's for short bobbed hair, cloche hats and dropped waist dresses. Her hair was dark, not quite black but a rich dark brown, and gathered into a loose curl at the nape of her neck, her eyes were a tawny brown, framed in thick dark lashes. Her clothes style was unique to her, that particular morning she was wearing a loose silk chiffon trouser suit in lilac topped by a tied silk scarf in shades of the palest lilac through to deepest purple.

They exchanged smiles, then breakfasted on little sweet milk rolls, with butter and cherry jam and cups of delicious black coffee.

Immediately after they had finished breakfast Samuel suggested they visit Schonbrunn Palace Gardens.

They boarded a tram which took them directly to Schonbrunn Palace. Sitting close together they simply held hands during the journey, for once they scarcely spoke, aware that their magical Viennese sojourn was shortly to end with Samuel's return to Glasgow.

Alighting at the Palace they decided to walk through the gardens as they had both visited Schonbrunn Palace, the glorious Imperial Summer Residence of Maria Theresa on many previous occasions.

April is the month of showers, suddenly the sky changed hue and large drops of rain started to fall. Holding hands the lovers ran towards the shelter of the Orangery.

Surrounded by tropical plants Samuel and Leah found a seat and an escape from the rain which was now falling heavily outside. As Samuel brushed a drop of rain from Leah's cheek he seized his moment, saying "My darling, beautiful girl, will you do me the honour of becoming my wife?"

Leah laughed as she kissed him, "Samuel Fischer, I thought you were never going to ask, you dour Scotsman, of course I'll marry you, the question is when my love. I have commitments at the University until December, I know, why don't you come back to Vienna in December and we can get married quietly without fuss?"

Samuel kissed his bride to be, totally impervious of the other people sheltering from the rain. He pulled her up from the bench saying. "Mrs Fischer to be, we are going into the city this very minute to visit a Jewellers, I want you to be wearing my ring before I leave for Scotland. And, I've got to get your Papa's permission, what do you think he'll say?"

"He'll probably say 'at last'. I think he has given up all hope of getting his youngest daughter married off, he'll probably offer you a dowry for taking me off his hands. Now, what's that you were saying about an engagement ring?"

As they left the shelter of the Orangery the sun came out and the rain ceased. Walking back towards the entrance gate Leah suddenly gasped. "Look, over there, a rainbow. Samuel it's an omen, we have both had our share of lonely days but now our rainbow is here, I'm so happy, so ecstatically, wonderfully, amazingly, I'm fast running out of adjectives, happy."

"Well before you do, we are going into town to buy you a ring. I'm not going to give you a chance to change your mind." Samuel said while holding her hand and walking faster and faster towards the exit.

Sitting in the tram Samuel asked his bride to be if she had any idea what style of engagement ring she would like.

"Something different, I would quite like a coloured stone, let's just see what they have in stock. Can we go to A.E. Kochert, they are probably the oldest firm of Jewellers in Wien, royal warrants and oodles of history. But I warn you they are quite expensive."

Samuel laughed. "Leah Goldbaum, soon to be Fischer, I never imagined meeting a wonderful girl I would want to spend my life with, I don't care what you choose but remember it will be on your hand for the rest of your days."

Alighting from the tram Leah led Samuel towards the shop in Neuer Markt from where the Kochert family had traded for over a hundred years.

The assistant welcomed them into the shop with great courtesy. Samuel tried to explain in halting German with a strong Scottish accent that they wanted to purchase an engagement ring. Seeing the confusion spreading over the poor man's face Leah explained in Wienerisch, the language of Wien, the purpose of their visit.

Of course Leah had given thought to what kind of engagement ring she would like, but she had no intention of telling Samuel she knew exactly what she wanted so she directed the shop assistant. "We would like to see something set in platinum, perhaps with a coloured stone and diamonds, possibly an Art Deco style."

The assistant disappeared into the stock room and returned with a tray of rings fitting Leah's description. One ring immediately spoke to her, it was a one caret diamond surrounded by a halo of natural French cut rubies, the shoulders were set with diamonds and the platinum setting looked like tiny beads. The other rings sported emeralds, sapphires, even semi precious stones such as amethyst and topaz, her birthstone, but the minute Leah saw the diamond and ruby ring she knew it was the one for her finger.

"Samuel I like this one, what do you think?" Samuel looked at the beautiful ring and knew it was perfect for his fiancé. He removed the ring from the pad and placed it on her ring finger, it fitted perfectly.

"Fits a treat Leah, another omen? Now can you please ask the gentleman the price and you can leave the store as my fiancé."

Samuel paid for the ring and they left the store in a whirl of love. "Let's go to the Metropole in Morzinplatz for a glass of champagne, Dutch courage before I speak to your Papa." suggested Samuel.

They sat in the beautiful surroundings of the elegant hotel which had been built for the Vienna World Exhibition. The waiter brought them two flutes of French champagne. As they clinked glasses Samuel said. "A toast to my beautiful fiancé. May we have a long and happy life together, l'chaim."

Leah responded "l'chaim my darling, l'chaim."

When they returned to the Goldbaum house in Dobling Leah ran upstairs to her bedroom and Samuel went through to the sitting room where Mr and Mrs Goldbaum were taking tea.

Mrs Goldbaum immediately said. "I'll ring for another cup Samuel, do join us. Now tell me have you enjoyed your springtime visit to our beautiful city?" Samuel was much too nervous for small talk, he cleared his throat and in his heavily accented German said. "Mr and Mrs Goldbaum would you do me the great honour of allowing me to marry your daughter Leah?"

The couple had been debating as to when, and if, Samuel would eventually pluck up the courage to propose to their daughter, so Samuel's request came as no great surprise to the couple. Mr Goldbaum stood up and shook Samuel by the hand. "My dear boy, welcome to our family, we will be more than pleased to accept you as a son. Now where is that daughter of mine, call her downstairs I want to congratulate you both."

Samuel ran into the hall and called. "Leah, Leah, please come downstairs, your Mama and Papa want to see you." She ran down the stairs at breakneck speed and the couple went through to the sitting room. Leah extended her hand. "You can't refuse Papa, Samuel has bought me this beautiful ring from Kochert's no less."

"I've no intention of refusing my liebling. Your Mama and I are both delighted to welcome Samuel into the Goldbaum family. No doubt you and your Mama will be bankrupting me with a lavish wedding. It's nearly ten years since your sister Anna married so it's definitely time for us to celebrate another wedding in the Goldbaum family."

The remaining two days of Samuel's holiday vanished as if by magic, making plans for the wedding in December and celebrating their engagement.

All too soon Daniel dropped his friend, and soon to be brother in law, at the Wien Sudbahnhof Railway Station. Sadly the day coincided with Leah's return to work at the University so she was not able to accompany Samuel to the railway station as he departed on his long journey back to Scotland.

While waiting for his train Samuel happened to see some beautiful silk embroidered postcards in one of the station shops, he chose one of a girl wearing Austrian national dress, which he bought and wrote to Mary back in Gartsherrie.

My dear sister Mary

I just wanted you to know that I have fallen in love with a beautiful and talented girl from Vienna called Leah, we hope to get married at the end of the year. I know it seems unbelievable, me Samuel finding love. Please be happy for me.

Your brother, Samuel

Samuel put the card inside a white envelope and addressed it to Miss Mary Law, then placed it in the post box.

During his journey home, Samuel's mind was busy hatching plans to move to a nice house in the South Side of Glasgow. And, he knew the very person to discuss his ideas with, Sarah. Before marrying Alan, Samuel's twin sister had owned an elegant flat in Shawlands. After they married, Sarah and Alan purchased a large detached house in Whitecraigs overlooking Rouken Glen Park, once again Sarah had waved her magic style wand and created a welcoming family home. That was the kind of house Samuel wanted for his bride, a home ready to be filled with happiness.

By the end of March 1929 the workload preparing Drumkiln House had intensified, even Alexander and Robert had been roped in to help. They were paid to get the long neglected garden back into good order. This was extremely important as Mary wanted to keep the day to day running expenses down by using home grown produce wherever possible, the secondary benefit being that gardening could act as a therapy for some of the women.

Jennie arranged appointments with local doctors and at the Out Patient Department of the Alexander Cottage Hospital to explain the service that Drumkiln House would offer and left cards with contact details. It had been unanimously agreed that women should be referred through the medical profession, with only five single and two family rooms available it was essential to ensure that each woman or family accepted was in genuine need.

Liz, who at the outset was frightened that her blindness would not allow her to participate in any useful way, was relieved to find that this was not the case. Mary Law became a frequent visitor to Liz's home where they worked on how the women would benefit from education and training. Mary was a practical woman and Liz an intellectual but as well as the teacher training lessons, together they planned the daily running of the Refuge, investigating suppliers, setting budgets, and thinking of ways that Ella's Friends could raise money as they couldn't rely on the capital to provide running costs forever.

Miss Mary Law and The Rt Hon Elizabeth Agatha Wallis-Banks became firm friends through their united desire to make Ella's Friends a resounding success.

Jessie, driven around by her daughter Mary, purchased linen, curtains, cooking utensils, additional furniture, in fact everything that was going go be required to fit out Drumkiln House as a comfortable and secure Refuge for women in need.

An unexpected benefit to the Law household was that as everyone was so involved with Ella's Friends Agnes Law had no option but to stop playing the matriarch and start doing some household work. After a few weeks of grumbling she found she was actually enjoying using her cooking skills again, even returning to going down to the Store each morning for her messages.

However, a great and totally unexpected sadness was the way some of the inhabitants of the Rows treated the Law and Johnstone families. In such a close knit community gossip was rife. As soon as the process of purchasing Drumkiln House had started so did the rumour mill. Two and two was put together and resulted in twenty two. Jessie Johnstone was the main focus of the gossip, sadly people she had known for decades seemed to harbour a wealth of jealousy, they did not seem to appreciate Ella's legacy had given Jessie a lot of hard work and worry. As she passed women talking in the Row or the Store, even in the bus, she heard snippets of conversation, 'you wouldnae credit the money' 'liv'n on steak and chicken, I've heard' 'an that daughter of hers, a car if you please'. As soon as she was spotted the comments would change to, 'morn'n Jessie, grand day', or some such. This was very hard for Jessie to thole, these were women whose families both her and Mary Law had helped over the years and yet there was no congratulations, no well done, there is an expression in Scotland used when someone does well or moves up in society, 'aye, but I knew his faither' and that attitude was prevalent towards the three members of Ella's Friends who lived in the Rows.

Mary and Jessie had a tiring day driving around various suppliers placing orders and organising delivery times. However, before dropping her mother home Mary suggested they call in to see her sister Agnes at her bungalow in Drumpellier.

As they caught up with each other's news over a cuppa Emily, Jessie's ten year old granddaughter, and the apple of her eye, came bounding in from school.

On seeing her Aunt Mary's car parked outside Emily was overcome with excitement, she ran into the living room and threw her arms around her Granny then started to talk ten to the dozen. "Granny where is my Grandpa? Why have you left him at home and Auntie Mary, where is my Auntie Liz, we are not a full family today, and my Daddy is also out at work.

I had a great day at school, guess what, I was first in arithmetic and I got all my spelling correct and Miss Bryce said my composition was excellent and that I have a very fertile imagination. And, and..."

"Miss, will you kindly take a breath," said her long suffering mother. "Honestly, I have never known a lass who could talk quite as much as you."

"I have," laughed Mary. "You! I remember you could talk for

Scotland, Sam was Mr Mischief and me, I was Mr and Mrs Johnstone's well behaved wean. Remember Ma, I was the quiet one who sat in a corner and read anything she could get her hands on."

Jessie laughed, "Actually Agnes, she is not wrong." Emily jumped in "See Mummy, Daddy is quite right when he rolls his eyes and says 'oh Emily pet you are just like your Mum'."

Mary rose saying. "Come on Ma, I had better take you home so that you can get the meal ready for Miss Emily's Grandpa and I have to get back to Airdrie to make sure her Auntie Liz is safe and well. Mrs Armstrong leaves for home at four o'clock so I have to make her evening meal."

Emily giggled, "Poor Auntie Liz, I bet Grandpa gets a better dinner." Mary chased her shouting "For your cheek madam I won't leave you that delicious bar of Cadbury chocolate I have in my handbag." But she did.

As Mary drove her home Jessie thought, 'what a lucky woman I am to have such a wonderful family and I think Emily is the glue that sticks us all together'.

Mary stopped the car outside her parent's home, saying. "I won't come in tonight Ma, I really had better get home to make Liz's tea and yes I know my offering will be inferior to yours, Emily really is a caution but she invariably gets it right. I'll collect you tomorrow about elevenish, we can go over to Drumkiln to check on how Hugh Mason's team are getting along downstairs. If the bed clothes have arrived as promised we could make up all the beds and possibly even hang some of the curtains. See you tomorrow Ma."

Ella's Friends were now reaching the final stages of the refurbishment and Jennie was being kept busy looking after the accounts.

One morning just as Mary was leaving home to catch a bus for Airdrie and another day working with Liz, the postman knocked. "Two letters this morning Miss Law, one for you from foreign parts and one for your mother."

Every communication that Mary received from Samuel or Sarah invariably found its way into the depth of the kitchen fire after being read. However, this postcard was so intricately made and carried such wonderful news that Mary simply could not bring herself to destroy something so lovely, she returned it into it's envelope and secreted it into the back of her Holy Bible.

Mary's peace was suddenly shattered when she heard her mother shouting. "Mary, you'll never believe what is in the letter that Postie brought this morning. It's from oor Charlotte and that useless man of hers Charlie, they want to send that boy of theirs back here to live with us. Honestly Mary I have had quite enough of Wee Willie and his funny peculiar ways. You'll have to write to that daft sister of yours and tell her NO, absolutely and definitely NO."

Mary wholeheartedly agreed with her mother. Willie had been such an oddity on the previous occasions he had stayed with the family in Gartsherrie. However, with the opening of the Refuge so close they definitely could not accommodate him. Besides her brothers Robert and Alexander would not relish having a ten year old share their bedroom.

Mary quickly put pen to paper.

Dear Charlie and Charlotte,

Ma is really upset at receiving your letter telling us you want to send Willie to live with us yet again.

I just have to be firm, the answer is NO, we have quite enough to deal with at the moment and a precocious ten year old does not fit into our lives.

Willie is your child, deal with him. Charlotte this time NO means NO.

I hope you and Charlie are both well and the children are all thriving.

Also, please give my best wishes to Alice Baird, I so admire the way she works on her husband's farm. Charlie is very lucky to have Farmer Baird as an employer.

I'm really sorry Charlotte but this time you and Charlie have to control Willie.

Love, your sister
Mary

Mary put on her hat and coat and headed off to Airdrie but first she posted her reply to Charlotte into the post box outside the Gartsherrie Store. As she dropped the letter into the red box Mary thought, 'Charlotte, you will certainly get the message this time, NO means NO'.

Mary quickly put Willie to the back of her mind she was so involved with getting Drumkiln House up and running.

Hugh and his team finished the decoration; furniture was delivered; beds made; curtains hung; kitchen equipped and stocked. Mary organised the little room off the kitchen as a clinic and a place where she could make Ella's healing ointments. With every day that passed the house neared completion and the Refuge for Women came closer to being a reality.

One evening towards the end of April Ella's Friends met in the sitting room of Drumkiln House. Jennie, Jessie together with Mary and Jessie Law were first to arrive. "Funny not being at your place Jennie." said Jessie. "It seems odd after all our planning in your morning room and now the reality. This beautiful house prepared as a Refuge for women in need."

Mary looked out of the window and saw the Vauxhall draw up outside. "That's Mary and Liz arrived from Airdrie, what are they not like? Your Mary is carrying a couple of bottles of champagne." Mary Law headed to the front door to help Liz inside.

As she opened the front door another car drew up, from which Andrew Cornwall and Hugh Mason alighted.

The men presented the ladies with a bottle of the finest malt whisky and a plaque which read:

> The Ella Millar Refuge for Women
> Opened April 1929
> By Ella's Friends

Jessie thought 'thank goodness I made a batch of sausage rolls, champagne indeed'.

There was congratulations all round and a toast to Ella, a truly remarkable woman. Everyone enjoyed the celebration and there was much talking and laughter and telling of stories.

Eventually Andrew Cornwall managed a word with Jessie on her own. "You know Mrs Johnstone when I first read to you and Miss Law the terms of Ella Millar's will, I realised you were taking on a very onerous commission. To be perfectly honest in all my professional career I have never come across anything quite like it. However, I must congratulate you on handling the task at hand with such enterprise and enthusiasm. I think your great strength has been realising you could not do everything alone and forming Ella's Friends. Then bringing in Hugh Mason as your Clerk of Works, that was a brilliant move." "Alas" said Jessie. "I can't take the credit for involving Hugh, that goes to my wee namesake Jessie Law. They are good friends, Hugh used to work for her late fiancé, McInnes."

Andrew Cornwall spoke quietly. "Yes, I do know the history, absolutely tragic. However, I hope involving Hugh and Jessie Law in Ella's Refuge will in some way help them both through their pain."

The champagne was drunk, the sausage rolls eaten and Hugh screwed the plaque onto the wall in the vestibule.

At last the Women's Refuge was officially open and the first part of Ella's legacy spent. According to Jennie, the expenditure to date totalled £898.14.3, well within budget.

CHAPTER 7
June 1929

Jessie Johnstone arrived home from Drumkiln House one beautiful summer evening, she quickly threw her bag and outdoor things on the bed and started to prepare dinner before Alex returned from work. Much as she enjoyed her role of managing Drumkiln House, supported every day by Mary Law and the other members of Ella's Friends, whenever they could make time, she greatly missed her leisurely time with Alex. Before opening the Refuge she had cooked, cleaned and fitted in her millinary work during the day. After clearing away the dinner her evenings were spent with Alex, talking, playing cards, perhaps reading a welcome letter from the family in Australia or just sitting holding hands in front of the fire. It did not really matter what they did, it was the companionship, the being together, that mattered.

Jessie had only just started making the dinner when she heard the Work's siren, indicating the shift was over and Alex would be home in a few minutes time.

He came into the kitchen looking tired after his long shift. "Well my darl'n girl how was life at the Refuge, and what's your craic today."

"Away with you Alex, get yourself washed while I finish the dinner. It's a lovely night, after we eat our meal why don't we go out for a wee walk."

After they had finished eating their meal and clearing away the dishes Alex and Jessie started out on their walk.

Children were playing on the greens, old men were sitting on chairs outside their homes, smoking their favourite baccy, women were standing in small groups gossiping while the courting couples had all headed off to Drumpellier Lochs for a spot of winching. The Johnstones' walked passed Shanks Farm towards Blairhill, for once in her life Jessie was glad to get away from the Rows, the idea that she was the subject of gossip, and nasty gossip at that, was extremely hurtful. Jessie felt she had to ask the question of her husband. "Alex, are you the butt of gossip at the Works?" He reached out and took her small hand in his large work worn one, they walked together in silence, as much in the throws of love as any of the young couples who had headed out for the Lochs. Eventually Alex answered. "You know the answer is 'yes' Jessie. Ella meant well, she was a kind auld wummin but I honestly don't think she could have imagined in a million years the changes her legacy would make to all oor lives. You running around with oor Mary in that fancy car spending money like its goin' oot of fashion, and Mary Law up at Liz's posh place in Airdrie every other day. Of course the auld biddies are going to make a meal of it, and yes, their men try and wind me up. But Jessie my lass it disnae work, I just ignore them or joke it off."

They were just walking past Jennie's home, when she saw them from the garden as she dead headed her roses. She called out.

"Alex, Jessie, out for a walk this lovely evening, come on in and have a cold drink, I made lemonade this afternoon."

This was the first time Alex had ever been inside Jennie's home, he was truly amazed not only at the comfort and beauty but at the size, he thought 'My my, a single wummin in a hoose this size. When I think we brought up three bairns and had the Laws as lodgers, with their brood, in two wee rooms, it's an ill divided world, so it is'.

"Come away in" said Jennie. "Make yourselves comfortable and I'll get the lemonade." She returned with a tray containing a pitcher of lemonade, glasses and a plate of little biscuits, saying. "I'm no Agnes Law in the baking stakes but I made a few biscuits this afternoon, I hope they are all right."

The three friends sat comfortably enjoying the refreshments for a few minutes when Jessie said. "Jennie, do you think for one moment Ella imagined the amount of gossip that would be created over the

opening of Drumkiln House? Even my Alex is being subjected to
nasty comments. On the one hand I can see that we can do an enormous amount of good. In a few months we have taken in six women,
two of which we have resettled with other family members, Helen
Watson and her little girl are growing in strength and Wilma
McDonald, well Mary has managed to get a job for her in Rankins, so
hopefully when she has grown in confidence we can help her find suitable long term accommodation. It shouldn't take long to get Mavis
back on her feet, she doesn't have any wee ones and her marriage to
Bertie Wilson didn't last too long. Biggest worry is Sadie Kane, she was
in such a poor state when she arrived that it's going to take a long time
to turn her life around. I know we are providing a worthwhile sanctuary to women at the end of their tether, but I also feel we are all paying
a personal price, I don't feel like me any more."

Alex laid his glass on the table and took his wife's hand, saying.
"Jessie Johnstone you have always been a brave resourceful lass, you
have brought up our bairns to be good decent people, you have
been a kind neighbour and no man on God's earth has a better wife.
Jess my girl, let the auld gossips blether. Remember the nonsense
they talked about Jennie here when her sister Margaret ran off to get
wed. It'll be a ten day wonder, you and the other lasses need to concentrate on the Refuge, you have the vote now, it's time to move on,
auld Ella has placed her trust in you, don't you go letting anybody
destroy that trust.

Do you think I'm right Jennie? If you do, give my wife a good
telling off and tell her to get on with her work."

Jennie laughed. "Oh Alex, indeed I will. You have no idea how
good your Jessie is at supporting the ladies who badly need a Refuge.
As well as the ones who have stayed with us she has counselled quite
a number of other ladies, perhaps one day they will find the courage
to leave a violent home and start their lives anew. Ella left a financial
legacy but you my dear Jessie are the guiding force behind Drumkiln
House, the force that makes it work."

As Alex and Jessie walked home companionably together he
turned to his wife and said. "Jessie, these years have been like nothing that has gone before in our lives. When we all sung Auld Lang

Syne to see in 1928, none of us could have imagined the changes we would all see. 1929 has been even more incredible, I have no idea what's coming next but in my heart of hearts I ken there is no stop'n a runaway horse."

Since the opening of the Refuge Mary Law was the happiest she had ever been in her entire life. At last she felt she had a worthwhile mission, she no longer had to work as a maid three afternoons a week or spend her days housekeeping under her mother's watchful eye. And, she was receiving a proper wage for her work. Now on a Friday evening, like her brothers and sister she gave her mother 'dig' money and her remaining cash was hers to do with as she wished. As for the gossips and their nasty little comments, Mary cared not a jot, 'sticks and stones may break my bones but names will never hurt me'. Her delight was at the age of nearly thirty she was at last having a worthwhile career.

For once Mary was at home by herself, Robert was out with his current girlfriend, Alexander at football practice, Jessie out walking with her friends and her mother had gone to visit the Ballantine family, taking some of her scones. Jimmy Ballantine had been off work ill for some weeks and she just wanted to be neighbourly.

Mary was using the quiet to enjoy reading 'The Mystery of the Blue Train' by Agatha Christie when her peace was interrupted by a visit from her brother James.

Mary put her book aside and put on the kettle, as she made the tea James told her the purpose of his visit. "Mary, you helped me get straight financially, Margaret will never be a housewife like our Maw, I realise that now and I manage the money. She is supposed to buy the food from her wages, sometimes she does, sometimes not. Well the news is she is expecting a bairn early in the New Year. Money will be even tighter but I promise we will not have the tick man knocking at the door again.

But what I'm really here to tell you about is my involvement with first aid. Mary, you are not the only one in this family interested in medical matters. I have joined the St Andrews Ambulance Association. Last year the Association opened a headquarters in Glasgow, in North Street. I have been attending classes in first aid and I will soon be able to attend events as a Qualified First Aider. However, I can't help but think it would be great if there was a well equipped First Aid Station at Gartsherrie Works, you know, to deal with minor accidents and to provide a place where men with injuries could be assisted until an ambulance arrives to take them to hospital. I know I am just a joiner but do you think I could put the idea forward to the works management?"

Mary was thinking on her feet. "James, I think it's a brilliant idea, but don't you think it would be better if you worked at getting more qualifications and experience before putting up such a plan. Particularly as you are about to become a father and that means you really must have a secure job."

"I know what you are saying Mary, and you are probably right, but every day I see accidents, I've even had a few myself. Men with flakes of metal in their eyes, burns, cuts, broken bones, you know as well as I do the amount of accidents at the works. Its criminal, pure criminal."

"Yes James, there is no arguing with the facts but I can only repeat my advice, get more qualifications, make a good case. Can I also suggest you have a wee quiet word with Agnes Johnstone's man, Tom Coats. He is a senior manager and he might be able to give you some good advice as to who you should approach. Plan quietly, that's my advice, it might take longer but you have a much better chance of success in the long run.

Now let's just sit down and enjoy a quiet cuppa before everyone starts returning and the peace ends."

The following morning Mary was in the kitchen clearing the breakfast dishes when Postie brought the mail. Mary's heart sank when she saw another letter with a Condorrat postmark.

With mounting trepidation she opened the envelope addressed to her in her sister's handwriting.

Dear Mary
Read the enclosed letter Charlie and I received from Willie's teacher, well the headmaster, Mr Gibson.
The other bairns are all fine and doing well at school, particularly our May, Irene is four this year and a wee charmer. Honestly, the others are all normal

Mary, I have no idea what sin we committed to get Willie.

I have addressed this letter to you as I thought you might be able to persuade Maw to let Willie come and live in Gartsherrie, I do understand it's a lot to expect Robert and Alexander to share their room with a ten year old and I wouldn't ask but we are at the end of our tether. Honest Mary, wait till you read the letter.

Send me a telegram when he can come and I will bring him myself. Please help us out.

Love

Charlotte

Mary carefully unfolded the enclosure, it read,

Dear Mr and Mrs Fyfe,

I am afraid it is once again necessary to write to you regarding the behaviour of your son, William. Numerous letters sent by his class teacher, Miss Williams, have been ignored. Therefore, as Headmaster I have no option but to formalise the situation.

Since returning from his last temporary expulsion William has continued to be a disruptive force in the school, here follows some examples of his misdemeanours: dipping girls hair in inkwells; spreading glue on Miss Williams chair; advising Miss Williams that he was unable to attend school as he had no shoes or boots (your other children confirmed this was an untruth); painted red spots on his face and pretended he had a fever; attended school wearing a sling and claimed he had a broken arm, another untruth.

The above examples are just part of a bigger picture of daily classroom disruption.

However, the final straw occurred last Friday, our local Church of Scotland minister Rev. Cowan was conducting his weekly service at Assembly. Afterwards William approached Rev. Cowan and asked if he could speak to him privately. The minister agreed and asked him kindly as to what was his question. William responded thus.

"Minister, I have been questioning my Christian faith and I was just wondering what I need to do to become a Roman Catholic?"

This school is simply not equipped to give your son the attention he demands, in my opinion he requires a private tutor to school him in the subjects he excels, arith-

metic and English, and to bring his serious behavioural problems under control.

In all my years teaching and as a Headmaster I have never encountered a child quite so determined to get expelled.

It is with regret that I must inform you of the immediate permanent expulsion of William Fyfe from this school.

Yours faithfully

Alexander Gibson

For all the seriousness of the situation Mary could not help but smile at the idea of Willie approaching the dour Presbyterian Minister, no doubt wearing his best poe faced expression, and asking how to convert to Catholicism.

Mary put the letters into her handbag, the eruption she knew would take place when her mother found out about the letters would have to be delayed.

Mary called out to her mother, "That's me away Maw, I should be home about six o'clock."

On the bus ride over to Coatbridge Mary could think of nothing else other than the dynamite she carried in her handbag. Arriving at Drumkiln House she said a cheery 'good morning' to the women breakfasting in the kitchen then went straight into her little medical room. Sitting at her desk she removed the letters from her handbag and carefully re-read them.

Mary could think of no solution other than Willie coming back to Gartsherrie. Charlotte and Charlie lived on a farm in the country and there wasn't another school within walking distance. There was no point in sending him to Charlie's family, they also lived on a farm and Willie's aim in life was to get as far away from farming as possible.

Jessie opened Mary's door. "Penny for them, you look deep in thought, is everything all right?"

"No Auntie Jessie it's all wrong. Just read these letters I received this morning from Charlotte and give me your opinion."

Jessie carefully read the letters, a smile breaking out on her face when she read of the meeting with the minister. "He really is a pure caution, does your mother know of this latest episode in the Willie saga?"

"No" answered Mary, "To be honest I couldn't face the fireworks this morning, I thought I would tell her this evening after we have our dinner, then all the family can have their say. Aunt Jessie, I can't cope with the wee blighter and the boys will be furious, I say boys, they are working men now and they don't need a ten year old sharing their room. As far as my mother is concerned she will be furious with Charlotte, she never approved of her marrying Charlie Fyfe, and landing us with her offspring is simply not on my Maw's agenda."

Mary spent the rest of the day making up various ointments and distilling cordials, courtesy of a fine crop of blackcurrants and raspberries from the garden. Jessie dealt with all the day to day goings on in Drumkiln House, leaving Mary to work alone, knowing she wanted some thinking time.

As she returned home on the bus Mary was dreading the family confrontation that awaited after they had eaten.

The family enjoyed homemade mince pie with potatoes for their dinner, accompanied with salad, courtesy of Drumkiln House's garden. Agnes Law was not always the easiest of women but she was certainly an excellent cook and baker.

As they finished dinner Alexander started to say that he was off out. Before he could finish the sentence Mary stood up and said. "Everybody please stay where you are I have some news that effects us all. Now before anyone says a word please just hear me out." Mary then read the two letters from Charlotte and Willie's headmaster.

As she finished there was an outpouring of voices, led by Agnes. The four siblings thought their mother was going to have apoplexy, she was absolutely furious. As Mary thought would be the case both Robert and Alexander were none too pleased about the grim prospect of Willie staying in Gartsherrie on a permanent basis and made their views felt.

Everyone was vying to make their voice heard when Mary took the initiative, all the lessons in public speaking from Liz were brought into play.

"Right everyone, I think we are all one hundred percent in agreement that we don't want Willie to move into our home in the Long Row. However, quite frankly I don't think we have a choice in the matter. You have all heard the content of the letters, Wille is a manipulative wee scoundrel, we all know that but we also know that if he is staying here he will play Willie the angel instead of Willie the devil.

Now very reluctantly I think I should write to our Charlotte and tell her to bring him here at the start of the new school term in August. We can advise the school that he has simply come to live with us again. Besides, he behaved himself at Gartsherrie Primary previously so they would have no real reason to refuse to allow him to attend.

At the end of the day it all comes down to family. Charlotte might live miles away on a farm in Condorrat but she is still part of this family."

Jessie stood up determined to quickly end the conversation. "Let's get the table cleared and Alexander if you want to get away out you had better get ready. Now Mary you put the kettle on and we can sit down with Maw and have a cup of tea."

Both Robert and Alexander took up the cue and quickly got out of the house. By the time the meal was cleared and the tea made Agnes had calmed down a little.

Mary went into the bedroom found her writing pad, and penned the letter.

Dear Charlie and Charlotte

As you can imagine all the family are furious at Willie's latest escapades.

However, we have reluctantly decided that you can bring him to Gartsherrie when the other children start school in August after the summer holiday.

One piece of nonsense and he is back on the train immediately, there will be no second chances. And, if he does get sent home he will NEVER be allowed back again. Now I suggest you tell him the rules and ensure that he behaves all summer, give him plenty of work to keep him out of mischief. Write with the details of your arrival.

Maw and all the family

Satisfied she had made their views abundantly plain, Mary addressed the envelope and it sat on the table ready to be posted the following morning on her way to work.

CHAPTER 8
August 1929

Mary Johnstone returned to her home in Airdrie one evening, tired after a busy day working at Drumkiln House. In a surprisingly short time news of the Refuge in Coatbridge had circulated and local doctors and hospitals saw it as a route to helping women who were living in fear. It was also often a way to pass on a problem case they did not particularly want to deal with themselves.

Ella's Friends had quickly discovered that the actual residence period at Drumkiln House should be short rather than long term, with each woman receiving help appropriate to her needs, in order to make her independent, in a safe environment, as quickly as possible.

As well as successes there had been a number of troubling moments. A number of women, for various reasons, had simply given up and returned to abusive homes. However, overall the successes far outweighed the failures. Mary Johnstone had found her niche as record keeper, writing a report on each client from the initial referral to detailing the help given and the final outcome. These reports were carefully filed in a cabinet in Mary's Medical Room which was always kept locked when Mary Law was not on duty.

Mary liked to think that Ella Millar was looking over her shoulder as she typed the reports, approving of how her legacy was being spent.

When she arrived home in Airdrie Mary hung her coat and hat on the hallstand then walked through to the sitting room, saying to Liz. "Fancy a cup of coffee sweetheart? I could do with a lift, I've never stopped today, between answering the phone, record keeping and can you believe amusing children honestly I've never halted. I'm going to suggest to my Ma that we buy some more story books and toys for the wee ones."

A distracted Liz answered. "Yes, that would be an excellent idea and Mary, I've got something important I'd like to discuss with you."

Mary made the coffee and they settled down companionably to talk. "Mary, I received a telephone call today from my Stockbroker in London. He wants me to sell the bulk of my stocks and shares and invest the money into property. Apparently he feels uncertain on a number of issues and he thinks bricks and mortar rather than shares would be a better long term investment in the present climate.

His words gave rise to a chain of ideas bubbling through my head. I'll try and make sense of them. What if I was to take his advice, sell my, or as I think of it now, 'our' portfolio and use part of the money to provide low rent housing for some of the women who are ready to move towards independence from Drumkiln House but can't afford commercial rents. It would free up space in the Refuge for desperately needy cases and the rents would cover the property maintenance expenses.

Also, your Pa is not getting any younger, and he works terribly hard at Gartsherrie Works. Now Mary how do you think your parents would respond to this idea. If we were to buy say a row of cottages for the women to rent we could gift a cottage to your parents. Now I know your Pa would not take anything he considered 'charity' but perhaps we could ask him to take a job overseeing the properties and to be on hand as a Warden. If there was any trouble from disgruntled husbands he would be on hand to contact the police, it would also give the woman an added level of security.

I have been rolling around the whole idea in my head all afternoon looking for possible flaws and I need you to do the sums.

Mr Green is adamant that we make a swift decision, I have followed his advice for many years and never regretted it, so Mary, what do you think about my ideas?"

"I think I am going to be up half the night crunching figures, that's what I think," replied Mary. "First I'm going to make us both some scrambled egg on toast for supper and then I'll get started."

It was quarter past two before Mary woke Liz, who was dozing in her armchair. "Liz, I have some thoughts and figures, I've also made us some cocoa, let's talk."

Mary put forward an outline business plan which included Liz's idea of making low rent properties available for women leaving Drumkiln House, together with her parents moving into a 'managing' cottage. It also included a diversifying strategy. Buying several apartments in the better parts of London or Glasgow which would produce good income. Possibly purchasing a small pied-a-terre for their own use in London, which would save a fortune on staying at the Savoy.

Finally, she said, I know you might think this is a bit radical but it might be an idea to purchase parcels of land on the outskirts of towns and communities that are expanding. Land is the one thing that cannot be produced, therefore if we own strategic plots, we just need to either hold the title deeds or get an income from renting as agricultural land and then simply wait until we are approached with an offer. Another thought, if Mr Green is jumpy about the market perhaps we should divide the money released between a number of bank accounts until we purchase the properties. What do you think Liz?"

"Mary my dear, I think we should speak to Mr Green tomorrow, give him an outline of the plan and see if he approves. Now let's go to bed, you must be exhausted and we have a seriously busy day tomorrow."

Mary might have gone to bed but she did not sleep, the ideas kept spinning around in her brain. However, the one thing that kept returning was how wonderful it would be to give her parents security and allow her father to leave his job labouring at Gartsherrie Works.

The following morning Mary telephoned Mr Green and presented him with a summary of her and Liz's ideas. He did not waste a moment. "Miss Johnstone, I wish all my clients were as proactive and businesslike as you and Miss Barns-Wallis. Can I speak to Miss Barns-Wallis now and receive verbal instructions to liquidate most of her portfolio. Please send me a confirmation letter by registered post, with her formal instructions, as soon as possible."

Mary wrote the required letter and read it to Liz who immediately signed the paper that was to be the most important communication of her entire life.

A life changing communication also arrived for Mary Law in Gartsherrie, it was a letter from her sister Charlotte.

Dear Mary

Willie has behaved quite well all summer, he knows any nonsense and he would have lost his chance to move to Gartsherrie.

The children return to school next Monday. I'll bring Willie on Saturday, I should arrive around noon.

Charlie has suggested I also bring wee Irene over to Gartsherrie so that my Maw can see her. Mary she has the most beautiful dark wavy hair and the family blue eyes, she is a picture and bright as a button but not manipulative like 'you know who'.

See you Saturday

Love Charlotte

Mary knew that her short reprieve had now ended and Willie would soon be once again living with the Law family in Gartsherrie.

Saturday dawned, Jessie was at her work in Shettleston, Alexander was at football practice and then he intended going to support his team Albion Rovers. Robert was spending the morning working in the garden at Drumkiln House and then he intended to join his brother at Cliftonhill to cheer their team on for the first home match of the season.

Mary and her mother prepared for their visitors, with Agnes constantly grumbling under her breath and Mary simply ignoring her and accepting the inevitable. Around half past twelve, the door opened and in came the Fyfe family from Condorrat.

Willie, wearing his new trousers, shirt and school shoes, stood in the background, carrying a large brown paper parcel containing his possessions. After welcoming Charlotte and admiring wee Irene, Mary turned her attention to Willie, who she could sense was up to something.

He went into his pocket and produced a paper poke containing black and white striped balls. With great aplomb he presented the bag to his grandmother saying. "I promise to be exceedingly good Granny, no nonsense, you will find a changed William Fyfe. A

William who will always show respect to his elders, and betters, and be a good hard working Protestant boy. A William who will make you proud of his achievements. A William..."

As Mary watched the scene being played out, her eyes met Charlotte and they both looked up to heaven.

Mary put an end to the drama. "Charlotte I've made some sandwiches, come away into the scullery and help me get the food served. As soon as she got Charlotte on her own Mary asked. "What in the name of goodness is all that acting about?"

"I know" said Charlotte desperately trying not to laugh. "He has been practicing his arrival speech in front of the mirror for weeks, he really is a caution." Mary snapped, "Caution? Caution? That does not begin to cover the contents of the letter from his Headmaster. Charlotte this is the last time we are going to take him in. One step off the straight and narrow and he will be on the train to Condorrat before you can say Jack Robinson and then he is your problem."

Bringing Irene had been a brainwave on the part of Charlotte and Charlie, Agnes was quite taken with the wee girl who had her colouring and bright blue eyes, Irene took the attention away from Willie, who had now put the second part of his 'Operation Granny' plan into action by quietly passing around the sandwiches and fruit loaf.

Mary could see right through him but kept quiet and simply enjoyed spending time with her sister and playing with her wee niece.

Charlotte and Irene left at half past four, in plenty of time to catch the five o'clock train home.

After saying a polite, rather than tearful, goodbye to his mother and sister Willie proceeded to wash and dry the dishes in the scullery.

Through in the kitchen Agnes relented. "Maybe it will no be too bad having him here, he can do a lot of the wee jobs around the place, and remember our Mary you are always away at that Refuge of yours. Perhaps he will be a help after all."

Mary doubted how much of a help he would really be but it was better having her mother accepting Willie's presence that constantly complaining, and Agnes could complain for Scotland if she felt the situation demanded.

Jessie, Robert and Alexander returned home, Mary made the

Saturday night tea of sausage, fried egg and chips, served with bread and margarine from the Maypole Dairy. There were now six at the family table and wee Willie never said a word other than, 'please, thank you and may I leave the table'.

CHAPTER 9
October 1929

The chain of events feared by Mr Green came to pass and the repercussions circled the world.

24th October 1929, Black Thursday, Wall Street stock market lost eleven percent of its value. Panic meetings ensued bringing a slight rallying of the market.

28th October, Black Monday. The slide continued.

29th October, Black Tuesday. Panic selling reached its peak. The market lost over 30 billion dollars in the space of just two days.

30th October, there was a slight recovery with the Dow Jones gaining around 12 percent.

By November 23rd the American Market had reached rock bottom and started to stabilise.

The crash followed the speculative boom of the 1920's and it would lead to the 'Great Depression' which would ultimately affect the entire world.

However, Germany under the Weimar Republic of President Paul von Hindenberg would suffer dreadfully because of the loans they had received from America, via the Dawes and the Young Plans, this eventually led to severe unemployment, even starvation, throughout the land and renewed anger against the Treaty of Versailles.

Germany was now a fertile breeding ground for the extremes of the political spectrum, both Communism on the left and the far right, as represented by the Nazi Party.

However, in 1929 not even the most pessimistic person could have predicted what the next ten years would hold for Europe and the world, as it moved from The Roaring Twenties to the Great Depression of the Thirties.

CHAPTER 10
November 1929

The events of the previous months continued to reverberate, even in a community as unsophisticated as Gartsherrie, most of the inhabitants realised that world trade was grinding to a halt, and the implications that would have on an industrial town like Coatbridge.

Mary and Liz were greatly relieved that they had taken Mr Green's wise advise and their money was now safely lodged in a number of separate bank accounts.

Just before the crash they had purchased a delightful little pied-a-terre in Kensington, providing them with a central base in the capital. They were now hoping to make a visit to London in order to furnish and decorate their flat. After the New Year they intended to return to London in order to purchase a number of other properties, then arrange long term leases for them.

The idea regarding the low rent properties for women leaving Drumkiln House would take longer to organise than they had initially imagined. After much research on the part of Mary she had been unable to find a suitable block of properties. Separate properties dotted all over the town was not really the answer, firstly the women would feel more secure having neighbours they already knew and trusted and secondly in order to get Jessie and Alex to accept one of the properties it had to be near the tenants so that Alex could be appointed to the job of Warden.

Mary and Liz had not yet discussed their property plans with the other members of Ella's Friends. They both felt their idea would stand a greater chance of success if they had a concrete plan to present rather than simply talking around an idea.

In Gartsherrie Willie had been enrolled at Gartsherrie Primary and his teacher, Miss McLeod, was soon holding him up to the remainder of her class as a sterling example of a boy who worked hard and whose behaviour was exemplary. Fortunately, she was not privy to Mr Gibson's letter to his long suffering parents.

There was a general feeling of pessimism in the town, the Wall Street Crash might have happened thousands of miles away in America but its repercussions were starting to touch all the industrial cities of Great Britain.

Towards the end of the month Jessie called a meeting of Ella's Friends. Rather than have to go out on a cold, dark, November night, they decided to meet at Drumkiln House on a Sunday afternoon.

Jessie opened the meeting. "Firstly, Mary and I would like to give our wholehearted thanks to Jennie, Young Jessie, Liz and my Mary. They have contributed so much to Ella's Friends without any thought of payment. We would not have a Refuge without them and all their hard work.

Friends, Drumkiln House is working, and working well, my Mary's reports confirm we are doing exactly what Ella wanted, giving women in distress a helping hand. However, I sense that our services are going to be required more and more. The 'crash' might have happened in New York but it's spread to London and there is already a feeling of 'depression' hanging over the town. Works have stopped overtime and it won't be long before they are laying men off. Men who are bullies will be worse without jobs, I just thought we should think about the coming months and try to prepare.

Liz thought about sharing her and Mary's property plan but she felt it would be unfair to offer something which could take months or even years to complete, she simply said. "Yes, Jessie I absolutely agree with you. As a short term measure why don't we use this room for accommodation. I know we agreed to use it as a meeting room but it's a nice big room, it would easily hold two people, probably three, and we could use the dining room for our meetings."

It was agreed unanimously that the erstwhile morning room would become another bedroom.

It was also agreed that the money made from the sale of Mary's creams, potions and cordials would provide income, the jams, chutneys and bottled fruit being used to supplement the food budget.

Mary announced that her and Liz were off to London for a few weeks, however they would be home well before Christmas and the New Year.

Jennie updated everyone on the Refuge finances. She also suggested that Jessie should contact Mr Cornwall and get him to recommend a good accountant, preferably one who would not charge a large fee. As it was now nearly a year since they had started the project.

They then discussed one or two other matters before bringing the meeting to a close.

Everyone went through to the sitting room where they joined the current residents in a cup of tea before heading home.

It was such a cold afternoon Mary insisted that everyone squeeze into her car and she would drop them all home. As the car pulled up outside Jessie's house in the Long Row she invited Mary and Liz to join her and Alex for a bite of supper. Mary replied, "Thanks Ma but I think we will get ourselves home, it's almost dark, besides we have to get organised for our trip to London, we leave on Tuesday morning."

Jessie hurried into her home to prepare the meal for her and Alex and then settle down to a quiet evening, updating her husband on the goings on at Drumkiln House.

Monday morning and the start of a new week. Jessie arrived at the Refuge to find Mary Law standing outside trying to calm a man who was worse the wear from drink and hammering on the front door, shouting. "Sadie, will you get yerself doon here this very minute, I've had enough of all your bloody nonsense. A wummin's place is with her man, no to bide in some fancy big hoose."

Mary and Jessie tried to pull the man back from hammering on the door. He turned and punched Mary full on, catching her just under the eye, the blood poured down her face.

Sadie Kane's husband again started to thump the door, shouting obscenities. Fortunately two policeman quickly came on the scene, a neighbour hearing the commotion having telephoned the Police Station in Muiryhall Street. The policemen tried to apprehend Jimmy Kane, however he put up a fight against the two officers, pushing one to the ground and causing him to break his ankle. As his colleague and the two women tried to help the poor constable, Kane ran off shouting. "Sadie Kane, I'll get you, so I will, don't you go think'n you can run away from me you stupid bitch, for you can't get away from me, not ever."

Jessie opened the Refuge door and managed to get everyone inside. The women came downstairs, with crying children holding onto their skirts.

Jessie and the young officer quickly got the situation under control, then he telephoned to arrange an ambulance to take Mary and his colleague to the Alexander Hospital. Meanwhile Jessie administered first aid to Mary and the young constable, who she found out was called Billy and that he had only started with the force a few weeks previously. Poor lad, he was more worried about what his Sergeant would say than his injury.

As Jessie was putting a cold compress on Mary's face Jennie appeared in the doorway. Awash with relief at having some support Jessie cried. "Jennie am I glad to see you, whatever angel sent you I'm grateful. "Actually," said Jennie "It was the book-keeping angel. I had a few errands in the town and I thought I would pop in and collect any paperwork you had available, I wanted the accounts to be up to date before I go off to spend Christmas with Martin and Margaret in Oxford."

A few minutes later the ambulance arrived to take Billy and Mary to the hospital, Jennie accompanied them while Jessie stayed at her post in the Refuge.

Jessie resisted telephoning her daughter Mary and Liz, as she knew that the following morning they were travelling to London and she did not want to upset their plans.

Eventually the nightmare of a day ended. Mary Law was assured there was no lasting damage to her face; the young constable was discharged with a plaster on his leg; Jennie took Mary home and later that evening she met Jessie Law at the train station to warn her what to expect when she arrived home in the Long Row.

During the day Jessie tried her best to comfort the women in Drumkiln House, particularly Sadie Kane, and get the house back into some semblance of order. Jessie also contacted a local locksmith and had him add security chains and bolts to both doors, she also arranged for him to come back the following day to fit bolts to all the windows.

Satisfied she had done everything she could Jessie headed home, where a worried Alex awaited her arrival.

As soon as she walked into the kitchen he embraced his wife. "My darl'n girl, Jennie came over and told me all that has been going on today. Honestly Jessie I never dreamed for one minute that you and the other lasses would be in danger. What in the name of all that's holy are we going to do?"

Jessie told him about the additional security she had installed and that the police had promised to keep an eye on the house. As Jessie talked Alex helped her off with her hat and coat and made her a cup of tea. They sat down in their chairs at either side of the fire, both silent with their own thoughts. Eventually Alex said, "Jennie brought down an ashet of stew, with sliced potatoes on top, it's in the bottom oven warming. I thought that was right thoughtful of her, she also brought some cake, it's in that tin on the dresser."

They ate their food then Jessie insisted they go down to the Law's house and check on Mary. As always, Alex and Jessie received a warm welcome and assurance that Mary had not suffered any permanent injury. However, Agnes and Alex were definitely 'singing from the same hymn sheet' on this one, they were both concerned that the attack could well have caused serious injury and they did not want to see their loved ones open to any further danger, they made their worries known.

In order to change the direction of the conversation Jessie suggested that she would pay Mr Cornwall a visit the following day and get some legal advice. "Jennie asked me to see him to get a recommendation for an independent accountant to audit our books. As well as getting advice on an accountant I'll update him on the goings on of today, see what he suggests. Now Alex, I think it's time we went up the road, I'm absolutely wabbit, besides I'm sure Mary could do with an early night."

Jessie did not sleep well, there were too many questions to which she did not have answers rumbling around in her head.

Tuesday and the Johnstones, got up to a cold, miserable November morning with frost underfoot. Alex ate his porridge followed by a mug of tea with toast and honey then he set off to his work. Jessie tidied up, prepared the vegetables for dinner then as it was so slippery on the cobbles, carefully walked down the Row to catch the bus. She was surprised to meet Mary Law at the bus stop. "Mary pet, I never imagined you would be going into the Refuge today, why aren't you having a few days at home?" Mary replied "Auntie Jessie need you ask, my Maw is prattling on ten to the dozen. I've had Robert, Alexander and even Jessie on at me to give up working at Drumkiln House. But I'm not giving up, if anything yesterday has just made me more determined. At last, here's the bus Auntie Jessie, another day and we're back to work, Jimmy Kane and his likes aren't going to beat us."

Earlier in the morning as Alex walked down the frosty Row in his tackety boots, bunnet and muffler, many other men were also leaving the warmth of their homes similarly attired for another day of grafting at Gartsherrie Works. He heard footsteps catching up with him and a voice behind him called, "Uncle Alex, what on earth is happening at that Refuge? Our Mary got a terrible punch in the face. I know that auld Ella Millar meant well with her legacy but I'm sure she would never have wanted to put the women folk in danger. And, is it true the man who bashed our Mary's face also injured a policeman?"

"Aye lad, it's true," confirmed Alex. "I hear the poor copper has a broken ankle. Look I am none too pleased at how this is all turning out either but what can I do? James lad, can you honestly see me telling my Jessie to give up on Drumkiln House or you, Robert and Alexander forbidding your Mary to work at the Refuge? My Jessie and her pals Jennie and Liz fought tooth and nail to get the vote, do you seriously think a wee naff from Coatbridge is going to stop them, I dinna think so." James laughed, "Oh Uncle Alex you're right, oor Mary would go doolally at me and the others lads if we dared to interfere."

They reached the Works gates where they separated, James to go to the Joinery Shop and Alex the Furnaces.

When Jessie and Mary reached Drumkiln House they were pleased to hear that there had been no further trouble during the night. As there was presently no school age children staying Jessie instructed the women to all stay indoors with the wee ones until she found out if the police had detained Jimmy Kane.

While the women started to tidy up the breakfast things, and see to the housework Jessie asked Mary if they could have a private word in her medical room.

"Mary, I'm going to go down to see Mr Cornwall this morning, not just about getting an accountant. I need to discuss with him the protection of the women under our care. I could hardly sleep last night for thinking about the whole security issue. I think we have all been right naive about potential dangers, yesterday fairly opened my eyes." Mary laughed, "and, closed mine. I've got a right black and blue keeker."

"Exactly," said Jessie "None of us signed up for violence, protecting the women is more than giving them a room and three meals a day."

There was a knock on the door, a young woman said. "Mrs Johnstone, there is a man at the door, he says he's here to fit snibs to all the windaes. Will I let him in?" Jessie replied, "Yes Helen, let him in, I asked the Locksmith to come back today and add extra security to all the windows."

As Helen left Jessie shouted after her. "Remember and offer him a cup of tea after he gets a few done. Thanks Helen."

Mary asked Jessie. "What on earth is it going to cost for all this extra security?" Jessie replied, "For once in my life I did not ask the price, what price someone's life. It had to be done and done quickly."

Just then Jennie joined them. "How are things this morning? I see that the Locksmith has started work on the windows, that's a step in the right direction."

Jessie spoke seriously to her two friends. "Jennie can you and Mary hold the fort here while I go down to Bank Street to see Mr Cornwall. I telephoned as soon as I arrived this morning and his secretary said to come in at around eleven o'clock. As well as engaging an accountant I think we really need some serious advice about protecting the woman and children while they are staying here, without turning the place into a prison."

Mary and Jennie assured her all would be well at the Refuge and she should get on her way down to Bank Street.

As Jessie entered Mr Cornwall's now familiar office he asked her to take a seat and instructed his secretary to bring a tray of coffee. Andrew Cornwall opened the conversation. "That was a right stramash yesterday Mrs Johnstone, was it not? Yes, I do know about the whole escapade, Superintendent McKinnon telephoned me, knowing of my connection with Drumkiln House, no secrets in a town like Coatbridge."

As his secretary brought in the coffee and a plate of shop bought biscuits, Jessie updated him. "Mary Law is back at the Refuge today, she has a black eye and her face is still very bruised but according to the hospital no lasting damage. Yesterday I had an extra lock and a security chain fitted on each of the outside doors, at the moment Mr Cameron the Locksmith from Whifflet is fitting snibs on all the windows." For the first time Jessie's voice started to break and she could feel tears gathering in her eyes.

"There there" said Mr Cornwall, "Mrs Johnstone, you have handled this incident in an exemplary fashion, please don't upset yourself. I will look at all the legal issues and advise you of any other steps that Ella's Friends should take as soon as possible. In fact I blame myself, I really should have looked at the possibility of such an occurrence before now and advised you accordingly.

Please Mrs Johnstone, pour the coffee, my secretary tells me there is also another matter you wish to discuss."

Jessie blinked away her tears and focused her attention on the coffee cups. "Yes, there is another matter. As you know Jennie Mathieson has been dealing with the accounts, however at the end of our first year she would like to have them audited independently, can you recommend a good local accountant?"

Mr Cornwall smiled "That's an easy request after this Kane business. I'll telephone John Cuthbert, he has a practice in the town. John is a good friend, and, I'll twist his arm to charge you a very low fee. Knowing Miss Mathieson I am sure the books will be in apple pie order, he shouldn't have a great deal of work to do.

Now Mrs Johnstone please return to the Refuge I am sure the residence could do with your calming presence and let me know immediately if there are any further developments. I'll have a serious think about the whole security question and I'll speak to you later in the week. However, remember if you do need any further help I would consider it an honour to be of assistance."

Jessie took her leave reassured that meantime she had done all that she could to ensure the safety of Ella's Friends and the women and children who were under their care at the Refuge.

Shortly before Jessie returned the telephone rang in Drumkiln House. Jennie answered the phone located on the hall table, saying. "Good morning, Drumkiln House, Jennie Mathieson speaking." A man's voice with a soft Western Isles accent enquired. "Can I have a wee word with a Mrs Johnstone please?" "Sorry" Jennie informed the caller. "Mrs Johnstone is out at present, can I help?" "This is a Superintendent McKinnon calling from the Police Station in Muiryhall Street. I just wanted to inform Mrs Johnstone that Mr Kane was arrested last night, drunk and disorderly. He has spent the night in the cells as our guest, when he sobers up we will have to release him, although he will be formally charged with a number of incidents. Would it be possible to send an officer to your Women's Refuge to take formal statements? I would also like to visit Mrs Johnstone personally, I think she could do with a wee bitty advice on security and the setting up of a procedure to be carried out in the event of a similar incident."

Jennie thanked Superintendent McKinnon for his kindness and diarised the times of the proposed visits.

Jessie, Jennie and Mary joined the residents for a sandwich lunch and Jessie took the opportunity to update and reassure everyone.

Completely oblivious to the crisis playing out at Drumkiln

House, Liz and Mary were sitting on the Royal Scot in a first class carriage heading towards London Euston and the excitement of moving into their new apartment.

"I think it was best to book into the Savoy for a week." said Liz. "You can shop in Heals and Harrods my dear. With a bit of luck the decorator will have completed the papering and painting by now. That was a really good idea of Jessie Law's to look through Mr Mason's sample books, engage a London decorator and instruct them on what you want. Fingers crossed they are as reliable as his team were at Drumkiln House."

"Yes, it was a great plan and Jessie helped me with the choices. You know she really has wonderful taste, it was so sad McInnes died, the two of them would have made a formidable business team."

They enjoyed a delicious lunch in the First Class Dining Carriage, Mary thought about the first time she had made this journey and the feeling of awe that had overwhelmed her. There were no such feeling now, Mary had moved on from the shy, studious lass from the Rows of Gartsherrie to being a well educated and sophisticated young woman.

They arrived without incident at Euston and hailed a taxi to take them to the Savoy Hotel on the Strand. Tired after the long journey they simply enjoyed a light supper in their suite and had an early night.

Wednesday morning Liz and Mary breakfasted early, happily planning their week staying at the Savoy and then the move into their new apartment. After breakfast Mary put on her outdoor clothes and caught a taxi to meet the estate agent and collect the flat keys. After visiting her new home in Kensington where she was delighted with the work of the decorator, Mary took some measurements and gathered up a selection of wallpaper samples, before taking a taxi to Harrods in Brompton Road, where she planned to start her shopping expedition.

Liz had arranged for Mr Green to call into the Savoy for morning coffee to have a chat about her finances. Luncheon she had organised in the hotel dining room with two friends from university days. Then she proposed to have a rest before Mary returned, no doubt full of news about their new apartment and her shopping adventures.

Back in Gartsherrie it was life as usual. Alex walked down to the Works with James Law, the two men once again discussing the Refuge and their concerns, Alex laughed. "James lad, can you just imagine what your auld faither would have had to say about the goings on with the womenfolk. Your Ma choosing fancy curtains, linoleum and rugs, and His Masters Voice playing all the latest music on the gramophone in your kitchen. He would have had an 'Annie Rooney', so he would. You know I often think of the grumpy auld bugger but hidden beneath all his bluster he had a good heart, so he did."

"He certainly kept it well hidden from all of us and especially my Maw," laughed James.

"Well lad, I often think of him, because he was my last link with County Fermanagh. You know, we often used to talk together about our homeland in Ulster over a pipe of baccy or a glass of porter.

Nearly there son, see you when we louse the night, another day of work and another few bob for the auld black pot."

Agnes Law cleared away the breakfast dishes, put on her coat and headed down to the store with her message bag. It had been a long time since Agnes had been so involved in the practical day to day running of the Law household, while she might grumble to any-one who would listen that she had been deserted by her daughters, secretly there were parts of her new life she enjoyed.

Mary and Jessie boarded the Baxter's bus as usual, knowing a busy day lay ahead, including visits from the Coatbridge Police Force.

Although carrying on with the usual routines they were both aware that since the Kane incident there had been a nervous atmosphere hanging over Drumkiln House. Mary said to Jessie. "I've been thinking we really need to get everyone boosted up a bit, all the women are in nerves and it's rubbing off on the wee ones. Let's try and make time today to come up with some ideas to lift the spirits. Jennie said she would drop in around lunch time, I think we definitely need an Ella's Friends brainstorming session, even if it's just the three of us."

The bell on the front door rang, looking out from the sitting room window Mary could see a police officer standing on the doorstep.

"That'll be the first of our police visits Auntie Jessie, I'll away and let him in. The sooner we make our statements and get the paperwork completed the better."

Mary answered the door to a young police officer, his face was pale and he seemed very nervous as he spoke in a diffident voice. "Are you Mrs Jessie Johnstone?" Mary looked at the constable and answered. "No I'm not but we were expecting you please come away in, I'll organise a cup of tea while we give you our statements. The young man followed her into the hall and removed his cap. He seemed slightly confused as he asked. "Excuse me miss, who are you exactly?" Mary answered. "I'm Mary Law, you are here to interview me, Mrs Johnstone and Mrs Kane regarding the incident outside the house on Monday morning. Now come away through to the sitting room while I get the others."

The officer touched Mary's arm, saying. "Miss Law I'm afraid you have got it completely wrong, I'm here to see Mrs Johnstone about another matter entirely.

Can I speak to you privately Miss Law?" Mary showed him into the sitting room. He cleared his throat and then said. "I am afraid I have some very bad news. There has been an accident at Gartsherrie Works, it's Mrs Johnstone's husband, Alexander Johnstone, there is no easy way to say this. I'm sorry he has been killed. Would you please help me to break the news to Mrs Johnstone?"

Just at that moment Jessie came into the sitting room carrying a tea tray. As she started to welcome the policeman she was suddenly aware of the tense atmosphere in the room and the expression on the faces of both Mary and the young policeman.

Mary took the tray and guided her Auntie on to a sofa, held her hand and said gently. "Auntie Jessie, I have some terrible news, the worst possible news, it's Uncle Alex, there has been an accident at Gartsherrie Works."

Jessie turned to the officer. "You must have made a terrible mistake Alex went off to work as usual this morning, he was in fine fettle, he can't have been injured, it's just not possible."

Now came the part Constable Muirhead had been dreading from the moment his Sergeant had instructed him to deliver the news.

"Mrs Johnstone, I am so sorry but it was a fatal accident.

Mr Johnstone was working at the furnaces, he fell into a molten slag channel, nothing could be done he must have died instantly, there is no body."

As the young Constable related the horrific details the colour drained from Mary's face, as he spoke Constable Muirhead could see her turn white and start to shake uncontrollably.

Jessie however did not seem to be processing his words, it was as though he was speaking in a foreign language.

Young Constable Muirhead was completely out his depth and he was greatly relieved when another woman walked into the room. She said, "Constable, my name is Jennie Mathieson, what is the problem." Not in her worst nightmare could Jennie have imagined what she would hear.

The tears were now pouring down Mary's face but Jessie still retained the same unhearing expression.

Jennie took Constable Muirhead's arm and led him into the hall. Managing somehow to hold her feelings in check, Jennie thanked him for his kindness in what must have been a very difficult act. The young man left the Refuge and as he walked down the hill he took out his handkerchief and blew his nose hard to hide the tears that were forming.

Mary and Jennie sat at either side of Jessie holding her hands. Eventually she said. "What was that young officer saying about my Alex? I couldn't really understand him." Somehow between them Mary and Jennie managed to convey to Jessie that her beloved husband had been killed in a horrific accident.

Jessie started to sob, quietly, but through her tears the others could hear her saying, "It's not true, it's all a terrible mistake, not my Alex, I'll see him tonight, I've made mince for the dinner, just need to boil the tatties, a favourite meal is mince and tatties, and I've got some turnip, he loves that, well champit with a wee bit of marge and plenty of black pepper."

They heard a knock on the outside door, somebody must have answered for into the sitting room came Jessie's daughter Agnes and her husband Tom Coats.

Agnes held her mother tightly, somehow the closeness of her oldest girl made Jessie realise that an accident had indeed taken place, she cried but her tears were for her daughter's grief, not her own.

Word of the accident ripped through the Refuge like wildfire. All the women and children gathered in the kitchen to give the family some privacy, and to allow them to talk of the tragedy in whispered tones.

Jennie went into the hall she looked at the telephone for ages, while hearing the sobbing coming from the sitting room. Eventually she plucked up her courage and placed a long distance call to the Savoy Hotel in London and asked to speak to Miss Barns-Wallis.

Liz was enjoying lunch with Caroline and Rose, two of her old university friends. They were laughing over some of the early wheezes they had got up to during their student days when they were all involved with the struggle to win the right to vote.

The maître d' approached their table. "Excuse me interrupting ladies, Miss Barns-Wallis, there is a long distance telephone call for you. I understand it is most important, would you like to accompany me to my office which will afford you a measure of privacy. Puzzled Liz could only imagine that something dreadful had happened at Drumkiln House. "Thank you so much I appreciate your kindness." said Liz, as she took the young man's arm while he led her into his office, where he handed her the telephone.

"Hello, Liz Barns-Wallis speaking, how can I help you." Over the crackling line Liz heard a familiar voice, that somehow sounded unfamiliar. "Liz, it's Jennie. Is Mary with you?" "No my dear, she is out on a variety of errands, I don't expect her back until late afternoon. What's the matter Jennie? You sound as though you have been crying."

"I have been crying Liz, you will have to give Mary some terrible news, her father has been killed in an accident at Gartsherrie Works."

In all her life Liz had never plummeted from joy to despair as she did in that moment. She braced herself to ask. "Jennie, what happened?"

Jennie could not bring herself to repeat over the telephone the whole truth. Instead she said. "Liz it was a terrible accident at the Works, Jessie is in complete shock. Can you and Mary please come home, we need you both here."

With a breaking voice Liz replied. "Of course Jennie, I'll see if I can get reservations on the sleeper tonight, if not, we will come home tomorrow. Jennie, does Agnes and Tom know yet?" Jennie reassured her. "Yes, Tom went home from the office to tell her, immediately after the accident happened, Agnes and Tom are with Jessie now. Oh Liz, I just can't take it all in, Mary Law and I need you and Mary here."

"Jennie, Mary and I will be home as quickly as ever we can, I promise you. Thank you for telephoning I know it can't have been easy. I'll go now and make arrangements for the train journey back home. Goodbye my dear, goodbye."

Liz came off the telephone with tears coursing down her face. The maître d' who had been standing discretely in the corner of the room came over to her and handed her a handkerchief, saying. "Miss Barns-Walls would you like me to arrange two sleepers to Glasgow for you and Miss Johnstone this evening?"

Liz thanked him, he then took her arm and led her back to the dining room where Caroline and Rose were still chatting animatedly.

Liz simply said. "Caroline, Rose, I've just received some very bad news. Mary and I have to return to Scotland immediately. I am afraid I cannot bring myself to discuss the telephone call I have just received. If you could walk me back to my suite I would be most appreciative."

As long term friends of Liz, Caroline and Rose knew she did not wear her heart on her sleeve but they did not miss the tears trickling down their friend's face.

Sitting alone in her room Liz had never felt her sight problem so acutely. There was nothing she could do but sit and wait for Mary to return. The telephone rang, Liz answered. The reassuring voice of the maître d' said.

"Miss Barns-Wallis, I have made reservations for you and Miss Johnstone on the Glasgow sleeper, I have also booked you a taxi for 9.00pm and cancelled the remainder of your stay. I trust that will be in order."

Liz thanked him for his kindness and then waited, it was the longest afternoon she had ever known. Mary did not return until almost six o'clock.

The door opened and Mary burst in full of her day. "Darling Liz, I can't wait to tell you about everything that's happened today. Well, the painter made..., Liz whatever is the matter, you've been crying, what's wrong?"

Not in her worst nightmare could Mary have imagined the news that Liz was about to break to her. "My dearest Mary, sit yourself down, I have some terrible news to tell you... and she said the words.

So you see my dear girl, you must pack and we will catch the night sleeper to Glasgow this evening."

Thankfully, Jennie had spared them the worst of the news, exactly how Alex had been killed.

Afterwards neither Liz nor Mary could remember how they travelled from the suite in the Savoy to Drumkiln House, where Jessie, Mary and Jennie had all spent the night.

In the early hours of the morning Mary Law heard the taxi pull up and Mary and Liz alight, she pulled on her red flannel dressing-gown and came to the front door to let them in quietly. The taxi driver brought their luggage into the hall and set it down. Mary just stood looking completely blank while Liz held on to her arm. Mary Law quickly went to find the petty cash tin and get some money to pay the driver.

Mary Law ushered Mary and Liz into the sitting room, she helped them remove their coats and sat the two women down. There were still some embers alive in the fire so Mary roused them with the poker and carefully added more coal.

Hearing Mary and Liz arrive Jennie got up and joined them, the four women were all in a state of shock. Eventually Mary broke the eerie silence. "I'll never see my Daddy alive again, will I? Only in his coffin, I'll have to say goodbye to him cold in his coffin. I could have had supper with him and my Ma before we left but I did the packing instead. I could have tried harder to find a property where he could have been the Warden and left off working at Gartsherrie Works. It's all my fault, where is my Ma?"

Jennie looked at Mary Law, they both knew they had to tell Mary and Liz the truth before they found out from somebody else.

The fire started to flicker into life. Jennie got up and lit the wick on the paraffin lamp on the table beside the fireplace, to bring some soft light to the dark winter morning.

Speaking with a trembling voice Jennie said, "Mary, we have sent a telegram to Sam and Maria in Australia. Tom has taken Agnes back home to their home in Drumpellier. Your mother is in Mavis's Room, and she has moved in with Sadie. Mary has given your Ma a draught of laudanum, we had to make her sleep for a few hours to remove her from the reality of what has happened."

Liz asked the question they had both been dreading. "What exactly happened to Alex?" Again Jennie and Mary looked at each other, neither able to offer the horrendous explanation.

Mary started to cry. "Please, just tell me exactly what happened, I need to know."

Jennie knelt in front of Mary, taking her hand she said in a soft voice. "My dear Mary, there is no easy way to say this, there is no body, no coffin, your Pa was killed instantly at the furnace."

Mary's grief took a life of its own. Neither Liz, Jennie or Mary Law could quieten her. All the women in their rooms lay awake and listened to the loud sobbing from downstairs, only her mother, Jessie, did not hear, she was cocooned in her drug induced sleep.

The following days passed in a mist of pain and tears. Rev. Maxwell called into the Refuge and offered to conduct a service in the Johnstone family home in memory of Alex. An offer which Agnes and Mary gladly accepted on behalf of their mother.

Agnes wrote the agonising letter to her brother Sam and his wife Maria in Melbourne informing them the details of Alex's death. The three Johnstone children, Agnes, Sam and Mary had always been close and Agnes was aware that every word she was writing would wound her brother to his very core.

It was agreed that while the Refuge would remain open, no new ladies would be accepted. Mr Cornwall and Hugh Mason called to offer their condolences to the Johnstone women. The Law family rallied round, but through it all Jessie remained in a state of shock, she scarcely ate, didn't cry, hardly spoke and would disappear into Mavis's erstwhile bedroom and sleep for hours on end.

Dr Murphy called in one morning to enquire how Jessie was bearing up. Mary Law thanked him for his visit and explained Jessie's condition. Dr Murphy, in his broad Irish brogue explained. "Mary lass, it's nature's way, so it is, it's her body trying to protect her. Try and get her to eat light meals and sleep a little less each day. And, you must realise one day the dam will burst, maybe days maybe weeks, even months, but burst it will, and only then can the healing process start. Now lass, don't you overdo things yerself, your heart isn't that strong, let the others help you. You gave the wumen in this hoose sanctuary, they owe you and the Johnstone wumen, mind what I'm saying now, don't you try and take on the world."

For once in her life Mary listened to the advice of a man and allowed, Sadie, Mavis, Helen and the others to give of their help and she accepted it all graciously.

At last the dreaded day arrived, Rev Adam Maxwell, the Johnstone family and all those who loved them, met at 130 Long Row, a house that had seen its share of; drama, poverty, sadness, happiness, fun and love, a home.

Rev. Maxwell conducted a short service celebrating the life of Alexander Johnstone. His son in law Tom Coats gave a moving eulogy, and Robert Law in his pure tenor voice sang Macushla, the song he had sang at the funeral of his father Robert Law, the song joining the two men from County Fermanagh, the land they had both loved and lived their lives in exile from. A Lodge sash and bowler hat sat on the table the only earthly signs of the man that was Alexander Johnstone.

After the service Agnes Law came through from the scullery with a tray of whisky drams and sherry. Her daughter Jessie carried a large platter of Agnes's little tattie cakes, that had been served as a celebration food to both families over the years. Mary Law looked at the tattie cakes, she no longer saw them as simply tattie cakes, they were latkes, food that had travelled down the years with Agnes from her time with Ben Fischer, the food of Hanukkah the food of light.

During the service Jessie had sat in her chair by the fire, looking at the empty chair opposite, no tears came from her eyes, she was in altogether another place.

People left and when only the immediate family remained Jessie spoke. "It's time now, I am moving back to the Long Row. I know you all mean well but it's time I returned to my home and my memories of my Alex. Please go home everybody, I need some time alone with my man."

Agnes Law shepherded everyone outside, she gathered them all around her and said. "It's time, we must leave Jessie to her grief. Don't worry, I'm just a wee bitty away, I'll see to her. Agnes, Mary, she needs her daughters but not yet, do you understand me. Now everyone away home. Agnes went back into the Johnstone home and held Jessie's hand until darkness fell, she lit the gas mantle then put on her coat and walked down the Row to her home.

When she arrived at number twelve her face was ashen, she sat in her chair and cried, her four children, Robert, Alexander, Mary and Jessie had never felt so proud of their mother as they did in that moment.

Over the next week Agnes attended to Jessie singlehandedly, she kept Mary and Agnes informed and assured them that the time would shortly come for them to take over but for now Jessie needed to live solely back in the past.

One morning Agnes had just got Jessie to eat a boiled egg with little toast soldiers. Agnes quietly talked to her. "Remember when your Sam had the croup, and we thought we'd never get him to eat and I went up to the farm and got a few eggs, we made him a soft boiled egg and soldiers and it was the turning point, do you remember Jessie?"

Just then a knock came to the door, it was a young man smartly dressed in a suit and overcoat to keep out the bitter winter cold. He stated his business. "Mrs Jessie Johnstone, I have a communication for you from the the Directors of Gartsherrie Works." He then handed Agnes a sealed envelope and swiftly walked away.

Agnes did not enlighten him that she was not Mrs Jessie Johnstone but took the letter through to the kitchen, saying. "Jessie a man in a bowler hat from the Works Office had just brought you a letter, will I open it up for you?"

Jessie replied. "Aye Agnes, just you read it, we've got no secrets us two." Agnes removed the letter from its envelope and put on her reading spectacles, she carefully read aloud.

Dear Mrs Johnstone

I am writing to inform you that this letter forms one weeks notice from today's date that you are required to remove yourself and all your possessions from the property known as:

130 Long Row, Gartsherrie, Coatbridge which is owned by Messrs. Wm Baird of Gartsherrie.

This property was rented by your late husband, Mr Alexander Johnstone, on the strict condition, Mr Johnstone, or another person resident at the said property was employed by the Company. As this is no longer the case you are required to allow the Company vacant possession seven days from the date of this letter.

Agnes crumpled the cruel missive in her hand.

Jessie spoke. "Agnes, did I hear that right? They are throwing me out of my home, Alex's home, in a few days. They can't do that, he died working for them."

Her voice had started to rise and the moment of grief Dr Murphy had told Mary about, and Agnes instinctively understood, came.

Agnes simply held her friend and rocked her back and forth, saying. "There there Jessie, get it out, cry, cry your tears."

While she was comforting her friend Agnes was thinking 'what are we going to do about the letter'?

Eventually Jessie could cry no more, Agnes got her to lie down on the bed and she held her hand until she fell asleep.

Agnes quietly put on her coat and walked up the hill to Blairhill and the home of Jennie Mathieson. Even as Jennie was welcoming Agnes inside, Agnes pushed the letter in front of her, saying. "Jennie, a man from the works delivered this to Jessie. Her grief has broken, she has cried herself to exhaustion and she is sleeping now. What in the name of the Lord are we going to do now?"

Jennie read the letter and thought she had never witnessed such a cold hearted act in her entire life.

Jennie reached for her winter coat. "Agnes, you had better go away home and get the dinner ready for the family, and take another look in at Jessie. I'll take this evil letter over to young Agnes, perhaps Tom Coats can do something, he is a Manager at the Works after all. And, Agnes will be able to telephone Mary and Liz in Airdrie and your Mary at the Refuge with this latest blow."

That evening everyone gathered together in Agnes and Tom's home in Drumpellier, except Jessie. Agnes Law had agreed to stay with her friend in the Long Row as Jessie was simply not yet ready to face dealing with an eviction threat.

Everyone started to express their outrage at the letter. Tom Coats a quiet, thoughtful man raised his voice. "Please listen everybody. When my Agnes brought the letter down to my office it did not come as a complete shock, we all know of families in the past who have had to move on or take in working lodgers to conform with the rules. However I went up to the Directors Office and put forward Jessie's case, bearing in mind exactly how Alex was killed I hoped they would reconsider. They used words of sympathy but would not consider breaking the rules for anyone. It was implied that if my mother-in-law was to keep her home, when others had been evicted, it would be assumed that it was down to favouritism due to my position in the Works and that would make my job untenable.

I am afraid I have done as much as I can, I have a wife and child to support and the way things stand at the moment I simply cannot risk losing my job.

However, I would be more than happy for Jessie to come and live with us and make her home with Agnes and me and wee Emily."

Liz had been angry beyond words when she heard about the disgusting letter, and she made her views felt. "Tom, I do understand your position and in the short term perhaps Jessie may choose to come and stay with you. However, I am not beholden to Gartsherrie Works and when Jessie is a bit stronger I intend to encourage her to take legal action against this cruel injustice, not just on her behalf but for other families who have been, or will be affected in the future."

Everyone saw the fiery Liz of old, the suffragette, Elizabeth Agatha Barns-Wallis, fighter of injustice, in all its forms.

"Besides, there is always a place for Jessie with Mary and me in Airdrie."

Mary Law too had a view to express. "I know Jessie will appreciate you both offering her a home but the truth is my Aunt Jessie is a very independent woman and perhaps she will not relish being under someone else's roof, no matter how much she loves her family. I think it might be a thought, possibly in the longer term, for Jessie to live at Drumkiln House. The old morning room is available, it's big enough for us to turn it into a good sized parlour with a sleeping area and Jessie would still have her own place."

Jennie immediately agreed with Mary. "I think that is an excellent idea Mary and definitely an option for Jessie to consider in the future. Although, if she wants she could always stay with me, I'm living alone in that big house, I would be delighted to have her come to live with me."

Mary Johnstone had been very quiet while everyone was offering opinions as to what would be best for Jessie, Mary now spoke up. "I think the one good thing that's come of us all getting together is that Ma now has a number of choices, both in the short term and for the future. Jennie, will you speak to my Ma tomorrow, tell her everything that has been spoken of tonight and get her decision. Then let's organise the move as soon as we possibly can. I don't want some jumped up little man in a bowler hat from Gartsherrie Works harassing her."

Everyone agreed with Mary that this was the way forward.

When she returned home Mary Law told her mother what had been discussed and the various proposals for Jessie's future accommodation.

The following morning she had just arrived at Jessie's with bread and milk when Jennie arrived. Agnes immediately said.

"Morning to you Jennie, I'm just away to make tea and toast for Jessie's breakfast, would you like a wee cuppa?"

"That would be lovely Agnes, thank you." "No bother" replied Agnes, "Now away and have a wee blether with Jessie while I go through to the scullery and mask the tea."

Holding the letter Jennie told Jessie what had transpired the previous evening and asked her what she would like to do. "Whatever you decide now isn't necessary for always. But you need to make a decision and move your things out as soon as possible. You don't want to be bullied into leaving, make your choice my friend and leave with your head held high. Agnes and I will help you pack.

Agnes came back through from the scullery carrying a breakfast tray of tea and toast with marmalade for Jessie, saying. "There you are Jessie pet, eat a wee bitty breakfast, I'll just away now and get a wee cup of tea for Jennie and me."

When Jennie told Jessie everything that had been discussed the previous evening surprisingly for the first time since the accident Jessie appeared to understand all that was being said to her.

As the three women sat in front of the fire drinking their tea Jessie said. "Jennie I have actually taken in everything you have told me and well I think I am a woman blest to have received all those kind offers of a comfortable home. However, I think perhaps Mary Law is right, I could live in Drumkiln House and have my own private quarters in what was the morning room. But I'm not quite ready yet, I'm not ready to be in charge, to be Jessie everyone's problem solver. Truth to tell, I just don't feel strong enough to run the Refuge. So I think I will take up Liz and Mary's offer and stay with them in Airdrie for a wee while.

I don't think staying with Agnes and Tom would be a good idea. I don't want to upset wee Emily, you know how she dotted on my Alex, well seeing me upset would be a constant reminder her Grandpa is gone. Besides I think I want to get right away from Gartsherrie for a time.

They started work on the move that morning. Telephone calls were made. Mary drove down from Airdrie and took some of Jessie's precious possessions to Drumkiln House and arranged for a van to take to the Refuge any larger pieces of furniture she wanted to keep, later in the day.

That evening Jessie left 130 Long Row with two cases, one containing some clothes and the other her hat making equipment. Sitting beside her daughter they drove past Gartsherrie Works, the Works that had robbed her of her husband, the man she loved. Jessie Johnstone silently vowed never to return to the Gartsherrie Rows and see the mocking furnaces ever again.

Jennie Mathieson and Agnes Law killed the fire, emptied the ashes and locked the door for the last time on the Johnstone home.

The two women then walked together as far as number twelve, the Law home. Jennie said. "Agnes, I'll return the keys, the Gartsherrie Works has no hold on me whatsoever, I can say anything that I damn well please." And she did.

CHAPTER 11
December 1929

As Samuel alighted from the train at Sudbahnhof Railway Station in Vienna his eyes searched into the crowds of people waiting to meet loved ones. Immediately he caught sight of his beloved Leah, she was wearing a bright red coat, trimmed with grey fox fur and a matching fox fur hat. He ran towards her and held her in his arms, murmuring caresses. "My darling, my leibling, my sweetheart. I've missed you so much."

"Darling Samuel, no more separations. We'll get married at the Standesamt," said Leah between kisses, "then we will be husband and wife."

The city around Sudbahnhof was busy with family and friends returning and leaving for the holidays. As they left the bustling station the winter cold enveloped them, however Vienna dressed in snow was exquisite to behold. They were lucky and managed to get a taxi to the Goldbaum home in the comfortable suburb of Dobling.

The entire Goldbaum family was waiting to welcome the lovers, Mama, Papa, Leah's brother Daniel, her elder sister Anna with her husband Rolf Bernhardt and their children Sophia, Hannah and baby Simon. Samuel was also pleased to see his old friend Leon with his wife Isabella.

Samuel felt privileged to be welcomed and accepted so wholeheartedly into this warm family. Mrs Goldbaum led the way into the dining room where there was champagne on ice and platters of blinis with soured cream, smoked salmon and caviar.

They ate, drank, laughed, made toasts. Samuel and Leah were floating on a sea of happiness.

Later that afternoon Samuel and Leah managed to get some time alone before dinner, which was to be a special celebration. "Darling" said Leah, "we will have to complete the registration for getting married at the Standesamt, did you bring all your paperwork?" "Yes, of course I did, this is Samuel your fiancé, otherwise known as Mr Perfectly Organised. However, I imagined we would get married under the canopy in the Shul." Leah looked surprised, saying. "Well we must have a civil ceremony, it's the law in Austria. Do you really want a religious service as well?"

"Actually Leah I do, I don't stick strictly to a kosher diet and I'm certainly not ultra orthodox but I was brought up in Glasgow by a family who had to flee Russia because of their religion, and I have an uncle who is a rabbi, so I'm not about to disregard all my Jewish traditions."

"Rolf isn't Jewish so Anna and Rolf only had a civil ceremony, Mama and Papa raised no objections, in fact Papa paid for a splendid wedding. I suppose I just never gave much thought to getting married in the synagogue." responded Leah. "However, and can you believe this, I too have an uncle who is a rabbi, he lives in Budapest. If you like I'll get Papa to telephone him, he's Papa's brother, our Uncle Gideon. Actually he is not affiliated to a Shul, he is a Lecturer at the Budapest Rabbinical Seminary.

"Yes my darling, ask your Papa to contact your uncle," said Samuel. "I would like a blessing under the chuppah, it's important to me to share the wine and break the glass, it would make our marriage complete."

I really wanted my sister Sarah and her husband Alan to share our wedding celebrations, and I also have an aunt and uncle I'm very fond of but the journey would be out of the question for them, too tiring a journey for Ruth and Dan and Sarah and Alan have the twins."

"Why can't Sarah and her husband come on their own, can't they get someone to look after the twins? I know it's a long train journey for a few days but I'm sure Sarah would want to share in our celebration. Telephone her, go on, do it now before dinner." said Leah impulsively.

Samuel went into the hall and lifted the telephone. It took quite some time to place an international call but eventually a call came back from the operator at the exchange and Samuel was connected to his sister's home in Glasgow.

"Is that you Alan? It's Samuel, I'm telephoning from Vienna, tomorrow we are going to arrange registration for our civil marriage service and afterwards a Jewish service. I know Sarah said she couldn't travel all the way to Vienna with the twins and in any case it would be too much for Aunt Ruth and Dan but is there any chance you and Sarah could come on your own for a few days, is there someone who could look after the twins?"

Alan spoke loudly and clearly. "Samuel, we'll have to look into this, phone us back tomorrow and I'll see what we can do at this end, no promises but we would love to stand with you and Leah as you make your vows."

"I'll phone back tomorrow Alan. Goodbye." Samuel returned the handset to it's cradle.

"Who were you yelling down the phone at?" asked Sarah, "I could hear you from upstairs."

"Believe it or not it was Samuel, at least he says it's Samuel, I think his body has been taken over. Have you ever known such a change in anyone? He wants us to go on our own to Vienna and leave the wee ones here?"

"What on earth is he talking about? He's gone mad. As if we would jolly off to Vienna and leave our babies," Sarah laughed. "Honestly you are right Alan, I think this Leah girl must be some sort of femme fatale. Could you for one minute imagine Mr Samuel 'I am the most sensible man on the planet' Fischer coming up with a wheeze like that?"

"No I can't my darling, you were always the impulsive one in your family. But is it entirely a mad idea? Perhaps we could ask your Auntie Ruth if she would come and stay with the twins. It would be lovely to spend a few days alone with you and travelling by train across Europe sounds very romantic."

Sarah sounded aghast. "For goodness sake Alan we can't possibly ask Aunt Ruth to look after two two year olds, it would be far too much for her on her own and Dan would be horrified, he loves them to bits for a few hours but that's enough for him. He likes to get back to his quiet house and bury his nose in a book or listen to music. There is only one person I'd trust to look after them and that's my sister Mary. If she would stay here with Aunt Ruth, between them I'm sure all would be well. So my romantic husband, no Mary no trip."

Alan conceded. "I take your point darling, terrible twos times two, we can't expect Ruth to manage on her own. Look why don't you send a note to Mary and see what her reaction is, and get the telephone number of the Refuge so that you can get in touch with her easily."

Sarah sat down at her desk and wrote.

My dearest Mary,

You are NEVER going to believe this story. Well, Samuel telephoned from Vienna, he wants Alan and I to hare across Europe to attend his wedding, well two weddings actually, one civil and one religious. The weddings of the century between, our brother Samuel and the extraordinary Leah.

Big deep breath, could you possibly come and stay here with Aunt Ruth and look after your niece and nephew for a few days, well probably a week?

I realise Alan and I are asking a lot but it would be wonderful for me to see my twin brother wed. And, I promise I will give you a full report, miss nothing, on the whole mad, exciting adventure.

What do you say? Can you please telephone me, also give me the telephone number at the Refuge so that I can contact you.

I won't be sad if you can't come, honest. But you and Ruth are the only people I would trust with my babies.

Your totally incorrigible sister
Sarah

The Law and Johnstone families were still coming to terms with the untimely and horrific death of Alex. No matter how they tried it seemed to be constantly in everyone's thoughts.

Ella's Friends had closed ranks and we're doing all they could to keep up the momentum of the Refuge while their inspiration, Jessie, was still in a state of shock.

Mary had not written to Sarah with the full details of how Alex had died. Somehow she could not bring herself to write the words detailing exactly what had occurred and the aftermath. Mary had decided that when they next met she would tell her all the horrific details of Alex's death and the unjust way her Aunt Jessie had been treated by the company.

When Mary saw the letter in Sarah's handwriting her heart jumped, at last here was some news outside the nightmare they were all living.

Mary read the letter several times, she had never met Sarah's Aunt Ruth, although she had heard a great deal about her. According to her mother she had been the one bright light when she was married to Ben Fischer, a kind woman who had eventually brought up her twins Samuel and Sarah.

Sarah too had often talked about her Aunt Ruth and Uncle Dan with great affection.

Mary could not imagine what reason she could possibly give the family if she was to disappear for a week or so but her instinct was 'yes Sarah, I'll look after my niece and nephew, and I would be absolutely thrilled to do so'.

As soon as she reached the Refuge Mary lifted the telephone and dialled Sarah's number in Whitecraigs, Glasgow. The bright voice of her sister immediately answered.

Mary spoke quietly, not wanting anyone in the house to hear. "Hello Sarah, I'm at the Refuge so I'll have to be quick, yes I would love to look after the twins with your Aunt Ruth, I just need to work out a convincing story to get away from home without creating suspicion.

As soon as you know the exact details when you will be leaving telephone me here, the number is Coatbridge 987. If I'm a bit curt don't worry, just means somebody is around. I'll speak to my, oops our mother tonight and see if she can come up with something, it's the very least she can do. Phone me, thank you goodbye."

Mary quickly ended the call as she heard footsteps on the stairs. Somehow she managed to get through the remainder of the day, functioning as sensible, reliable Mary on one level, while her brain was buzzing with escape plans.

Thankfully when she reached home it was only her mother who was in the house. Mary knew it would not be long before her brothers, Willie and Jessie arrived home from work so she did not waste a moment. Agnes was seated by the fire knitting, her work for the day done and the dinner prepared. Soup on a simmering hob and a tray of links sausage in batter browning in the oven.

"Mother" said Mary. "We don't have long before the others come home and I have something important to tell you. Don't interrupt me, just listen."

Mary told Agnes about the forthcoming wedding and Sarah's plan. "So you see Maw we need to find an excuse for me to disappear for a week or so without arousing any suspicion. Now get your thinking cap on and we will talk about it in the morning after the others leave for work."

The explanation ended not a moment too soon as Alexander returned home, shortly followed by Jessie, Robert and Willie.

The following morning when the others had left for work and school Mary said to her mother. "Well Maw, have you been thinking of a story we could tell everyone to explain my absence? We can't use Charlotte as an excuse, the others would soon find out that was a lie, particularly with Willie staying here.

"Look Mary" said Agnes. "Do you really think it's a good idea to go rushing off to Glasgow as a nursemaid while Sarah swans off to Austria, it's no that long since we were fighting them Germans. Besides after what happened to your Uncle Alex do you really want to desert your poor Auntie Jessie in her hour of need."

"Look Maw" snapped Mary. "I can read you like a book. You don't want me to go because you are frightened your secrets will all come tumbling out. I want to go and spend time with wee Miriam and David and I know how much it means to Sarah to see her twin brother married to Leah. I am going to Glasgow, now do you intend to help me work out a good reason to disappear for a week or do I just pack a bag and go? Your choice Maw, but go I will."

Agnes realised that Mary was absolutely serious in her intent to help Sarah and she could not risk Mary simply disappearing with all the questions that would provoke.

"You were always the headstrong one, Mary Law." snapped Agnes. "Well if there is no talking you out of this madcap idea, keep the story simple. Just say my relative, Ruth, has contacted us and needs some help. And, we will just say I have asked you to go and stay with her for a few days, that'll do absolutely fine. Best keep it simple and it's also almost truthful."

Mary never ceased to be amazed by her mother, she might drive her to distraction with her drama queen ways but she could certainly knit a story together when she had to.

Mary left to catch the bus to the Refuge. Jennie had postponed her trip to Oxford to see her sister and her family and between the two of them they were keeping Drumkiln House open.

This was the difficult part for Mary, asking Jennie to hold the fort alone for a week, with perhaps some help from Mary Johnstone.

Mary had just entered the hall when the telephone rang, she quickly answered and a familiar voice said. "It's me Sarah, we have spoken to Samuel and Aunt Ruth, I've also investigated travel arrangements. If we are going, we need to leave Saturday morning. The ceremonies are being held on Tuesday first. Aunt Ruth has agreed to help, providing you stay. Quite rightly she thinks it would be too much for her on her own. We would return home the following Saturday. Mary can you?"

Seeing Jennie appear out of the corner of her eye Mary said. "Yes, those dates are absolutely fine, I'll confirm travel details tomorrow. Thank you for getting in touch, I will be more than pleased to help."

Jennie was now in the hall. Deciding to tell as much of the Ruth story as necessary, Mary came off the phone, saying. "Jennie, a relative of my mother's is needing help. I have been asked to go into Glasgow on Saturday and stay for a week. I know we are stretched here but do you think you could hold the fort for a week? Perhaps Mary would come in to help out, in fact it might be good for her to leave the house and do something practical."

As always Jennie stepped up to the bar. "Of course Mary, I'll cover as best I can for you, and yes I do agree it would be good for Mary Johnstone to get herself out of the house. Mary has taken losing her father very badly and I think her mother being turfed out of the family home was the last straw. It just shows we still have a long way to go in the fight for women's rights. Besides, Sadie Kane will see to the cooking, the other women will look after the children and the housework and I'll just deal with any enquiries and administration. One thing I won't be able to do is the first aid or any nursing, that's your province Mary."

"Actually you don't need to worry about first aid." Mary explained. "Mavis Wilson will deal with any minor accidents. I've been training her up and I have managed to help her get a place in the next intake of trainee nurses at the Glasgow Royal Infirmary, it's live in accommodation which is a bonus. Mavis is thrilled, she can now see a new life opening out before her."

What she did not tell Jennie was that Sarah, with her nursing contacts at the hospital, had been instrumental in getting Mavis an interview.

'First part organised' thought Mary, 'phase two this evening, I'll get my Maw to make the announcement after dinner'.

It was a full table at number twelve Long Row, James's wife was visiting her brother so Agnes had all three of her sons and two daughters at the table, plus of course young Willie. After everyone had finished their rice pudding Agnes announced.

"I've just received a wee note from my cousin Ruth, she needs a bitty help. Our Mary has kindly said she will go into Glasgow on Saturday for a few days to help, so I'll be needing a hand here. And, that specially applies to you Master Fyfe."

This was a perfect opportunity for Willie to manipulate the situation for his own ends. "Granny, don't you worry yourself I will rush home from school every day and get your messages and I'll peel the tatties and veg, in fact you'll hardly miss my Auntie Mary, honest."

Jessie and Mary exchanged looks but Mary was thankful to the wee beggar, his outburst had taken the attention away from her.

Willie still had the floor. "Uncle Alexander, will you help me with my arithmetic homework, you are best at helping. My Auntie Jessie is quite good but Uncle Robert and Auntie Mary, well it's not really their subject, now is it?"

Mary could cheerfully have throttled him.

Saturday morning dawned clear and crisp, despite the time of year not an unpleasant day for Mary to travel into Glasgow.

Mary had spoken several times to Sarah and knew that her and Alan were leaving Glasgow Central on the early train to London from where they would catch the boat train. Aunt Ruth and Uncle Dan were staying at Whitecraigs on the Friday night and would be in charge until Mary arrived later on Saturday. After Mary's arrival Dan said he fully intended to return home to Newlands, for some peace and quiet.

Mary arrived at Sarah and Alan's beautiful home in Whitecraigs around lunchtime Saturday to be greeted by two little people shouting "May May, May May, at last you're here, come and play, come, come, see our new swing."

Ruth and Dan managed to quieten the children, and welcome Mary all at the same time.

"Come my dear" said Ruth. "I'll show you to your room Mary, come away upstairs. And, Dan, please put the kettle on for coffee, I'm sure Mary could do with a bite of lunch. I've made up some salmon sandwiches and I brought over a honey cake."

Ruth showed Mary up to the spare bedroom which was decorated with Sarah's superb taste in calm peaceful colours. It was painted a soft shade of eau de nil with cream curtains and bedcovers. The wardrobe and bedside tables, with their cream ceramic lamps, were a light oak. The floor was also oak with a cosy bedside rug. In the window recess there was a green Lloyd Loom chair with a gold edging and a little matching table which held a selection of books and magazines, together with a pretty vase of autumn coloured chrysanthemums.

Against the vase was propped an envelope addressed to Mary.

Darling Mary
Words cannot express how grateful I am to you for your great kindness. I know it must have been incredibly difficult for you to arrange to 'disappear' for a

week, particularly after the sad death of your Uncle Alex.

Mary, attending Samuel's marriage to Leah is incredibly important to me and I will be forever in your debt.

Love
Sarah

Ruth took Mary by the hand. "I've always hoped we would meet one day my dear. Sarah has kept me up to date with the lives of the Laws of Gartsherrie. However, I've so wanted to speak to you. Is your mother well? You know I never agreed with what the family did to her after Ben died. However, there was nothing I could do, only bring up Sarah and Samuel to the best of my ability."

"Ruth, my mother really did appreciate everything you did for her and she always speaks of you with great warmth. In order to survive I think she just closed the chapter of her life that was her marriage to Ben Fischer and the twins and got on with bringing up her Law family. Unfortunately it's really very difficult for me as I am the only one who knows about her past. I can't talk about Sarah and Alan and the wee ones, or show happiness that Samuel is about to marry, everything is a ghastly secret."

"Well Mary" said Ruth, "This week you can acknowledge your Fischer family and I hope you will enjoy spending time with Miriam and David. Actually, I think we are going to have a very busy and probably exhausting week but together I am sure we will manage. Now let's go downstairs, rescue Dan and have a little lunch."

Sitting around the kitchen table, eating sandwiches with Ruth and Dan and listening to the twins chattering Mary relaxed and for the first time since receiving Sarah's letter really looked forward to her week in Whitecraigs.

After a hectic afternoon Mary fed, bathed and put the children to bed while Ruth prepared the dinner. She had cooked a fine piece of pickled brisket which she just had to slice and warm through, served with boiled potatoes and home made horseradish sauce it was a dinner fit for the gods.

As they ate Dan said. "I thought it would be nice to take the children a run down to Ayr tomorrow, as long as this dry weather lasts. We could wrap them up warmly and take them for a walk down on the beach. Then we could all go for a high tea to Invercloy Hotel, it's quite near the sea front. Invercloy is kosher you know, but it's also a very fine hotel, excellent food, and it even has a synagogue. What do you think Mary?"

"I think it sounds a lovely idea, I'm sure the twins will be thrilled with a visit to the seaside." What Mary did not mention was that at nearly thirty years of age this would be her first trip to the Clyde Coast. Instead she said. "Actually Dan I didn't realise you would be helping us with the twins."

Dan laughed. "Ah Mary, the trip to Ayr is my swan song, duty done. I intend to go home Sunday evening for a week of peace and quiet with visits to my favourite deli in Newton Mearns for supplies. I'll return the following weekend and hopefully find you both still in one piece after a week of caring for two toddlers.

Sunday morning dawned as a crisp cold December day. Mary awoke in the warm comfortable bed, for the first time in her life she had experienced sleeping in a bedroom all to herself and enjoyed the luxury of being able to lie in bed with the lamp on reading magazines. Mary looked at the clock on the bedside unit, it showed seven thirty. Then she heard scuffling outside her bedroom door, accompanied by giggles, "You first, you, go, go, let's wake May May." The door opened and in rushed the twins calling "Wake up, it's morning, wake up May May."

The week had started...

After breakfast, and with the winter sun giving promise of a lovely day, Dan organised everybody for the trip to the seaside. Ruth managed to find buckets and spades in the back of the toy cupboard. Mary offered to make a picnic but Dan said "No my dear, when we arrive in Ayr we will have coffee and a wee something in the Invercloy, we can book a meal there for later. Then we'll take the wee ones down to the beach. It's only a short walk from the hotel."

Mary thoroughly enjoyed the drive in Dan's car from Glasgow to the Clyde Coast, seated in the back seat with her niece and nephew. The children chattered and then played games, spot a cow, spot a sheep, spot a car. They eventually started singing: 'Polly Put the

Kettle On', one of their favourite songs, extremely loudly and emphasising the last word Teeeeeee. By the tenth rendition all the adults were glad that they had reached Racecourse Road in Ayr, where the hotel was situated. Dan parked the car and they all went into the lounge to enjoy a well deserved coffee and strudel, with milk and biscuits for the wee ones.

After everyone had enjoyed their drinks in the warm comfortable lounge they headed off for the beach, Miriam and David with buckets and spades in hand. They walked down Seafield Road to the sea front, and Mary's first view of Arran, looking magnificent in the low winter light, the Goat Fell range of mountains scattered with a good dusting of white snow.

There were more people on the beach than they imagined would be out and about, the winter sunshine having attracted a lot of folks with their dogs as well as families and hand holding courting couples.

Mary suggested to the twins that they could leave a trail of sandcastles to follow back to Seafield Road. The two children ran in front quickly making a line of castles along the beach.

As they walked Dan said, "Ruth, remember when we used to bring your mother down to Ayr or Troon for the day, it's certainly cheaper bringing the twins, you two would head straight for the shops and a spend, before we finished the day with a meal at Invercloy."

Ruth laughed, "Yes I do, we always enjoyed a wee visit to Hourstons, it's a lovely department store. Mind you Ayr is a popular place for shopping, lots of nice shops and you can always get something a wee bit different. The Italian ice cream down here is a real treat, we must come back in the summer Mary and have pokey hats. My Mum always enjoyed a wafer when we came down to Ayr."

Dan pointed out the ruin of Greenan Castle to Mary. "Looks magnificent on the headland doesn't it? I believe there was a Kennedy fortification on that sight right back to the twelfth century. Kennedy is an important name in these parts, everywhere you go in Ayrshire and further south the name keeps cropping up. Nowadays they live in Culzean Castle just down the coast. Lot of history in these parts."

Mary thought the sea wall looked magnificent, like a fairytale castle. Mentally she was already planning how she could bring Jessie down by train for a day trip, and another adventure in Ayr.

They walked a good distance along the beach, to the point where they could see the elegant Pavilion Ballroom and the magnificent Ayr County Buildings. Mary marshalled the twins up the stone ramp and they all found a bench to sit and draw breath, and from where they could all take in the breathtaking views of Arran and the Carrick Hills.

The twins wanted to go back along the beach, following the trail of sandcastles, however Dan and Ruth were happy to take up Mary's suggestion that they return to the hotel by the sea wall pathway alongside the Low Green.

By the time they all met up at Seafield Road the sun was starting to go down and deliver what promised to be a beautiful fiery sunset.

The heat inside the hotel from the glowing fire welcomed the walkers and they removed their outdoor clothes before settling down to peruse the menu and order their meal.

Realising that Mary would be unfamiliar with many of the dishes on offer Ruth suggested they all have, fried fish with latkas and grated beetroot. To which the twins started to chorus, "we love latkas, we love latkas" and were firmly told to wheesht by Mary and Ruth in unison.

Before the food arrived Dan asked Mary if she would like to see the synagogue. Mary was astounded, "A synagogue in a hotel Dan, I can't for the life of me imagine a church in a hotel."

Dan smiled as he took his kippah out of his pocket and placed it on his head, saying. "Come with me Mary." He led her into the hallway and opened the door almost directly opposite the dining room and sure enough there was a synagogue.

On the return journey the children had barely started on 'ten green bottles' when to everyone's relief they fell sound asleep beside Mary on the back seat. The journey home was uneventful and while Mary got the wee ones ready for bed Ruth made a cup of tea for the adults.

As they finished their tea and cake in the sitting room Dan announced, "Well ladies that's my duty done, I'm off home now for a well earned rest. I'll see you both on Saturday morning. If there are any problems phone me immediately, however with you two capable ladies in charge I'm sure all will be well."

The following five days were hectic but enjoyable for both the carers and the children. Between them Ruth and Mary quickly set up a routine with Mary doing the lions share of caring for the twins and Ruth doing the cooking and organising clothes. With it being such a big house there was a daily who came in to help with the housework, a Mrs McWilliams. She was a godsend as Mary did not fully realise just how hard it would be to amuse and keep safe two two year olds.

In the evenings after the wee ones had been told a story and were sound asleep Mary and Ruth enjoyed sitting by the fire and having a blether. Mary felt she understood her mother better after hearing Ruth's version of the events that took place over thirty years ago. And, Ruth enjoyed hearing of the Law family's life in Gartsherrie.

Mary told Ruth all about Ella's legacy and the money she had secreted in the Airdrie Savings Bank. "To be honest I have no real idea what to do with all that money. However, I feel it's somehow my security, and I should treat it carefully. I almost gave my brother money to help him out of a fix but then I found a way where he was able to clear his debts himself and I think that was probably a much better way for him to deal with the problem, he isn't so likely to get into debt again, hopefully.

You will have heard from Sarah about the death of my sister Jessie's fiancé, well I think Jessie is so broken hearted that she may well not marry, I'll never marry so perhaps the money might provide us with security in our old age. Look what happened to my Auntie Jessie, thrown out of her home within weeks of Uncle Alex being horribly killed at the Works."

"Yes Mary I think you are right." agreed Ruth, "However, have you ever thought of investing your money in a little property and then renting it out. That would give you some extra income and you would have a home waiting should you ever need one. Dan used to be a jeweller, however he owned his three shops outright, when he retired he sold the business but leased the shops and that provides us with a nice annual income. If you like I'll speak to Dan and you can have a talk with him about how you would set about investing in property."

Mary was flabbergasted at the idea of her owning property but her life had taken so many strange turnings during the last few years that she immediately thought 'why not, why can't a girl from Gartsherrie own her own home'.

"Ruth, I would really appreciate speaking to Dan about buying a property. I've never given it a thought but it makes a lot of sense. Once Sarah and Alan return and life in Coatbridge settles down perhaps I could talk to Dan."

"Of course my dear, before you leave on Sunday morning I'll give you our telephone number and address. Dan is very discrete and we won't say anything to Sarah, if that is what you wish."

"Good heavens no," said Mary "I'll certainly tell Sarah if I decide to buy, we don't have secrets, there are quite enough secrets in my Gartsherrie life without having secrets from Sarah."

Dan did in fact return on Friday evening and they celebrated Shabbat together, with Ruth lighting the candles, and saying the kiddush blessing over the challah bread and wine.

Dinner was home made chicken soup with knadles followed by roast chicken with vegetables. The children ate small portions of the Sabbath meal and little David proudly wore a tiny kippah.

After the children were safely tucked up in bed the adults ended the evening sitting around the fire with a glass of Russian tea.

Saturday morning everyone attended the synagogue and after the service the meal was a cholent made from lamb, vegetables, pearl barley and butter beans that had been gently simmering away all night. Mary thought it was truly delicious and fully intended to try and find out from Ruth exactly how to cook a Shabbat stew.

Mary, who was a devout Christian felt very privileged to have been invited to join in the celebration of the Sabbath, she thought 'This is what Jesus and his earthly family would have done all those years ago. Mary silently prayed: 'God bless these good people, I am very blessed to join with them to celebrate their Sabbath'.

Sarah and Alan arrived home early on Sunday morning having

travelled on the overnight sleeper from London to Glasgow and then taking a taxi home to Whitecraigs.

Everyone was up early and had prepared a welcome home breakfast to celebrate the travellers return. The children were beside themselves with excitement knowing Mummy and Daddy would soon be home.

Hearing the key in the lock Miriam and David charged into the hall to greet their parents. They launched themselves at Sarah and Alan, crying. "Mummy, Daddy we have had great fun with May May and Auntie Ruth, we went to the Ooken Glen Park nearly every day and Uncle Dan took us to make sand castles in his car and May May cut the crusts off our toast and honey and did you bring us a present? And, did you have a lovely time in Otria? And..."

As Sarah cuddled her babies Alan shook hands with Dan and kissed Mary and Ruth. Saying. "Thank you all so much for allowing us to go charging across Europe. It was a wonderful experience, we wouldn't want to have missed it for the world."

Sarah interrupted. "Wait until you see the photographs we have brought home, Leah is absolutely beautiful. Honestly, tall and elegant and Samuel well, he looks happy fit to burst. They are off to Prague and then they are coming home via Paris, opera and galleries all the way. The Goldbaum family were all very welcoming, they have a beautiful house in a lovely suburb of Vienna or as we say now Wien.

Let's have a decent cup of tea and some toast and I'll tell you all, or maybe a bit, before I fall asleep. They make fabulous coffee in Austria but you can't beat a good cup of Glasgow tea."

They all sat around the kitchen table talking ten to the dozen, drinking tea and eating toast with marmalade or honey.

Ruth and Mary were desperate to know what the bride's outfit had been like. Sarah opened her travel bag and produced some photographs. Leah was stunning, almost as tall as Samuel and her wedding outfit was perfect." Sarah elaborated. "Honestly, her outfit was truly magnificent. It was a long medieval style dress in white velvet, trimmed with white fur, she wore a matching velvet hairband holding her veil in place and when they were outside she had a beautiful cloak over her shoulders, it was a sort of peacock blue colour with a band of embroidery. Her parents gave her a magnificent sapphire

and diamond pendant, perfect with her outfit. Oh, and she carried a
spray of lilies. Samuel, well he wore a morning suit, nothing more to
say really. Leah's mother and her sister Anna were both beautifully
dressed and the whole family really spoiled us. Her father certainly
didn't skimp, lots of money spent but they were not in the least 'We
are incredibly rich' they were all amazingly kind hospitable folks.

Now, I am absolutely dead on my feet. Would it be all right if I
went to bed for a couple of hours? I promise I'll give you all the rest
of the news later."

Mary said. "Sarah, I'm really looking forward to hearing all but I
have to get back to Gartsherrie and prepare for a busy week at the
Refuge. Dan has offered to run me to the train station. It'll take me
a good few hours to get home. I've had a wonderful time here with
Aunt Ruth and I'm so glad all went well with your Austrian trip."

Hugs and kisses then Mary put on her outdoor things and prepared to leave with Dan. As she left the house Alan handed Mary a
little box tied with ribbon, saying. "Mary, we can never repay you but
please accept a little token of our thanks and love."

On the short ride to the railway station Dan said. "I hear from
Ruth that you might be interested in buying a little property Mary.
Think about it carefully and if you want a listening ear give me a call
and come over and have a meal with us one day in the New Year.
Not long now and it will be a new decade my dear. The Roaring
Twenties will end and it will be the 'who knows what' Thirties."

Mary accepted Dan's card and thanked him for his kindness. As
she waved goodbye and entered the station, Mary Law from the
Rows of Gartsherrie realised loudly and clearly that she did not like
this double life she was living one tiny little bit.

Settled in the train to Glasgow Central Mary carefully
unwrapped the little box Alan had given her to find it contained a
beautiful silver brooch with blue and white enamel edelweiss flowers,
the national flower of Austria. A present that would be absolutely
perfect to wear with her best blue coat.

When Mary got off the train at Blairhill, light snow was starting to
fall and even in the early afternoon the winter sunlight was fading fast.

Walking down the Long Row she passed number 130, the house

that her Aunt Jessie and Uncle Alex had lived in for so many years, the house where her parents had lodged, her first home. A strange woman came out, holding the hand of a toddler who she walked over to the toilet block. Mary felt a lump rise in her throat as she walked past, knowing she would never again share time there with her beloved aunt and uncle.

As she passed James and Margaret's house Mary noticed the curtains were closed and thankfully all was silent, too many times in the past she had heard noisy arguments raging between her brother and his wife from their home in the Long Row.

As Mary approached her family home Willie, who had been taking out her dog Rags for a walk, caught sight of her and ran towards his aunt. He handed Mary Rags's lead while taking her bag to carry and then started talking ten to the dozen.

Willie launched into his tale in his usual theatrical manner. "Auntie Mary what a time we've had since you've been away helping Granny's cousin in Glasgow. Auntie Margaret has had a wee girl, she is no at all well and is sleeping in your room, Auntie Margaret that is, she is no well, the wee baby is fine. My Auntie Jessie is staying in Airdrie with her friends and my Granny is no happy at all. It makes a change for me not to be the naughty one, it's Uncle James and 'That Margaret One' who are getting the sharp edge of her tongue at the moment."

Mary's heart sank to her boots. What now? Her feet had hardly got into the house when Agnes started. "Am I glad to see you home our Mary, what a right to do we've had here. That eejit Margaret goes out in this weather with high heeled shoes if you please, and her pregnant, falls over breaks her wrists and then she goes into labour. The Alexander Hospital plastered her wrists and the babe was born at the hospital. Now we have her and her attention seeking ways here.

James has got to go to his work, and Lady Muck can't attend to the wee baby with her wrists in plaster, so yet again I've been landed. Honestly Mary I don't know how I would have managed if it hadn't been for young Willie, he has been a wee treasure, running errands, and nothing too much trouble for him. I really can't think why we were all so reluctant to have him come to live with us here in Gartsherrie."

Mary had not taken off her coat and already she had walked into trouble. A corner of her mind thought. 'I wonder if there would be room for me at Liz's house in Airdrie'?

Mary went straight into her bedroom, Margaret was laying in her bed, wrists plastered, just as her mother had described. Beside the bed in a little crib, lovingly made by James, lay a tiny baby, with her father's black curly hair and blue eyes.

"Oh Mary" cried Margaret "You can have no idea what I've been through, between breaking my wrists and having little Lillian."
"Lillian?" enquired Mary. "Where did you get a name like that from?"

"Actually" replied Margaret "My daughter was named Lillian, after my very favourite star, Lillian Gish and her second name is Constance after Constance Bennett. Lillian Constance Law now that's a bit more like the thing than your Agnes or Jessie do you no think?"

Mary thought it was Margaret and James's right to call their bairn exactly what they wanted but she doubted if her Mother would see it that way, Lillian Constance Law, would no doubt be yet another excuse for Agnes to complain. Mary contented herself with saying. "Well Margaret I hope you feel better soon and you certainly have a lovely wee baby girl."

Mary went back through to the kitchen. Without stopping to take off her coat she said. "Maw there is no room for me to sleep here. I'm going to go over to Drumkiln House and see if I can get a bed there for a couple of nights. Don't worry I'll give you a hand. I'll do some cooking and bring it over tomorrow."

Before Agnes could get into her stride Mary was heading down to the bus stop. Willie ran after her shouting "Auntie Mary, Auntie Mary, I'll carry your bag." Mary let Willie catch up and handed him her bag and together they walked down to the bus stop.

Mary opened her purse and handed Willie a threepenny bit, saying. "There's a wee something for your savings box or sweeties, and thank you Willie for being helpful."

It was almost a relief when he put on his best 'exasperated' face and said. "Well Auntie Mary what do you think of Lillian Constance as a name? Poor wee wean, her name is longer than she is. And, I'll tell you this Auntie Mary, my Granny is no best pleased, she thinks wee Lillian Constance should have been called wee Agnes after her, so 'That Margaret One' and my Uncle James are right in the bad books I can tell you."

Mary couldn't help but laugh at Willie's observations, knowing they were probably all completely accurate.

"I'm going to stay at the Refuge Willie so you are now in charge. Keep an eye on things for me, I'll see you tomorrow after school."

Mary arrived at Drumkiln House, tired from her journey but exhausted from the goings on in the Long Row. The ladies all greeted her warmly, everyone was pleased Mary was now back at the helm.

The transformation of the downstairs morning room into Jessie's parlour was not quite finished. It might be some time before Jessie felt strong enough to return but everyone felt it was important that her room should be ready and waiting to welcome her home to Drumkiln House. The new furniture had been delivered and Mavis gave Mary a hand to make up the bed with fresh linen giving her a comfortable temporary bedroom.

Before unpacking Mary telephoned Liz's home in Airdrie. Mary Johnstone answered, saying. "Mary Law am I glad to hear from you, your mother wouldn't tell us how to contact you. Have you heard about the accident that happened to Margaret?"

Mary confirmed that she knew what was happening at home and that meantime she had moved into the Refuge.

"I'll get your Jessie, I'm sure she would like to speak to you." said Mary. Jessie picked up the phone, saying. "Mary, what on earth is going on? My Maw wouldn't tell us how to get in touch with you. Have you heard, Margaret and her wee baby are in our bedroom at home. Liz and Mary have been really kind and put me up here in Airdrie, it's all been such a carry on and one we could well have done without, after losing Uncle Alex."

Without giving too much away Mary said. "It's fine Jessie, I know what is happening, I'm staying at Drumkiln House meantime. However, we have to make a plan. Tuesday is your half day, come over here in the afternoon and we will discuss the whole situation. I've promised to take some food over tomorrow so that will give me a better idea as to the lay of the land. Jessie, tell me, how is Auntie Jessie bearing up?"

"The answer is she isn't. She hardly eats enough for a sparrow and her eyes have black shadows. Mary, to be honest I am seeing in her what you must have seen in me when I first lost McInnes. Mary too is in a terrible state, she has given herself a terrible burden of guilt because she did not go to supper with her Ma and Pa after the Ella's Friends meeting we had on the Sunday afternoon. And, together with Liz they were making a plan to get Uncle Alex to leave the Works, she blames herself for being too involved with the flat in London and not concentrating on her parents. I've tried to tell her it's not her fault, so has Liz but she won't believe us. As for Aunt Jessie, well she hardly speaks."

Mary felt as though her world was tumbling around her. One minute she was relaxing in Sarah's graceful Glasgow home and enjoying life with her niece and nephew and the next her responsibilities once again seemed overwhelming. Mary ended the call. "Look Jessie there is not much more I can say on the telephone. Come straight here from the train station on Tuesday and we'll talk everything out then."

As promised Mary went back to the Long Row the following afternoon, taking with her a large ashet of shepherds pie and a dozen scones, cooked by Sadie Kane. Mary also took with her a jar each of her home made jam and chutney.

Mary had timed her visit to coincide with Willie's return from school. His presence would prevent her mother quizzing her on her stay at Sarah's home, she was also starting to think that in this situation it might be useful to have young Willie on her side.

As Mary was in the scullery unpacking the food from their wrapping of spotless tea towels Willie bounded in from school.

"Hello Aunt Mary, nice to see you, is that one of your lovely home cooked dinners by any chance? And, scones, great. Can I please have one now? I need to feed my brain, I've been working exceptionally hard today."

"Yes Willie you can have a scone." agreed Mary. "Now I'm just going to have a wee word with your Granny."

Agnes was sitting nursing baby Lillian when Mary went through into the kitchen. Mary immediately took in the tired look on her mother's face. "Maw you look done in. I've brought dinner, you just need to warm it through, and some scones, Willie is in the scullery sampling one now.

Agnes, looked up and said. "Honestly Mary I don't know when I last felt as completely worn out, I'm fair trauchled. Between the death of your Uncle Alex, and 'That Margaret One' constantly moaning, honestly Mary my hair is turning white. You were away in Glasgow when this carry on started and then our Jessie has to leave and stay away in Airdrie and now you having to leave your own home, it's all too much. Besides I'm far too auld to be caring for a wee wean, I've had my time changing dirty hippens and wind'n wee weans.

For once Agnes's complaints fell on sympathetic ears. "Actually Maw, I completely agree with you that it's not fair to expect you to be a nursemaid, look after the house, and care for Margaret. I've got the makings of an idea, just be patient another couple of days and hopefully we will get something sorted out."

The following afternoon Jessie arrived at Drumkiln House, cold and drenched on a truly miserable December day. The two sisters settled themselves in front of the roaring fire in the sitting room with a plate of toasted cheese and a pot of Lipton's tea.

As they ate Jessie said. "Honestly Mary, while you were helping Maw's cousin Ruth in Glasgow it was a nightmare here. Have you come up with any ideas as to what we are going to do about Margaret? It's too much to expect Maw to look after three men, Willie, Lady Margaret and young Lillian Constance."

Mary agreed and confided in her sister the plan she had been hatching.

Knowing that she had the security of her Airdrie Savings bank book, which was now carefully secreted in the Refuge Medical Room, Mary said. "Jessie, I'm getting a decent wage for working at the Refuge so I would be able to pay for some help.

Now this is my idea. One of the girls here, Mavis, has been accepted to train as a nurse at Glasgow Royal Infirmary, however the next intake is not until April. Mavis is a very capable girl and I've been giving her some instruction on home nursing and first aid.

Margaret can move back home, Mavis will look after her and wee Lillian Constance during the day and then return to the Refuge for dinner and accommodation. James will just have to do his bit in the evening. We can return home and generally help out until Margaret gets the plasters off, probably about another three or four weeks. On Mavis's part, it would be an opportunity for her to save a little money before starting her training. What do you think?"

"Inspired Mary, honestly I think it is an absolutely brilliant plan." said a smiling Jessie. "That would be the first positive step forward. Only question is, do you think Mavis will agree to your plan?"

"No time like the present." said Mary. "I'll take the lunch things back through to the kitchen and see if I can find her."

About five minutes later she returned with Mavis. Mary invited her to sit down and then explained her idea.

Mavis jumped at the chance to help. "Miss Law, you have been wonderful to me, giving me a decent place to stay, well away from that brute of a man I stupidly married. And then, helping me to get accepted for a nursing course at the Royal Infirmary. Of course I'll help look after your sister-in-law and her wee baby. When do you want me to start?"

Jessie laughed. "Would tomorrow be too soon? Our poor mother is fair exhausted. Mary and I will take Margaret up to her own house tonight and get her settled. If you take the bus over to the Long Row tomorrow morning, and come to number twelve about eight o'clock, I'll take you up to my brother James's house on my way to Blairhill Station where I catch the train to my work.

Mavis, it's only fair to warn you, Margaret is not the easiest of people to deal with. Baby Lillian is a good wee soul but Margaret, well Margaret's Margaret."

Having organised care for Margaret and the baby, Jessie decided to telephone Mary and Liz and let them know she would be moving back home. Mary kindly drove down to Drumkiln House from Airdrie with Jessie's things and then drove the sisters over to their home in Gartsherrie.

When Mary's Vauxhall stopped outside the Law home, Alexander happened to be looking out of the window, he said to

Robert. "Robbie, remember when McInnes used to come to Gartsherrie in his Morris Cowley and he would take us for rides, we were so chuffed at all our pals seeing us in his car. It's rather sad seeing our Jessie getting out of Mary Johnstone's car."

"What's that your saying?" said his mother. "Jessie getting out of Mary's car." "Yes Maw" confirmed Alexander. "And our Mary is there too, and they've both got their bags."

The three women rushed into the house through the rain. Willie greeted them. "Aunties, Miss Johnstone can I make you all a nice cup of tea, my Granny is busy nursing wee Lillian Constance."

As much to get rid of him into the scullery as anything Mary agreed that some tea would be lovely and handed him a parcel of shortbread.

Mary sat down and explained the new arrangements for the care of Margaret and the baby. Everyone was delighted, then a shrill voice was heard from the bedroom. "What is going on out there, are you lot having a party or what?"

Mary and Jessie looked at each other. Jessie said. "Toss you for it, who tells her you or me." Agnes stood up, all five foot nothing of her, handed the baby to Alexander, who happened to be nearest, and said. "There will be no need for either of you to tell her, it will give me the greatest of pleasure."

When James arrived for his dinner he found a full house. Baby Lillian was well wrapped up and the outdoor tartan plaid laying in waiting. Margaret was also dressed warmly to keep out the cold, however she was certainly not keeping quiet.

Agnes snapped at her. "Margaret for once in your life stop your constant girning and thinking about YOU, think about your family, and think about me and the girls and the work and upset you have caused everyone, and particularly think about your man. Now, our James get up to your place and lay a fire. Jessie, you go with him and make up the bed with clean linen, you had better take a fresh set from my kist. Mary pet, will you run Margaret and the bairn up to James's place in your car, our Mary will go with you and get them settled in. Robert ladle some of the soup from the big pot into a bowl and cut some bread, you can wrap it in a tea towel, that'll do for their tea tonight."

As Agnes was issuing her orders with all the authority of a Sergeant Major in the H.L.I., Margaret continued to whimper and cry. Agnes was having none if it, as everyone jumped to carry out their tasks Agnes once again rounded on her daughter in law. "Will you stop that snivelling my girl and think about how lucky you are, not another word mind, just get ready to go back up the road to your ain hoose, where you belong."

Within an hour James, Margaret and wee Lillian were back in their own home. Meanwhile in number twelve Agnes had organised soup followed by tea sandwiches and shortbread for her family and Mary Johnstone, who was after all near as dammit family. It was a jolly meal with everyone laughing and joking. Willie was in top form doing his impersonation of 'That Margaret One'.

As Mary was leaving to go home Jessie walked her to her car. Mary took Jessie's hand and said. "That was the first time I've laughed since my daddy died. Jessie, I now realise how truly terrible it must have been for you when you lost McInnes." Jessie replied. "Mary, tonight was the first time you laughed, there will be lots of other firsts. You just have to walk the road at the pace that is right for you. But can I tell you, my Uncle Alex would have been laughing fit to burst at Willie's antics tonight, remember that and relay all the funny stories to your Maw and Liz."

As planned Mavis arrived the following morning and Jessie took her up to meet Margaret. As they left Jessie felt like she was leading a 'lamb to the slaughter' but it was only a short time to Christmas and having Margaret out of her bedroom was the best present Jessie could have asked for.

A new pattern quickly developed with Mavis looking after Margaret and the baby during the day and James collecting a cooked meal from his mother to take home for him and Margaret each evening.

Agnes asked Willie if he would like to go home and spend the Christmas school holidays with his parents in Condorrat. To which suggestion Willie had politely answered. "That is extremely kind of you Granny but I think it would be better if I stayed here in order to assist you as much as I can, it's much too cold for you to go down to the Store." Not for the first time Agnes wondered if she had not been too hard on her grandson.

Mary made up a Christmas stocking for Willie containing tangerines, a shilling, a Cadbury's chocolate bar, liquorice laces, a 'Just William' book by Richmal Crompton, (Mary did have some reservations about this gift) and a metal savings bank in the shape of a red pillar box.

While appreciating his improved behaviour Mary had no illusions that Devil Willie was still lurking, behind the Good Willie facade.

After everyone returned home from work on Christmas Day, dinner was the usual celebration treat of home made steak pie, mashed potatoes and boiled marrowfat peas. However, there was a new woman in the Refuge from Poland called Katya, who had insisted on making Mary a traditional Polish Christmas gingerbread, to be served with plum conserve for their Yuletide celebration. Everyone enjoyed this tasty departure from the traditional dumpling or trifle.

Mavis joined the women and children at Drumkiln House for her Christmas dinner. Sadie sat at the top of the table and said a grace, giving thanks to the Lord and his helpers, Ella's Friends, for bringing them all to a place of safety.

Mavis was rather quiet and thoughtful, her thoughts were a mystery. Nobody would have guessed that she was thinking. 'How on earth did a kind, decent and handsome man like James Law end up marrying someone so truly self centred as Margaret'.

Mavis found Margaret's attitude towards Lillian particularly hard to understand. When she had a visitor she was all over the baby, the picture of maternal love. However, when it was just the two of them she completely ignored her beautiful bairn.

Jennie having given up on her plans to visit her sister and family in Oxford, joined Liz, Mary and Jessie in Airdrie. It was not the most joyous of Christmas days. However, at the dinner table Jessie said. "Mary you must tell Jennie about the brouhaha at the Laws when Margaret was sent packing."

Mary who was also a good mimic gave a comic rendition of the goings on and relayed Willie's antics which helped lighten the mood. Especially when Mary said "Honestly, my daddy would have laughed fit to burst."

Christmas over, it was now time to start thinking about and preparing for the New Year. Willie was on holiday from school and was feeling mighty bored when he managed to get himself involved in a new adventure.

He was returning from the Store where he had been buying messages and posting some mail. A blue Baxter's bus pulled up and a young man got off, he caught sight of Willie and shouted. "Are you one of the Law lads?" "Who wants to know?" responded Willie.

The young man had now caught up with Willie. He was handsome, well dressed and seemed friendly. "Don't worry son I just want to know if you are part of the Law family, I know your sister, Jessie." Feeling a bit more confident now Willie launched into a tale of how he was in fact Jessie's nephew, William Fyfe, and had left his home and family in the country to assist his Granny in Gartsherrie.

The man introduced himself. "My name is John Sharp, I used to work for the same firm as your Aunt Jessie. I would really like the opportunity to meet up with her again, can you tell me where she works now, and how she travels every day?"

The bright light of opportunity lit up in Willie's brain. "Tell me Mr Sharp, exactly why would you like information about my Auntie Jessie? I'm not the kind of boy who would tell tales out of school you know, I've never been a clype."

"I didn't for a moment think you would indulge in tittle tattle William, I just wondered where I could casually bump into Jessie one day."

"Well" said Willie thoughtfully "My auntie is a very refined lady and I could not possibly give information as to her whereabouts, unless of course I felt it was greatly to her advantage. Mr Sharp, exactly what are you asking of me."

John Sharp was fair bamboozled, here was a young lad of ten or eleven trying to negotiate with him as if he was an adult. "Look son" said John. "Simple question, how does your aunt travel to work? That's it, now are you going to tell me or not?"

Not wanting to miss out on what looked like a money making opportunity Willie adopted his innocent look, saying. "Mr Sharp I think if you would like me to assist you it would be only fair if you assist me. I am presently hoping to do a science project at school which requires I purchase some chemicals, litmus paper and one or two other things. I really don't want to ask my Granny for the money as she can ill afford to buy luxuries for the likes of me. If you were to help me out, naturally I would in turn help you and give you the information you require."

John knew when he was beat. "All right, William Fyfe, how much do you want?"

Willie was taken aback with the ease John agreed to making him a payment. Now the problem was, how much? If he set as sum too high he risked John walking away, if however he set it too low, he could lose out. Willie stammered, Mr Sharp it's very kind of you to offer to assist me with my school studies. I was wondering how much do you think would be appropriate?"

John Sharp was no fool and he now had the full measure of Willie. "Look my lad, here is my first and last offer, one shilling. You tell me details of how your Aunt Jessie travels and at what time and I'll give you one shiny shilling."

Willie smiled. "Done Mr Sharp, my auntie works in Shettleston, Dickson's Drysalters, and she travels by train to and from Blairhill railway station, can I now have my project money?"

John handed him a shilling saying. "Now you little tyke, what train does she normally travel home on?"

Willie laughed. "Mr Sharp that information will cost you another sixpence."

John saw red. "Look here William, it's cold, the snow isn't far away and I am fast losing patience with you, now tell me the time her train arrives each evening and I'll give you threepence, now that's my final offer. Do you understand?" Willie knew just how far he could go but sixpence had been well worth a try.

John handed Willie a threepenny bit and in return Willie gave him chapter and verse on train times. He then rushed home where he accepted one penny from his grandmother for going for the messages. One and four pence was carefully inserted into his new bank, Willie went to bed delighted with his days work.

The Hogmany celebrations for the move into the new decade of 1930, were very subdued in the Law household. Too many sad and worrying events had taken place over the previous months. It would be a long time before everyone came to terms with the horrific death of Alex.

However, within Gartsherrie, Coatbridge, Lanarkshire, Scotland in fact the whole of the British Isles people were feeling a sea change approaching. The optimism of the Roaring Twenties now seemed well and truly over and who knew what changes the Thirties would bring to the country and the entire world.

CHAPTER 12
January 1930

On New Year's Day 1930 Mavis arrived at James's home ready for another day looking after Margaret and baby Lillian. She was greeted with the smell of frying bacon and the sight of James buttering rolls. "Fancy a roll'n bacon Mavis? We had a very quiet Hogmany this year, Alexander and Robert came up here to first foot. Margaret was sleeping so we just had a wee glass of ginger wine and a blether, then the boys went home. No playing records on the gramophone and dancing at Maw's this year, far too soon after my Uncle Alex's death."

As he talked James made three mugs of tea, and cut Margaret's roll into small pieces. After taking Margaret's breakfast through to the bedroom James and Mavis sat in the kitchen with their roll and tea and for the first time really talked together. Up until now their conversation had simply been changeover information. Like, 'Lillian has had quite bad wind today but she has settled down now' 'Margaret hasn't eaten much today, just picked at tea and toast.' 'Your mother called in and left some pancakes'.

However, today James asked Mavis about her life. How a pretty young woman in her early twenties had found herself in a Woman's Refuge? What she intended to do with her life? Did she have any family?

It was a long time, in fact never, since a man had asked Mavis how she felt and was actually taking an interest in her answers. Eventually the conversation turned to James and Margaret.

Enjoying the luxury of a sympathetic ear James told Mavis how the family had all warned against his marriage but he had felt trapped and against all advice had gone ahead. He also told her about the debts and Margaret's earlier abortion.

Without really thinking Mavis took James's hand and said. "Now that you both have a beautiful little girl perhaps Margaret will take her responsibilities as a wife and mother seriously. Does she not realise how incredibly lucky she is to have a kind, handsome husband who doesn't drink or hit her."

James laughed. "No Mavis, Margaret does not consider herself in the least bit lucky. I think she lives in a sort of fantasy world, not the day to day reality of life, and she tried to draw me into her fantasy. For a time I got caught up in it all but not any more. Thanks to my sister Mary I have the debts under control and I am now studying and taking exams in the St Andrews Ambulance Association. I'm really interested in first aid, in fact I think the Works should take it a lot more seriously, so many accidents and no immediate professional assistance. I want to put up an idea that they set up a fully manned first aid post but Mary suggested I waited until I have more qualifications under my belt."

Just then Margaret called. "Jimmy Law, I can hear you in the kitchen blethering away, will you not come in and get the baby, she needs her napkin changing."

James rose to go through to the bedroom, as he opened the door Margaret caught sight of Mavis. "My oh my, I didn't realise the maid was coming today, give the baby to her, she can attend to all her needs." Margaret instructed.

James snapped at his wife. "Margaret, Mavis is not your maid. Our Mary has very kindly arranged for Mavis to help us until you get the plasters off your wrists. You should be right grateful for her help, not speaking to her like she is some kind of servant."

Margaret retaliated. "Oh yes, your perfect sister Mary, she is the one who rules your life, Jimmy Law. Well she'll never in a million years get a man of her own, so I suppose that's why she interferes in our lives."

Mary was something of a hero to Mavis and to hear her mentor miscalled by Margaret disgusted the young woman.

James just sighed and said. "Margaret, it's a New Year, a new decade, you've got a lovely wee baby for goodness sake try to be pleasant and grateful for everything the family have done for you, particularly our Mary."

Mavis took Lillian and changed her, then she wrapped the baby in the tartan plaid and said. "I think I'll take the wee one out for a walk, give her a wee bit fresh air." James lifted his trench coat from the hook behind the door and said. "I'm coming with you."

New Year's Day in Airdrie, Liz and Jessie were enjoying a coffee together, while Mary was in the kitchen preparing the evening meal. Jessie passed her friend a home made biscuit. "I actually made these yesterday, first practical thing I've done since losing my Alex. Liz, I just wanted to thank you for taking me in after the Works made me homeless, do you know I can't stop thinking of the callous way I was treated. And, I was one of the lucky ones I had a choice of four comfortable places to go to, very few women in my position are that fortunate.

But the time has now come Liz, it's a New Year, and I must get out from under your feet and start to work again. I am truly grateful for all you and my Mary have done for me but tomorrow I intend to go back to Drumkiln House and sort out my room. The old morning room will make a fine bedroom and parlour for me, somewhere I can spend a bit of private time. I might even start making a few hats again, just to keep my hand in."

Liz reached out to take her friends hand, saying. "Jessie, you don't have to stay permanently at Drumkiln. Make your home here with us, you know you are welcome, besides you might make us the odd batch of biscuits if we're lucky."

Jessie laughed. "No Liz, I needed time not to have to think about the practical things of life, between you, my Mary and Mrs Armstrong I have been wrapped up in cotton wool these past weeks. However, Ella gave me a task and I feel I need to carry out that task, not only for Ella but for my Alex. You know Liz, he was so proud of Ella's Friends and I can feel him on my shoulder saying, 'Get on with your work lass, the auld yin chose you, so she did'."

They both smiled. Liz said. "Yes, m'dear I can hear Alex saying those words so clearly. Oh Jessie if only we had been able to buy a suitable property, we could have..." Jessie interrupted. "Liz please stop talking like that, you are as bad as my Mary. We both know 'if ifs and ands were pots and pans'. It just wasn't meant to be, you know I was never a great churchgoer but I am a believer and it was Alex's time. My mother used to say, 'If you knew what was in front of you, you would never live to see it'. Thank God, not in my worst nightmares could I ever have imagined the horror of the past weeks. Liz, my mind is made up, tomorrow I move back to Drumkiln House. But I might still make you some biscuits from time to time."

New Year's Day in Paris, Leah and Samuel woke up in their bedroom in the romantic Le Belmont Hotel, near the Champs Elysees in Paris on what was to be the last full day of their honeymoon as they were due to catch the boat train on the last leg of their journey to Glasgow on the 2nd of January.

Laying in the big four poster bed Samuel took Leah's hand and whispered. "My darling, you know my flat is very much a basic home for a bachelor? However, I thought, well truth be told, my sister Sarah thought, it would be better for you to choose our new home, rather than me buying something before you arrived in Glasgow." Leah laughed, "Samuel Fischer, I don't actually care where we live, as long as we have a comfy bed where we can make love together. What a wonderful honeymoon we have had my darling, but it's nearly over and I'll have to find a useful job when we arrive in Glasgow, I'm not an Austrian hausfrau you know."

Samuel was stunned. "Leah, you don't have to go out to work. The business will keep us both in comfort, besides I can well afford to buy us a nice house in one of the better parts of the south side of the city."

Leah snuggled up to her new husband, she kissed him on the forehead then down his face to his lips, where she lingered. She then whispered in her soft voice with its seductive Austrian accent "Samuel Fischer, I have no intention whatsoever of being a kept woman. I intend to pursue my career in Glasgow, now don't argue, love me my darling, love me."

The Law family and young master Fyfe breakfasted together on New Year's Day, possibly one of the few families without any hangovers. Robert and Alexander as bandsmen in the Salvation Army were both teetotal and the womenfolk had welcomed in the New Year with nothing more than a small glass of sweet sherry.

Immediately after breakfast Willie announced he was going to take Rags out for a walk, he put on his coat and was gone before anyone could challenge him. Robert and Alexander too donned their coats, setting out for the Salvation Army Citadel to help decorate it for the New Year Social to be held later in the evening.

As they walked towards Sunnyside Alexander said to his brother. "Robert, I've something I want to tell you. I have met a really beautiful girl called Judith, she has long red hair and she is nearly as tall as me. Her family are definitely not Gartsherrie Row material, they have a big house near to the Refuge in Drumkiln House and her father is quite senior in the police. Now before you say a word, I know I am still an apprentice joiner but I have something else to tell you. You know I have always loved maths and the sciences, well whenever I get a chance I go over to the laboratory where the metallurgists work. I've spoken to Agnes Johnston's man, Tom Coates, well apparently he was sponsored through the Works to get his engineering degree, and he wants to put me forward to get a scholarship to study in Glasgow at the Andersonian Institute to qualify as a metallurgist."

"What!" exclaimed Robert "Alex that's a lot to take in, you're not even half way through your apprenticeship. Maw will go doolally, if you go off studying for years there goes your dig money into the house. Besides, can't you remember the stooshie she created about oor Jessie getting above her station in life, what with managing a shop and getting engaged to McInnes. It would be ten times worse if you gave up a steady apprenticeship to go and study. And, is this posh lassie, Judith, really keen on you because that would be another can of worms, we live in the Gartsherrie Rows and her folks are living in a fancy house up near the Hill Kirk."

"I know it's not going to be easy" explained Alexander "Robbie, I have discussed my studying metallurgy with Judith. She is at secretarial college and supports me one hundred percent, her family think that a good education is the passport to a better life. Besides, the Works will give me a bursary to cover fees and during the long holidays from college I will work at Gartsherrie Works and get paid. Hopefully, I might also get some part time work to help out the finances."

Robert was astounded at his young brothers ambitions. "Well our Alexander, you have certainly thought it all out. I wish you well, both with your studies and your red haired beauty. Just give me the wheeze when you are going to tell our Maw and I'll make sure I'm well out of the firing line, I might even take that young rascal Willie Fyfe with me.

Thinking about it Alex, why on earth don't you tell our Mary before speaking to our Maw, she knows how to handle her and if she is on your side your half way there."

Alexander thought about this idea. "For once in your life our Robert I think you are one hundred percent on the ball. I'll get Mary on her own and sound her out."

In Whitecraigs Sarah was busy setting the table, with the help of David and Miriam, for the New Year lunch while Alan was opening a bottle of kosher wine. The doorbell rang out, heralding the arrival of Aunt Ruth and Uncle Dan.

Over lunch the conversation was predominantly about Samuel's wedding and the Austrian trip. Sarah confided. "Samuel is totally besotted by Leah. I rather like her but I think she is quite career minded and could be quite feisty." The twins picked up on the new word. "Fity, fity, is our new aunty going to be fity Mama? Fity, what is fity?" Sarah rolled her eyes as Aunt Ruth said. "Little jugs have big ears."

The conversation was quickly changed as Dan told the family. "I received a telephone call from Mary yesterday. She is coming to lunch with us next Sunday and I'm going to talk her through purchasing a small property as security for her and her sister, Jessie. Now I'm not telling tales out of school she has given me permission to tell you of her plans. We would love you all to come for tea on Sunday to see Mary and we thought we would also invite Samuel and Leah. It might be too soon after their travels but we can always ask."

Sarah enthused. "Oh Uncle Dan, Aunt Ruth, what a super idea. What time do you want us to come over, the twins will be thrilled to see their aunties, Leah and May May?"

Ruth replied. "About four o'clock my dear, Mary is arriving around noon so that her and Dan can have a good talk before lunch."

Mary Johnstone drove down to Blairhill to collect Jennie who was going to join her, Liz, and her mother for the New Year meal.

As they travelled along Coatbridge Main Street towards Airdrie Jennie said. "Mary, something excessively peculiar has happened to me over the past weeks. Would you mind if I tell you about it, I'd really value your private opinion."

Mary smiled, "Oh ho, that sounds mysterious Miss Mathieson, fire away, I won't tell my Ma and Liz, honest injun."

"Well it was like this." started Jennie. "Do you remember I asked your Ma to ask Mr Cornwall the name of a good accountant. Well, he recommended a Mr John Cuthbert. Honestly Mary when I put it into words it all sounds so ridiculous at my age. Well, we got on rather well and he invited me out for dinner. We have started a lovely friendship, in fact I'm meeting him again next Saturday, and..."

Mary burst out laughing. "Jennie Mathieson, that is the nicest thing I have heard since, well you know, since. Come on spill the beans, tell your Mary all about him. Will I approve? And, much more to the point, will my Ma approve?"

Jennie blushed. "Mary, you are making me feel like a schoolgirl. Well, John, err Mr Cuthbert is a widower, his wife died in childbirth many years ago, he has no children and lives alone in a bungalow on the Glasgow Road. John is nearly two years younger than me, and he has a naughty wee Jack Russell dog called Minx."

"Not enough information." laughed Mary. "Is he handsome? Does he have any frightful relations? Is he rich? Has he fallen head over heels in love with you? And, have you fallen for him? And, does your sister Margaret know about said Mr John Cuthbert?"

"Mary Johnstone you are the nosiest girl imaginable but I suppose I deserve to be questioned after letting you into my secret. To the best of my knowledge he doesn't have any frightful relatives. I don't know if he is rich but he is certainly comfortable, he has a lovely car and a chartered accountancy practice, and he has promised to prepare our accounts for free as a way of supporting Ella's Friends. He is indeed quite distinguished looking, wears gold rimmed spectacles and dresses smartly.

I haven't said a word to Margaret yet, you know I had a relationship with a wonderful man many years ago, his name was also John and he was a great friend of Margaret and Martin. The man I loved was killed at Ypres, and I never for one moment considered I would ever have another relationship. My life became the Suffragettes, the cause. Ella's Friends was going to be my new cause. We spinsters need a cause, and then out of the blue this wonderful man has come into my life. It's all moving a bit fast but at our age, why on earth not? In answer to your question, yes I think we are falling in love."

As they neared their destination Mary said. "Jennie, I know you know about the relationship I have with Liz, the love that can never be spoken about. Well I'm so pleased that you too have found your special person. I hope this John Cuthbert fellow is worthy of you. Liz and I are so very happy together that I can't help but wish the same happiness for you. Mind you, we will check him out thoroughly. You will have to invite him to Airdrie for the 'once over' and I promise we will try not to behave too much like a coven of witches.

Actually Jennie, why don't you tell us all about your romance at the dinner table? It will cheer everyone up, and take everyone's mind of my frightful cooking."

"Do you know Mary, I might just do that, we have had precious little to make us smile these past weeks, perhaps the very idea of me having a romance might bring a little bit of joy. And Mary, I'm sure your cooking will be wonderful, you couldn't have Jessie Johnstone for a mother and not pick up something about cooking."

New Year's Day and with nothing special to do John Sharp had taken a walk over to Gartsherrie on the off chance that he might run into Jessie Law. He was just passing the Institute when he saw a young lad leading a little scrap of a black dog. The boy was wearing a navy trench coat, a grey cap and a blue and claret striped scarf, the colours of his football team, Albion Rovers.

John quickened his step to catch up with the boy and said. "Well well, if it isn't Miss Law's scheming young nephew. What are you up to today William my lad?"

Willie smiled, mentally working out if there was any more mileage and money to be made from the encounter. "I'm exceedingly well Mr Sharp, just taking my Aunt Mary's wee dog out for a walk."

John questioned him. "Does your aunt return to work tomorrow young William?"

Knowing full well who he meant Willie replied. "What aunt would that be Mr Sharp? There is my Aunt Mary or perhaps you are referring to my Aunt Jessie."

"You little tike you know perfectly well it's your Aunt Jessie I want to meet," muttered an exasperated John. "Will she be off the six o'clock train at Blairhill tomorrow evening?"

Willie laughed and said slyly "Mr Sharp, that's for me to know and you to find out. However, I am sure a coin or two might assist the information flow."

By now John could cheerfully have throttled Willie, as many could have done in the past. "Information flow indeed! How come you are a wee lad at Gartsherrie Primary school and you talk like a bona fide lawyer Master Fyfe?"

"It is indeed interesting you should say that Mr Sharp, I had intended to study for a career in engineering but perhaps my gifts would be better suited to the law, especially considering my family also has the name of Law."

John couldn't help himself he burst out laughing. "William Fyfe, I don't know about the law but you could be on the stage. Alright, I give in, how much money do you want this time?"

Willie was well acquainted with the art of 'just how far can I go'. He piped up. "Since we have done business previously sixpence ensures I tell you what day my Aunt Jessie returns to work, and as a bonus I promise not to meet her off the train. I often meet her and carry her bag home."

John knew that once again Willie had bested him, but it was almost worth it to listen to his patter. But John was not going to give him sixpence, he handed the young entrepreneur a threepenny bit. Without hesitating Willie whipped the money from him saying. "My Aunt Jessie is back at work tomorrow and as a bonus I promise not to play a wee goosegog by turning up at Blairhill Station. I'll give you a clear field Mr Sharp."

With that he ran off laughing, with Rags running behind him, as fast as her wee black legs could carry her.

CHAPTER 13
January 1936

Five years had now passed since the tragic death of Alex and the birth of Lillian. As the auld ones used to say, 'one in and one out'.

It was the night of 31st December 1935 and folks were gathering to welcome in the year of 1936, yet another Hogmany; a night to reflect; a night marking out the many changes that had taken place in the lives of the Laws, Johnstones, Fischers and Jennie, no longer Mathieson, but Mrs Jennie Cuthbert, during the first five years of the 1930's.

At number twelve Long Row Agnes presided over the celebrations of the Law Family to welcome in 1936.

The music on the gramophone was everything from 'Your the Tops' by Ethel Merman to the latest Bing Crosby. Dancing to one of the crooner's popular ballads was Alexander and his new fiancé Judith. Judith had done well at secretarial college and for the past few years had been working as a secretary to the financial accountant of a firm of insurance brokers in Glasgow, during this time she had been saving every penny she could towards her future marriage. Alexander was nearing the end of his studies and was due to receive his degree in metallurgy in a few months time.

A handsome couple, Judith and Alexander were looking forward to marrying soon after Alexander's graduation, they saw a happy and prosperous future unfolding before them. Alexander often pondered on how lucky he was to have received a good education and the opportunity to study for a degree, his father had not even had the opportunity to learn to read and write. Yes, Alexander fully appreciated how far a Law had travelled in just one generation.

Robert and Molly were now a couple, when they were youngsters the pair had often gone to dances or out for a walk together. However, over the years both had romances that did not work out for various reasons. The two had recently found themselves seeing each other as a couple again and this time round there was undoubtedly the spark of a romance. It was just that, a little spark, whether they would turn it into a fire, that was still in the lap of the gods.

James was dancing around the kitchen with his little girl, Lillian Constance. Much to Agnes's disgust he was in the midst of a nasty divorce from his wife Margaret. Sadly poor wee Lillian was the pawn, handed around from pillar to post. Every so often Margaret would ride into her life, whisk the little girl off for a few weeks, buy her ribbons, perhaps a pretty dress and then tire of the wee soul. Lillian would then be returned unceremoniously to her father who had to find people to look after her while he was out at work. Naturally the Law family did the lions share of providing loving care but sadly even at the tender age of five the child was already showing signs of the constant disruptions in her life.

Willie won the Dux medal when he was in the Qualifying Class at Gartsherrie Primary which allowed him to be accepted to attend the High School in Albert Street. Willie moving to the local Grammar School was yet another strain on the family finances, as he was required to wear a smart uniform and there were many other additional expenses. His parents, Charlie and Charlotte could not possibly afford to meet all the costs of having their son at Grammar school, with four other children to feed and clothe. Alas, once again the Law family had to step up to the bar. Unsurprisingly, the brunt of Willie's education expenses were met by his aunts Mary and Jessie.

Tonight Willie was dancing with a pretty young girl called Susan Cross who was in his year group at 'The Albert'. Susan lived nearby and her family were impressed that Willie, together with his Uncle Robert, collected their girl and promised that she would be escorted home no later than one o'clock. Besides, the Cross family knew that the Laws were one of the most respectable families in all the Rows.

The music finished and Willie took to the floor. "Granny it's a New Year and I know you are a Glasgow Girl, so I'm going to sing a special Glasgow song for you." He cleared his throat and gave an elaborate rendition of 'I Belong to Glasgow' by Will Fyffe, beloved by Glaswegians the world over.

Willie sang the verses and everyone joined in the rousing chorus, which Willie had changed to.

> *'I belong to Glesga*
> *Dear old Glesga toon*
> *Well, what's the matter with Glesga*
> *For it's going roon an' roon*
> *I'm only a great wee Granny*
> *As anyone here can see*
> *But when I enjoy my tea and a pancake*
> *Well, Glesga belongs to me'*

This led to uproarious laughter, Willie was now a firm favourite with Agnes and there had been no further talk of decamping him back to his parents in Condorrat for quite some time.

Everyone enjoyed the generous food including Agnes's traditional New Year offering of her wee tattie cakes, dumpling, cherry cake and shortbread, with home made ginger wine and sweet sherry for the ladies.

As she was about to leave young Susan thanked Agnes for her hospitality. "Mrs Law, I've had a great Hogmanay, thank you for going to so much bother, the food was delicious."

With a twinkle in her eye and enlivened by Willie's song Agnes replied. "Well pet, as my auld Granny used to say, 'Och, it's no the bother, it's the expense'." Everyone was in peals of laughter, especially since Agnes, as far as food was concerned, was always the most generous of women.

The house emptied and before they went to bed Mary and Jessie cleared away the remnants of the celebration and washed the dishes leaving everything spic and span for the following morning.

New Year is always a time for memories and laying in bed Mary thought back to the time when she had not a penny to bless herself with and the little money she had earned working with Ella Millar and as a maid for Mrs Watson were pounced upon by her mother.

Even after all these years she couldn't quite believe that with the help of Dan she now owned a little bungalow in Seafield, Ayr. The property was on a long let to two retired schoolteachers who treated the property as if it was their own. Their pride and joy was the garden which they tended with loving care, their only enemy the salt winds blowing in from the Firth of Clyde.

Every quarter day Mary took a trip down to Ayr to collect the rent and enjoy a cup of tea with her two tenants. Sometimes Dan and Ruth would run her down to the coast and they would all meet up for a high tea at the Invercloy Hotel, after Mary had completed her business.

Even after purchasing the bungalow there was still a healthy balance in her Airdrie Savings Bank account but Mary's greatest joy was, despite her heart condition, having a real job, working alongside her Aunt Jessie managing the Refuge. Drumkiln House had been successful beyond their wildest dreams and thanks to Mary Johnstone and her careful reporting, they were now receiving financial support from the Coatbridge Municipal Council and grants from a number of local charitable organisations.

Mary still hugged her secret life, two families and never the twain to meet. Many times she had been tempted to confide in her sister Jessie, or her Aunt Jessie about her Fischer family. On a number of occasions she had come within a hair's breadth of telling Liz. However, her fear of a scandal had always won the day.

Mary was moving into 1936 happy and optimistic about her future, despite The Great Depression.

Sadly, Jessie's thoughts on entering another year were simply 'more of the same'. Although she had tried to enter into a normal life for a young woman, her life had stopped when her fiancé McInnes died in 1926. Could it really be nearly a decade ago.

John Sharp, a painter from the McInnes days and Graham Jones, who owned the butcher's shop two doors down from where she worked, had both taken Jessie out. While she enjoyed their company she didn't want a serious romance, she simply wanted friendship.

John Sharp would not give up easily and they had gone out together on and off for years. Jessie shed a tear as she decided never again to go out with him, or with Graham, again. Carrying on these friendships just wasn't fair on any of them.

Probably the person who had seen the biggest life change in the previous five years was Jennie Mathieson, now Jennie Cuthbert. The year 1930 saw Jennie blossom from a middle aged spinster who spent her life working for worthy causes to a woman in love.

After losing his wife and baby in childbirth John Cuthbert had no intention of ever marrying again, he simply couldn't contemplate once again suffering the pain of a lost love. His life became his work, his love a procession of Jack Russells, and his hobbies reading, playing chess and gardening. Then he met Jennie and his world was turned upside down.

They met as client and accountant in November 1929 and were married in the Maxwell Manse in April 1930. Jennie's sister Margaret and her husband Martin were the witnesses and the happy couple were supported by their many friends and family.

Jennie looked beautiful in a sophisticated calf length dress of pale grey with a matching jacket, topped by a chic grey and black hat, made by Jessie, her shoes were high heeled black patent leather and she carried a bouquet of white orchids. John's wedding gift to her was a double string of graduated pearls with stud earrings to match, this jewellery perfectly completed her stunning outfit.

About three months into her marriage Jennie had happily settled into life with John in his bungalow. Minx the Jack Russell had accepted her into the household, as had the housekeeper, Mrs Cameron, who worked Monday to Friday, and whose help allowed Jennie to continue working with Ella's Friends.

The couple were blissfully happy together and it seemed a contented future together was about to roll out before them.

However, one day in the heat of summer Jennie was in the kitchen at Drumkiln House, pouring glasses of cold lemonade for Jessie and two of the women who were working in the garden, while chatting to Mary who was working in her medical room. Suddenly, the doorbell rang with great urgency, over and over it chimed. Jennie hurried to the front door and there found a heavily pregnant woman standing on the doorstep.

The young woman gripped Jennie's hand and started crying. "Please, please help me, I've run away from him. He has a right terrible temper and he has jist been given his cards, and he's powerful angry. If he finds me it'll be yet anither beating, I jist can't take any mair, he caused me to miscarry last year, this latest wee wean will be due soon, and it deserves a chance to live."

Mary Law joined Jennie on the doorstep, just in time they caught the woman as she fell to the floor and her waters broke. Mary, who had helped at many births with Ella, immediately took charge of the situation.

"Jennie, go quickly and get Jessie and the girls in from the garden, Room 1 on the top floor is empty. Ask my Aunt Jessie to prepare the room for a birth. Rose and Ellen can help us get this lass upstairs."

Once the mystery women was settled and Mary had treated her as best she could for her superficial injuries, her swine of a husband had not only bruised her he had put cigarettes out on her arms. Mary and Jessie decided it would be best to telephone for Dr Murphy.

Although she regained consciousness and the difficult labour progressed, the words the woman uttered seemed to make no sense whatsoever. The Drumkiln ladies did their best to help this needy stranger, although they had absolutely no idea who she was or where she came from.

Jennie answered the door to Dr Murphy and explained to him the little they knew. He addressed Jennie in his broad Ulster accent. "Well m'dear we'll just have to do whit we can do for the poor lass, so we will."

Rose came downstairs and said to Jennie. "Jessie wants you to telephone the police station, the woman upstairs is very poorly and we still have no idea who she is." Jennie made the telephone call, she then decided to 'phone Andrew Cornwall and update him on what was happening at the Refuge.

Two police officers arrived within a short time. Even as Jennie was showing them into the sitting room Dr Murphy was coming down the stairs. He followed them into the sitting room saying. "Well lads we have a right mystery for you the day. The lass who came to the door of the Refuge was nearly at full term, I've brought the wee bairn into the world, she is small but should survive, the mother, God love her, is in a right bad way. Miss Law and Mrs Johnstone will give her good care but to be frank I dinna hod oot much hope for the lass. Miss Law has checked through her bag and claes, but there is nothing to show who oor mystery wuman is."

As Dr Murphy was giving a description of the woman to the police Jessie burst into the sitting room calling out. "Dr Murphy can you come upstairs this minute, I think the lass is on the way out." By the time Dr Murphy Jessie and Jennie had made their way upstairs Mary was closing the sad woman's eyes, and the tiny baby was laying in her dead mother's arms.

Mary lifted the child and handed her to Jennie saying. "Jennie, take the wee one and find something to wrap her up in. Jessie and I will deal with the mother, poor soul."

Jennie carried the baby downstairs while Rose found a nappy and a shawl to swaddle her. Jennie sat herself in an armchair in the sitting room, cuddling the little girl, bathed in a sea of calm, while chaos seemed to be filling the entire Refuge.

Andrew Cornwall arrived. The young police officers telephoned the station for instructions. Dr Murphy arranged for the undertakers to come and take the body to the mortuary.

John Cuthbert walked into the sitting room and saw Jennie holding the baby. He found Mary and said. "You can't possibly look after a newborn baby in the midst of all this upheaval. Jennie and I will take the wee one to our bungalow and tend to her in the meantime."

The baby never left the home of Mr and Mrs John Cuthbert, she was adopted by the scarcely married couple and given the name Louise Christine Cuthbert.

Investigations eventually found that the mother was called Christine McLean and she came from Motherwell, there was no trace to be found of the errant husband and it was never ascertained how she knew about the Refuge. Jennie and John decided that the least they could do was to give Louise the middle name of Christine and one day tell her how brave her mother had been in finding her way to the Refuge, in order to save the life of her unborn child.

As 1936 dawned Louise Cuthbert was now ready to go to school, a beautiful little girl with blond hair and blue eyes she was the apple of her parent's eyes. A child who brought John and Jennie unmeasured joy and the totally unexpected blessing of parenthood.

Jennie, with the agreement of her sister Margaret, rented out the family home in Blairhill to women who had left the Refuge as, a 'stepping stone', but still needed a link with Drumkiln House and who were happy to house share. In a strange way Jennie saw this as a 'giving back', a payment for the happy life she was now enjoying with John and their beautiful daughter Louise.

Mary and Liz had brought in the New Year of 1936 at their favourite hotel, Gleneagles in Perthshire. They were still devoted to each other and despite Liz's blindness, well content with life.

They now owned a row of eight terraced houses in Whifflet which they let out to women who could not afford commercial rents and needed a 'stepping stone' on the road to independence.

In addition to their pied-a-terre in Kensington Liz and Mary had purchased three other properties in London and a town house in the West End of Glasgow all of which were earning them excellent returns. Taking Mr Green's advice immediately before the Wall Street Crash had ensured they had weathered the Great Depression a great deal better than most.

After the tragic death of her beloved Alex, Jessie threw herself into the work of the Refuge. On a number of occasions, Mary and Liz offered to buy her a small property but she always refused, preferring to stay in her parlour at Drumkiln House.

Over the years Andrew Cornwall had become Jessie's friend, not just her lawyer. He often called into Drumkiln House to share a cup of tea with her, sometimes they would listen to a concert or a play together on the wireless, while Jessie sipped a sweet sherry and Andrew drank his favourite tipple of a Glenlivet Malt with a drop of water.

During the summer months he would regularly drive her up to the Clyde Valley where they would enjoy lunch at the Popinjay Hotel and return with boxes of ripe Lanark tomatoes, their stalks smelling of mint.

In Jessie's eyes Andrew would never take the place of her Alex, for all his position and wealth. However, he helped her feel like a person in her own right again as well as being her faithful friend and sounding board.

Andrew, on the other hand, loved Jessie with all his heart. He had developed feelings for her almost from the day they first met, and the years had simply reinforced why he loved her. However, he respected her love for Alex and never showed her any feeling beyond friendship.

Alan, Sarah and the twins were joined by Aunt Ruth, Uncle Dan, Samuel and Leah to see in the year of 1936.

Sarah had cooked a celebration dinner, which they ate at the table adorned with the silver candlesticks that her grandparents had brought from Russia. A poignant reminder of Jews fleeing oppression.

The twins, Miriam and David were allowed to stay up to see in the New Year and hear the ringing of the bells. After the singing of Auld Lang Syne and the traditional toasts the children were sent off to bed.

Alan refreshed the drinks but the mood had become somber. While the children were with them everyone had kept up a front of celebration but now the adults were alone the conversation turned to serious matters.

Ruth reminisced. "When my parents left Russia my oldest brother David was just a baby, Ben and I were both born in the Gorbals. My Mama and Papa left Russia because of the pogroms. They didn't want to up sticks and come to Scotland where they had nothing, knew nobody and they didn't even understand the language, but their lives were in danger, so they did what Jewish people have always done, packed their bags and travelled on to pastures new.

My uncle Isaac, Mama's younger brother had initially intended to emigrate to New York but then for some reason, and I've no idea what, he ended up in Glasgow and got involved in the clothing business. He was quite an entrepreneur was Isaac and built up the business of Salmond's Clothing which you inherited Samuel.

He was the one who sent the money back to his homeland enabling his sister, her husband and little boy to escape to the safe haven of Scotland. He was a good uncle, he financed our eldest David to train as a rabbi and he intended the factory for Ben and then when Ben died in that terrible accident you became his heir Samuel. Me, well I was a girl, the best I could have hoped for was a nice wedding."

"Nothing ever changes for the Jew" said Leah. "We are continually persecuted, the young, the fit, the clever, the courageous take off for safer climes, and the old, the infirm and the timid die. Ruth, it's people like your brother Isaac who stop us being exterminated altogether."

Samuel took his wife's hand. "My darling, I know how worried you've been since Paul von Hindenberg died and that guttersnipe Hitler became the President as well as Chancellor, the undisputed Fuhrer of the German people.

With every month that passes there are more restrictions against us. Since the start of the Depression the Nazis have bit by bit taken over Germany and the German conscience."

"Not just Germany," interrupted Leah. "My sister Anna wants to get out of Austria with the children but her husband, Rolf, won't hear of emigrating. He isn't Jewish and he just says 'don't be ridiculous, the children are only half Jewish, besides I'm a doctor AND Austria isn't Germany'. He is wrong, clever Jews need to get out of Germany and preferably out of Europe. The February Uprising in Austria should have convinced any doubters. The Patriotic Front have now consolidated power. In a short time it will be too late to escape the Nazis."

The conversation did not lighten, six Jews from the one family, sitting together in the comfort and safety of a beautiful home in a Glasgow suburb - but what about their brothers and sisters in Austria and Germany. Not just those with filial ties but the thousands of people with whom they shared a racial bond.

Dan commented. "My feeling is there will be a window of opportunity to leave during and just after the Olympics in August, even the Nazis are bowing to pressure from the international community and on the surface cleaning up their act in Berlin. We all know it's just window dressing but I reckon Berlin would be the safest place to leave from. And Leah, I agree with you, the answer isn't to emigrate to the Netherlands or France, Jews should aim to leave mainland Europe altogether.

With Dan's words ringing in their ears the party broke up with Ruth and Dan going upstairs to the spare room and Samuel and Leah, after saying their goodnights, walked to the local taxi rank. Holding hands they got into a taxi and headed back to their flat in Gartnethill.

When Leah first arrived in Glasgow Samuel had been keen that they should purchase a nice property in the southern suburbs. However, Leah was essentially a city girl and had no desire for a house in the suburbs. Within a short time of arriving in Scotland she acquired a position at Glasgow University, working as an assistant to the Director of Modern Languages.

Having a property near the city centre was not only convenient for work it was within easy reach of theatres, concert halls and museums, all of which both Leah and Samuel loved to visit.

However, after a few years of marriage the Fischers decided to purchase a home on the Ayrshire coast at Troon, where Samuel kept his car. This home was a retreat, convenient for weekends and holidays. They could easily travel from Glasgow by train and it was also ideal when friends or family visited from Austria.

Sadly, Samuel and Leah did not have any children, all the family simply assumed that as they were both so wrapped up in their careers and each other that they had decided not to have a family. However, this was far from being the case, Leah had suffered several miscarriages but they kept their disappointment a secret from both their Scottish and Austrian families.

Neither actually said the words aloud but they both hoped that 1936 would be the year they welcomed a child.

Over the following weeks Sarah could not get the thought of Anna and her family out of her head. It was one thing to be concerned for the plight of Jews under the Nazi Reich but when she thought of one family, the Bernhardt family, it was altogether different. She had drunk champagne with them celebrating her brother's wedding. She could visualise each of the children, Sophia now aged ten, Hannah just turned eight and dear little Simon the youngest, five now. Bless, he was just a baby when Samuel and Leah were married, how the years had flown past. She welcomed the home made Hanukkah cards they sent to Scotland every year. She remembered laughing with Anna as they helped Leah dress for her wedding. Together with Alan and the twins she had accepted their hospitality and they had all holidayed together, sharing a chalet in Salzburg, just four years ago. This family wasn't just Jews in Austria, it was her Jewish family in Austria and they needed help, and no matter how she tried the thought of them in danger would not leave her.

Mary and Sarah met for one of their regular lunches at Miss Cranston's in Sauchiehall Street on Tuesday 21 January 1936

As always they greeted each other warmly and then quickly headed into the Mackintosh decorated tearoom and out of the dreich Glasgow January weather.

They settled down at a table looking down on Sauchiehall Street and removed their winter coats and gloves, which the waitress hung on the coat stand together with their umbrellas.

Sarah's first words were. "Well Mary, it's the end of an era with the old King passing yesterday. We'll now have a new young King, King Edward VIII, he certainly seems to be very popular and in touch with what's happening in the country. When do you think the coronation will be held?"

Mary replied. "I shouldn't think it will be this year, there will have to be a state funeral for the old King and no doubt a mourning period. No, the coronation will probably not be celebrated until early next year.

But don't you think the whole world seems to be in a state of change now, and not a good one. Between the King dying, and the Depression. Worst of all the fascists seem to be on the rise everywhere, Spain, Italy, Czechoslovakia, Germany, Austria, even here in Britain.

Did you know a lot of the women who were leading suffragettes are now involved with the British Union of Fascists. They must have seen joining as their 'what now'.

I'm glad that shortly after we got the vote in 1928 Ella left us her savings and Liz, Mary and Jennie joined with my Aunt Jessie in opening the Refuge. Liz told me they were all having a 'what now' moment and then the Refuge became their focus. All except dear Jennie, she still helps quite a bit and our accounts are immaculate but her main focus is being a wife to John and mother to little Louise. You couldn't make it up, one minute she was a middle aged spinster, and the next a wife and mother, we are all so happy for her and John. I think Jennie's happiness has helped my Aunt Jessie. She will never get over losing Uncle Alex but she is such a good soul she shares in other people's joy."

After ordering sandwiches and catching up on all the family news. Mary was first to tackle the political situation. "Sarah, with the fascists all on the rise in Europe, do you have any relatives or friends in Germany being persecuted by the Nazis?"

In Scotland in the year 1936 Sarah could scarcely believe that she was being asked that question, once again the Jews were the victims of persecution, she answered. "We lost touch with any Salmond and Fischer relatives left behind in Eastern Europe when my grandparents emigrated. My Uncle David's in-laws and Dan's family also originally came from the shtetl, I don't know if they are still in touch with family but the Nazi's evil tentacles are well away from Poland or Russia, they have their own set of problems.

Alan's family are Sephardic Jews, most of his relatives are in or around London, although I believe some of his family live in Portugal which is fine at the moment under Salazar but who knows? No, our major worry is Leah's family in Austria. Her sister, Anna, is desperately worried and wants to get out but her husband, Rolf, is not Jewish and he thinks everything will settle down. We had a fairly miserable New Year, Auntie Ruth, Dan, Samuel, Leah, and both Alan and me think Anna's instincts are absolutely right and she should get out with the children."

Just then the waitress brought their lunch of smoked salmon sandwiches, and a pot of tea for two. They poured the tea, added slices of lemon then quietly ate for a few minutes.

Sarah suddenly said. "Mary, do you remember the first time we met, we sat at this very table and you told me the story of our mother's past and all about the Law family. We could never have imagined on that day the paths our lives would take, and despite everything we have still managed to share so much, as loving sisters.

It must have been truly dreadful for you keeping our secret all these years, it's only recently I realised just how it must feel to say something while thinking something completely different. It's difficult to explain and as usual I am probably getting it all wrong but I've got to tell you how I really feel about something, something scary and important.

Mary, I suggested to Alan that we go to Berlin during the Olympics and spirit Anna and the children back home to Scotland. Honestly, I have never seen Alan so annoyed with me. He said that my first priority was the twins and on no account were we, as two Jews, going to enter Germany or Austria, and it was not up for further discussion. Honestly Mary he was absolutely adamant that we could not risk such a journey. I telephoned Samuel and he agrees with Alan, in fact he has also told Leah that if Anna and her family get out he is happy to let them stay at his house in Troon and he will help them financially but as Jews it would be madness for him and Leah to risk a trip into Mr Hitler's Reich.

I haven't mentioned to Leah how I feel, we get on fine but her and Samuel are very wrapped up in each other and I always feel as though I'm not quite clever enough for her. That sounds really dreadful. I'm very fond of her and she has never been anything but lovely towards us and a wonderful aunt to the twins, it's just I've always felt I have more in common with her sister Anna. Her husband Rolf is a paediatrician, as well as looking after their children she manages his practice. You know, like us, practical rather than intellectual.

And, Aunt Ruth and Uncle Dan are also against my going to Germany. Aunt Ruth said to me, 'After all the sacrifices my parents, your grandparents, made to bring us to safety you cannot think of dishonouring their memory by going to a country where your life is in danger by just being a Jew. Then she gave me the 'you have two children' lecture, but in all conscience I feel so strongly I want to do something to help, I really do."

Mary thoughtfully replied. "Sarah, they are all absolutely right, none of you can risk going into Germany, the news gets worse by the day. It's only a matter of days until the Winter Olympics start and then the games proper at the beginning of August. I simply do not understand how they have been allowed to host the games and at the same time behave so appallingly. The really awful thing is the ordinary German people seem to be in a state of denial about the horrendous crimes of the Nazi Party, although I suppose having a job and bread on the table makes you look the other way.

In saying all that, look at the way the blackshirts under that creature Oswald Mosley are behaving in London. Never mind London, it's happening in Scotland. That mad Billy Fullerton and his Billy Boys in Bridgeton are also supporters of Mosley's Mob.

But that's not really the point, the point is, Ruth is absolutely right, you can't throw away the sacrifices of your grandparents. Sarah, you nursed throughout the War and ended up a Lecturer in Nursing at the Royal Infirmary. Samuel runs a successful factory providing jobs for umpteen people, jobs that are still putting food on the table for families throughout this terrible Depression. You have both given back to your adopted country a hundredfold. There must be a way you can help Anna's family other than travelling to Germany."

The waitress cleared away the sandwich plates and brought a fresh jug of boiling water to refresh the tea and a three tiered plate with a selection of teabread and cakes. The two sisters were silent while she worked.

Mary poured the water into the teapot, as she looked up she saw tears streaming down Sarah's face as she fingered the gold Star of David around her neck, a present from their mother Agnes on her wedding day.

Sarah said in a quiet serious voice, quite unlike her normal self. "Mary how many times have we met for lunch or we have been together at Aunt Ruth's or over at my house in Whitecraigs, we know each other so well so I must tell you, I have never felt so helpless as I do now, not even during the War. My head is telling me that you, Alan, Samuel, Ruth, everyone is absolutely right but my heart says I should try and help in the way my Great Uncle Isaac helped my grandparents and gave them and ultimately me and Samuel life.

Mary took her sister's hand, saying. "Sarah my dear, Isaac helped with money and support, he didn't return to the Pale. You must find a way to help without endangering your own life. Perhaps you could start by writing a clever letter to Anna asking her how you can help without giving away that by help you mean her escaping the Nazis."

Sarah brushed her tears away. "I knew you wouldn't shout me down altogether, I'll start the ball rolling tonight, it won't be easy but surely I can write a letter.

Now enough of my bubbling, are we going to do our usual, share a scone then a cake?"

Mary smiled. "Sarah, I think this is the most serious conversation we have had since our first meeting. Please remember if there is anything at all I can do to help I will do it. Now fruit or plain scone? Daft question, fruit."

CHAPTER 14
June 1936

The schools had just broken up for the annual summer holidays and Willie was bored. He was fed up being ordered to help in the Refuge garden or carry out errands for his grandmother, William Fyfe craved a new adventure.

He had heard all about The Barras in Glasgow's East End and it sounded just the sort of place he would like to visit. Knowing that the family would be horrified at the idea of him on the loose at The Barras he decided to concoct a tale.

"Granny, you know I am doing several school projects during the summer holidays, well I really need to visit a reference library, do you think it would be alright if I go into Glasgow on Saturday morning and visit the Mitchell Library? I won't be allowed to bring any of the books home, I'll have to take notes so I'll be away most of the day. I could catch the train with my Aunt Jessie and then stay on it until Charing Cross Station, apparently North Street, where the library is located is just across the road from the railway station."

Agnes could think of no real reason why Willie should not spend a day in Glasgow studying so she agreed that he could leave after breakfast with his Aunt Jessie on the following Saturday to visit the Mitchell Library.

Now Willie, never a boy to be unprepared, acquired a lined jotter, covered it in brown paper and visited the Carnegie Library in Coatbridge where he took copious notes which he knew would be useful when he returned to school.

Saturday morning dawned and Willie set off with his Aunt Jessie to catch the train to Glasgow. He left with a packet of sandwiches and his train fare from his Granny, Unbeknown to her he had also received his train fare from both his Uncle Robert and Aunt Mary. When they arrived at the station his Aunt Jessie paid for his ticket. 'This looks like the start of an excellent day', thought Willie. 'Fare paid and three in my pocket'.

"Aunt Jessie." said Willie, "I really am going to work very hard today, look I bought a jotter out of my savings money." He produced the jotter and opened it up showing a series of blank pages, what Jessie did not know was that Willie had carefully turned the book so that the work undertaken at the Carnegie was at the back, ready to be produced on his return home. There were no flies on Willie!

As she left the train at Shettleston Jessie gave her nephew a cake of Fry's Five Boys chocolate. Alone at last, he congratulated himself on how well his plan was working with the added bonus of sand-wiches and chocolate.

Willie alighted from the train at High Street, took a deep breath and set out on his adventure. He walked down High Street, past Bow's Furniture Emporium to the Tollbooth Clocktower on the Trongate. Ever thorough, Willie had found a map of Glasgow dur-ing his research at the Carnegie Library, which he had carefully copied to ensure he knew exactly where he was going.

As Willie left the Merchant City and headed towards Calton he was aware that the accents were getting broader and the streets were busy and bustling. Before starting out on his adventure Willie decid-ed to treat himself. He saw an Italian cafe and walked boldly inside, passing the small tables he sat himself down on a wooden bench in one of the four booths. A man wearing a white coat approached Willie. "Iva no seen you aboot hera son, whit are you want'n?"

Willie had to listen carefully to understand the strong Glasgow Italian accent. With a show of politeness Willie removed his cap and said. "Good morning sir, I've just travelled from Coatbridge, I'd like a cup of tea please, two sugars and a splash of milk."

The proprietor, Luigi was astounded at this schoolboy who spoke like a lord. He just shook his head and shouted to his wife. "Maria, wul ye git a mugga tea furra the wee fella, milka an twa sugars."

Maria brought the tea over to Willie who had picked up a copy of an Evening Citizen someone had left laying on the bench the previous night. The newspaper served two purposes, something to read and a way to hide his sandwiches. Willie thanked her politely and appeared engrossed in the newspaper.

As other patrons entered the cafe and Maria and Luigi were distracted serving them Willie proceeded to enjoy his Granny's egg sandwiches and his tea. 'Delicious' he thought 'perfect way to start my adventure'.

After leaving the cafe he walked into the busy market. Fascinated, Willie stood listening to the patter of the salesman making their pitch selling everything from books to bananas. People were selling second hand goods from the back of carts, clothes, curtains, tools, whatever you wanted you were sure to find it at The Barras. The indoor market sold old furniture, pictures and bric a brac. Willie was sure there were valuable antiques hiding away amid all the junk.

He passed the food stalls laden with fruit and vegetables, sweeties, fresh bread rolls, winkles, some were even serving hot food, hot peas served in bowls, bowls which were just dipped in cold water and then refilled for the next customer. Willie was sorely tempted by the delicious aroma of frying sausages and onion which were served in rolls but he was still full to burst'n after his tea and sandwiches.

He watched a man setting up his stall with blue bottles of various sizes which looked as though they contained medicine. The tall, thin, grey haired man in the shiny black frock coat saw Willie and smiled a secret smile as he approached him, saying.

"Hello son, how are you today?" "In the pink sir." replied Willie, "in the pink." The man introduced himself. "I'm Dr Josiah Hardbottle and I supply medicinal relief to the population of Glasgow and beyond with my efficacious potions. Now my lad would you like to earn yourself five shillings, two shiny half crown pieces?"

Ever susceptible to earning money, but full of streetwise caution Willie replied. "Well Doctor Hardbottle what exactly do I need to do to earn the money?"

"Look son, this will be the easiest five bob you will ever make. Now what's you're name boy." "My name is William, William Fyfe sir." Responded Willie. The man raised his eyes heavenwards. "Too highfalutin by far son, I'll call you Billy. Now Billy this is the plan, see that wooden chair, you must sit in it and whatever I say to the crowd you will acknowledge as the truth by nodding your head in agreement. Right. And, once I've sold my stock you get your five bob, now how easy is that?"

Doctor Hardbottle pulled a set of black curtains across the front of his stall and sat Willie on the elaborate wooden chair. All was quiet, then after a few minutes a voice full of confidence started to speak enticing a large crowd around the booth.

"Ladies and gentlemen, you all know of Dr Hardbottle's headache powders, and the relief they bring. You have purchased my efficacious spring tonic which sets you up after the long winter, puts the zip back in your life does my spring tonic, as I am sure many gentlemen here will willingly testify. And, who among you has not had relief from my Dr Hardbottle's liniment which treats all arthritic complaints in man and beast.

However, ladies and gentlemen I want to introduce you all to my special potion which treats one of the worst scourges known to man, and woman - and, especially children - TAPEWORMS!. He then produced a glass jar containing the longest tapeworm imaginable in all its awfulness.

Opening the curtains with great aplomb to reveal Willie sitting on the chair he now got into his stride. "This young man sitting here goes by the name of Billy. He suffered excruciatingly ladies and gentleman, excruciatingly, by having this evil tapeworm in his intestines. However a few doses of my patent medicine and it was excreted and now young Billy here can once again enjoy life and eat his food knowing that it will not be gobbled up by this vile creature. He walked around Willie showing off the worm to great theatrical effect. Looking at Willie he said "Tell me son was the removal of this evil creature not the greatest moment of your entire life."

He knew he was just supposed to nod but Willie was thoroughly caught up in the moment. "Dr Hardbottle you did indeed induce a miracle in my life, the wicked creature is now gone and my parents are rejoicing in my new found health. You are a saint among men, a saint to bring relief from all my suffering. I am now able to return to my studies, Dr Hardbottle you are truly a genius, a genius."

Even Doctor Hardbottle knew when enough was enough. "Right my lad, you have testified to your cure. Ladies and gentleman do not allow anyone of your acquaintance to suffer as young Billy here has suffered, purchase my patent medicine at the special price of two shillings per bottle. Now form an orderly queue to purchase my limited stock, you will never make a better contribution to the health of those you love.

The reaction was instant, people were falling over themselves to hand over their money, not only for the patent tapeworm medicine but for his other powders and potions. The stock reduced and the money grew until at last he put up a sign, 'sold out'.

Doctor Hardcastle drew the curtains again and addressed Willie. "Well my lad, you were only supposed to nod agreement but that speech was a masterstroke. I have sold out my entire stock for the day and it's just after 11 o'clock, what are you doing next Saturday lad?"

Not wishing to push his luck Willie said he would try and return the following week but could not promise. Doctor Hardbottle handed Willie not two but three half crowns. "A bonus Billie, you are without a doubt the best stooge I've ever employed."

Willie accepted the money and headed into the crowds where he enjoyed his cake of Fry's Five Boys chocolate, thinking 'I am definitely the 'Realisation' boy. I now realise there is money to be made in the big city'. However, a wee part of him was suddenly fearful that a tapeworm was going to gobble up all his Fry's Five Boys, from Depression, Pacification, Expectation, Acclamation through to Realisation.

He then spent a few hours looking at the stalls and carts containing second hand books, tools, furniture. Absolutely anything could be found at the Barras but for Willie the best thing was the banter. He thought he would never tire of listening to portly men with red noses playing the crowds in strong Glasgow accents.

"Come own noo missus, if you give yer man a mug of my beef

extract fur his tea the night that will see him right, if you know what I mean. And I'm no 'Extracting the Michael'. Ladies, ladies, buy this at Coopers in Howard Street and it will cost you a shiny shilling. Buy it here from Honest Jimmy and it will cost you, NOT a shilling, NOT a ninepence, NO - not, eightpence or even sevenpence, a jar. Ladies of Glesga I'm a fool to myself... the bottom price is sixpence a jar, a silver sixpence, I'll even accept two thrupny bits, or six pennies bearing his late majesty's head, God Bless Him. Now come on girls I'm not here today and gone tomorrow, Honest Jimmy is here every week with a selection of groceries at the best possible prices..."

As soon as the patter stopped and the selling began Willie moved on to the next stall, he was particularly impressed by Cheeny Charlie who sold tea sets, he practically juggled with his stock, while blethering ten to the dozen. "My teapots are not chocolate, no misses they are China, Not English, Not Welsh, Not Irish, NO they are Chinese, guaranteed no ta melt when you put your Lipton's finest into the pot for the cup that cheers."

Eventually Willie felt his tummy rumbling, it was now nearly three o'clock and a long time since his mug of tea and egg sandwiches. He contemplated, 'Do I go back to the food stalls and have a roll n' sausage? The Italian cafe and check out their offerings? Or, buy a hot pie from the bakers shop?'

However, this was a wonderful adventure of a day and caught up in the whole experience, with plenty of money in his blazer pocket, Willie decided to finish the day with a spectacular 'blow oot' treat. He went into another Italian shop, this time selling fish 'n chips, the smell was mouth watering. Willie handed over some of his extra rail fare money and in return received a parcel well wrapped in newspaper containing, haddock in batter, small portion of chips and as an extra special treat, three large scallops (sliced potato dipped in batter and deep fried). He took his treasure down to Glasgow Green where he found an empty park bench. Sitting down he carefully opened the fragrant package containing food fit for a prince, all liberally sprinkled with salt and malt vinegar.

To say Willie enjoyed his meal does not do the experience justice.

He savoured every single mouthful. Eventually the last wee bit of crispy batter eaten, he headed back to Luigi's cafe and there enjoyed another mug of tea, with two sugars, before heading home.

He caught the train before his Aunt Jessie's but instead of going straight home he sat on a bench in Blairhill Station and adjusted the cover on his jotter to now show his work on the front pages.

When Jessie got off the train, tired after a busy Saturday working in the shop, Willie was there to greet her.

"Auntie Jessie, what a busy day I've had, honest. Would you take a look at my jotter, is that no some amount of work for one day? And Auntie Jessie, thanks for the chocolate, that and the egg sandwiches from Granny were the business, really kept me going. Now let me carry your bag."

Willie hardly needed to utter a word, Jessie told the family how hard working he had been. However, Willie now had to find room in his tummy for a plate of bacon, eggs, chips and bread spread with margarine, from the Maypole Dairy, followed by a pancake. Otherwise, suspicions would have been aroused.

CHAPTER 15
July 1936

Over the previous months Sarah had been conducting a secret correspondence with Anna in Vienna. While life for Austrian Jews was much better than in Germany the wind of fascism was indeed blowing through the whole of Europe.

Anna's husband Rolf was now much more sympathetic to Anna's desire to leave Austria but he was still reluctant to leave his homeland. Another complication was Mr Goldbaum had suffered a heart attack, while both of Anna's parents were also keen to emigrate her father's medical condition was a real concern.

Sarah and Mary were once again meeting in Glasgow for one of their regular lunches. Over the past months the conversation at their meetings had been dominated by the political situation and what was going to happen in Germany after Herr Hitler's Olympics were merely a memory and he was free from caring what the rest of the world thought about his party's rampant anti-semitism.

Standing outside Fraser's Department Store Mary watched Sarah walking down Buchanan Street. Gone was her usual cheery positive gait, she was walking like a woman with the cares of the world on her shoulders.

The two sisters greeted each other warmly then headed into Fraser's, taking the lift upstairs to the restaurant.

After ordering their lunch Mary tackled Sarah. 'Sarah, I have just watched you walk down Buchanan Street and it wasn't my bright, joyous sister. Tell me what is wrong, although I scarcely need to ask, it's about Anna's family in Austria isn't it?"

"Yes it is, none of us can go to Germany to help Anna and the children in their escape bid. They have booked tickets to go to Berlin to see the Olympics, the intention is to leave Berlin and then travel by train to London via Cologne and Paris. They have Austrian passports and the story is the family are on a big holiday; Olympics then visiting family in Scotland. Samuel intends to meet them when they land in England as she will need proof that she will be financed by her family and not be a burden on the state, isn't that a horrible phrase, 'a burden on the state' when we are talking about four lives, three of them children.

However, it's a big ask for her to manage on her own with three little children all the way from Berlin. Rolf is staying at home and working as normal to add credence to the story of a family vacation.

The one bit of good news I have for you is that Leah is pregnant. We are all over the moon about the news but it just adds fuel to Alan and Samuel's view that we are Jews and as such should stay out of Germany, Olympics or no Olympics."

They ate lunch catching up on family news. James's divorce was now complete, much to the relief of the family. Alexander and Judith were planning an Autumn wedding, now he had his degree in Metallurgy and was employed at the Works Laboratory, where he was receiving a good salary. The twins had both passed their school exams. Aunt Ruth and Uncle Dan were thinking about selling their house in Newlands and buying a flat in Newton Mearns.

After the waitress had cleared away the plates and produced the tea bread and cakes Mary decided to once again address the 'elephant in the room'.

'Sarah, how would it be if I went to Germany and met up with Anna, the main problem is I can't speak any German but I guess I might manage as thousands of foreigners will be descending on Berlin from all over the world."

Sarah felt the tears well up in her eyes, they never seemed to be far away these days. 'Darling Mary, you are so wonderfully kind to offer but your health is not of the best and I simply can't risk you travelling. Besides, I think you are underestimating how hard it

would be to cope with a long journey, and umpteen train changes
without at least a working knowledge of the language. Especially as
we simply do not know what obstacles Anna is likely to encounter."

Mary did not mention going to Germany again but as she travelled home that day the thought stayed with her.

The following day at the Refuge Jessie accosted her as she
worked in the medical room. "Mary Law you might as well tell me
what is wrong with you? You have not been yourself for weeks now
and since your day off yesterday you are a million miles away."

On the spur of the moment Mary decided to unburden herself
to her Aunt Jessie. "Aunt Jessie can we go into your parlour and I'll
tell you over a cuppa. This is not a two minute story, it's a secret I
have been holding for years and I think the time has come when I
need to share it."

They settled down on the two comfy arm chairs with a tray of
tea on the low mahogany table between them.

Mary did not know where to start so she just jumped in. "Aunt
Jessie, you are going to find this tale unbelievable but I assure you it's
true, my involvement in this story starts shortly after my Pa died.
One day my Ma received a letter from a man called Samuel Fischer
asking to meet her, he was, is, her son. I went into Glasgow on her
behalf and met Samuel, I found he was a really decent man. Shortly
after the first meeting I met his twin sister Sarah, she is the most joyous person you would ever hope to meet. We meet up regularly and I
also know her husband Alan and their children Miriam and David.

My Maw was married to their father, Ben, when she was young.
She converted so that the children would be born Jewish, so techni-
cally all her Law family are Jewish as well. Sadly Ben was killed in an
accident and his family brought up the twins and rejected my mother. Eventually she married my Pa and the rest you know."

This was a highly censored version which Mary relayed to her
Aunt Jessie but the whole truth would be just too fantastical, besides
she did not think it was necessary to reveal all of Agnes's secrets.

'You know what is happening in Germany, well all over Europe
really, the fascists are persecuting the Jews. Some years ago Samuel
married a Jewish girl from Austria called Leah, she has a sister Anna

who desperately wants to get out of Austria with her three children. Anna is going to take the children to the Olympic Games and then travel via Cologne and Paris to London, on the pretext of a family holiday, Samuel will meet her when she arrives in Britain. He will have to vouch for all their expenses while her and the children are living in Scotland. Her husband Rolf, who isn't Jewish, is going to stay at home in Vienna to add weight to the holiday story.

Sarah desperately wants to go to Berlin to help her get to Britain but her husband, quite rightly I think, says definitely not. Leah is pregnant so she can't possibly travel, besides Samuel wouldn't let her.

I offered to go but Sarah is adamant that my not being able to speak any German, plus my heart condition makes the idea of me travelling also a definite no.

I was wondering if there was any possibility of Liz and Mary, taking on the journey. I know Liz speaks good German, and they both speak fluent French. But before I would ask them I wanted to sound out your feelings. I do realise there is an element of danger."

Jessie was absolutely dumbstruck. 'Mary, I just can't take all this in. Are you telling me that your Ma has another Jewish family, a family you have been in touch with for years and not a soul knows about, not even your sister Jessie."

'That's about it."replied Mary. 'Obviously there is a great deal more but that's the gist of the story. I have almost told you on so many occasions but I always managed to hold back, you have no idea what its been like living a double life all these years. The only reason I'm telling you now is I think it's only right to get your permission before I approach your Mary. Auntie Jessie, will you think about what I've said and give me an answer in the next few days. And Aunt Jessie, I know you will respect my secret."

Just then a young woman called Susan knocked the door. 'Sorry to disturb you but I wonder if you could come to your medical room Miss Law. Wee Josie Conner has fallen playing oot in the back garden. She wis tumbl'n oor her wilkies and she has two badly skint knees. Her Maw is at her wee cleaning job so I wondered if you could clean her up, she is girning like nobody's business."

Mary went off to attend to wee Josie leaving her Aunt Jessie in a state of shock.

To say Jessie was dumbfounded hardly touched how she felt. How could her friend Agnes have kept a secret like that all these years and in her turn how could Mary have kept her secret, two families, one Jewish, one Christian kept firmly in two separate boxes.

Jessie decided she had to get out of the Refuge to think straight, go a walk and clear her head, she put on her outdoor shoes, hat and gloves, then lifted her handbag.

Before going out she went into the medical room where Mary was bathing wee Josie's knees with Dettol, while wee Josie was tucking into a piece of Highland toffee, her injuries forgotten.

"Mary, I've decided to go out for a walk to clear my head. What a bombshell, I need time to think this one through. I'll be back before teatime, there is nothing urgent I need to attend to this afternoon."

Jessie walked down to Main Street and then turned right towards Bank Street, her destination being Drumpellier Park. As she passed the offices of Cornwall & Prentice she hesitated for a moment. Over the years Jessie had got used to Andrew Cornwall being her confidant, her sounding board, she was just wondering if she should go in and see him when she felt a hand on her arm and a weel kent voice said. 'Well Mrs Johnstone, what can the firm of Cornwall & Prentice do for you today?"

Jessie jumped, "Oh Andrew you did startle me. Yes, I was just wondering if I should come in and see you."

"Well wonder no more my dear, come on in." said Andrew. "Actually it's after one o'clock, do you fancy going over to the City Bakeries for a spot of lunch? I have just spent the morning with some rather trying elderly clients getting their affairs in good order. I could really do with a coffee and some cheery company."

Jessie laughed. "Cheery company is that what you want Mr Cornwall? Well I bet my morning at the Refuge was considerably weirder than yours, I'm afraid I can't guarantee cheery company today."

They crossed the road and went into the City Bakeries. Downstairs was the shop selling an assortment of sweet and savoury deliciousness, the aroma unique among all the shops in The 'Brig. They headed upstairs to the tearoom where they ordered coffee and sandwiches.

"Well Mrs Johnstone what is your 'weird' tale from Drumkiln House?" enquired Andrew.

Jessie replied. "Honestly, I don't know where to start or even if I should tell you, it's someone else's secret and normally I would never dream of discussing something told to me in confidence. Some of the stories I hear at the Refuge would make your hair curl but I never pass them on. This time it's different, it's dangerous, and my Mary could get involved in this whole incredible story. And, I'm not making much sense am I Andrew?"

"No my dear you are not, look why don't we just chat about mundane things and eat our lunch. Afterwards you can come back to my office and tell me the whole story in private, too public here for discussing secrets. Besides, I would be lying if I said I was not intrigued."

After lunch they did indeed go back to Andrew's office where Jessie repeated to him Mary's tale. "Actually Andrew, I think what I have told you is the censured version of events. I dread to think what the full story might be."

Andrew sat quietly for a few minutes then he rose and went over to his mahogany bookcase, opened the cupboard door and took out the sherry bottle. He poured two glasses, handed one to Jessie and said.

"I speak fluent German Jessie, during the War I was a Major in the forces, however my main duties were behind the lines acting as an interpreter and translating documents. Why don't we go to Germany, nothing wrong with a middle aged Scottish couple going to the Olympics, now is there?

I think the fewer people who know about this saga the better, besides I don't know what Mary Law is thinking about suggesting sending a blind women into Germany. Knowing Liz she would be all in favour of her and Mary going off to Berlin on some half baked idea or other but I don't think it would be at all helpful, do you? Besides if this woman and her family want to seek asylum it might be prudent to have a lawyer onboard."

Jessie could scarcely believe what Andrew had just proposed. "You never cease to surprise me Andrew Cornwall, I had no idea you spoke German. You have never spoken about your War service but then a lot of people never mention their experiences so I never pried.

As for us going off to Germany together, Andrew I've never been out of Scotland, I've never even been to Edinburgh. We really need to have another serious talk with Mary Law."

"Yes we do" agreed Andrew, "No time like the present, telephone her and ask her to come down to the office. Nothing is ever private at the Refuge, also there are constant interruptions."

Jessie telephoned Mary and asked her to come to Andrew's office immediately, as they needed to have a private discussion with her.

By the time Jessie and Andrew had finished their sherry and talked through the whole situation once again Mary had arrived at the offices of Cornwall & Prentice and was attempting to get past the receptionist.

"Mr Cornwall, Miss Law is at reception and she says she must see you immediately, I have told her you are presently in conference but she insists, she says it's most important."

"Please show Miss Law through to my office Miss Morgan, then no more calls or visitors until I tell you." Andrew instructed.

As soon as Miss Morgan closed the door Mary burst out. "Aunt Jessie, you've told Mr Cornwall, haven't you. I told you everything in confidence, secrets I have held for years and it's only taken you an hour to pass it on. I'm so disappointed in you, I really expected better."

Before Jessie could reply Andrew said. "Mary my dear please calm yourself, Jessie did exactly the right thing in telling me. Now I have a proposal I want to discuss with you.

Firstly, the whole idea of Liz and Mary galavanting off to Germany is not going to happen. I have advised Jessie that on no account should any of this business be discussed outside the three of us. Now Mary, I have a positive proposal to make, I speak fluent German and I have no health issues or for that matter any dependents. Jessie and I are willing to consider going to Berlin.

Now as a first step you must immediately contact your sister in Glasgow and organise a meeting between all the parties. Time is now of the essence, it's only just over a month until the games start. Mary I am sure you want a bit of privacy, Jessie and I will go and sit in the meeting room while you use my telephone, and Mary, you can arrange the meeting at any time, we will make ourselves available."

Completely flabbergasted by this swift turn of events Mary quickly put a call through to Sarah and related Andrew's proposal to her. Sarah promised to telephone Samuel immediately and call her back.

Within a few minutes Miss Morgan, put through a call, "a Mrs DeSilva for you Miss Law." Mary heard her sister say. "Can you all come to my place this evening, anytime after six o'clock I'll make some supper?" Mary agreed, "Yes Sarah that will be fine, see you this evening."

Mary sat for a few moments, her heart beating a mile a minute, feeling as though she had ignited a blue touch paper and now she had no control over what was going to happen next.

Andrew and Jessie joined Mary in the office where she told them the details of the meeting and they started to make plans. Jessie instructed Mary to telephone her sister Jessie at the drysalter's shop and tell her that she would be late home so as her mother wouldn't expect her for dinner. 'In fact" said Jessie 'tell her you might stay at the Refuge tonight, goodness knows what time we will get back to Coatbridge. We will tell Sadie that we all have to go out together and she is in charge this evening."

Sadie Kane had never recovered from the fear of her vicious husband and almost without anyone realising she had become a permanent resident who helped in untold ways, from cooking to listening to the stories of women when they first arrived at the Refuge. Drumkiln became her home, the women and children who sought refuge, her family.

Mary and Jessie returned to the Refuge, Andrew having arranged to collect them later in the afternoon. He wasn't quite sure why but Andrew sent Miss Morgan out to the florist to purchase a bouquet of flowers for Sarah, it just seemed the right thing to do.

Fortunately Andrew had a street map of Glasgow so they were able to find the DeSilva house in the southern suburbs quite easily, in fact they arrived early.

Jessie was impressed by the beautiful houses and bungalows with their manicured gardens in Whitecraigs and the other suburbs they travelled through, quite unlike the city tenements which was the only part of Glasgow she had previously seen.

As they got out of the car Miriam and David ran out of the house calling. 'May May, we are so pleased you are coming for supper, what a lovely surprise, we didn't think we would see you until Mum's birthday tea."

David welcomed the three travellers into the house and Sarah accepted the beautiful bouquet of flowers from Andrew. Sarah showed her guests through to the sitting room where Dan and Aunt Ruth were awaiting their arrival.

There was a flurry of introductions, then Aunt Ruth said to Jessie. 'When I heard you were coming Jessie I just had to be here to meet you, you are such an important part of Mary's life, just as she is an important part of ours, welcome."

Sarah came into the room carrying a large platter of blinis adorned with smoked salmon while Miriam carried a plate of warm potato latkes. As she started to pass them around the doorbell rang. 'That'll be Samuel and Leah arriving, Alan can you get the door please?" called Sarah. Alan did as he was bid and welcomed his brother in law and his pregnant wife.

Jessie accepted one of the latkes, tasted it, then said to Ruth. 'I'd recognise these anywhere, Agnes calls them her special tattie cakes, many's the one of these I've eaten at New Year or on special celebrations."

Ruth was thrilled, 'After all these years and she still makes latkas, my word, I learned from my Mama and she learned from my Bubbe, that's the Yiddish word for grandmother. You can trace the history of that recipe back to Russia. And Jessie, do you know the secret? Starchy potatoes, simple as that, summer salad potato, useless my dear, useless. Now you have the secret you will be able to make latkes as good as Agnes."

The DeSilva sitting room was full, the children passing around the canopies and Alan glasses of Austrian sparkling wine. Everyone was talking and enjoying each other's company, Mary found she had quiet tears streaming down her face, at long last two of the threads of her life had joined.

Eventually everyone adjourned to the dining room where Sarah had laid out a buffet. she apologised, 'sorry I didn't have time to cook a full meal I just raided the delis of Newton Mearns like a woman possessed and Aunt Ruth contributed the honey cake and apple 'n sultana kugel. Everyone filled there plates then sat down at the table. Before they started to eat Samuel rose, saying. "I would like to say a special thanks to our new friends Jessie and Andrew for offering us their assistance during these terrible times. The blessing:

Blessed are you O God, our Lord, King of the Universe, who has sanctified us with his commandments.

The company all started to eat and talk, there were so many things to discuss, but the German trip was firmly off the agenda until the children had left the room. After the meal Sarah said. 'Lets all adjourn to the lounge for coffee, Miriam, David, upstairs and get ready for bed, you can take a glass of milk with you. And, you can read until nine o'clock but then it's lights out, promise.

The twins tried weedling their mother to allow them to stay downstairs, however Alan used his occasional 'don't dare argue' voice saying. 'Upstairs you two and do exactly as your mother says, conversation ended." They called goodnight and disappeared.

Sitting in the lounge over coffee Leah explained the numerous daily persecutions Jews were suffering in Germany and how these were spilling into Austria. 'Antisemitism is rife in Europe now, a lot of Jews have already left for Palestine, America, Canada, in fact any safe country that will take them. My sister wants to get her children out of Austria while she still can. Our parents were also keen to leave but my father's recent illness means they have had to postpone their plans meantime.

Anna and Rolf have told the children they are going to see the Olympics in Berlin, or as Herr Hitler calls it 'Games of the XI Olympiad' and then as a huge treat they are then going to have a lit-tle holiday with Aunt Leah and Uncle Samuel in Scotland, my preg-nancy is the perfect excuse. However, they will be home in Vienna for the start of the new school term. Anna must try to keep every-thing light and jolly until they arrive in Britain and can apply for refugee status. To complicate things further she is hoping to bring jewellery and some gold coins with her.

Mr Cornwall, Andrew, we can't thank you and Jessie enough for offering to go into the Lion's Den and support Anna and her brood with their escape plan."

Andrew waved aside her thanks. 'Leah, we will do our best to help your sister. As you know I speak fluent German so language won't be a problem. My suggestion is that tomorrow I make the rail reservations for our entire journey, I'll need to know Anna's travel arrangements from Berlin to London so that we can accompany them. It's not essential that we share the same hotel in Berlin, this afternoon I booked a suite at The Adlon and they are going to arrange to purchase tickets to a number of the events for me. Do you have a note of the tickets Anna has purchased?"

'Yes we do" replied Samuel. I have taken the liberty of typing out her travel and accommodation plans, together with the Olympic tickets she has pre-booked. Andrew, it goes without saying we will reimburse you for all your expenses. I'll give you a cheque this evening to get things rolling and you can let me know whatever else we owe you. Actually Andrew, Jessie the truth is we can't possibly repay you for the debt we will owe you if you get our little family out of Europe.

The conversation flowed, not just about politics and the humanitarian crisis in Germany but Mary's friends found they got on extremely well with Mary's Jewish family. Ruth and Jessie in particular found they had much in common and by the end of the evening were making plans to meet again.

It was fortunate Mary had telephoned her sister Jessie and told her of her intention to stay at Drumkiln House as they did not get back to Coatbridge until well after midnight.

The following morning Mary joined the breakfast table at Drumkiln House. While Sadie cleared the table Jessie and Mary adjourned into Jessie's parlour to make plans.

"Honestly Mary, yesterday you were confiding in me about your secret Jewish family and today Andrew and I are planning a mission to Berlin to spirit a family away from the Nazis. You couldn't make it up in one of those Agatha Christie books you like to read so much.

While I'm away would you stay in my room Mary, I'll feel happier knowing the Refuge has you living on the premises. Sadie will no doubt give you a good hand and Jennie deals with all the book-keeping and money matters. The problem is what on earth am I going to tell my Mary and Agnes and young Emily for that matter, that their mother and grandmother, the woman who has never had the slightest interest in sport, is going off to the Olympic Games in Berlin with her solicitor."

Mary giggled. "Put like that Jessie you're in a right pickle of bother. Look you have always supported your girls in whatever they wanted to do so I suggest you just tell them you and Andrew are going away for a wee holiday and leave it at that. Plenty of time for explanations when you get home.

But to practical things, you are going to need some new clothes. Esme Black is a great dressmaker, you could pay her to make you a few new dresses, it would be no bother to you to make the matching hats. And Miss Aitken's has some lovely things in her window just now, you must buy yourself a nice comfy travelling suit and perhaps an elegant evening gown. You'll have to look the part if you are going to stay in a fancy hotel."

Just then Sadie knocked the door. "Jessie that's Mr Cornwall on the telephone for you."

Jessie left to take the call leaving Mary still smiling.

Andrew spoke with some urgency. "Jessie we'll have to get busy if we are to complete all the arrangements in time. Firstly we need to get you a passport and go on a shopping trip to Glasgow and a hundred other details need to be sorted out. Can you come down to the office at lunchtime today, bring some sandwiches, and we'll make plans."

Jessie promised to call into his office at one o'clock then put down the telephone. Reality had just set in.

Meantime in Glasgow Leah was telephoning her sister, ever mindful that anyone could be listening. "Anna darling, how are you? I've got such lovely news. Remember Uncle Andrew, Papa's friend, well him and his dear friend Mrs Johnstone are going to be in Berlin for the Olympics around the same time as you and the children. I've given him the details of the apartment you have rented, he'll contact you when they arrive. We are so looking forward to your little vacation with us in Scotland, a girl needs her sister when she is going to have a baby. Such a pity Rolf is having to hold the fort at home, perhaps he can holiday with us another time."

Anna quickly picked up the information her sister was trying to relay to her. She immediately enthused about how wonderful it would be to see dear Uncle Andrew again and how the children were excited about their holiday in Scotland.

The following weeks simply flew past. Jessie acquired a beautiful wardrobe of clothes and accessories, all the travel arrangements were made, a passport for Jessie obtained, traveller's cheques and German currency purchased, carefully phrased letters sent to Vienna to ensure that the train reservations were co-ordinated. All this and the normal day to day work of the Refuge and Andrew's practice still had to be attended to.

Mary and Liz were surprised and delighted in equal measure at the idea of Jessie going off on a jolly with Andrew Cornwall. Her other daughter Agnes and her family in Drumpellier while initially shocked were pleased that for once Jessie was doing something for herself. Jennie and John Cuthbert were thrilled with the idea of their friends going off on an exciting holiday but Jennie was quietly convinced there was a great deal more to this trip than simply visiting the Olympics.

Strangely, or perhaps not so strangely, the only person who thoroughly disapproved of the proposed trip was Agnes Law. Her three sons and her daughter Jessie were fed up listening to her disapproval. 'I don't know what that Jessie Johnstone is thinking about going off with a man to another country, and them not respectably married. When I think your Pa and I were her and Alex's lodgers, they had hardly a penny to bless themselves with and here she is fancy clothes and travelling first class to Germany of all places, Germany! It's an ill divided world so it is'.

Mary escaped the worst of her carping as she was staying most nights at the Refuge to help her Auntie Jessie. How her sister Jessie envied Mary's freedom.

CHAPTER 16
August 1936

Sitting on the train to London in her new suit and smart accessories Jessie was an exceedingly handsome woman and Andrew Cornwall's heart was fit to bursting at the idea of having her all to himself for nearly three weeks.

Jessie was as excited about experiencing a first class train journey as her daughter Mary had been when she had first accompanied Liz to London many years ago. This was going to be a long journey, firstly to London Euston, then a taxi to Victoria from where they would get the train to Dover and then the P&O boat over to Calais where they would board yet another train, travelling to Berlin via Paris and Cologne.

"Well Jessie, it has been a remarkable few weeks, has it not? I can scarcely believe we have managed to accomplish all the planning in such a short time and we are actually on our way. Mary Law is looking after your empire and James Prentice mine, so all is in safe hands. Well Jessie, in addition to carrying out our mission we might as well enjoy all that Berlin has to offer.

As we are arriving at The Adlon a few days before the opening ceremony I thought we could do a bit of sightseeing. Berlin is such an interesting city with lots of modern buildings, as well as historic, like the Brandenburg Gate, which we will be able to see from the hotel. We can visit the Tiergarten, perhaps go to the zoo there if you want. And, we mustn't miss Potsdam and the beautiful Grosser and

Kleiner Wannsee Lakes."

"Andrew Cornwall, I think you are starting to forget the purpose of this visit, it's not to spend our time enjoying sightseeing it's to help Anna and her little family escape from the Nazis." scolded Jessie.

"Indeed and I have not forgotten why we are going and Jessie this is something important that you must remember, the only time we can talk openly is when we are outside, and even then we must be extremely careful."

From London they boarded the boat train, sailed to Calais, train to Paris then across France to Berlin, via Cologne eventually arriving at Freidrickstrasse Railway Station, two days after leaving Glasgow. Andrew had booked two sleeper compartments and Jessie rather enjoyed the whole experience of sleeping in her own miniature bedroom, with the cabin steward bringing her early morning tea.

On arriving in Berlin they took a taxi to the luxurious Hotel, The Adlon, in Unter den Linden. They were shown to their suite, which consisted of two en suite bedrooms with a salon between them, the suite enjoyed a magnificent view of The Brandenburg Gate. Jessie's reaction to such luxury was similar to Mary's when Liz had first taken her to the Savoy in London. That of complete awe and a real awareness of the enormous divide between how the rich and the poor live their lives.

As the porter who carried their bags left, adequately tipped, Jessie exclaimed. "Andrew Cornwall this hotel must cost a fortune we can't possibly expect Samuel to..." Andrew drew her a look and raised his fingers to his lips. Jessie immediately completed the sentence. "...imagine what a lovely hotel we are staying in, him and Mary will be awestruck, and ever so jealous."

To avoid risking any further indiscretions Andrew said. 'Let's go downstairs and have some tea or in the German tradition 'kaffee und kuchen', the maid will unpack for us. Besides I want to check with Reception if they have our Games tickets available."

The coffee lounge was packed with locals, as well as tourists from all over the world. It was not lost on Andrew that there was a high proportion of men in uniform, or in civilian clothes but wearing Nazi Party badges on their lapels, circling around.

The couple were seated at a delightful window table and Andrew ordered, in German, coffee and cake for them both. Sitting in the famous hotel taking in the atmosphere Andrew had the advantage of understanding the language and some of the snippets of conversation that he heard he found distinctly worrying.

A waiter arrived with their coffee followed by a young waitress pushing a trolley laden with a delicious assortment of cakes. They made their choices and settled down to relax and enjoy.

However, Andrew did not feel completely relaxed the atmosphere was not that of his youth when he visited Germany before the War or for that matter a short holiday he had spent in Berlin during the time of the Weimar Republic. He couldn't quite define his misgivings but Andrew felt there was certainly an undertone of black menace behind all the show of bonhomie.

Thinking it was best to make casual mention of Anna, Andrew said. 'My friend's daughter Anna is due to arrive with her children the day after tomorrow. That will give us a day for touristing Jessie before we catch up with them.

Not long then until the Games start. It's all so exciting being in Berlin for the Summer Olympics and seeing Anna and her wee ones again, well that will be an added bonus."

They dined in their salon on the first evening, Andrew felt he had listened to enough bombast in the coffee lounge for any one day. Although Jessie did not understand the language she certainly caught the atmosphere. A tete a tete dinner in the privacy of their salon definitely seemed a better option than facing a sea of intimidating uniforms downstairs in the dining room.

The following morning Jessie and Andrew decided to go downstairs early for breakfast so as to have a full day for sightseeing. They had just finished eating boiled eggs and toast and were enjoying a cup of coffee when a uniformed man approached their table. Speaking in heavily accented English he said.

'I hope you are enjoying your stay at The Adlon Herr Cornwall and may I congratulate you on speaking such excellent German. I wonder are you simply attending the Summer Olympics or is there any other reason why you and your good lady are visiting our capital city? Herr Cornwall, I wonder can I be of any service to you during your stay in Berlin?"

Andrew was not at all happy about being approached by a member of the SS but he decided the only option was to play along. 'Thank you for your kind compliment, I studied your language at university, and I have visited your beautiful country on a number of occasions over the years but this time it's quite simply to enjoy the Olympics with my friend and companion Mrs Johnstone. The Reception staff at this fine hotel have kindly organised the event tickets for us, thank you very much for your concern but there is no further help we require."

Politely dismissed, the officer bowed saying. 'Enjoy your visit to our country Sir, Madam." and walked smartly back to Reception, where he checked their passports. The only slightly suspicious indicator he found was that Mrs Johnstone's passport had only been issued a few weeks previously.

Andrew and Jessie returned to their suite to freshen up before going out. Andrew would have preferred for them to see the sights under their own steam, using public transport. However when Andrew had enquired about the Olympics tickets the receptionist had 'suggested' they join an escorted tour leaving the hotel at ten o'clock. Although the receptionist had 'suggested' the tour, Andrew was aware of the unspoken subtext that it was not so much a suggestion as an instruction that they should travel around the city with an approved group.

Wanting to draw as little attention to themselves as possible Andrew had no option but to agree to joining the tour and thank the receptionist for all his help with a smile on his face.

The twelve people on the tour were mainly from the United States, a couple from London and Andrew and Jessie. As they drove around the city both Andrew and Jessie were horrified at the amount of Nazi iconography to be seen. The Nazi propaganda machine had been out in force, everywhere was covered in red, black and white, the swastika emblem taking pride of place. Historic German architecture and the true identity of the German nation appeared lost in a sea of evil symbolism.

They behaved like all good tourists; asked appropriate questions, expressed enjoyment at the food and drink supplied, offered congratulations on the high standard of the many Olympic stadiums and the facilities at the village in Elstal. Secretly they just wished the tour would quickly end.

After a day of non stop propaganda Jessie and Andrew were exhausted when they were finally dropped off at The Adlon. Andrew suggested they immediately return to their rooms and have a rest before dinner.

After her nap Jessie had a bath and dressed carefully in one of her new dresses, a midnight blue lace over silk with long sleeves, decorated with tiny beads, she wore her black patent shoes with the shaped heels and the ensemble was completed with pearl ear studs, a Christmas present from Mary and Liz, and a little evening purse made by Jessie with some of the left over material and beads.

Andrew was also looking the part, dressed in his black double breasted dinner suit. As Jessie came through the door into the Salon, Andrew felt his heart would stop she looked so beautiful. He took her hand and said. "Mrs Johnstone, it is my pleasure to escort you to dinner."

They had a delicious meal in The Adlon's famous dining room, accompanied by a bottle of fine German hock. Knowing they had to keep the conversation away from the real reason for being in Berlin Andrew asked Jessie questions he had often wanted to ask but in Coatbridge he would have felt they were intrusive. However, here in Berlin in this totally surreal situation anything seemed possible.

They shared stories about their youth. Jessie told Andrew about how she met Alex and talked of their happy marriage, despite their poverty, and their pride in their three children.

Andrew then shared a secret with Jessie the reason he had never married. Everyone thought he was a crusty old bachelor from choice, however that was far from being the case. He confessed to Jessie that he had been deeply in love with a beautiful ambulance driver during the War.

'Jessie, I really thought we would make it, we spent over two years in that hell seeing each other whenever we could, we even managed one leave together to her parents home in the Borders, where we got engaged. We made plans: where we would live; what kind of house we would buy; how many children we would have. But it was not to be, we were another casualty of the War.

At the outbreak of hostilities Margaret joined up and trained as a nursing auxiliary and then an ambulance driver. For a young girl from a sheltered background she saw some terrible sights. Truth be told Margaret had a much harder War than me. I am ashamed to say I spent most of my War in an office well behind the lines.

My Margaret was killed a few weeks before the end of the War, her ambulance was involved in a collision, she wasn't even driving, she was applying a tourniquet to a soldier in the back of the ambulance. Margaret was thrown against some equipment and hit her head, she died of a brain haemorrhage later that day. As you know there are many woman all over Britain who have never married because they lost their love in the War, I must be a bit of a rarity, a man who lost his bride.

So you see my Jessie, I really did understand your sorrow when you lost Alex. However, you two had the blessing of many years together and three wonderful children. I have just had to live with what might have been.

Jessie took her dear friend's hand and saw a tear in his eye. "Andrew, I can tell you have not spoken Margaret's name for a long time. It's being here in Germany that's evoking memories. Or, perhaps it's just we are getting older. Let's go through to the lounge and have our coffee, you can indulge in a wee dram, I might even join you, and we can talk some more."

By the time they returned to their rooms it was nearly midnight. They said their good nights and retired to their respective bedrooms. Jessie had just settled down in the comfy big bed when she was aware of a light tap on her door, Andrew came in and knelt at her side in the darkened room, he put a finger over her lips and whispered in her ear.

"Jessie it was a huge mistake coming to The Adlon, too many important people stay here, it's full of secret service, this is the only way we can talk openly in the hotel. I don't want us to lead the Gestapo to Anna's flat tomorrow. We'll telephone her and arrange to meet in a busy public place. Night night Jessie, and remember always measure your words. Jessie felt a gentle brush on her cheek and then heard the door softly close. Laying awake she spent a long time wondering if she had imagined the gentle kiss."

After an early breakfast, and before they could be offered another tour Andrew and Jessie quickly put on their outdoor things and set off into the city, both wondering what the day would bring. They took a tram ride to Tiergarten and then chatting animatedly they strolled towards the Zoological Gardens, as they walked Andrew was continually checking if anyone was following them. Stopping at a busy café for a coffee Andrew said. "All is well Jessie on this beautiful morning", a phrase to indicate nobody appeared to be following them. After ordering two coffees he stood up and headed for the gentleman's toilet. Again assured all was well he went into a little public telephone booth in the corner of the restaurant and rang Anna's apartment. When a woman's voice answered he said, "It's Uncle Andrew my dear. I wonder can we all meet outside the monkey house in the Zoological Gardens at Tiergarten around noon?" Anna acknowledged. "Perfect see you then."

Andrew and Jessie sat in the café people watching and enjoying their coffee but even in a café full of tourists the swastika was still evident. On each table there was a small white vase containing a red carnation, also adorning each vase was a little Nazi flag.

They left the café in good time for the rendezvous in Berlin Zoo, here in a popular place of leisure for Berliners they were surrounded on all sides by the ever present propaganda, swastikas on banners attached to every lamp-pole, flags and bunting, gift shops selling Olympic souvenirs, adorned with swastikas. At various strategic points in the Zoological Gardens there were choirs of Hitler Youth singing patriotic songs. No tourist in Berlin for the Olympics could fail to return to their home without knowing that Germany was held in thrall by the Nazi Party.

Standing outside the monkey house at the appointed time Jessie was first to notice the woman with two girls and a little boy heading towards them, the children were all carrying little swastika flags, which they had been given on entering the gardens. With their blond hair and blue eyes and their little hands clutching Nazi flags this family would certainly be presumed to be of good Nordic descent.

Andrew approached them with an innocent greeting. "My dear Anna, it's been so long since I last saw your dear father, how lovely for us to meet you and the children while we are all attending this wonderful German Olympiad."

The three adults walked together, out in the open allowing them to converse quietly, while the little ones ran on ahead.

Andrew introduced himself and Jessie to Anna. Initially he spoke in German but Anna quickly reverted to English as she did not wish to exclude Jessie from the conversation.

"I'm so grateful that you are going to travel with us all the way back to Scotland. You can have no idea how much safer I'll feel knowing you are both giving us your support.

My husband Rolf is keeping up the appearance that we are simply attending the games then going to Scotland on holiday, after a few weeks I will send letters home saying that I am having to extend our trip to support my sister during her pregnancy.

Rolf intends to start looking for a post at a hospital or clinic elsewhere in Austria. He'll then quietly put our property up for sale and try to get the money out of the country. Wherever he gets a job he will rent somewhere big enough for us all, in order to give the impression I am returning with the children. As soon as my father is well enough to leave Rolf will try and get out with my parents.

Well, that's the plan. Hopefully all will be well and I'll actually manage to reach the safety of Scotland with the children."

Whenever people walked anywhere near them as a precaution Andrew and Anna reverted to speaking German and kept the conversation to generalities.

They found a table at an outdoor café where they all sat around a table and Andrew ordered ice creams. Anna introduced the children to Andrew and Jessie, telling them that Andrew was a friend of their Opa (Austrian for Grandpa) and Jessie was his friend from Scotland where Auntie Leah and Uncle Samuel live."

Jessie quietly whispered to Anna. "Remember and keep the little flags, and get the children to carry them on the train when we travel back to Scotland."

In that one sentence Anna realised that in Jessie she had a friend, a practical woman who would be clever, creative and help her on the journey to Scotland, the journey to freedom.

The following day was the opening of the games. The day of the culmination of Hitler's hopes and dreams that this display at the Berlin Olympic Stadium would show Germany and the Nazi party to the world as a powerhouse and ensure the further glorification of its Führer.

In order to record his achievements for posterity Hitler had commissioned Leni Reifenstahl to film the Olympic Games, this would eventually be released as the film Olympia in 1938. But that was all in the distant future.

At the Opening Ceremony representatives of each nation, dressed in national costume paraded around the stadium, led by Greece with Germany being the final group to march. Each country acknowledged Hitler, some even giving the Nazi salute.

The President of the German Olympic Committee gave a speech and this was followed by Hitler opening the games from his box then the Olympic Hymn by Richard Strauss.

There was one moment of humour within all the pomp, ceremony and Nazi worship. 25,000 pigeons were released, as the pigeons were circling overhead a cannon rang out loudly. The birds were so frightened they pooed and pooed and pooed. It covered hats and hair. At least one little humorous flaw in the Germans 'oh so perfect' Olympics.

Over the following days Jessie and Andrew attended a number of events, sometimes with Anna and the children. Andrew thought it would be best for the meetings to seem casual.

One evening they all adjourned back to the ground floor flat Anna was renting to enjoy a casual supper. They set up a table in the garden and the children and Andrew enjoyed conveying a series of crockery, cutlery glassware and platters of food outside, while the ladies were on kitchen duty. Andrew was extremely popular with the children, he would keep them amused with magic tricks and he was always very generous with ice creams or sweets.

After their meal Anna offered to show Jessie around the garden.

Out of earshot of the children Anna whispered to Jessie, "I am trying to smuggle jewellery and some gold coins to Scotland. I managed to get them here without too much of a problem but I'm really worried about the customs inspection when we leave Germany."

The ever inventive Jessie said. "What kind of quantity are you talking about?" "I've got about a hundred Krugerrands, some 50 and 20 gram gold bars, a few 5 and 10 oz silver bars, perhaps 30 other gold coins. The jewellery varies, some gold chains and I inherited a diamond brooch and earrings, a friend removed the gems from the settings so that's a little pile of diamonds. Then I have a number of other pieces, as well as the rings I always wear. Jessie, can you think of any way I could take them through the border control?"

Jessie did have an idea but she wanted to see how well it worked before committing herself. 'Anna, I do have a thought, now this is what I want you to do. Go into the house and get some of the valuables, preferably some of the smaller pieces, secrete them inside some cake, you can wrap it up and give it to us as we leave, say in front of the children it's cake to have with coffee when we return to The Adlon. We'll talk about this again soon."

Anna did as Jessie requested and shortly afterwards Andrew and Jessie caught a tram back to Unter den Linden, with Jessie carrying a little cake box.

Before going into the Hotel Jessie suggested they go for a short walk and enjoy the evening air. Berlin was busy and bustling, full of people speaking many different languages. Jessie thought it would be better to talk surrounded by a babel of voices in the street, rather than the hotel.

Speaking quietly while smilingly appearing to be joining in with the outwardly joyous atmosphere Jessie updated Andrew. "Andrew, Anna has brought a lot of bits with her, some inside the cakes. Got to think of hidey holes. Show you my ideas in the room, I'm not a milliner for nothing."

In the safety of her bedroom Jessie drew the curtains and proceeded to dissect the cake. Andrew took the valuable contents into the bathroom and gave them a good wash while Jessie cleared the cake into a napkin, ready to be disposed of the following day.

Opening her manicure case where it was hidden in plain sight she removed some of her hat making paraphernalia, which she had brought with her for just such an eventuality.

First she examined the jewellery carefully, she found a beautiful round sapphire and diamond brooch. Jessie removed a blue velvet hat from her wardrobe and sewed the brooch on at a jaunty angle, it now looked as though it was simply a piece of costume jewellery adorning a hat. A pair of diamond and ruby clip earrings were sewn on either side of the square neckline on a simple deep maroon dress. Andrew gave her a 'thumbs up'.

Next came sixteen Krugerrands. This time Jessie unpicked the hem on an eight pleated skirt, she removed the little metal weights inserted to ensure the skirt hung nicely and replaced each one with a golden rand coin. Again Andrew gave her a 'thumbs up'. While this was going on they were chatting inconsequentially about their day, just in case anyone was listening.

Satisfied she had made a good start Jessie put the skirt weights beside the cake and secreted them in her handbag. The following morning a trip to the park and ten minutes throwing cake out to the ducks removed all traces of her handiwork.

Over the next week Jessie worked every evening on her secret sewing. The weights on Andrew's dinner suit jacket were replaced with coins; gold chains were sewn inside the brim of hats; Jessie took to openly wearing Anna's engagement and eternity rings. Gradually Jessie was able to sew into hiding places all the jewellery and coins. However, the bullion was presenting a bit more of a challenge.

One morning at breakfast Jessie had a sudden brainwave. A smile started to spread over her face until it turned into a little giggle. Andrew asked her. "Jessie what on earth is the matter?" She replied her lips still trembling. "Andrew I've just had an amazing idea for some interesting undergarments!" Poor Andrew blushed to his socks.

Later in the day when they were able to whisper quietly Jessie shared her idea, the one that had nearly made Andrew choke on his toast. "Corsets, that's the answer, I will carefully unpick seams and insert the little squares of gold, then sew them up again, no problem. What do you think?"

Andrew burst out laughing, taking her arm he said. "Jessie Johnstone you are one incredible woman," and they walked still laughing towards the Olympic event for the day.

The corset sewing took several evenings as Jessie was very particular to ensure that there would be no visible changes to the stitching. Jessie tried on the finished work then dressed in her taupe travelling suit topping the ensemble off with a taupe and brown hat, which was lined with gold chains. Jessie sashayed into the salon where Andrew was reading a paper saying. "Well Andrew Cornwall what do you think of my new outfit?" Andrew gently took her in his arms and whispered, "Jessie, you are truly my golden girl."

The 1936 Olympic Games were passing into history, every day the medal tables were eagerly watched and the Nazi Party were no doubt basking in the international success. Although the United States impressive medal total was no doubt annoying to the Führer, particularly the Jesse Owens Gold Medals and his 200 metres record.

A few days before the Olympiad ended the day of their journey back to Scotland arrived, Jessie did not get much sleep the previous night thinking about the journey and if they would get safely over the border into France. The train to Cologne was scheduled to leave at 8.40am. The station was busy with travellers and Andrew felt the group did not stand out particularly. Anna Bernhardt and her three blond children carrying their Nazi flags, together with a well dressed, middle aged Scottish couple was hardly the stuff of spy novels. Although one cause for concern was the number of uniformed men boarding the train.

They settled themselves into a first class compartment and Andrew produced some packets of cards and games to keep the children amused on the journey. As the train puffed its way out of Berlin Jessie sent up a silent prayer that the good Lord would protect them on their travels.

About an hour into the journey they all started to relax, apart from a ticket check by the Inspector all was as you would expect on a normal train journey. The children had played, snap, happy families and Andrew was now teaching them dominoes.

Jessie said to Anna. "My dear why don't we leave the four children playing for a wee while and enjoy a nice coffee in the restaurant car?" "Good idea Jessie, perhaps we could manage a little something to eat, I missed out on breakfast." "Me to," agreed Jessie.

They settled down in the First Class Restaurant Car, ordering coffee with brotchen and strawberry jam. They were actually enjoying their belated breakfast and starting to feel a little relaxed when two men wearing SS uniform halted at their table and spoke in German. Anna replied and then turned to Jessie saying in English. "These two gentlemen would like to join us as the Restaurant Car is rather full. I have told them it is our pleasure." The roll turned to sawdust on Jessie's lips.

Aware that it was imperative that all seemed normal a little voice went off in Jessie's head it was Mary Law in the Long Row saying, 'Auntie Jessie have you thought about going into the films, Greta Garbo, Mary Pickford, Clara Bow you can out act them all'. And outact them she did.

Using Anna as an interpreter Jessie bombarded the young men in their intimidating uniforms with questions. "What an absolute pleasure for you to join us, we are just returning home after a visit to your Olympics, an experience of a lifetime. But tell me gentlemen where are you travelling to?" One of the soldiers answered, "Cologne Frau" Jessie was now on full steam. "Cologne, is that where they make the perfume? Are you going on leave or are you joining your regiment? I am sure two handsome young lads like yourselves have pretty girlfriends, are they in Cologne or Berlin?"

By now the two SS officers were starting to regret their choice of seat. Jessie didn't let up. "Have you been fortunate enough to attend any of the Olympic events? We were at The Opening Ceremony, what a memorable display that was, we also had tickets for a number of events, we even managed to get several for the athletics."

Quickly finishing their coffee the soldiers rose to leave. "Have a good journey home Frau." They bowed and walked at speed out of the restaurant car. Anna and Jessie looked each other straight in the eye, Jessie giggled first and Anna followed. Jessie whispered, "Anna, I'm a wee Scottish woman from Gartsherrie and a right blether: blether is a Scottish word. It means I could get an Olympic Medal, probably a gold, for talking."

They finished their coffee and roll then headed back to their compartment. Jessie thought she would save the story of the encounter with the SS men and regale Andrew with it when they were safely sitting in Drumkiln House enjoying a cuppa, please God.

With an hour to go before they reached Cologne the children were getting bored with games, both Sophia and Hannah were reading and Simon had fallen asleep leaning against his mother. Jessie envied their innocence.

At Cologne Railway Station the little group had to gather all their possessions and change to another train for the next leg of their journey to Paris. They had only fifteen minutes to complete this feat at an incredibly busy mainline station, a hub for trains travelling all over Europe.

Andrew managed to engage the services of a porter which ensured he transported his charges to the connecting train with time to spare, they were now commencing the crucial part of the journey with the customs and passport checks due to take place before entering Belgium.

Once again they all settled into a first class carriage, supplying the children with games and books. Jessie thought it would be better to present a casual family, slightly messy scene when they presented their papers for inspection at the German - Belgian border.

After they left Cologne the journey to the border went in very quickly. The train stopped in a siding and was boarded by a number of German customs officers, escorted by soldiers. After what seemed like hours waiting for the inspection a uniformed customs official entered their carriage, two gun carrying soldiers standing on guard outside. Andrew and Jessie presented their passports, all correctly stamped. The man took a cursory look at the paperwork, he then asked in German if they had been attending the Olympiad. Andrew replied, also in German that they had and that it was a thoroughly enjoyable occasion. He then turned to Anna who gave him the Austrian passports for herself and the three children. This time his inspection was more thorough and he asked a number of questions about the purpose of her trip and when she intended to return to Austria. He then requested that she open several of the cases, his thorough inspection revealed nothing untoward. A smart bow and he bid them good day, leaving the compartment, followed down the corridor by the soldiers.

Relieved beyond words Jessie took this opportunity to open the picnic box prepared by The Adlon as she wanted everyone to keep busy and engaged until they left the siding and entered Belgium.

The children's eyes lit up at the delicious picnic, complete with paper plates, napkins and little individual bottles of lemonade with straws. It was about fifteen minutes since the customs officer had left and everyone was eating the delicious little crustless sandwiches and the children were all eyeing the cake and buttered fruit bread.

Just then the carriage door opened and a boy of about ten or eleven peaked through the door. He addressed Andrew saying. "Sir, you have been inspected, can I hide in your carriage please, I don't have any papers. My mother put me on the train in Cologne, I have a brother in Paris and I am trying to reach him. My name is Felix."

Just when the adults had at last started to relax this was definitely not what they needed. Speaking quietly Andrew told Jessie what the lad had said. Jessie responded. "Ask him if he is Jewish." Andrew asked the question in a whisper. Felix nodded and said "Ja".

Jessie quickly issued orders. "Get three cases down from the rack, now form a table. Andrew get the lad underneath". She threw a travel rug over the top of the cases and placed the picnic box on top, setting some of the food out on the makeshift table.

The scene was set not a moment too soon. The Customs Officer and the soldiers had started to make their way back along the corridor. Once again the Officer slid open the carriage door saying. "I hope you are all enjoying your picnic." Anna agreed they were and offered him a sandwich. He quickly declined, thanking her but stating in a very formal fashion that he was on duty.

Again relief as the train chugged out of the siding, unfortunately it only travelled a short distance before entering yet another siding on the Belgian side of the border where another series of checks would be made.

Anna told her three children not to indicate in any way that they were hiding Felix, and Felix was told to be as silent as a little mouse. This time the inspection was carried out by a customs officer without any soldiers present. The Belgian officer checked their passports and confirmed that they were all in transit with a final destination of Scotland. The inspection was over in a few minutes.

Felix stayed silent under the makeshift table until the train was once again steaming through the countryside. Andrew stood up and pulled down the carriage blind then Jessie gently prised Felix from his hiding place, she lifted him onto her knee and cuddled the boy, a brave little lad with tears now running down his cheeks.

The customs check in Belgium and then France were fortunately fairly cursory, however with Felix now hiding in their compartment they were still the stuff of nightmares. Once they were on their way after the inspection at the French customs post Andrew asked Felix if he had a passport, as expected the answer was "nein".

Andrew reverted to English and addressed Anna and Jessie. "If the wee soul had a passport it would be relatively easy, we could say he had lost his ticket on the train while going to visit his brother, he was desperately upset at being so careless and I would buy him a ticket from Cologne to Paris. But it's not as easy as that, an unaccompanied child, no ticket, no passport, they are not daft, checks will be made and Felix here will be back on the train to Germany before you can say Jack Robinson."

"When we arrive at Paris what if we created a diversion," suggested Jessie. "What kind of a diversion asked Anna?" "Well, I have a friend in Scotland who has a wee monster for a nephew, he's a clever wee blighter and his tricks were always carefully thought out to ensure he got his own way. When he lived with his parents he wanted to get expelled from school so that he would be sent to live with his Granny in Gartsherrie. One if his tricks was to paint his face with spots and claim he had an infectious disease.

What if we made our three look ill and caused a bit of a diversion going through the ticket barrier? Perhaps Felix could slip through and disappear into the crowd."

"I'll give him some money so that he can pay for a taxi." added Andrew. Reverting to German he asked Felix where he was going when he reached Paris. "I have memorised my oldest brother's address, he is a student in Paris. I also have an aunt and uncle in Holland, he might send me there because I don't suppose he has enough money to send me to school and feed me. I'm the youngest and my parents just wanted me out of Germany."

"Right" said Jessie, "this is my plan. We have two sleeping compartments booked. When we arrive in Paris early tomorrow morning we have a few hours to get breakfast at the station before we catch the boat train.

Felix can sleep with Andrew and Simon in the boys compartment, the girls will be as planned. Anna you stay with the children while Andrew and I go to dinner, I am afraid you will just have to share the remainder of the picnic.

Andrew and I will tell anyone who will listen that the children are most unwell, I suggest a tummy bug, we don't want to go down the infectious route in case the authorities organise an ambulance, the last thing we want to do is get stuck in Paris.

Felix must walk beside people just behind us as though he is with them. Then we'll create a diversion with the ticket collector that's his chance to walk through quietly, no running, and disappear into the crowd.

Now, Sophie, Hannah, Simon, we have a God given opportunity to help young Felix here and I'm asking all three of you to be very grown up and do exactly what you are told. Do you think you can pretend to be ill with bad tummy ache?" Hannah laughed, "Auntie Jessie, we are all good at pretending to be ill, especially Simon. He says, 'Oh Mama I'm not feeling well can I have a hot milk with sugar to help me sleep please'. Then he says, 'Oh Mama a story would make me feel so much better', and there is nothing wrong with him."

Everyone laughed, the adults were all relieved that the little girl had broken the tension.

Andrew said. "I think that's a plan Jessie, now let's head off to the Restaurant Car, sorry Anna my dear, no dinner for you tonight."

Jessie let her acting skills rip. First she tackled the waiter. "I'm most concerned, the three children we are travelling with have all got terrible tummy upsets, are you sure all the food on this train is safe?"

Andrew loudly translated everything Jessie said, between English, German, French and Jessie's mime most of the diners must have understood that three children were suffering from serious stomach problems.

The Restaurant Manager then came to their table and assured them that all the food served from the kitchen was of the very highest quality and served Andrew and Jessie with a complimentary glass of champagne.

Jessie saved her best act for a party of Americans who had also been to the games and were avidly listening to Jessie's tale. "Can you believe three little children, their poor mother is nursing them now, and we have the English Channel to cross tomorrow." The Americans were immediately full of sympathy. One lady said in a broad New York accent. "Is that a Scottish accent I detect? My ancestors came from Scotland you know. Do you know of any McLeans?" She pronounced it MClean but Jessie didn't care a jot she wanted this group on her side.

Jessie engaged them in a spirited conversation about all things Scottish. Working out what she was up to Andrew insisted in buying them all a malt whisky.

When it came to ordering their food Jessie said to the waiter. "I think I'll just have a cheese sandwich, no harm ever came to anyone from eating a nice cheese sandwich, besides it goes very well with a wee malt. The Americans joined in with this idea, ten rounds of cheese sandwiches were ordered, the chef was furious. However, bar takings were probably up, the amount of malt whisky that was put away by the company. Jessie and Andrew were very careful, they gave the impression they were drinking without very much passing their lips. They both knew clear heads were the order of the day.

Eventually the party broke up with the Americans swearing eternal friendship and inviting their new Scottish friends to the good old U.S. of A.

Jessie and Andrew were shattered by the time they got back to the compartment but they had achieved all they had set out to do.

While Jessie and Andrew were forming an alliance with the Americans Anna took the opportunity to coach the children on what would be expected of them the following morning. In order for Felix to try and get a little sleep Anna had put the two boys into bed 'top to tail' with instructions that Felix had to keep his head covered at all times so that if any railway staff looked in they would only see Simon.

As can be imagined none of the adults slept well, however the four children slept like tops.

The following morning everyone was up early and dressed with the children moaning, on cue. They had now left the countryside behind and the train was travelling through the outskirts of Paris.

As the train slowly pulled into the station Jessie felt the butterflies in her stomach, like an actress about to step onto the stage and give an award winning performance.

Again Andrew managed to engage a porter, which was a great help. As they walked towards the ticket collectors their new friends from across the ocean joined them. Meantime, as coached by Anna, Felix had found a space walking quietly beside the Americans.

The three Bernhardt children had been whimpering and holding their tummies as the adults helped them along the long platform. As they neared the exit they moved the performance up a few gears. There were two ticket collectors, one standing at either side of the gate, which was secured open.

Just as they reached the gate Simon let out a yell, 'Tummy Mama, I feel sick, agh. Oh Mama I feel so sick. Hannah joined in. 'Simon, it's not just you Sophia and I feel just as bad, I want to go home Mama, I want to go to my own bed". They were now blocking the exit and Andrew appeared to be searching his pockets for the tickets. Just as Jessie had hoped they would the Americans started to interfere. 'Gee whizz, these poor babies, they've been sick all the night through. Andrew, can we help at all? The queue to get out was now backing up and the Ticket Collectors distracted by the crying children. Felix used his opportunity to slip through the exit gate and mingle with the crowds in the station, clutching the money Andrew had given him to pay for a taxi to his brother's apartment. He was never seen or heard off again but Felix was never forgotten by Jessie, Andrew, Anna and the Bernhardt children.

After the stress of the Berlin to Paris train journey, Jessie felt she had aged ten years. How she longed to see Drumkiln House again. Andrew felt much the same, thinking 'I'm too old for all this malarkey, I just want to get home to Coatbridge now'.

Samuel had travelled down to Dover to present the correct paperwork at the entry point to Great Britain, enabling Anna and the children to come into the country on a temporary basis, provided all their expenses were paid by the host family and they did not accept paid employment, the procedure took hours but eventually they were able to continue on the final leg of their journey to Scotland.

The train journey from London to Glasgow felt never ending. When they reached Glasgow Central Leah was waiting at the station to welcome her sister and take her and the children down to Troon.

Andrew engaged a taxi to take him and Jessie home to Coatbridge. He dropped Jessie at Drumkiln House where Mary bombarded her with questions.

Jessie just muttered. "Mary, I'm pure done in, I'm away to bed just leave me to sleep. I'll tell you everything soon but for now I just need a good sleep." Andrew too headed for bed immediately he entered his bungalow in Drumpellier and slept the sleep of the dead for twelve hours.

The following day Andrew called into the Refuge and found Jessie telling Mary all about their adventures. After a little while Jessie said. "Mary can I have a wee word in private with Andrew please."

Alone they looked into each other's eyes. Andrew said, "Jessie, did all that really happen or was it a dream? Felix, you sewing gold coins into our clothes, The Adlon, the Americans, all those damned Nazis in their intimidating uniforms, Berlin covered in swastikas and those bloody pooping pigeons. Oh, Jessie we are too old for all this cloak and dagger stuff. John Buchan could write a novel about our adventures over the past weeks."

"I know Andrew, I'm just a wee body from Gartsherrie, I never knew there was a world out there of champagne, first class carriages on trains and luxury hotels, hotels where they do your washing for you! It's going to take a bit of getting used to living an 'auld claes and purridge' life again.

Andrew, we have one more job, I have got to remove all the coins and jewellery from our clothes and return the haul to Anna."

"I knew you would want to get that job out of the way, any of my clothes you used are in the car. I'll go and get them."

Andrew returned with a suitcase and the door was once again firmly closed on Jessie's parlour. It was quite straightforward removing the booty but Jessie knew she would have a lot of work over the next few days sewing the seams back into place. When it came to the corsets they both dissolved into fits of laughter, Jessie laughed until the tears came. Once started she couldn't stop them, Jessie cried, she cried for Felix and all the other folks who were trapped, living in fear in the German Reich.

Andrew gently took her in his arms and soothed her pain. Jessie closed her eyes and she thought of Alex.

The following Sunday Jessie and Andrew drove down to Troon where they were warmly welcomed not only by Anna and the children but by Samuel, Leah, Ruth and Dan. They had a joyous day where the stories never stopped.

At last Jessie managed to get Anna on her own in the kitchen when all the women were preparing a meal. She whispered, "Anna I need to see you on your own I have something for you." They went upstairs to Anna's bedroom where Jessie opened her handbag and handed her a box containing her treasure. Anna gasped, 'Jessie, how on earth did you manage to get everything out, I hoped you might manage to bring out some of my things and I was grateful beyond measure when you handed me my engagement ring and the ring Rolf gave me when Sophia was born. Jessie, where did you hide everything."

Jessie gave a wry smile. "Anna, Andrew and I thought it best that you didn't know where everything was secreted just in case you gave something away with a glance. I sat in The Adlon and sewed everything either on or in our clothes, weights in skirts were changed to coins, I just pinned a brooch on a hat, but the absolute best was the gold ingots, I sewed them into my corsets, you should have heard us laugh. Mind you, it wasn't such a laugh wearing them on that long journey home."

Anna called everyone into the sitting room. 'Look everyone" and she opened the box full of her 'independence'. "Leah, Samuel, thank you from the bottom of my heart for allowing us all to stay in your beautiful home. But look what Jessie has done, thanks to her ingenuity I'll be able to pay my own way."

Jessie quietly thought, 'once again I've been able to help a woman become independent, Ella wherever you are God Bless you.'

CHAPTER 17
October 1936

Anna and the children were now safely ensconced in Samuel and Leah's house in Troon and the secret heroes Jessie and Andrew, were back working as normal in Coatbridge. Nobody in the 'Brig', with the exception of Mary Law, had any idea of their bravery.

However, at night Jessie often lay in the comfort and safety of her bedroom in Drumkiln House and thought of the many families, families like the Bernhardts, who were trapped in Nazi Germany and Austria and of little Felix.

When Ella Millar died and left Jessie with the responsibility of using her life savings to 'help women', together with the other members of Ella's Friends the decision was taken to open a Refuge in Coatbridge for local women, and their children who needed a safe haven from abusive husbands or sometimes fathers and brothers. Subsequently this care had been extended to offering subsidised housing as a 'stepping stone' to full independence.

Since returning from Germany Jessie began to wonder what was being done for refugees arriving in Scotland from Europe, and would it be possible for Ella's Friends to help them, after all women in need were women in need regardless of nationality and religion. These women were escaping an abusive regime and not an abusive man, abuse is abuse, regardless of where it emanates.

However, normal life in Gartsherrie continued and the next event due to be celebrated was the marriage of Alexander and Judith which was scheduled to take place in the Hill Kirk on Saturday 10th October 1936, it was to be quite a lavish affair, paid for by the bride's family with an evening dance reception in the Co-operative Halls.

Robert was going to stand as best man to his younger brother, he was pleased and proud to carry out this duty, unlike when he had been best man to James and Margaret, on that occasion he had felt a complete hypocrite. They were now divorced and the 'sky had not fallen down' as predicted by his mother Agnes.

Willie was greatly looking forward to the wedding where he would be carrying out the duties of usher for his favourite Uncle and the gorgeous Judith. On the day he would also have the opportunity to meet up with his parents and siblings from Condorrat who would all be attending the family celebration.

Once Willie was absolutely sure that he was not going to be sent back to live permanently with his parents in Condorrat he had deigned to honour his family with occasional visits. Willie would never be entirely comfortable as part of the Fyfe clan. However, he had a fondness for his youngest sister Irene who he sensed, even at an early age, would also have aspirations beyond working on a farm.

Jessie, while being outwardly supportive to Alexander and Judith by wallpapering and painting the downstairs flat they had rented in Lefroy Street, as a wedding present, was inwardly feeling very depressed thinking about the chance of a married life she had lost with the death of her beloved fiancé, McInnes.

It had been a long wait for the devoted young couple to find their way to the alter but at last the wedding day dawned dry and bright. All the arrangements went as planned. The bride was stunningly beautiful, the groom handsome, and love was shining from both their faces.

A dance band, The Sandy Brown Four & Isabelle, had been engaged to play in the evening after the guests had enjoyed their meal. The dancing was in full swing when Jessie decided to slip outside, away from all the celebrations for a quiet few moments. As she got to the bottom of the stairs she found she was not the only one who wanted to escape from all the jollities.

James was standing by himself outside in the cool evening air.

He greeted his sister. "You escaping too our Jessie, I couldn't stand another minute of all that wedding falderal. What a pair we are, I got a wrong one, and you had a real good one in McInnes then tragically he died before you could wed. I truly hope their luck holds and our Alexander makes a go of it with his bride Judith."

"I really think they will" replied Jessie. 'Hopefully it will be third time lucky for a Law love match."

"The only good thing that came out of my marriage to Margaret was Lillian but the poor wee soul is thrown about from pillar to post, she doesn't have the security we did Jessie. We didn't have much money but we always knew who we were and the family we belonged to. Whatever happened in our world Maw would make sure we were clean and well fed and we did have quite a lot of fun together. Poor wee Lillian, what kind of family life does she have?

Jessie, I think I need to get away from here. I'm not sure exactly what I want to do but I do know if I don't get away soon I'll never get a life for myself.

Have you heard Ma's latest ploy? She wants me to give up my house and move back into number twelve, taking Alexander's place and sharing the bedroom with Robert and Willie. It's not going to happen, against all the odds even our Mary has managed to escape, I'm going to follow her example Jessie, honest to God I am.

You know I have now completed many of the First Aid, Nursing and Advanced courses available with St Andrews Ambulance Association and I can drive an ambulance. I'm a Section Leader at the moment and I'm now working towards Deputy Commandant. I'd really like to use the skills I've learned with them, I'm fed up being a joiner, I want to do something entirely different, and I honestly cannot stand the thought of finding myself living under Ma's roof again.

Jessie, there is so much happening in the world just now, even Maw realises. The other night she put down the paper and said. 'Whit a state the world's in: We're all going to Hell in a handcart'."

They laughed together. "Trust our Maw" said Jessie. "Never short of a couthy expression is Maw Law. I must tell you this one, Mary and I took Ma to see a Shirley Temple film. We had been going on at her for ages, everyone but everyone goes to see Shirley Temple films except her. Well, she dressed in her Sunday black with the matching hat Auntie Jessie made for her and off we want to see 'Wee Willie Winkie'. At the end of the film Mary and I said, "Well Maw did you enjoy yourself? What did you think of Shirley Temple?" She drew herself up to her full height, all five foot nothing, and said. "I think she is a right precocious wee lassie, that's what I think." Mary and I were in fits of laughter.

But back to your issues, I know what you mean James, Lilian is with Margaret and her new man at the moment, what have you really got here. You are a qualified joiner as well as having your St Andrews Ambulance qualifications. You must just keep looking and the right opportunity will come.

Look we had better go back upstairs and show face, you can give your wee sister a dance, come on big brother we've got to put a face on."

CHAPTER 18
January 1937

Christmas and Hogmany, with all the attendant celebrations were now well and truly over, sadly the New Year of 1937 did not promise well.

10th December 1936 the Abdication had been announced and the following day the King made his poignant or treacherous, depending on your viewpoint, broadcast on the BBC. The new King to be crowned at Westminster Abbey would now be George VI, together with his wife Elizabeth and their two daughters, they would be the new Royal Family of Great Britain and her Empire.

In addition to the Abdication crisis the newspapers and wireless were relentless in their diet of political crisis which were happening all over the world. Not only were these daily reports depressing but the possibility of another war seemed to hang over the world like a black cloud.

It was 4th January, after a hard days work Jessie's train arrived at Blairhill Station. It was bleak, dark, and a light snow had just started to fall, a truly bitterly cold miserable evening. Much to her surprise Willie was waiting to meet her.

"Aunt Jessie, I have a letter for you from Uncle James. He asked me most particularly to meet you tonight and give it to you before you go home." What he didn't tell her was James had given him a shilling for his trouble.

Jessie accepted the letter and before leaving Blairhill opened the envelope and read it under the dim yellow station light.

Dear Jessie

Remember we talked at our Alexander's wedding and I said I wanted to get away and do something different. Well, I've joined the International Brigade, by the time you read this I'll be on my way to Spain. I'm going as a medical orderly but I do think the fascists under Franco need to be sorted out, and boys from Lanarkshire and Glasgow are just the ones to give them a bloody nose.

I've given up the keys of my house and sent the contents to Margaret. She can keep everything or sell it, I honestly don't care. Not a lot of happy memories in that house.

Jessie, will you break the news to Maw and the family, I'll write when I can. Sorry to land this on you but I thought you were the only one who would truly understand.

James

Jessie read the letter twice then she handed it to Willie to read. He let out an exclamation - "Wow, my Granny will be as mad as a box of frogs."

Walking home Jessie and Willie talked about James's decision to join the International Brigade and the likely reaction of the family.

Jessie told Willie the story of the day in 1918 when the War ended. "I was just a slip of a lass at school, I was terrified by all the noise from the church bells and works sirens blaring out. As I reached our house in the Herriot Row I was so relieved to be home, there in the kitchen my Ma was crying her eyes out, I've never seen her as upset before or since, sobbing her heart out she was. When I asked her what was wrong she said. 'The War is over and my boys are all safe'. She was terrified that if the war continued long enough James would be called up. The idea that he has joined up to go and fight in a foreign civil war, honestly Willie I expect she will be upset beyond belief."

Knowing she could not delay telling the family of James's decision, as soon as she entered number twelve and without even taking time to remove her coat, Jessie called the whole family into the kitchen and read the letter aloud.

Everyone was horrified at the news. Mary immediately suggested that somebody should go down and tell Alexander and Judith before they heard it on the grapevine. Mary said, "As sure as eggs is eggs, it won't take long for the gossip mill of Gartsherrie to start turning."

Robert put on his coat and together with Willie they immediately set out for Alexander and Judith's flat in Lefroy Street, armed with James's letter. Leaving Jessie and Mary to deal with their mother.

Agnes sighed. "I have had a feeling he was up to something for weeks now. I've known in my heart he was planning and plotting but to be honest I thought he was going to move to Glasgow, he was always right sweet on that Mavis lass. Mary, you told me she is still single and is now a qualified midwife living in a flat in Cathedral Street. I was starting to jalouse he might be going to Glasgow after her. But going to Spain, not for one minute did I suspect he was going to behave this stupidly. A girl, yes, my James has always had an eye for a well turned ankle. Fighting, no, that's no my James, he would never pick a scrap, not even when he was a wee laddie."

Jessie interrupted her Mother. "Ma, he's not going to fight, he's going as a medical orderly, James will be well behind the lines. Quite honestly I don't think there is anything we can do, he's well over twenty one. We've just got to wait for his letters."

Surprisingly, Agnes agreed with Jessie and did not enact the drama scene her daughters had fully expected she would.

When Robert and Willie returned after breaking the news to Alexander and Judith the family sat around the table and ate bread and home made broth. Everyone was thinking of James, where he was on his journey and when would he next have a decent meal to eat.

Robert commented succinctly. "Look Maw, our James is no the first and he won't be the last to head for Spain singing The Internationale. Europe is full of fascists and the Government simply don't want to know, that's why the people are taking it into their own hands and there is so much support in Scotland for the Republicans in Spain.

I'm proud of our James, it might not have been a hundred percent conviction on his part, I know he wanted to put distance between him and his broken marriage but he's no stupid. James is in Spain to help people, so good on him, as soon as we get an address I think we should all write to him and tell him how damned proud we are."

A few days later Agnes received a letter from James, posted in London, apologising for any upset he had caused and promising to try to keep in touch. Agnes wasn't the only one who received a letter. Mavis in Glasgow received one too.

James asked her to wait for him, he also asked if she would marry him on his return from Spain.

When his Auntie Jessie heard the news about James Law heading out to Spain to serve in the International Brigade she felt an inordinate pride that the man she had known since he was a baby was in Spain using his medical skills to help the injured during the bloody civil war.

Later that evening when Andrew called in for their evening catch up she told him the news. "Andrew, it's not just us oldies who want to fight the fascists in Germany, there are fascists in Spain, and Italy too, that Mussolini started it all off. Agnes Law's lad, James, has joined the International Brigade as a medical orderly and he is now on his way to Spain.

The world really is in a terrible state, do you know Andrew I can't sleep at night for thinking about Jews escaping Europe. And, I wonder if Ella's Friends can do anything to help the refugees, now I'll be thinking about the Civil War in Spain as well. Andrew, Andrew. What is wrong? You look worried."

"Jessie, I had a telephone call from Samuel today. Anna's parents have left Austria, they have crossed the border into Switzerland. However, the bad news is Rolf has been arrested. That's as much as we know, a friend of the family found out and telephoned Samuel. Leah was so upset she has gone into an early labour, Samuel has taken her to The Rottenrow, and he has promised to let us know immediately there is some news."

"Does Anna know?" asked Jessie.

"Yes, I expect she does by now, Sarah was going to take the train down to Troon and tell her, obviously they didn't want to break the news over the telephone."

No listening to the wireless or playing cards that evening, Jessie and Andrew just sat and talked, not just about the political situation but also about the confidences they had shared in Germany and the fragility of life.

Later that evening one of the younger girls knocked on Jessie's door. "Telephone call for you Mrs Johnstone, I think it must be a long distance call it's a right crackly line."

When Jessie returned to the parlour her face was white. "Andrew, that was Anna, telephoning me from Troon. Sarah has left for home now, she spent the day with Anna after she broke the terrible news but now the poor girl feels completely alone and she hadn't told the children yet. The lass is absolutely distraught.

Andrew, I'm going to go down to Troon tomorrow, I can easily get a train, Mary and Ella's Friends are perfectly capable of holding the fort here for a few days."

"Indeed you are not going yourself by train. I'll run you down." said Andrew, in a voice that did not brook argument. "I'll go down to the office first thing in the morning, I need to make some arrangements before we leave. I'll collect you at around half past nine, Mary will have arrived by then and you can update her with all the news."

Just as he was leaving the telephone rang again and Jessie answered. This time it was Samuel telephoning from the hospital. "Good news, Leah has safely delivered a beautiful little boy, she had quite a bad time and is very tired but all is well. Can you please pass on the news to Mary in the morning, I'll be in touch soon. Good night Jessie, and thank you for everything."

Jessie passed on the good news to Andrew but they did not have a celebratory dram, they knew tomorrow was set to be a busy and emotional day.

The following morning Mary was both delighted and saddened by the news from Glasgow. Jessie was still updating Mary on what required to be done while she was away when Andrew arrived promptly at nine thirty. They set out for Troon promising to keep Mary informed of any further news.

Little did Jessie realise as she left Drumkiln House that winter morning it would be over four weeks before she returned.

During their time in Berlin and the subsequent nightmare rail journey back to Scotland Jessie and Andrew had become very close to Anna and the children and they were now both anxious to see them.

Andrew drove carefully down to the Ayrshire coast, as usual the stretch over the Fenwick Moor was dreich, rainy and gloomy. Andrew remarked, "I hate driving across the moor, the light is more like eleven o'clock at night than eleven in the morning. I'd hate to live in Eaglesham or any of the villages hereabouts." Jessie agreed, "It certainly feels like a setting for a Burns poem:

> *The wind blew as 'twad blawn it's last;*
> *The rattling showers rose on the blast;*
> *The speedy gleams the darkness swallow'd*
> *Loud, deep, and lang the thunder bellow'd"*

"I didn't know you were an expert on Burns," said Andrew. "Hardly an expert, but Agnes Law and I used to sing his songs when the bairns were wee. They loved them, particularly 'Charlie, He's My Darling'."

"Go on", said Andrew "sing me one of the Bard's songs, I'd love to hear you."

Jessie sat silent for a few minutes and then in her beautiful clear voice, unaccompanied, sang:

> *Ye banks and braes o' bonnie Doon*
> *How ye can bloom so fresh and fair*
> *How can ye chant ye little birds*
> *And I sae weary fu' o' care*
> *Ye'll break my heart ye warbling birds*
> *That wantons thro' the flowering thorn*
> *Ye mind me o' departed joys*
> *Departed never to return*

As the last notes died away they drove in silence for a few minutes, then Andrew said. "Jessie, that was truly beautiful. I never knew you had such a lovely singing voice."

Jessie laughed softly, "Ah ha Andrew Cornwall there are lots of things you don't know about me."

At last they emerged from the Fenwick Moor and eventually reached Troon, and South Beach where Samuel's house was located.

Anna answered the door and by the look of her she hadn't slept a wink since hearing of Rolf's incarceration.

Thankfully the children were all at school, Hannah and the youngest, Simon, at the local primary and Sophia at Marr College. Language was not really a problem as both Anna and Ralph were fluent English speakers, besides since her decision to escape from Austria Anna had been giving all the children extra language tuition.

What do you say to a woman who's husband has been imprisioned by the Secret Police? Jessie was used to providing council to women in many situations but this time she found herself bereft of words, she simply hugged Anna, a young woman who had become very dear to her during their time together in Germany.

Somehow they got through the day, Andrew collected Simon and Hannah from school, much to their delight, and Jessie took over the kitchen.

After supper, Andrew was enlisted as 'Homework Helper' while Anna and Jessie cleared the table and started the washing up. Jessie said gently. "My dear girl, I think you must tell the children what has happened to their father. It's impossible for you to keep pretending everything is normal. They are not stupid. They know you are upset and you can't keep up this pretence that nothing is wrong for a long period of time. And, much as I hate to say this, we have no idea how long Rolf will be held.

And on another matter, have you any idea how your mother and father are going to travel to Scotland from Switzerland?'"

"Not really" replied Anna. "They have friends in both Geneva and Bern, I don't even know where they are in Switzerland. If it's Geneva they could travel through France but if it's Bern I suppose they might try and fly out.

I honestly can't believe the way all our lives have changed, one minute we were a perfectly normal family, My Papa is retired and together with Mama they really enjoyed their grandchildren, and their other hobby was nagging Daniel, my brother, to settle down and get married. They were so happy when Leah married Samuel, not happy that she moved to Scotland, but delighted she had found love. Rolf and I were perfectly contented, we had a loving marriage, a good medical practice, we had a beautiful apartment over the surgery. Rolf's patients were children of Jew and gentile and nonbelievers for that matter. He simply did not care. He only wanted to help children who were sick and these, these wicked people have put him in jail, and it's all my fault. If I hadn't insisted in running away to Scotland with the children we would all be at home now. Oh Jessie, Jessie, what on earth have I done to my husband?"

Anna burst into tears yet again and Jessie tried to comfort her but how could she give comfort when the tentacles of the Gestapo were possibly involved.

The telephone rang in the hall, Andrew answered. It was Sarah. "I'm so glad you and Jessie are with Anna, I don't see how I can come down to Troon at the moment. Leah had a very bad time giving birth to her son and she is going to need a lot of care. We have decided to bring her and the baby to Whitecraigs for a few weeks, their flat in Garnethill is on the top floor, not at all practical. Is there any chance Jessie could spend a few days with Anna, I know it is a big ask considering all you have already done but we would be so very grateful."

Andrew replied, "Sarah, Jessie is with Anna just now and it's not the moment to interrupt them. I'll speak to Jessie later and phone you tomorrow. Is there any more news of Rolf and have you heard any more about Leah's parents in Switzerland?"

"I'm sorry to say no, absolutely nothing. It was a friend of Samuel's called Leon who telephoned with the news about Rolf but he was very brief, I suppose he is frightened as to what could happen to him."

Andrew and Jessie stayed the night with the little family. Before the children went to bed their mother told them that their father was trapped in Austria and it might be a very long time before he was able to contact them. Anna did not use the words 'prison or police' but all of the children were old enough to know that their father's plight was serious.

The following morning Andrew travelled home, promising to return at the weekend to collect Jessie who had decided to stay with Anna and the children in the meantime.

Back in Coatbridge Andrew decided to call into Drumkiln House to update Mary on the latest happenings in Troon and Glasgow. As they sat in the sitting room and shared a cup of tea together the conversation moved from the Bernhardt family to the bigger political picture in Europe, and how the whole continent seemed to be heading at breakneck speed toward yet another war.

Mary went into her handbag and took out a letter in a crumpled envelope, handing it to Andrew she said. 'Please read this letter, it came a few days ago from my brother in Spain.''

Andrew put on his reading spectacles and carefully read aloud the letter received from James serving in the International Brigade in Spain.

Dear family

It doesn't get any easier. We do our best to help the injured but sometimes it is a relief when they die and leave their agony behind.

There are shortages of just about everything, even simple things like soap, everyone smells. As you can imagine medical supplies are very scarce and if it wasn't for the goodwill of people from many countries who send medical aid all would be lost.

Ma, you would be horrified at the food here, even horse meat or rat is a luxury. I lie at night and remember all the wonderful food you cooked for us as bairns. Great steaming pots of soup or porridge to fill us up and then a boiled egg and bread. You really are a great cook Ma, and if I concentrate really hard I can smell your pancakes, fresh off the girdle, pancakes and tattie scones were our favourites.

The fighting here is fierce but the real evil is the Nazi and Italian bombers. I have always believed in God, attended church and the Salvation Army. But what is happening here makes me doubt the existence of any higher identity, least of all a God of goodness and love.

I can hardly write this, do you know, the bastards even drop little metal boxes with labels to make it look as if they contain sweets, naturally all the wee weans open them, they are so excited to get something nice, having so very little. But, they are not sweets, they are a kind of bomb. As soon as they are opened they explode taking off the children's hands, arms, faces. The lucky ones die instantly. What kind of human beings could think up such wickedness?

Despite everything I am glad I joined, some days I really feel I am helping in this war against the fascists. However, I would be a liar if I didn't say there aren't moments when I wish I was back in the 'Brig', walking down to the Gartsherrie Work to start a shift carrying my piece box.

I hope you are all well, please look after wee Lillian for me, tell her I think of my dear little girl and send her all my love.

James

"The war has begun Andrew," said Mary, as Andrew replaced the letter into its fragile envelope and handed it back to her.

"Mary, that letter just brings it all home. When Jessie and I were in Germany there was Nazi propaganda everywhere, it's as though the entire nation were being brainwashed to comply with whatever their Führer ordered. You cannot imagine the atmosphere; on the surface everyone is very pleasant and polite but you know it's all an act and if the finger was pointed they would have no compunction in imprisoning you, or worse. I suspect it's exactly the same in Italy and Spain. What am I talking about, even here in Britain we are not exempt, what about Mosley and his crew? Who would have believed that in London, our capital city, The Battle of Cable Street would have been fought last year. It's like being on a runaway train, you just know it's not going to stop.

Mary it's not only the Jews getting a hard time in Germany, the Nazi's are killing mentally retarded people; Universities have to toe the line; political dissidents are being sent to camps for what's called 're-education'; books and paintings are being destroyed. It's beyond me how a civilised and cultured nation like Germany has allowed itself to be pulled into this evil maelstrom.

Jews can still get out, they can emigrate to Palestine under a special agreement but they leave Germany with absolutely nothing, all their assets are confiscated. Thanks to Jessie's ingenuity Anna managed to bring quite a bit of jewellery and gold coins with her but most Jews are lucky to get out with their lives.

Mary, are you managing to cope with all the demands of the Refuge? Jessie feels guilty at leaving you yet again so soon after our trip to Germany."

Mary laughed, "Would you listen to yourself Andrew, only Jessie

Johnstone could feel guilty about going to Germany to help a family, people she didn't even know, to a safe refuge here in Scotland. Ella's wish was that we helped women who were abused, women in danger of losing their lives. What on earth was Jessie doing in Germany but helping a woman and her family who were in fear of their lives. Does she think it doesn't count if the help isn't given in Coatbridge?

Of course I'll manage, Jennie and Mary are wonderful. Liz also comes in and gives counselling sessions. My sister Jessie helps when she can find time after her work and Sadie Kane is a real stalwart. So you see Ella's Friends all pull together, when you see Jessie tell her not to worry all is well at Drumkiln House."

When Andrew returned to his home in Drumpellier he couldn't get the conversation with Mary out of his mind, he decided not to leave passing on Mary's reassurance to Jessie until the weekend, he picked up the telephone and called Troon.

Jessie answered the 'phone and as always was delighted to hear Andrew's voice. He passed on Mary's words and assured her that she was doing Ella's work whether she was in Troon or Coatbridge. Promising to see her on Saturday and stay overnight, coming home Sunday. Andrew bid his dear Jessie goodnight.

Jessie slept better after hearing Andrew's words. Which was just as well for the following day was the start of an avalanche of terrible happenings.

After the children had breakfasted and left for school Jessie brewed a fresh pot of tea and made some toast for her and Anna. "Come on Anna, you really need to eat a little." coaxed Jessie. "You have three children to care for, you have to keep your strength up. Besides I think today we should start preparing for your parents arriving. We need to move beds around and prepare a double bedroom for your mother and father. Besides it's better if you keep busy."

They were interrupted by the ringing of the doorbell. Postie handed Jessie an architects tube, carefully sealed and postmarked Wien, Austria. Jessie gave the package to Anna who immediately opened it. She removed the top cap and saw that the tube contained rolled up canvas, carefully taking it out of its container and unrolling the canvas Anna was delighted to find two portraits, her maternal grandparents, which had always hung in the hall in the family home in Dobling.

Anna shed a tear as she said, "My dearest Jessie, this is a sign, Mama and Papa are on their way. If only we had some news on Rolf. He isn't Jewish why on earth would they imprison him?"

Jessie ignored the rhetorical question, saying. "Anna eat up your tea and toast. Now don't you think it would be a really nice idea to have the paintings framed and hung before your parents arrive." This was all part of Jessie's plan to keep Anna busy.

Anna had just left to pay a visit to an art shop in Prestwick that she thought could arrange framing when the telephone rang. When Jessie answered, it was Samuel calling from his office in Glasgow. "Jessie, I'm glad it's you I'm speaking to. I've just received a telegram from Austria, it just says: 'Rolf is now in Germany' no signature, sent from the main Post Office in Vienna. I know there is nothing we can do but it's so terribly worrying.

Also, Leah has gone into a depression, Sarah says many women suffer from this type of depression after childbirth but I think it's due to the worry about what's been happening in Austria. Thank God Sarah and Aunt Ruth are looking after Leah and the baby, they are also organising a brit milah for the baby on Thursday. The Mohel will perform the ceremony at Alan and Sarah's at four o'clock. Can you organise Anna and the children to come up to Glasgow. I'll phone Mary and invite her and Andrew." Slightly puzzled Jessie asked, "Samuel what on earth is a brit milah?" Samuel laughed, "Oh Jessie, Jessie, it's when a Jewish boy baby has his foreskin removed. We always make it into an occasion, we actually normally just say 'bris'. However, with Leah quite unwell and everything that's happening in Austria it's just going to be the immediate family and our very special friends. Sarah will lay on a nice tea afterwards.

Can I rely on you to break the news to Anna about the telegram? Jessie, you and Andrew have done so much for us and here I am asking you to do even more. I can only say thank you from the bottom of my heart."

Jessie in her practical way said. "Samuel it's our pleasure to be of help, these are strange times we are living in, all the more reason for people to support each other. Now remember let me know instantly if there is any more news from Europe." Promising to keep in touch Samuel said his goodbyes.

Later that morning Anna returned home with some shopping, pleased that two of her precious family portraits were now safely in Scotland and being reframed.

Jessie had been working away in the kitchen, dreading Anna's return and the news she would have to give her, when she heard her key in the door, Anna called out. "Jessie, I've got the rolls and I bought sausages for supper tonight. I'm so pleased to be able to get the portraits framed, the ones that I have chosen look very similar to those we had at home in Wien...

Jessie, what's the matter you look as though you have seen a ghost."

Jessie took a deep breath and relayed the news from Samuel's telephone call. As she had expected Anna was distraught, and the worst thing was there was absolutely nothing they could do, there wasn't even proof that the telegram was genuine.

Reverting to her strategy of keeping Anna busy Jessie insisted that they should go up to Glasgow with the children for the bris and that they should telephone Sarah to see if they could bring any baking or savouries with them. Planning ahead Jessie was thinking, 'I'll get her to come with me into town to purchase any ingredients needed and then keep her busy cooking. And, we must arrange for the girls and Simon to leave school early on Thursday.'

Jessie was just about to lift the telephone to ring Sarah when it rang incoming. Jessie answered. Once again it was Samuel. "Jessie I feel as though the troubles at our door will never end, yet another telegram, this time from Paris, Papa Goldbaum has taken ill again. We have decided that Alan will travel immediately to Paris, being a doctor he will be more useful than me. I'm so sorry that once again I have to give you more difficult news to break to poor Anna."

Jessie could hear the worry in his voice and simply said. "Samuel we have to deal with what the good Lord sends us. Don't worry, I'll tell Anna this latest news. Perhaps you could telephone back later this evening and speak to her, give her a bit of family reassurance." Samuel promised he would 'phone later and Jessie took a deep breath before imparting this latest news bulletin from Glasgow to Anna.

To Jessie's surprise her immediate reaction was "Oh Jessie at last something I can actually do, I'm going with Alan to Paris. I'll telephone right now and make the arrangements. Besides I'll actually be in Europe, and nearer Rolf."

As good as her word Anna telephoned and found out Alan's travel details, Sarah immediately promised to book tickets for her. She then flew upstairs and packed a small case, while Jessie went out to collect Hannah and Simon from the local primary school.

By five o'clock in the afternoon Anna was on the train headed for Glasgow where she would meet Alan and Jessie had found herself in sole charge of three youngsters who had suffered more than their share of trauma over the past months.

Later that evening when the children were settled for the night Jessie 'phoned her confidante Andrew and told him all about the happenings of the day. He promised to update Mary and explain that her visit to Troon was now open ended and Drumkiln House would have to tick over without the redoubtable Jessie Johnstone for the foreseeable future.

Promising to see her on Thursday at the bris Andrew said his goodnights. Mary was not the only one who would be missing the presence of Jessie in Coatbridge.

The following evening Anna telephoned Jessie from Paris, the news was not great, not only had her father had a relapse and was now in hospital but her mother was in a state of near collapse due to the stress that she had been under over the past weeks and months.

Jessie reassured Anna that she would 'hold the fort' in Troon and that she had arranged for the children to leave school early on Thursday to allow them to go up to Glasgow for baby Isaac's bris.

Over the next few days more architects tubes arrived at the house in Troon and at Samuel's office in the Gorbals, his flat at Garnethill and Alan and Sarah's house in Whitecraigs. Mama Goldbaum had decided to spread the risk by sending pictures to four different destinations from a variety of post offices in Austria. A strategy which worked, in total 33 pictures arrived in Scotland, including a number by French impressionists, such as works by Berthe Morisot, Mary Cassatt, Eva Gonzales and Marie Bracquemond. There were also some beautiful works by Alexander Mann and Thomas Dow from the Glasgow School and an exquisite work by Margaret Macdonald Mackintosh.

The Goldbaum family left behind their home in Austria but they managed to bring part of their family heritage to Scotland.

On Thursday afternoon, Jessie and the children arrived at Whitecraigs to find Ruth in the kitchen and Sarah upstairs trying to persuade Leah to get up and dressed before the Mohel was due to arrive.

The three children were delighted to meet up with David and Miriam. In the way that children do they all disappeared off somewhere to do goodness knows what, leaving Ruth and Jessie free to talk.

"Is this not a right pickle of bother" exclaimed Jessie. "Honestly Ruth I have got to the point I absolutely dread the 'phone ringing."

"I know exactly how you feel Jessie, I'm most worried about Rolf, I've never even met the man but the idea he is in the hands of the Gestapo is terrifying. I think they know that Anna and the wee ones are not going to return to Austria and they suspect she has taken valuables out of the country. They are none too pleased at the thought of missing out on the family's assets, that is what is behind his arrest, I'm sure of it - money."

In fact Aunt Ruth was absolutely right. An innocent remark by the Goldbaum's friend Leon at a party saying that he thought 'Anna had no intention of returning to Austria', was overheard. Investigations followed, it was then discovered the family property was up for sale and her parents had also disappeared.

Sarah rounded up the children and everyone gathered in the sitting room to await the arrival of the Mohel, as well as Mary, Jessie and Andrew the only other guests were Samuel and Sarah's three cousins. Their father, Uncle David, was in poor health and unable to attend. Baby Isaac was laying cuddled up in his Moses basket, happily unaware of what was shortly about to take place.

The Mohel, Dr. Mendel, arrived. He welcomed the guests then commenced the ceremony which was going to take place in the dining room. Leah handed her baby to Dan who had been given the honour to carry little Isaac. He then handed the baby to Alan who would hold him while Dr Mendel performed the ceremony.

Everyone gathered in the room, however Mary and Jessie stood as far back as they could not really wishing to witness the proceedings. Dr Mendel welcomed the little one and then carried out the surgery.

The child was blessed and Samuel also said a blessing over his son. The Mohel prayed and blessed the wine, a few drops were given to Isaac and his parents both drank of the wine. The ceremony now over, the crying infant was gently soothed and the celebration commenced.

The women brought the food from the kitchen and the buffet was served after Dr Mendel recited the blessing.

CHAPTER 19
Spring 1938

Rolf was arrested in Austria by the Vienna Secret Police, the Geheime Staatspolizei, after a time he was sent to Germany where he was questioned about the disappearance of his wife and children from Berlin. The Gestapo did not care in the least about another four Jews having left the country, what they cared about was that they had not gone through the process of being 'legally robbed' before receiving the required paperwork to leave the Reich.

Rolf wasn't tortured in the sense that he was beaten or electrocuted. However, he was mentally tortured, locked in a cold cell in solitary confinement for weeks on end, fed on a diet of bread and water while suffering the constant fear of not knowing what was going to happen to him next. There was also the humiliation of becoming dirty and unshaven with tangled hair and long nails and the indignity of having to use an old metal bucket as his toilet. Together with the mind blowing boredom of having nothing to do and nothing to read, that was the torture the Gestapo inflicted on Rolf Bernhardt.

Several times he was interrogated but he never deviated from his story that the only reason his wife had not returned to Austria was because her sister was having a baby. He was questioned in detail about his finances and 'requested' to supply details of all his assets and any assets belonging to his wife that she had left behind in Austria.

The fact that his Jewish parents-in-law had left the country leaving behind very little had not helped Rolf's case. The house in Dobling was inspected and it was found that there were no pictures hanging on the walls and the only items of value in the house were large pieces of furniture. Confirming they too had avoided the exit taxes.

One day without any warning a soldier took Rolf to a light clean office, not the green painted room where he had previously been interrogated. A uniformed officer sat behind an imposing desk, there was also a second desk at which sat a low ranking soldier behind a typewriter the desk strewn with piles of files and forms.

The officer spoke in a perfectly pleasant voice, as though they were conducting a normal business transaction. Saying, "Herr Bernhardt tell me, do you wish to leave the Reich and join your wife and children in Scotland?"

Rolf decided less was probably best so he just said. "Yes."

The officer continued. "In that case we simply have to process some paperwork, are you agreeable?" Again Rolf said "Yes."

The soldier handed the officer a file and the exit administration process lasted for approximately two hours. Signatures, stamps, affidavits, title deeds, documents witnessed, lists of personal possessions perused and confirmed. The soldier typed up various forms which he checked and handed to the officer for signature.

The officer eventually made a neat pile of the paperwork, signing and stamping the documents, he then smiled and said in his calm reassuring voice. "The transaction is now complete. Herr Bernhardt I am pleased to inform you that all the administration required by the Reich has now been dealt with. We will now arrange for you to have a shower and return your outdoor clothes. This evening you will be conveyed to the railway station, where you will be issued with a travel pass to leave Germany, a train ticket and five Reichsmarks, as you have now paid your Exit Tax in full."

In return for his freedom Rolf had been required to sign away all his property in Wien, the entire contents of his house and surgery, his bank account containing around ten thousand Austrian Schillings, a joint bank account with his wife, bank accounts in the names of his three children over which he was guardian. Every possession he owned was confiscated in exchange for his life.

The officer put out his hand, still mesmerised Rolf shook it, as he walked from the office he heard a voice say. "A pleasure doing business with you Herr Bernhardt."

The rail ticket which Rolf received with his 'Travel Exit Pass' was only valid as far as Strasbourg where he had to disembark the train. At ten o'clock at night he found himself standing in the Gare de Strasbourg with nothing but five Reitchsmarks in his pocket between him and complete destitution.

Rolf sat on a station bench looking at a row of telephone booths. Weary beyond words all he could think was 'I don't know Leah's telephone number in Troon, I don't know the telephone number. I can't contact Anna and the children. Tears slid down his cheek and he didn't know whether they were tears of relief or despair.

He had no idea how long he sat on the bench but eventually he stood up and exited the railway station into an unknown city.

Rolf just walked without purpose through the town, he was cold, hungry and he felt vulnerable in a way that just a few weeks earlier he would never have dreamt possible. He found himself making a promise: if I ever get out of this situation, if I ever reunite with my darling Anna and our children, if I ever practise my profession again, if I ever feel safe. I will do whatever I can to help people who have lost their way in life, in whatever country I find myself.

Eventually he found a bench where he sat down and slept soundly for the first time since having been taken into captivity. Waking in the early hours of the morning he started to walk again, eventually coming to the medieval centre of Strasbourg, the Grande Ile. Few people were about, the predominant noise being the birds welcoming the day. His senses were suddenly awakened by the smell of baking bread, his feet followed the yeasty fragrance.

Rolf stood outside a small bakery, taking all his courage he walked inside and saw metal trays full of baguettes and rolls still warm from the ovens. An elderly boulanger had just put another tray of baguettes in the ancient oven when he turned around and saw Rolf. The man immediately realised that he had no need to fear, this was a man in trouble not one out to make trouble.

The boulanger lifted a baguette and handed it to Rolf, no words were exchanged. Rolf bit into the crispy crust, at the same time his nose absorbed the aroma in a sensory overload. The taste would never be replicated if Rolf lived to be a hundred, he slowly savoured the deliciousness of the loaf for a few minutes before thanking the old man in his halting French.

The man replied. "I will get my daughter, she runs our family boulangerie." Rolf sat on the floor and ate the remainder of the bread, slowly savouring every mouthful.

A middle aged woman returned with the baker, she spoke a little German and told him her name was Ines. Rolf managed to convey to her that he was an Austrian doctor and had just left Germany with nothing.

He tried to explain that his wife was in Scotland and he wanted to contact her. At the mention of Scotland the woman's face lit up. Ines smiled and then hurried out of the bakehouse. Meantime the baker had prepared a large cup of coffee au lait and handed it to Rolf. Sipping the ambrosial milky liquid Rolf thanked whatever God had brought him to this place.

Ines returned with a red haired man who immediately started to speak to Rolf in a broad Scottish accent. "Hello son, whit's been happening to you? Ines here thinks it's the bloody Nazi Hun that's involved."

Although he spoke excellent English Rolf struggled with the man's broad accent, however he tried to explain clearly what had happened to him and that his Jewish wife and children were living in Troon.

At the mention of the Scottish seaside town the man became animated. "Troon, yer lass is in Troon? I worked as a lad in the pits at Auchinleck, so I did. I'm an Ayrshire man maself, och by the way my name's Jimmy. Ines, Pierre, we've got to get this poor lad sorted oot." He laughed, and then reverted into French to speak to his friends.

The baker, his daughter and Jimmy from Auchinleck had a conflab which resulted in Jimmy shepherding Rolf out of the bakehouse and taking him to his home where his wife was getting breakfast ready for their three children.

Jimmy introduced his newfound friend to his wife. "Julie, this lad has jist got away frae they damned Nazi's, we need tae help him get in touch with his wife, I canna believe it she is liv'n in Troon, back in Ayrshire, my auld stomp'n ground."

Julie answered him in English with a similar accent to Jimmy. Nae worries, first aff, give the man some of your claes 'n I'll wash his and I expect he widnae say no to a bit of meat and a hot bath.

Rolf was taken upstairs where he removed his clothes and luxuriated in a hot bath and a shave. He dressed and came downstairs wearing an outfit of Jimmy's two sizes too big for him but by now he was just so relieved to have met with friendly faces that he was grateful to wear whatever he was given.

Downstairs the children had all left for school and Jimmy was heating something in a pot on a range type cooker. "You look a bit mair like the thing noo son." said Jimmy, "sit yersel doon an I'll dish you some hotchpot stew, it's got a fancy French name but I ca' it hotchpot because it's a right mix of things." He dished the stew into an earthenware bowl and gave it to Rolf, with a spoon, another hunk of good bread and a glass of local red wine.

As he ate, savouring every single mouthful, Rolf asked Jimmy how a Scottish man had ended up living in Strasbourg.

Jimmy sat down beside Rolf at the kitchen table and lifted his coffee cup. "Well it wis like this son. I served in the forces dur'n the War, afterwards we were due to go back tae Blighty to get demobbed. I jist didnae fancy goin' back doon the pits, I wis a young, single lad so I joined the war graves folk and worked with them all over France. Then I met my Julie, she wis originally frae Strasbourg so we moved back here an' stayed with her Ma, when the auld yin passed away Julie inherited the hoose. I'm a sort of odd job man here, we won't get rich but it keeps us in baguettes." he laughed.

"Noo son, first things first, we need to get in touch with your lass in Troon. Whit is the 'phone number?" Rolf looked blank. "I've no idea, Anna and the children are staying at a house belonging to her sister and brother-in-law, his name is Samuel Fischer." "Right" said the ever practical Jimmy, "all we need to do is 'phone the international directory folks and ask them whit the number is, they will connect you to Troon nae bother."

Suddenly it all seemed so easy but after the events of the past weeks Rolf had not been thinking logically.

Jimmy took charge. "Finish up your food first then we'll go

round and see Ines at the boulangerie, they have a 'phone."

Jessie had just received a long letter from Anna in Paris. Alan had now returned home to Glasgow, the immediate crisis over. Anna was staying with her parents while they convalesced and they were all planning to return to Scotland in about a weeks time.

'Thank goodness' thought Jessie, 'Mary will be thinking I have deserted Drumkiln House altogether. I'll telephone her this evening and let her know I'll be home a week on Sunday, and I'll give Andrew a 'phone, he'll come down and collect me'.

Later that morning the telephone rang and Jessie immediately thought 'what now'. When she answered an international call was connected and a male voice she did not recognise said.

"Hello, can I speak to Anna Bernhardt please?" "Sorry" replied Jessie "Anna is not here." The voice took on a disappointed note. "It's very important. When will Anna be home?" Jessie was very reluctant to hand out too much information to a stranger, so she asked. "Who is speaking please?"

In a breaking voice the man said. "I'm Rolf her husband, I'm in France and I need help to travel to Scotland." Excited Jessie shouted. "Rolf, Anna is in France with her parents, where are you?" She took a note of Jimmy's address in Strasbourg and the telephone number at the boulangerie.

"Rolf, your speaking to Jessie Johnstone, I'll telephone Samuel and we'll get a plan together we'll get back to you soon. Don't you worry son the worst is over now."

Over the next few hours the telephone lines between Troon, Glasgow Paris and Strasbourg were red hot. Anna managed to get a train to Strasbourg that very afternoon. On arriving at the Gare de Strasbourg Anna immediately took a taxi to the Grande Ile and Jimmy's home. Julie heard the taxi draw up and opened her door to see a beautiful woman alighting from the vehicle. The McGregor family warmly welcomed Anna into their home where the couple were joyously reunited.

Back in Troon Jessie phoned Mary with the latest news and explained she was hopeful that she would return home to Coatbridge on the following Sunday. Thankfully Ella's Friends had gathered round and all was well at the Refuge, any problems that had occurred Mary Law and her troops had dealt with quietly. Mary reckoned Jessie had quite enough worries without adding to her load.

Jessie then 'phoned Andrew with the good news and he promised to collect her the following Sunday, they had a long catch up and it wasn't until Jessie put down the receiver and went into the kitchen to make a cup of cocoa that she realised just how much she had come to rely on Andrew Cornwall over the years.

The following day before setting out for the journey to Paris to meet up with Mama and Papa Goldbaum Anna and Rolf thanked their benefactors Pierre, Ines, Jimmy and Julie profusely for all the kindness they had shown to a stranger in their midst.

The previous evening when Jimmy had been reminiscing about his life in Ayrshire, he had told his guests.

"Och my auld maw is deed noo and my brithers and sisters are in awe airts and pairts. I've no notion to go back to Scotland, besides look at the bobby dazzler of a wife I've got in Julie, naw the only thing I miss is sliced sausage and sweeties. We had a rare wee sweetie shop in the village, tablet, macaroon bars, boilings, and luxury of luxury Cadbury's chocolate, you name it - they were all stonking."

Anna immediately worked out her plan.

As soon as Anna and Rolf arrived back in Paris at the apartment her parents had rented Rolf telephoned Troon and spoke to his children. After the call Hannah and Simon were ecstatic, running around shouting "Papa's coming home, Papa's coming home, eh oh my daddy oh, Papa's coming home."

However, Sophia spoke thoughtfully to Jessie. "Do you really think my Mama and Papa will come to Troon with our grandparents and it's all over?" Jessie reassured her that her parents would definitely be home in a few days time with her grandparents. However Jessie used the opportunity to talk about the situation.

"My dear Sophie, I would be lying if I said it was 'all over', in a way it's just beginning pet. Your life here in Scotland with your parents is going to be very different from the life you all lived in Vienna, you will all have to get used to a complete change in circumstances. In a way I am sure the past weeks have seemed very temporary, like a holiday. However, the next few months won't be easy and I hope you will give your Mama lots of support and help. I'll have to go back to Coatbridge and carry on with my work at Drumkiln House, where we try and help women and children who are having a difficult time."

Tears in her eyes Sophie said, "Auntie Jessie, please don't leave us, we are having a difficult time too. You and Uncle Andrew helped get us out of Berlin safely, Mama told me all about the coins and jewellery and how you hid them. I had to promise not to tell Hannah and Simon, Mama said she'll tell them when they are older and can fully understand the danger we were all in."

Jessie reassured the young girl, who was having to grow up much too quickly, that her and Andrew would always keep in touch with them but she had other work that she had to carry out.

Over the next few days while her brother and sister were getting more and more excited Sophie clung to Jessie and helped her get everything ready for the arrival of her family.

Anna took Rolf shopping to buy some basic toiletries and clothes in Paris before the next stage of their journey. As they boarded the train Anna was greatly relieved that she was not hiding any valuables on this journey. On the other hand her Mama had several little stashes of diamonds, carefully wrapped and inserted into wads of cotton wool which she placed into various bottles of pills prescribed for her husband. Papa would probably have had another heart attack if he had known what his wife was up to!

Samuel had arranged to meet the family at Dover in order to comply with British rules and sign the paperwork that he would stand as guarantor for Mr and Mrs Goldbaum and Rolf and confirm that they would not require financial assistance from the British taxpayer.

When they eventually arrived back in Troon there was an ecstatic welcome from the children. This was the first time their entire family had been together in many months and often during that time it seemed as though this reunion would never happen.

Andrew had also come down to Troon to welcome the travellers home and to take his beloved Jessie back with him to Coatbridge, where she belonged.

The following morning, the start of their new life in Scotland,

Anna walked hand and hand with her husband along the beach at Troon, they scarcely spoke, words were not necessary. Eventually they would tell each other of their experiences but for now it was enough just to be together.

'Let's go into the town before we go back home." said Anna, 'I've got something I really need to do. They stopped at the sweetie shop and Anna had them fill a box with pounds of sweets, all in quarter pound pokes, soor plumes, black and white stripped balls, pear drops, treacle toffee, puff candy, she just worked her way along the jars then she added cakes of Cadbury Chocolate and Duncan's Walnut Whips but the one sweet she sent a whole pound of was home made Scottish tablet. The sales assistant packed the sweeties beautifully and Anna and Rolf each enclosed a postcard from Troon, written with gratitude to Jimmy, their Good Samaritan.

About two weeks later the parcel eventually arrived in Strasbourg to the great delight of Jimmy and the entire McGregor family, naturally their friends Ines and Pierre received a goodly share of the sweet bounty.

Three generations sharing a house in a small Scottish town was far from easy. Rolf was not allowed to work which he found incredibly frustrating. The grandparents felt that their grandchildren were turning into little ragamuffins, their present life was so far removed from the cultural life to be found in Vienna. Poor Anna, she felt that she spent her entire life trying to keep the peace and make everyone happy.

After a short time living in Troon all the children spoke English with a Scottish accent. Simon became an Ayr United supporter, he enjoyed playing football and what he lacked in skill he made up for in enthusiasm. Simon loved sport, playing golf, table tennis and later badminton. The girls enjoyed Scottish Country Dancing and they also helped at a local stables in return for riding lessons. Together with their school friends they attended the local Church of Scotland, Sophia and Hannah joined the Brownies and Girl Guides and Simon the Cubs and Boys Brigade.

As the months turned into years the children gradually lost any desire to return to Austria, their home was in Scotland. The opposite was true of their grandparents, the desire to return to Austria and their old life at times became overwhelming.

Andrew and Jessie never forgot their charges and regularly visited them in Troon.

CHAPTER 20
November 1938

The final wake up call was Kristallnacht. In their heart of hearts everyone in Great Britain now knew a second war with Germany was inevitable. The horrors of Kristallnacht not only affected people of the Jewish faith in Britain, every right minded person was horrified at what was happening in Germany. Not only were the Nazis burning the synagogues, they were burning books, works of art, their culture, everything that makes for a civilised nation. Now their persecution against the remaining Jewish population was unrelenting.

The seemingly inevitable Anschluss had happened in March '38 Austria was now part of the Reich. In September '38 with the Munich Agreement Hitler had 'walked' into the Sudetenland, another land grab to which France and Great Britain had capitulated.

In Coatbridge as had happened in the war there was now a demand for coal, iron, and steel, the heavy industries were once again entering a time of full employment as rearmament was the order of the day. The town would again see prosperity but for all the wrong reasons.

Sarah's time had come to answer her call, stop making chicken soup with knadles and help her people.

Following Kristallnacht the Kindertransports of unaccompanied children started to arrive on the south coast of England. These children had to be guaranteed accommodation, whether or not it was with Jewish families was irrelevant, a place of safety was all that was required.

Sarah together with Leah and a friend Catrina from her Royal Infirmary days started to organise accommodation in and around

Glasgow for refugee children. As a linguist Leah's main role was organising classes to teach English while Sarah vetted prospective families and tried to match children to homes where they would fit in and feel wanted and loved.

Ella's Friends accepted the Kindertransports as a new challenge and worked with Sarah and her team to find temporary homes for some of the children in Coatbridge and the surrounding area.

CHAPTER 21
January 1939

It was almost time for the welcoming in of another New Year but this year was different, the folks of the 'Brig' could almost taste the coming war, they could certainly smell it with the increased output from all the heavy industry in and around the town.

On Hogmanay as Jessie and Sadie Kane were baking and making the traditional dumpling a wee germ of a thought came into Jessie's head. 'Sugar, I bet that's the first thing that'll get rationed if we go to war. I'd better organise a stockpile, I'll also get in some treacle, syrup, dried fruits, mixed spice. Mmm and it wouldn't be a bad idea to have a few sacks of dried peas, butter beans, lentils, barley and rice squirrelled away either'.

"Penny for your thoughts, Jessie?" said Sadie as she topped the clootie dumpling up with boiling water. "I was just thinking it might not be a bad idea to lay in some sugar, spice and other things that might be in short supply if there is another war. We don't want to be caught out, especially since it's not just us that have to be fed, it's the women and children who arrive here depending on us for help and sustenance.

You know Sadie, when my Agnes got married during the last war we had a right bother trying to organise a wedding cake. Liz managed to get a hold of some dried fruit, probably best we didn't ask from where. Another of our pals in the movement contributed eggs and Agnes Law performed a miracle of the bakers art. Icing sugar defeated us but Agnes put a wee posy of flowers on top of the cake and it looked, and tasted, lovely. Just a memory Sadie, just a memory."

Mary Law was taking a short holiday from the Refuge spending time at home with her family in Gartsherrie, where they were preparing for the expected full house as all the Law family gathered to see in 1939.

A few weeks previously a letter had arrived at number twelve from James. The envelope was crumpled and covered in postal stamps, the letter was dated September 1938

Dear family
We are being pulled out on the orders of the Prime Minister, all the International Brigades are having to leave Spain. I'll be heading home soon. Hope to be in Gartsherrie to see in the New Year.
James

James arrived back in London but instead of heading straight for Coatbridge James made his way to Glasgow.

Mavis walked back to her flat on a cold December morning after a long night shift at the Rottenrow, tired and longing for tea and toast then bed. She climbed the stairs to her third floor flat and there, sitting on the doormat, with his back against the door, was James Law, sound asleep.

Mavis woke him from his slumbers, they said not a word just wrapped themselves in each other's arms. They went into the single end flat, didn't bother with the tea and toast they just fell into the recess bed. Too tired for anything but sleep they cuddled together and slept all day until the winter sun was starting to set.

Mavis rose first and James was wakened by her making tea and scrambled eggs on toast. "My lass that smells delicious, like something my Maw would make." Mavis laughed, "Right lazy bones, get up and tell me all about your adventures."

"No I will not," said James. "Spain was just too dreadful, and it will get worse before it gets better, what a mess. Mavis I want to talk about us, we've wasted enough years, let's get married now. Never mind the minister, we can go up to Martha Street and do the paperwork. I want to take you back to Gartsherrie as my bride." They exchanged a long lingering kiss, ate their food, washed and dressed and were at the Glasgow Registry Office before it closed for the day. The wedding was arranged for Tuesday 27th December 1938.

Mavis and James spent the weeks until their wedding together in Glasgow, telling nobody that he was back home. These weeks gave them time to normalise their relationship and allow James time to distance himself from the horror that was Spain.

Their wedding was simple, Mavis wore her Sunday best coat and hat with the addition of a corsage. The witnesses were her friend Jean, a nurse from the hospital, and her boyfriend Alf. After the ceremony they all had lunch in The Rogano, an Art Deco restaurant in Exchange Place that everyone was talking about.

On Hogmanay the newlyweds travelled by train to Gartsherrie where they were congratulated and welcomed back into the fold. Both James and Mavis had been apprehensive as to how they would be received but their worry was unfounded, everyone was overjoyed to see them and none more so than James's mother Agnes.

The cooking finished and Drumkiln House cleaned from top to bottom Jessie went back to her bedroom to change her clothes for the welcoming in of the New Year.

On her bedside table there was a photograph of her beloved Alex taken in a studio in Glasgow on the day they were married. Jessie picked it up and gave herself over to a little reminisce.

After spending many years in her kitchen drawer in the Long Row the photograph of Alex was now encased in a beautiful silver frame, a present from Rolf and Anna. Oh how Jessie wished she could turn the clock back and sit with Alex in front of the range in their homely wee house in the Long Row. She would tell him about her Jewish friends; tell him how Mary and Liz had helped so many women through their 'Stepping Stone' properties and Jennie, dear dear Jennie, so happy with John and Louise, and how she too was allowing her beautiful Blairhill home to be used in the 'Stepping Stone' project.

In her head she could hear him say, 'My lass, Ella's Friends has done well, so they have. Auld Ella would be right proud of you all, so she would.'

Giving herself a shake so as not to bring on the tears Jessie put on one of her good dresses and a dab of 4711 Cologne, looking at the bottle a smile lit up her face. 'Cologne indeed, Andrew and I will never forget Cologne'.

Andrew joined the ladies in the Refuge to welcome in the New Year, as well as the residents of Drumkiln House, they were joined by many of the ladies who lived in the Stepping Stone housing.

The bells rang out and the sirens blared at midnight, the company sang Auld Lang Syne, glasses of sherry were passed around and the toast proposed. This year there was no celebration dancing or merriment, everyone ate a little something and quietly chatted before the evening ended and Andrew and the ladies from the Stepping Stones housing returned home.

January 1st, Sadie Kane was in the kitchen cooking the New Year's Day dinner with help from some of the current residents. This year everyone seemed to be having their celebration dinner at home, apart from Mary and Liz who were following their tradition and were spending the holiday at Gleneagles Hotel in Perthshire.

Jessie spent a quiet day reading and indulging in her latest hobby needlepoint embroidery. Just as it was getting dark, before four o'clock, on the winter afternoon Andrew arrived armed with a large box of chocolates.

After thanking him Jessie poured a good measure of his favourite malt and they settled themselves down in front of the fire in her parlour.

'It's been a funny sort of a day, very quiet, nobody has popped in. Quite a few telephone calls though. My Agnes and Mary both telephoned, Jennie and John 'phoned, all is well with them. Anna 'phoned from Troon, I promised we would go down and see them soon. Ruth 'phoned, her and Dan are at Sarah and Alan's so I also had a wee chat with Sarah. However, I've not heard a word from the Laws.

Coorie doon in yer ain nest, that seems to be the way of things this year."

Andrew sat quietly for a few moments then said. "Jessie, I'm here with you, Drumkiln House seems to have become my nest.

I've been doing a lot of thinking lately and I've decided to retire. My partner, James Prentice has a son who works for a large practice in London, and he would dearly like to return with his family to

Scotland. I intend to offer him the opportunity to buy my share of the practice."

Jessie took his hand. "Good decision Andrew, that will give you time to do what you want to do."

Andrew looked into her eyes and said. "Jessie, what I want to do is marry you so that we can spend our retirement years together. I understand Alex's place in your life but I am sure he would like to think that you were loved and cherished during your autumn years.

Mary Law is well able to take over the helm of the Refuge and you can still be an Ella's Friend on a voluntary basis, same as Jennie."

"Phew" exclaimed Jessie, "Andrew Cornwall, that's a awful lot to take in. In many ways we have been a couple for years, especially since Berlin. I hadn't considered retiring but perhaps the time is now right to hand over the reins to the younger generation. Perhaps Jessie Law might like to work full time for the Refuge with Mary, I know that she could do with a greater challenge than working in a shop she doesn't own.

I hadn't considered marriage either, but thinking about it in lots of ways we are like an auld married couple, sitting here on New Year's Day in front of the fire, enjoying a dram together before our dinner.

Andrew, it would be an honour to become your wife, I will also cherish you and look after you for the rest of our days. But tell the truth Andrew Cornwall, are you sure it's no just for my cook'n you want to marry me?"

Andrew laughed. "You silly lass, even if you couldn't boil an egg I'd still want you at my side."

Just then there was a knock on the parlour door, it was Sadie Kane. "Jessie, that's Mary and Jessie just arrived, they are through in the sitting room. Do you want me to bring a tea tray through?"

"That would be lovely Sadie." said Jessie, sure that she was blushing like a schoolgirl.

As Jessie and Andrew walked hand and hand into the sitting room Andrew whispered. "Jessie, can we tell them? Please." Jessie replied. "Yes, let's tell them."

The following months were a time of great change. All who knew them were delighted at the news that Andrew and Jessie were about to wed. However, there was a great many practical details to be put in place before the wedding could take place.

There was an 'extraordinary' meeting of Ella's Friends. Jessie talked of their early days, the purchasing of Drumkiln House, setting it up as a Refuge, the women they had helped and the force they had become in the community.

"My dear friends, I could never in a month of Sundays have honoured Ella's legacy without us all working together. Mary, your work of healing and training for independence has not only helped the women to move on to a better life but the sale of products has helped towards making us self financing. As has my Mary getting grants and donations from various sources. And, after ten years we still have well over £5,000 in the coffers, at least so Jennie tells me. Then there is the Stepping Stone housing thanks to Liz, my Mary and Jennie, what greater gift than a safe place to stay that is affordable.

As you all know Andrew and I are going to wed this year, and I am going to retire from my post in Drumkiln. However, you are not going to get rid of me that easily, I will still be an Ella's Friend and help in whatever way I can."

At that point the cheering broke out and laughing Jessie called out.

"Will you all shoosh, this is the last time I'll lead an Ella's Friends meeting. Mary I'm handing you the baton and Jessie, my wee namesake, welcome as a full time member. I'm handing over to the young ones and none better. Mary will you finish the meeting please?"

Mary stood up and simply said. "Auntie Jessie, nobody, but nobody could have done more to help women and children than you, and not just women and children from Coatbridge. We are all so proud how you have taken Ella's legacy and turned money into a helping hand. God bless you."

Liz, thinking tears were not far away said, "Right ladies, there is some champagne lurking in that new Kelvinator Refrigerator in the kitchen. Mary, go and open a bottle. Mary had also brought a large platter of little triangle smoked salmon sandwiches from Airdrie. The celebration commenced.

Over the next weeks and months Andrew and Jessie dismantled their working lives and started to plan their retirement

CHAPTER 22
April 1939

Andrew and Jessie were married on 9th April 1939 in the Maxwell Manse with Jennie and John as their Witnesses. The bride, although now turned sixty looked radiant dressed in a midnight blue suit with a matching hat of her own creation and wearing a corsage of pink roses.

Afterwards they held a small celebration at Drumkiln House for all their friends and family. A place that had not only been a refuge for abused women but a refuge for Jessie when she too needed sanctuary.

Sadly they could not invite all their friends, because of the secrecy of the relationship between the Laws and the Fischers, Jessie and Andrew were unable to invite their Jewish friends to attend their wedding and celebrate with them. This made them fully realise just how difficult it must be for Mary to constantly keep her life firmly in two totally separate boxes.

They started their wedded life by spending a month touring Scotland together then, at long last, Andrew took Jessie to share his home, a place that Jessie made warm, welcoming and full of love.

CHAPTER 23
Friday 1st September 1939

Judith was sitting in Dr O'Flannery's surgery with her fingers crossed and thinking a little prayer mantra, 'please let it be Yes, please let it be Yes, please let it be Yes'.

The surgery door opened and Dr Murphy's new young assistant called out 'Mrs Law, won't you come through please". Judith went into the surgery and sat down. Her heart was in her mouth and she could scarcely process the words he was saying, "Mrs Law I'm delighted to tell you that your test has come back positive you will be having a new addition to the Law family next year."

Judith left the surgery on a cloud of joy, desperate to put her arms around her husband Alexander and tell him the news, the news that their lives were about to change forever.

Neither Doctor O'Flannery or Judith were aware that a few hours earlier the German tanks had invaded Poland, the Blitzkrieg, the 'lightening war' had begun.

Sunday 3rd September 1939 - 11.15am

The entire Law family, with the exception of Mary and Jessie who were at Drumkiln House, were gathered around the wireless at twelve Long Row listening to the announcement from the Prime Minister, Mr Neville Chamberlain.

"This morning the British Ambassador in Berlin handed the German Government a final note staying that, unless we heard from them by 11 o'clock that they were prepared at once to withdraw their troops from Poland, a state of war would exist between us.

*I have to tell you now that no such undertaking has been received, and that
consequently this country is at war with Germany.
You can imagine what a bitter blow it is to me that all my long struggle to
win peace has failed. Yet I cannot believe there is anything more or anything
different that I could have done and that would have been more successful..."*

The same broadcast was being listened to at the DeSilva home in
Whitecraigs, Glasgow by Alan, Sarah, Uncle Dan, Aunt Ruth, David
and Miriam.

It was also heard in Troon, by Samuel and Leah holding their
toddler Isaac; together with Rolf, Anna, and their children Sophia,
Hannah and Simon, listening with them was the older generation
Papa and Mama Goldbaum.

The sitting room at Drumkiln House Refuge was full, as everyone gathered around the wireless: the women and children under the
care and protection of Ella's Friends together with their mentors
Mary and Jessie Law; Andrew and his new bride Jessie; the Cuthbert
family John, Jennie and young Louise had all congregated there to
support each other at this solemn time.

The broadcast ended with the words.

*"Now May God bless you all. May He defend the right. It is the evil
things that we shall be fighting against - brute force, bad faith, injustice,
oppression and persecution - and against them I am certain that the right
will prevail."*

As the final words of the broadcast were still ringing out Mary
and Liz arrived from Airdrie, they were joined shortly afterwards by
Tom, Agnes and Emily who had listened to the broadcast at their
home in Drumpellier.

At this time there was an overwhelming desire to join with family and friends for mutual comfort and support.

Another War in Europe was about to commence. All those who
remembered the last war and had experienced its horrors felt a deep
fear, together with a certain knowledge that all their lives were now
about to change forever.

EPILOGUE

ROBERT took his girlfriend Molly's hand, immediately after Mr Chamberlain's announcement that the country was at war. He shepherded her outside and there and then he proposed. They were married within the month. Eventually they had one daughter who was her parents pride and joy. The couple never left Coatbridge, Robert and Molly never aspired to move from 'The Works' or 'The Rows'.

ROLF was interned in the Isle of Man as an enemy alien, he was eventually released in 1941. On his release he converted to the Jewish faith, after spending time studying with a Rabbi during his internment. The Bernhardt family settled in Scotland, eventually purchasing a home near Alan and Sarah. Rolf practised at the Royal Hospital for Sick Children but he never forgot his promise in Strasbourg and both him and Anna worked as volunteers helping the homeless.

ALAN, SARAH, DAVID and MIRIAM, they spent their entire married life in the house in Whitecraigs, a home which was always full of love. Both children followed their father into the medical profession David as a surgeon and Miriam as a gynaecologist. Sarah and Mary never lost their sisterly love. And, May May was a much loved Auntie.

JAMES and **MAVIS**, they settled in Coatbridge and had a son and daughter. His relationship with Lillian was always very difficult, she never fully recovered from all the moves and absences. James followed a career with St Andrew Ambulance Association. After their children were well settled at school Mavis returned to her profession as a midwife.

PIERRE, INES, JIMMY and JULIE, joined the French Resistance and saved many lives during the war, their inspiration being Rolf. After the war Rolf and Anna made contact with them again, every year at Christmastime they sent a large box of sweeties from Glasgow to Strasbourg.

SAMUEL, LEAH and ISAAC, after the war they bought a property in Glasgow's West End. In the late 1950's Samuel sold Salmond's Clothing, their son Isaac having no interest in commerce, Isaac was an academic and became a Professor of Mathematics. Leah recommended her profession as a linguist. In a complete career change, after selling Salmond's, Samuel wrote a number of best selling crime novels.

While they rejoiced at the founding of the State of Israel in 1948 they never considered emigrating. And Mary, she always remained a much loved part of their lives.

ALEXANDER and JUDITH had three children, a son and two daughters. All of whom inherited Judith's flame coloured hair. Alexander enjoyed an interesting and worthwhile career, Judith too carved a career for herself when the children were all at school. They too settled down in Coatbridge, although they had a number of opportunities to move to pastures new.

UNCLE DAN and AUNT RUTH bought a flat in Newton Mearns where they lived happily until Uncle Dan passed away. Ruth spent her last years living with Alan and Sarah. Ruth and Jessie became great friends often enjoying lunches in Glasgow with Sarah and Mary.

AGNES, TOM and EMILY. Emily served in the WRENS during the War, afterwards she studied architecture at the Andersonian Institute and the Macintosh School of Art. Agnes and Tom happily lived out their lives in their bungalow in Drumpellier.

ANDREW and JESSIE had a long and happy retirement together. During the war years they opened their home and hearts to evacuees. After the War Samuel and Maria came back to Coatbridge on holiday to visit their families. This was a joyous occasion for Jessie, an opportunity to spend time at long last with her beloved son and his wife.

LIZ and MARY remained devoted to each other until Liz passed away shortly after the end of the War. Mary then became an extremely wealthy woman, she used this money for great good, including the education of her niece Emily.

MARY never married, however she had a rich and fulfilling life giving aid to countless women and children. Mary always kept her two strands of family completely separate.

After her mother died she moved into her little bungalow in Ayr where she spent many happy years. She was never lonely, the kettle was always on to welcome her family and friends and the many women and children she had helped over the years. Mary also joined the congregation of a local Church of Scotland where she was an active member.

When she died Mary's Bible was buried alongside her and with it the card Samuel sent from Austria - the only written connection to her Fischer family.

JESSIE never stopped loving McInnes however during the War she met a kind, generous man who had suffered terrible injuries. They eventually married in 1947 and had one daughter. Although Jessie spent her married life in Glasgow there was always a very special place in her heart for Gartsherrie, the place where she had grown up.

HUGH MASON passed away after the War leaving his house and estate to Jessie Law. Hugh was Jessie's last real link to McInnes and she greatly mourned his passing.

MAMA and PAPA GOLDBAUM they lived in Troon for the duration of the War with Anna, Rolf and their grandchildren. In 1947 they returned to Vienna, leaving their paintings with their daughters Leah and Anna (their son Daniel having died during the War). With help from the Red Cross they managed to again acquire ownership of their once beautiful house in Dobling. The Goldbaum family could never again live there knowing the S.S. had been billeted in their lovely home. They gifted the house to a Jewish Organisation resettling people who had been in the camps or were otherwise casualties of war. However, before they left the house for the last time Mama dug up a box which she had buried in the garden, the proceeds from the contents kept them in great comfort for the remainder of their days.

JENNIE, JOHN and their adopted daughter **LOUISE** had an extremely happy family life together. Louise qualified as a chartered accountant and eventually inherited her father's practice. Jennie never stopped being a kind carer and was much loved by all who knew her.

WILLIE was called up before he could finish his long planned university education. He served with distinction in North Africa and later in Europe. After the war he married a young woman he met while serving in the forces, jilting a pretty Gartsherrie girl in the process. He eventually completed his studies and acquired his law degree. William Law Fyfe became an eminent barrister in London, where his 'acting talents' stood him in excellent stead.

AGNES, lived a long life, thanks to the ministrations of Dr O'Flannery and her family. She never entirely lost the desire to control her children but had a wonderful relationship with all her grandchildren, particularly Willie, who was her special favourite. All her secrets were taken with her to the grave.

And **ELLA MILLAR**, well she looked down from her place among the Angels, proud and happy at all the achievements of Ella's Friends.

THE END

Retired and looking for a new interest, like many of my generation, I started to research my family tree.

I was saddened to find that Gartsherrie, a place that my mother had greatly loved, appeared to have been almost wiped from the pages of history.

With the demolition of Wm. Baird Iron & Steel Works and the flattening of the Rows to make way for new council housing the history of Gartsherrie and its people, during the years when it was so closely affiliated to Wm. Baird & Sons, appears to have simply vanished.

The Laws of Gartsherrie and Beyond Gartsherrie are my contribution to keeping the memory of Gartsherrie and its people alive.

Alexandra J Morris

www.AJMorris.me.uk

·

Printed in Great Britain
by Amazon